Hawley Smart

At Fault

A Novel

Hawley Smart

At Fault
A Novel

ISBN/EAN: 9783337044404

Printed in Europe, USA, Canada, Australia, Japan

Cover: Foto ©Andreas Hilbeck / pixelio.de

More available books at **www.hansebooks.com**

BY HAWLEY SMART

AT FAULT

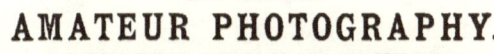

AT FAULT.

A Novel.

BY

HAWLEY SMART,

AUTHOR OF
"BREEZIE LANGTON," "BROKEN BONDS," "SOCIAL SINNERS,"
THE GREAT TONTINE," ETC. ETC.

" For the lords in whose keeping the door is
That opens on all who draw breath,
Gave the cypress to love, my Dolores,
The myrtle to death."

WARD, LOCK, AND CO
LONDON: WARWICK HOUSE, SALISBURY SQUARE, E.C.
NEW YORK, 10, BOND STREET.

CONTENTS.

CHAPTER XXXII.

AT FAULT.

CHAPTER I.

"JOHN FOSSDYKE, SOLICITOR."

UGHT to have a theatre, sir—of course, it ought to have a theatre—the idea of a thriving, go-a-head place like Baumborough being without such a thing! We've a mechanics' institute, assembly rooms, hospital, college, covered market, Conservative club, public gardens, a town band—the most thick-headed and irascible municipality in the kingdom, school of Art, and all the latest fads of the times we live in, and no theatre. It can't be—it mustn't be. Do you mean to elevate the masses or do you not? Are these not days in which culture is everything? What are mutton-chops to mezzotints, or ducks to dados? Who would think of table sensualities when the intellectual banquet of Hamlet by the great Dobbs awaited him. No, Baumborough, with its thirty thousand inhabitants, is astir with dramatic interests. We have local artists, sir, who only want opportunity; suckling Shakespeares in our midst who merely want some slight study of stage craft to blossom into metropolitan fame. No, Dr. Ingleby, despite the supreme stupidity and obstinacy of the Corporation, you and I have pulled through a good many ticklish matters, and we'll work this. Baumborough must have a theatre, and when I, John Fossdyke, tell you so, you know the thing will be."

That was the keynote to John Fossdyke's career—his indomitable self-assertion. Fifteen years ago he had settled in Baumborough as a solicitor, a young man with no introductions, not an acquaintance, much less a friend, in the place, and now he was practically their leading citizen. From the very commencement it signified little what it might be, but whatever there might be to be done in Baumborough, about it Mr. Fossdyke had much to say. Shrewd, hardheaded, pachydermatous, and a fluent speaker, he had proved from the first totally irrepressible. He began, as naturally all leading citizens do begin, in the opposition, and speedily demonstrated that to have John Fossdyke's fluent tongue and keen brain against a thing was to make its accomplishment a matter of some trouble. A man this to be propitiated, and cookers and contrivers of snug local jobs came quickly to the conclusion that this was a man to have on their side, and made overtures accordingly. Energetic, irrepressible John was in no humour to turn up his nose at well-buttered bread, and speedily had not a finger but his whole fist in every pie worth baking. Practice came rapidly to him, and he had plenty of ability to take advantage of it, and having succeeded in marrying the daughter of a well-to-do clergyman in the neighbourhood, who had inherited a nice bit of money from her deceased mother, he conjoined the lucrative profession of money lending to the selling of law. It was soon spread about amongst the farmers round Baumborough that lawyer Fossdyke had clients ready to advance a little money on decent security should the banks prove rusty, and in his early days John Fossdyke took care to outbid the banks and demand one per cent. less interest than they did. He throve and waxed fat in substance year by year, as men with this vehemence of clutch always do, obtained the appointment of town-clerk and a monopoly of all legal pickings connected with the Baumborough municipality. At the time this narrative commences, and Mr. Fossdyke feels it incumbent on him to express his sentiments concerning the erection of a theatre for Baumborough to his esteemed friend, Dr. Ingleby, he had acquired for himself a pleasant villa about a mile outside the town, with about a hundred acres of grass and pleasaunce around it, and was as leading and prosperous a man as any in Baumborough. The building of this theatre, which now occupied his restless mind, was another of those local improvements which he so persistently floated, and which had in no little measure made him. His fellow-townsmen appreciated the public gardens, mechanics' institute, &c., all of which were in great measure brought about by his unwearied agitation, and which he took good care should more or less contribute to his advantage. "A warm man, and a good sort, and likes a bit of sport," said that large country side of which Baumborough was the market town, and the popular solicitor so far endorsed the latter laudation as to be ever open to the offer of a day's shooting or coursing, and to generally put in an appearance at the cover-side, when the hounds met within easy distance. But with all these virtues there was one allegation sometimes made against Mr. Fossdyke, namely, that though he doubtless had made a good bit of money, he was a very difficult man to get money from. These detractors were chiefly the tradespeople of Baumborough, who, though perchance mere scandal-mongers, it could not be denied were certainly in a position to form an opinion.

"Well," said the doctor slowly, after a pause, "I suppose if you have made up your mind, Fossdyke, we are to have a theatre, a theatre we shall have. You generally carry out what you go in for, but it's no use pretending your schemes are always successful. You shook us up to begin with. We had got stagnant, and the municipality wanted new blood, but you re over-doing it now. The assembly rooms are not open twice a year, the covered market draws no custom, and the public gardens so far are mere sand, ashes, and sticks."

"Things must have a beginning," rejoined Mr. Fossdyke, cheerily. "You must educate your public to prefer legitimate space for dancing to the delights of crushed and torn flounces. Trees must have time to grow, while as for the covered market, I'll leave the climate to bring that into fashion. Walk out to the Dyke with me, have some lunch, and discuss the theatre."

But Dr. Ingleby declined that offer, and the prosperous solicitor strolled home by himself.

Prosperous, well-to-do men's houses are not quite so pleasant inwardly at times as their exterior would indicate. Good Lord! there are many things we hanker sadly after that, could we only take a peep behind the scenes, we should never wish for more. John Fossdyke had married well, so said all Baumborough. It was regarded as a considerable step up the social ladder when he, at that time a struggling solicitor, won for himself the hand of the only daughter of the Rev. Maurice Kimberley, J.P., and rector of Bimby, a parish lying some two or three miles outside the town. It was true Mary Kimberley was no chicken, and some years older than the aspiring attorney, but still Mary had a nice bit of money, and was considered at the time to have thrown herself away rather, although it did not seem quite so clear what other matrimonial alternative was open to her. Marriage no doubt is no necessity for women, but when she has passed five-and-thirty, if she has any inclination that way, it behoves her to give due consideration to such proposals as may fall to her. Mary Kimberley was a little tired of Bimby rectory; life there was somewhat stagnant, and she had a vague longing to change it for a world with somewhat more "go" in it. She was a sensible young woman, and when John Fossdyke asked her to marry him replied she would give him an answer in twenty-four hours. She had "a good think" over the business, and having arrived at the conclusion that .

there were only three courses open to her, namely, to remain mistress of the rectory, to marry some impecunious curate, or say yes to John Fossdyke, made up her mind to the latter, and said yes the next day. So far Mary Kimberley had shown wise discretion, but the pity of it was, that as Mary Fossdyke she forgot to continue it. Many a man has been indebted to his wife for his first start in life, but if ever a man feels that he has borrowed the capital that floated him at usurious interest it is when his wife persistently reminds him of the fact. Mrs. Fossdyke always kept before her husband that it was her social pre-eminence that placed him where he was, that it was her money which was the foundation of his fortune. Perhaps it was; no doubt there was considerable truth in it; but the perpetual recapitulation of conferred benefits is about as trying as any known method of exasperation. Nobody accused the Fossdykes of living a cat-and-dog life, but it was generally conceded that Mrs. Fossdyke, though a well-meaning woman, was a little trying at times, while it was urged on her behalf that she had fair cause of complaint about the manner in which she was often left alone for weeks at a time. Mr. Fossdyke's business was extensive, and by no means in these days confined to Baumborough. He was a man with a good many irons in the fire, and such irons, as we all know, require constant watching, and energetic John Fossdyke was not the man to let the kettle boil over from being out of the way.

Mrs. Fossdyke, dear good lady, although honestly fond and proud of her lord, could no more resist that irresistible luxury, a grievance, than the rest of us, and was wont to murmur over these constant absences in plaintive manner to her intimates. "After all I've been to him, my dear," she would say, "after my lifting him into society, after my even finding him the money with which he was first enabled to embark in these great undertakings. John's clever there's no denying, energetic I grant you. Few men, even with all his advantages, would have achieved what he has done, but

John is not considerate. He should remember what I have been to him, that I occasionally require change, and am not above roughing it a little when necessary ; in short, he might, I think, take me with him on some of these business excursions."

But John Fossdyke remained impenetrably deaf to all such hints as these. When his business required him to leave home he went, but never found it incumbent on him to take Mrs. Fossdyke. That estimable woman possessed the advantages of a steely grey eye, an aquiline nose, and much fixity of purpose, but she was fain to admit in moments of confidence that John would have his way in some things, and one of those things was the transacting of business without counsel from his better half. It had taken some time to instil this into the good lady's mind, for she was by no means diffident concerning her abilities to conduct anything, of any kind, and from laying out a flower-garden to the buying or selling of Egyptians, from the cooking of an omelette to the question of what had become of the lost tribes of Israel, never hesitated to express a decided opinion. About this last question, indeed, she was deliciously feminine and illogical. She said the Jews were unbelievers, and therefore not entitled to credence, consequently there was no real reason to believe that there were any lost tribes, such evidence as there was concerning them being utterly unreliable—an ingenious bit of sophistry more easy to deny than disprove, and which caused Mrs. Fossdyke to be spoken of by the surrounding clergy as a clever woman, but with rather unsound opinions. So John Fossdyke went his way silently and solitarily on these business excursions, while his wife aired her imaginary grievance with much petty satisfaction. She was not exactly the woman to take a real wrong quietly, and, though she was very far from suspecting it, neither was John Fossdyke the man to put up with anything but absolute submission to his will when the occasion waxed strong enough. People may live a long time together, and while life progresses

in the ordinary grooves, form a very mistaken estimate of
each other's character. The indolent man thoroughly roused
for instance, the dictatorial bully sharply collared, the meek
patient woman at last outraged past endurance, or the shrinking shy girl, suddenly called upon to play a heroine's part,
constantly astonish those who fancy they know them
thoroughly. It is some sudden discovery of this nature,
which labelled incompatibility of temper, very often furnishes
employment for the divorce court.

Seated in the drawing-room at Dyke, in desultory conversation with Mrs. Fossdyke, was a tall rubicund elderly
gentleman, who, sad to say, was wont to be the cause of some
acrimony between the lady and her spouse. Mr. Totterdell,
by appearance, should have been devoted solely to his own
comfort, the pleasures of the table and port wine. So he
was, but he unfortunately conjoined with these tastes a most
insatiable curiosity. No child could have been more exacting
as to "the why" of this, that, and the other, and his presence
on one occasion of the packing of John Fossdyke's portmanteau had driven that gentleman to the verge of madness.
He wanted to know why he took dress things with him; why
he took shooting boots, when he said he was going to London.
Whom did he expect to dine with, &c. ? In short, he possessed one of those petty inquiring minds that are very trying
to a quick, energetic temper. He was Mrs. Fossdyke's godfather, had made a comfortable bit of money at some business
in the city, and had now retired and settled at Baumborough,
where his principal occupation was the supervision of his
neighbours' affairs. Notably was he much exercised concerning the goings and comings of John Fossdyke, and that
energetic gentleman was the last man in the world to
succumb tamely to such supervision of his affairs. What
with Mrs. Fossdyke thinking that her advice would be invaluable, and old Mr. Totterdell's doddering curiosity concerning them, there was a good deal of friction in the domestic
life of John Fossdyke.

" He's too venturesome, Mary ; I've said so all along ; he's always starting something new in the town," wheezed old Totterdell from the depths of his easy chair. " What does he want with all those new notions down here ? they are all very well in London, but Baumborough can't support such things. I have heard that a theatre is a profitable speculation in the metropolis, but we don't want one, and what can John know of matters theatrical ? Mark me, my dear, I don't want to croak, but your husband will get into trouble by meddling with matters he don't understand. What is all this business that requires his perpetual absence ? Something, Mary, that he knows his old friends would pronounce hazardous if they knew of it. No, no, you ought to exert your influence. A wife should be her husband's confidante."

" It's too true, godpapa, and John makes me miserable by the mystery in which he insists on enshrouding his business transactions."

"Not only those, but I can't understand him at all," returned the old gentleman, fidgeting in his chair, and toying with a heavy pair of double gold eye-glasses. " I have only settled down here about a twelvemonth, and can consequently claim no longer acquaintance with your husband than that ; but now who is this companion you have got ? Where did she come from ? Nothing wrong in it, no doubt, but still where did she come from ? "

" How should I know ? " rejoined Mrs. Fossdyke. " Miss Hyde's account of herself is plain and straightforward enough. Her people are not rich, and she was tired of living at home. John—and it was kind of him to think of it—thought that it must be dull for me while he was away, and suggested I should have a companion. Miss Hyde answered our advertisement, and here she is."

" And a very nice-looking, lady-like girl she is to look at, I admit ; in fact, if anything, perhaps a trifle more good-looking than most ladies would care about as a companion."

" Don't talk nonsense, godfather," retorted Mrs. Fossdyke,

sharply. " John has never made me uncomfortable in that way, and Bessie Hyde is no coquette."

" Quite so, my dear ; but still, where does she come from ? "

" Good gracious, what can it matter ? She's a nice lady-like girl, and whether her father is a retired tradesman or a broken-down professional man is no consequence," and Mrs. Fossdyke's foot tapped the floor with somewhat unnecessary vehemence.

Her godfather's insatiable and absurd curiosity occasionally exasperated Mary Fossdyke, but there were, unfortunately, times when it roused distrust in her surroundings. The old proverb of the Romans tells us that the constant drip wears the stone ; the constant friction breaks the spring, the nerves, or the temper, and when once the why of all the actions of those with whom we habitually live becomes matter of inquiry, suspicion must be the inevitable consequence. This was exactly what was gradually arising in Mrs. Fossdyke's mind. She had indulged in natural curiosity concerning the business that took her husband so much from home in the early days of their wedded life, but when also it was made manifest to her that John Fossdyke brooked no inquiries into his business affairs, she, like a sensible woman, made up her mind to acquiesce in this decision. When he suggested that as they had no children it would be pleasant for her to have a young lady as a companion, Mrs. Fossdyke felt very grateful to her husband for his forethought, and she had found Bessie Hyde as bright, pleasant, and good-tempered as it was possible for a young lady of nineteen to be. Miss Hyde had arrived at Dyke nearly two years before the commencement of the narrative, while Mr. Totterdell had settled in Baumborough some twelve months later. It is necessary to mention these facts to explain the manner in which Mrs. Fossdyke, who was in the main an honest, good-hearted woman, gradually allowed her imagination to be inflamed and her judgment to be perverted by such a cackling curiosity-monger as Mr. Totterdell. That gentleman, since his retirement from

business, found time hang heavy on his hands, and endeavoured to lighten it as best he might, by laudable watch
over the concerns of his neighbours. He inflicted a considerable amount of his leisure on his goddaughter, and
though Mrs. Fossdyke was by no means enchanted by the
attention, she bore with it for prudential reasons. The old
man had beyond doubt a considerable sum of money to
leave behind him, and Mrs. Fossdyke was about the nearest
relative that he had. But the result of Mr. Totterdell's
perpetually " wanting to know " had slowly resulted in en-
gendering distrust in Mrs. Fossdyke's mind. She had got
used to her husband's constant and at times long absences
from home, but Totterdell's perpetual speculation as to what
he went about had brought back uncomfortable thoughts to
her mind that she had long since done away with ; while his
perpetually harping upon " where did Miss Hyde come from "
was inoculating her with unwarranted suspicions concerning
the girl. Mrs. Fossdyke was half ashamed of both these
feelings herself, but nevertheless she could not help showing
them to the two people from whom it most behoved her to
conceal them—her husband and Bessie. The former re-
senting all reference to his movements fiercely, speedily
discerned who it was that prompted his wife's interrogations,
and was rude and curt enough in his remarks to Mr. Totterdell
to have banished a more sensitive man from his house ; but
that old gentleman in his thirst for information was accustomed to encounter rebuff : he was case-hardened, im-
pervious to snubbing, and callous to sarcasm, and short of
telling him in plain English that you would have none of
him, was no more to be got rid of than Sinbad's " Old man
of the sea." To shut your door against your wife's relations
requires some justification, and when you belong to the community of a country town, the ordering of your *menage* is
public talk. John Fossdyke, though not a man to be cowed
by popular opinion, did see that to close the gate against Mr.
Totterdell would by no means close that garrulous old gen-

tleman's mouth, and as the broadest hints that his company was undesirable had proved useless, had finally elected to bear it as best he might. Still his face darkened a little as he entered the drawing-room and discovered his *bête noir* ensconced in the easiest chair, babbling, as he had little doubt, over his, John Fossdyke's, affairs.

A dark, portly man of florid complexion, scarce a tinge of grey in his black hair, and with an eye keen as a hawk's, John Fossdyke looked what he was—a prosperous man; shrewd, with an air of *bonhommie* that disarmed suspicion. He had a rich mellow voice, could, indeed, troll out songs of the "jolly nose" type in rather superior fashion, an accomplishment that stood him in good stead amongst the farmers of the neighbourhood, who, moreover, liked the jovial attorney none the worse because, if he could snatch a day, he had rather a *penchant* for attending the local races, and having what he facetiously denominated a few " spangles " on the principal event.

" Good morning, Mr. Totterdell," he said, as he advanced. " What is the best news with you to-day ? "

" Dear me, I've heard nothing, positively nothing at all ; nor has Mary, she tells me. There must be something new to talk about. What have you heard, my dear friend ? "

" I have nothing to tell. I had nothing to do out of the office except attend the meeting about establishing a theatre in Baumborough ; of course there are obstacles and there is opposition, there always is. We shall overcome them—people always do who persistently stick to a thing, and I'm a rare sticker."

" But godfather is quite sure a theatre in Baumborough can never pay, John," interposed Mrs. Fossdyke.

" And pray what does Mr. Totterdell know of either theatricals or Baumborough. He has only been a twelvemonth in the town. I have been fifteen years and more."

" I never heard that you had any experience of theatricals," wheezed Mr. Totterdell.

"I was very fond of them as a young man, and knew a good many theatrical people, and occasionally look in at a theatre now, when business takes me to London," replied Fossdyke, a little tartly.

"Then all I can say, John, it's a great shame that you don't take me with you when you go away, when you know how I enjoy a theatre," chimed in Mrs. Fossdyke.

"Eh! you mixed a good deal with theatrical people in your early days! Now what made you do that?" inquired Mr. Totterdell, eagerly. "How did you get thrown amongst them? Tell us that, it will be very interesting."

"I shall not gratify your curiosity in any way," rejoined the solicitor. "I only mentioned it in proof that I had some slight knowledge of matters theatrical. As for you accompanying me, Mary, on business trips, it is simply impossible. I rarely know when they may take me to London, and I have told you before that you would be only uncomfortable and disappointed."

"I should like to go once though," rejoined Mrs. Fossdyke, like a true daughter of Eve, none of whom would ever flinch from discomfort to see what any man they cared about might be doing under any circumstances.

"Are theatrical people pleasant acquaintances?" inquired Totterdell, who was all alive at the bare idea of getting a little insight into Fossdyke's early life, a subject on which he was singularly reticent; indeed, even his wife knew very little of his career previous to his settling in Baumborough, and it was the knowledge of his goddaughter's ignorance on the point that so whetted the old inquisitor's curiosity.

"Cultivate them and judge for yourself," rejoined Fossdyke brusquely, who, though a genial and tolerably good-tempered man, was wont to wax irritable under Mr. Totterdell's endless questions.

"Much doing in the office?" croaked the insufferable one.

"Pshaw!" ejaculated the solicitor. "Whatever may be doing in the office you surely know is not to be talked about.

I shall go and look at the roses, Mary. Send and let me
know when tea is in."

" It's very odd," remarked Mr. Totterdell, as Fossdyke
stepped through the window, " but that is just what Miss
Hyde went to do half-an-hour ago. Bad-tempered man your
husband, my dear ; bad mannered too, rather," and the old
gentleman sunk back in his chair with a benevolent smile on
his countenance.

" He's not bad-tempered, godfather," rejoined Mrs. Fossdyke, firing up, and by no means as yet prepared to hear her
husband found fault with by any one but herself. " He can't
bear being questioned, and you always irritate him by doing
so

" But, God bless me, how's conversation to be carried on
without you ask questions ? " rejoined Mr. Totterdell. " I
thought he would have been delighted to tell us all about his
theatrical life. I dare say he was something in a theatre."

" He was nothing of the kind, and it's downright wicked of
you to suggest such a thing," cried Mrs. Fossdyke, indignantly.

John Fossdyke made his way amidst the flower-beds to the
further side of the trimly-kept turf, where the grass ceased
to be studded with the gay masses of colour, and ran down
green and velvety towards a prettily-planned rosary, the
denizens of which were now in all the glory of their summer
bloom. In their midst a tall, dark-haired maiden, her hands
cased in gardening gauntlets and armed with a large pair of
scissors, was busy, snipping off the faded blooms and casting
them into a small basket at her feet.

" Hard at work again, tending your favourites, Bessie ? "
said the lawyer, as he advanced.

" Yes," returned the girl, as she welcomed him with a smile,
" they are worth taking care of this year. Did you ever see
a more magnificent show than they make ?—but you are
home early to-day."

" There was little business to be done, but old Totterdell

cross-examined me out of the house, so here I am. How my wife can endure that garrulous old nuisance I can't imagine. He ought to leave her a good bit of money, and not be long before he does it, I'm sure. Does he ever bother you, Bessie?"

" Yes; he embarrasses me at times. He wants to know so very much about my antecedents; but I usually escape on the plea of seeing about some household duty, and Mrs. Fossdyke is very good, she generally acquiesces and covers my retreat."

" Quite right; whatever you do make no confidant of him. My wife never troubles you in this wise?" inquired the lawyer, burying his hands in his pockets and casting a keen look at the girl.

" Never; Mrs. Fossdyke after the first has never questioned me about my home. But is it not time for tea?"

" I suppose so; and here comes Robert to tell us," and the pair sauntered slowly back to the drawing-room windows.

There was nothing much in this conversation, and yet if Mrs. Fossdyke had heard it she would have decidedly thought there was something in her godfather's suspicions after all. There was no sign of the slightest flirtation between the two, but the few foregoing sentences did rather point to an understanding of some sort between Fossdyke and Miss Hyde. His calling her Bessie was nothing: both he and his wife had commenced doing that before she had been six months under their roof, and made no disguise that they were very fond of her, and regarded her more in the light of a niece than a dependant. Still it was not difficult to gather from those few words which passed between them in the rosary that John Fossdyke knew more of Miss Hyde's antecedents than that young lady had thought fit to confide to his wife.

And it may here be at once stated, in justice to a very charming girl, that Bessie was no impostor, and that her statement was in the main correct. She had been brought up by her aunt, and had got on very well with her cousins, until she arrived at the age of seventeen, and commenced to mingle

in such society as her aunt, the widow of a well-to-do partner
in a large silk and millinery establishment at the West End
of London, had arrived at. Then her superior attractions
and attainments dwarfed the goods her two cousins had to
display, and it was the old story of Cinderella and her sisters.
They made home uncomfortable to her, and she sought to
leave it. She had a skeleton of her own in the closet—but
there's few of us have not—likely if discovered to prove
detrimental to obtaining such a situation as she wished to
obtain. It was no great harm, but society has its prejudices,
and no country on the face of creation is so miserably cant-
ridden as England. She knew John Fossdyke, and consulted
him. His answer was prompt and decisive: he knew all
about that skeleton.

"Say simply that you were brought up by your aunt, Mrs.
Lewisham, and are tired of home. Say nothing about your
other relatives, and, above all, never hint that you have any
previous knowledge of me, and I will find you a comfortable
home in my own house. My wife is a good woman, and will
be kind to you, but if she once suspects I have any previous
knowledge of you she will want to know the whole particulars,
will never rest till she does, and then, poor thing, she has
her prejudices, and, Bessie, I doubt whether she would tolerate
you at Dyke."

At first the girl flamed fiercely up at this, but gradually
John Fossdyke made her comprehend that, let her seek a
situation where she might, it was imperative that skeleton
should be kept out of sight.

"It is prejudice and sheer nonsense, child, of course, but
we cannot convince people of that. They will not want to
see what you are, but will at once decline your application.
You may just as well be mute about it in my house as another,"
and at last Bessie consented, and at the end of two years was
fain to confess Dyke was more a home to her than any other
place. The Fossdykes treated her precisely as if she was a
near relative, and being a handsome, lively, attractive girl,

Baumborough generally made a great deal of her. At the time this story commences the Fossdykes very rarely got an invitation in which Miss Hyde was not included.

" Come and pour out the tea, Bessie dear," exclaimed Mrs. Fossdyke, as the girl stepped through the window. " We are quite ready for it."

" I hope I haven't kept you waiting, but there was so much snipping to be done I forgot how late it was getting."

" Anything new this morning in "—Baumborough, Mr. Totterdell was about to ask; but John Fossdyke's darkened face checked him, and turning to Bessie, he concluded his question with " in the rosary ? "

" Yes, caterpillars," growled the lawyer.

Bessie bit her lips to control her laughter. Totterdell beamed benevolently, as if it was something even to learn that ; while Mrs. Fossdyke frowned meaningly at her husband.

A few minutes later, and Mr. Totterdell rose to take his departure, not influenced in the slightest degree by the undisguised irritability of the master of the house, but simply that no further question occurred to him, indeed his last, if completed according to his original intention, was a mere repetition. He shook hands affectionately all round, and then rolled out of the room with all the assured manner of a favoured visitor.

" Your godfather, Mary, is getting more unbearable every day," remarked John Fossdyke snappishly, as the door closed behind the old gentleman.

" He is somewhat trying I admit, but we can't well close our door to him ; besides, some of these days he will leave something very comfortable behind him ; and I don't know how it is, John, but we always seem to be in want of money, considerable though your income must be."

John Fossdyke uttered an impatient pshaw. Even to the wife of his bosom he was extremely reticent about his affairs, but she did know that she brought him a nice bit of money, and that he held the appointment of town-clerk, which

carried a very handsome salary with it, then surely his business as a solicitor must be tolerably profitable; yet she knew
from practical experience that he always parted with money
most grudgingly, and was wont to be querulous even over
the household expenses, an eccentric trait this in John Fossdyke's character, men of his genial temperament being usually
free-handed, unless compelled to be otherwise from circumstances, and that could hardly be his case.

"By the way, John," said Mrs. Fossdyke, after a slight
pause, "godfather told me he had been asked to come forward
as a candidate for the municipal council."

"He!" exclaimed her husband. "I trust he won't think
of such a thing. He's very unfitted for it. We have a great
deal too many fussy, interfering fools there as it is. Besides,
it is rather *infra dig* in a man of his position. Mind you
impress that upon him."

"I feel sure I couldn't. It was the height of his ambition
to achieve that distinction in London, though he never
succeeded. I assure you he is quite keen about it; besides,
he has nothing to do, and it will amuse him."

"You won't find him more untractable than some of the
others, Mr. Fossdyke," remarked Miss Hyde, "and you know
you contrive to have your own way pretty much with the
council."

"Nevertheless," he replied, decidedly, "I don't want Totter-
dell there. Remember, Mary, if you can choke him off it, do.
You also, Bessie, dissuade him if you have an opportunity.
As for me, I shall endeavour to prevent his election."

"Lor'! John, it surely can't matter much to you," exclaimed Mrs. Fossdyke.

"Please do what I ask you. It may be a small matter;
but, believe me, I have my reasons for not wishing to see
Mr. Totterdell on the council."

CHAPTER II.

THE Syringa Music Hall in the City Road was a place of mark known not only to Clerkenwell and Islington, but occasionally visited by adventurous spirits from the West End, whose insatiable thirst to see the last thing in "great and glorious comics," or eminent acrobats, led them to penetrate to distant suburbs. The Syringa had been established about ten years, but in its earlier days had been only a modest concert-room, under the name of Moffat's, where harmony and refreshments were nightly dispensed. Whether Moffat was unequal to the times, failed to discern that mystic problem, "what the public wanted," or whether Moffat lacked capital, it is impossible to say, but it is certain that Moffat did not flourish. He reduced his vocalists' salaries, whereby the music went from bad to worse; the quality of his liquors fell off, and his customers also in like proportion; in short, after sustaining the struggle for five years Moffat was glad to avert bankruptcy by disposing of the whole concern, including the remainder of his lease, to Mr. James Foxborough.

James Foxborough was a man of a very different stamp from the late proprietor. He was a go-a-head, energetic man, with evident command of capital. He knocked the old concert-room down, got possession of an adjoining house or

two, and proceeded to build a commodious modern music-hall
in its place, which he christened the Syringa. Whereas
Moffat's had been comparatively unknown, except to the
initiated, gaudy-coloured posters and extensive advertising
proclaimed the birth of the Syringa; star artists were
engaged, a capital entertainment organized, the catering
carefully looked to, and in less than three months the new
music-hall was drawing crowded houses.

Mr. Foxborough might be said to be in the profession. He
had married Miss Nydia Willoughby, the celebrated serio-
comic vocalist, some twenty years ago, and in the beginning
of his career had been chiefly indebted to that lady's earnings
for his support; but of late years he had made money, chiefly
it was supposed by travelling about the country with theatrical
companies. He was an admitted shrewd judge of such things,
and was, moreover, presumed to be considerably assisted
therein by his wife. Mrs. Foxborough was wont to say, "I
don't pretend to be a judge of either the play or the acting,
but I know when there's money in a piece, and it is by no
means the best plays that bring in the most money." In
which assertion the lady was in all probability right. At all
events she managed the Syringa, while her husband was away
on his numerous theatrical tours, exceedingly well, was very
popular with her company, and sure to note those who
" drew " and those who failed to do so; and though she knew
well it was her business to get rid of these latter unfortunates
as quickly as possible, yet the kind-hearted manageress, when
aware that employment was a very serious object for them,
on account of the narrowness of their means, would allow
them at times to hang on some weeks after their engagement
had expired, sooner than turn them adrift with nothing to do.

It was not often that Miss Nydia Willoughby appeared on
the stage herself now-a-days. It was not that her voice was
gone at all, far from it; perhaps it was as good as ever it had
been, the result of not being unduly worked. If her figure
was a little fuller and more matronly than in her younger

days, she was still a tall, handsome woman, verging on forty
it might be, but with not a thread of silver in the rich
chestnut hair, while the dark blue eyes flashed as brightly
and archly as when they had riddled the heart of Jim Foxborough years ago ; but Miss Willoughby thought it judicious
not to give the frequenters of the Syringa too much of herself.
She always got an immense reception when she did sing,
which she dearly loved, for she was clever in her line and
very popular with the public, and she had sense enough to
know that if she was continually in the programme her
welcome could hardly be expected to be so enthusiastic. She
was a brave, plucky woman, who had had a hard struggle
with the world in her younger days, and had battled it out,
neither flinching nor complaining. Now things were easy
for her, and she had leisure to enjoy life, and was never so
happy as when she had her vagrant husband at home for a
little between his tours.

Mrs. Foxborough dearly loved her husband and Nid. Nid
was their only daughter, a sweetly pretty girl of sixteen, with
her mother's chestnut hair and deep blue eyes, but with no
promise of ever attaining her mother's stature. She was a
bright, piquant little thing, with rather irregular features,
but with a charming smile and most beautiful teeth. She
had been highly educated, especially in music, for money had
been tolerably plentiful ever since Nid had been of age to
require masters, indeed the hard times of her parents' early
career had been over before Nid was old enough to understand such things. She had a dim recollection of living in
somewhat poky lodgings, compared with the pretty cottage
standing in its own garden on the north-east side of the
Regent's Park which they now occupied, but she could only
just call to mind the time when her mother had no brougham
of her own, but had to go about in cabs. The little lady,
indeed, had been brought up, if not in luxury, at all events
in easy circumstances, and had acquired a somewhat contemptuous estimate of the value of money.

She was seated now, coiled up in a big easy chair, in the drawing-room of the cottage, talking in animated fashion and with very flushed face to her mother.

" Yes, mamma, quite an adventure, I assure you. I was just entering the park at the upper end, one of the side gates not far from the Zoological Gardens, you know, when a rough-looking man accosted me, and asked me to give him some-thing. I glanced round in hopes of seeing some one, but, as far as I could see, there was nobody in sight. I hurried on, but he easily kept alongside of me, and I suppose it quickly dawned upon him also that he had got me all to himself. Suddenly he changed his tone, and exclaimed gruffly, ' If young women like you ain't larnt to be charitable it's about time they wos taught. Do you know, miss, it's the tiptop-pedest of all the virtues—leastways that's what the chaplain taught us in Millbank, so tip us that purse I see in your hand—quick, or I'll twist your blessed little head off.' Oh, mamma, I could have dropped, and mechanically held out my purse to him. ' This is a somewhat hasty conwersion,' he continued, as he pocketed it, ' but a well-educated young woman like you don't require to be reminded that " He who giveth to the poor lendeth to the Lord," and so off with that necklace and those bracelets, and look sharp, for if I have to help you I shall, perhaps, turn out a roughish lady's-maid.' This so frightened me, mamma, my hands trembled to that extent that I could not undo the clasp of the necklet. The man got impatient and suddenly seized hold of me and wrenched it from my neck. Up to this I had been paralyzed with fear, but now I screamed in downright earnest. ' Stow that,' exclaimed the man, fiercely, ' or I'll strangle you. Come, off with the bangles, quick, or I shall have to assist you again.' I unclasped one bracelet, and then my legs fairly failed to sustain me, and I sank half fainting to the ground. The ruffian uttered a savage oath, and advanced towards me. Suddenly I heard a quick step on the grass ; a man with a white hat dashed at my assailant, who had barely time to confront the new-comer. There was a quick interchange of blows. I saw my footpad acquaintance drop as if shot, and then I fainted."

"My darling, you must never go out again in that way by yourself," said Mrs. Foxborough, as she came across from her own seat to fondle the little chestnut head in the arm-chair.

"Nobody ever was rude to me in the park before, mamma, and you know I have been there by myself over and over again."

"Yes, dear, but this shows it is insufficiently policed. When your papa comes back we must get him to see the authorities about it. It is monstrous that a young lady living near the Regent's Park should not be able to walk in it unattended. But let me hear the end of your adventure, Nid, as I have got you here safe and sound I can afford to listen to it."

"Well, when I came to, I found the gentleman with the white hat supporting me, and dabbing my face with a wet handkerchief, which he kept damping from a watering-pot held by a park-keeper. I came round pretty quick then, mamma, as you may imagine. If finding herself in a strange gentleman's arms, while her face is being dabbed in a most uncomfortable and manlike fashion, with a park-keeper superintending the operation, isn't enough to bring any girl to, I don't know what is. Anyhow, I gave a gulp or two, got on my legs, shaking as they were, and asked for some water to drink. He of the white hat and the park-keeper looked helplessly at each other for a moment or two—it was obvious I couldn't drink out of the watering-pot, and then my preserver started the park-keeper off for a jug and a tumbler. I felt so damp that I half suspect they had used the watering-pot and treated me as if I were a geranium while I was unconscious.

"'I am afraid you have been terribly frightened,' he said, quietly, 'but I trust are not hurt. I was unluckily a little

late in coming to your assistance, though I assure you I came
as soon as I heard your screams, and as quickly as I could—
any one naturally would. Has the ruffian robbed you of
anything? I found the bracelet on the grass, but you may
have lost more.'

"'He has got my purse and my necklet,' I stammered,
'but don't, please, don't trouble. I can't thank you now, I
am too nervous, but you have been very good—and—and
I'm very much obliged.' It was tame, mamma, I know, but
I really was all abroad, and could not do the thing prettily.

"'I'm sorry about the purse, and also that the scoundrel
has got away, but though I knocked him down very clean,'
rejoined my hero, 'he was on his legs and making marvellously good use of them in a twinkling. I thought of giving
chase for a moment, but I couldn't leave you here insensible.'

"'It would have been very inhuman if you had,' I answered
with a gulp, for I could hardly repress a slight tendency to
hysterics."

"I should think not, darling," said her mother, softly, as
she bent over the girl, fondling her.

"'The scoundrel will probably get off,' continued my friend,
'and you will probably never see his face again. But there
is one consolation for you—had he been apprehended you
would have had to appear against him at the police court,
and that is not very nice for a young lady.'

"'I would rather lose ten purses,' I replied, hastily.

"'That depends a little on what is in them,' rejoined my
new friend, laughing. 'But are you well enough to think of
going home yet? Ah, here comes the park-keeper with the
water.'

"Well, I drank some water, and he escorted me to the
outside of the park, and walked with me till we met a cab.
Then he put me into it, asked where he should tell the man
to drive to, hoped I should soon recover from my fright, and
lifted his hat in farewell. He was very nice, mamma."

"And I suppose very good-looking, Nid—the heroes of

little romances like yours always are," replied her mother, laughing.

"Well, that is just what I don't think he is. I can't say I ever had a really good look at him. I was so frightened, and it was so awkward, you know, but I should call him a tall, red-headed man. He was thoughtful, too, to the last, for he checked the cabman a minute just as I was going off, and leaning forward said, 'Do not think me obtrusive, but remember you have lost your purse; can I be of any further use?' Of course I thanked him and said no."

"I suppose he is a young man?" said Mrs. Foxborough, interrogatively.

"I hardly know—not very young, certainly; but, mamma, the more I think about it, the more convinced I am he is ugly."

"Ah, well, my dear, I don't suppose we shall see him again, though I own I *should* like to thank him for his kindness to my little girl," said Mrs. Foxborough, as she stroked the girl's chestnut locks.

"Perhaps not," replied Nid; but in her own mind she felt pretty certain that she should see her red-haired, white-hatted acquaintance before long. And the girl was correct in her surmise, for the very next morning the trim parlourmaid brought in a card, on which was inscribed "Mr. Herbert Morant, 6, Morpeth Terrace."

"Please, ma'am, the gentleman wants to know if you will see him, as he has recovered Miss Nydia's necklace which the thief stole yesterday."

"Certainly; show him in, Ellen, and let Miss Nydia know he's here," and Mrs. Foxborough, with no little curiosity, awaited the appearance of the hero of yesterday's adventure.

He speedily made his appearance, a tall, gentlemanly-looking man, with hair, though not glaringly red, still of a most decidedly warm-coloured tint, clean-shaved all but a trim moustache, a quiet mobile face, with a pair of bold keen eyes that met your own without a blink or a droop in them.

" Mrs. Foxborough, I presume," he said, with an easy smile. " It was my good fortune yesterday to render your daughter some slight service, and though I should hardly have ventured to intrude upon you on such grounds, yet it is incumbent on me to restore this to her " (here he produced the necklet), " and I could not resist the temptation of doing so in person in order that I might inquire if she is really none the worse for the rascally attack made upon her."

" It is very kind of you to take so much trouble," rejoined Mrs. Foxborough, " and the more so because it enables me to thank you and express my gratitude for your protection of my daughter. I do thank you from the bottom of my heart," continued the lady, extending her hand ; " but for you there is no saying how far that brute's ill-treatment of her might have been carried ; and she is very, very dear to me, Mr. Morant, as you will understand when you know us better."

" I don't think I need see much of you to understand that," said the young man, with a frank smile, for though he might not be young, from Nid's point of view, he lacked a year or two of thirty. " I ought to tell you, Mrs. Foxborough, who and what I am ; but that is just what is rather difficult to convey to you. It is much easier to tell you what I'm not. I am neither barrister, doctor, soldier, sailor, in short, I am nothing. I am that anomaly known as a gentleman of independent means, which might be translated in this wise—I have sufficient money to dispense with working for my living, and yet not enough to do what I want. Then why don't I work, you will of course ask, like every one else ; to which I reply, I am just about to begin. I have been about to begin now," he added, ruefully, " about six years, but somehow I don't seem to get any nearer to it."

Mrs. Foxborough could not help laughing. " An extraordinarily frank, open-minded young gentleman, this," she thought ; and yet this guileless young man was even now practising a slight deception on her. The necklet which he had called to restore he had picked up at the same time as

3

the bracelet, but he had been so struck with Nid's beauty that he had quietly put it in his pocket so that it might serve as an excuse for calling upon that young lady.

"Forgive me," he said, after a slight pause, "but I am haunted with the idea that we have met before."

"I think not," she replied, "although it is very likely that you have seen me. I am a professional, you know, and that you have heard Miss Nydia Willoughby sing is very possible—that is my stage name."

"Of course; how very dull of me! I have heard you with great pleasure many times, but it did not, as you may suppose, occur to me to connect Miss Willoughby with Mrs. Foxborough, and so I was at fault."

"My husband is the proprietor of the Syringa, Mr. Morant, and as he has to be a good deal away conducting country companies, I am usually manageress. But here comes Nydia to thank you in her own proper person."

Very pretty the girl looked as she once more blushingly expressed her gratitude. "Ah, Mr. Morant," she said, "I am so glad you have come to see us. Mamma can say for me all I am too foolish to say for myself. I am sure she has thanked you properly for coming to my rescue yesterday."

Mr. Herbert Morant was as self-possessed a young gentleman as there was about town, but even he was a little taken aback by the expression of Nid's gratitude; there was a tremor in her voice, and the tears stood in her eyes as she gave him her hand and uttered the above speech. The girl's nervous system had received a shock from the fright, and, as is often the case, she felt it more the day following the occurrence than at the time. She had told her mother her rescuer was not good-looking; but he was her hero all the same, though an ugly one. Her girlish imagination had magnified the exploit considerably. It may be no great feat to knock a cowardly scoundrel down, but a woman feels great gratitude to the man who does that for her in her hour of need. To an athlete like Morant, who had been in his college Eight, been one of the best racquet players in the University, and had always enjoyed the reputation of being very smart with the gloves, it appeared a very small matter; but Nid viewed it in a very different light.

"You are making much of a trifle," he rejoined gaily, at last. "You don't know what relief it is catching a fellow to knock down occasionally—an impudent rough, or something of that kind—quite an outlet to the suppressed energy of my nature. I am afraid I shall recover no more of your properties, and that you must be content to suffer the loss of your purse."

"We dine what no doubt you will call very early, Mr. Morant. It was a necessity of my vocation at one time, and has now become habit with me. If you will take us as you find us, we shall be very glad if you will join us and accompany us to the Syringa afterwards. I must go there to-night to keep my eye on things."

The genial, off-hand manner in which the invitation was given would have impelled most men to accept it, and Herbert Morant closed at once with the offer. Mrs. Foxborough had no reason to mistrust her *ménage*, nor could any one reasonably have complained of the neat little dinner her cook served up. Mr. Morant, at all events, was perfectly satisfied with this the immediate result of his adventure. His hostess could be excessively pleasant when she liked, and upon this occasion it pleased her to be so. Not only was she under some obligation to the young man, but his quiet, easy assurance, without a particle of either swagger or affectation, amused her. Herbert Morant, indeed, with his perfectly unconscious manner, could perpterate in society without giving offence what would have been deemed impertinence in another. This, though in some measure the result of manner at first, was to some extent a matter of calculation now. He was licensed in his own set to do cool things, and he did them. Society as usual, when two or three of its leaders have accepted eccentricities from any one, followed suit, and

it was "only Herbert Morant's way" was the conventional
explanation of anything that gentleman might choose to do.
He was careful not to abuse the privilege he had somehow
acquired, and if he did cool things he took care they should
never be offensive. In fact, he was a very popular man, and
his table in Morpeth Terrace was usually pretty well covered
with cards of invitation. The talking at dinner was chiefly
done by Mrs. Foxborough and her guest. She was a quiet,
clever woman, and though she knew but little of his world,
she contrived that the conversation should turn mostly in
that direction. She was much more *au fait* of what was
going on in London generally than most of her class, whose
knowledge and interest are usually confined exclusively to
the doings of the profession in its various branches. He was
candour itself. He made no secret of his position in any
way; he owned that his means were very moderate, that he
was a great fool not to follow a profession or business of some
sort; but said gravely that he never could quite make up his
mind whether to make profit out of people's litigious tempers,
their ailments, their spiritual necessities, or their credulity.
The result was that he had embarked in no calling whatever,
and was still considering how to make that fortune which he
declared would require no consideration about spending.

"Now what do you think, Mrs. Foxborough? What
should you recommend me to turn my ever-wandering attention to? I've implicit belief in myself in any capacity,
and that, as a rule, usually insures the belief of the public."

"Upon my word, I cannot say," laughed the lady. "In
my case I only know belief in oneself is by no means so
readily reciprocated by the public, otherwise there are ladies
I have met with who would occupy a very different position
on the stage, oh! yes, and men too. Vanity is no specialty
of our sex."

"No, I quite agree with you there. A woman is apt to be
vain of her appearance, but, bless you, there's no end to *our*
conceits. Our good looks, our talents, accomplishments,

meaning a capacity for lawn tennis and valsing. I know one man who is vain about his collars, and another who piques himself on his boots. Oh! no, Mrs. Foxborough, you can't give us points about that."

"I am glad you admit it, for, honestly, in my profession I declare there is not a pin to choose about vanity between the sexes, nor about jealousy neither."

"Yes," rejoined Morant, "I have always understood theatrical people were very sensitive to criticism on their efforts, but it has never been my good fortune to encounter them before to-night," and here he bent his head laughingly to his hostess. "Do you mean to enter the profession, Miss Foxborough?"

"Oh! that is still in the same category as your own start in life, Mr. Morant—not yet decided."

"Nid can do just as she likes," interposed her mother. "She has no need to go on the stage, as I had, nor is she ever likely to have; but if she does, I insist on the legitimate theatre, my dear. I'll not have you in the music-hall business. I was glad to take an opening where I could, and when my chance of an engagement for a regular theatre came, found that I could command a much higher salary where I was. We can always find an opening for you if you wish to try the boards, and then, dear child, you can give it up if you don't like it. And now, Mr. Morant, we will leave you to your coffee and cigarette for ten minutes, while we get our hats on, and then it will be time to go down to the Syringa. Come, Nid," and the two ladies left the room.

"Well," muttered Mr. Morant, as he lazily inhaled his cigarette, "I have been some years making up my mind with regard to a profession, but it strikes me that the stage is about my form. Deuced nice little dinner. I'd like to be insured champagne as good all the year round, and, by Jove! what a charming woman the mother is! and as for the daughter, she is simply lovely. Bless my soul, if knocking down roughs is going to lead to this sort of thing only once

in six times, I'll go into the business heavily. It is so easy,
so simple—a brute of that sort, when you once get in a real
straight one, has always had enough—he's always a cur.
Upon my soul, I think Nid Foxborough is the sweetest girl I
ever set eyes on. Rather fun this going down to the Syringa
protected by authorities," and here his meditations were cut
short by the opening of the door, and an intimation from the
parlour-maid that the brougham was at the door. He threw
the fragment of his cigarette into the empty grate, and pro-
ceeding to the hall, found the ladies, hatted and shawled,
awaiting him. Trust I haven't hurried you," exclaimed Mrs.
Foxborough, "but you must bear in mind that it is business
with me. I shall send you to my box when we get there, and
leave you and Nid to amuse each other while I am engaged
in my own room with various people."

Now, though Mr. Morant knew the Syringa very well by
name, he had never been there. He had heard it mentioned
at times by some of the fastest of his acquaintance, young
men who were perpetually ransacking the town in pursuit of
novelty, as a fine music-hall, but he had expected to see a
very much rougher place, and was quite unprepared for the
gorgeously decorated and spacious theatre the place really
was, for the Syringa rejoiced in a large stage and elaborate
scenery, and as nearly enacted stage plays as it dared to do ;
indeed, Mr. Foxborough had for the last twelve months been
thinking seriously about applying for a license and turning it
into a *bonâ fide* theatre. But then, as his wife urged, there
was a risk about this—the place was a very paying, thriving
concern as it was ; turn it into a theatre, and it might
cease to be so, and nobody knew better the marvellous
uncertainty that characterizes matters theatrical than Jim
Foxborough.

Seated in an extremely well-fitted stage-box, looking lazily
on at a ballet, as well mounted as could be seen at any West-
end theatre, and *tête-à-tête* with his pretty companion,
Herbert Morant felt that he had indeed fallen on his legs,

and that his interposition in favour of injured innocence was
bountifully rewarded. "If those knights of the Round
Table got half such payment in kind, Miss Foxborough, as
you and your mother have bestowed upon me this evening, I
don't give them much credit for riding up and down to right
wronged maidens."

"I suppose the damsels they rescued ministered to their
wants," replied Nid, "though perhaps they did not comprise
cigarettes and music-halls."

"Hush, Miss Foxborough ; you must not speak lightly of
the laureate."

"Oh dear! Who commenced, I should like to know?
Yesterday when I was frightened I could have given you my
glove to wear in your helm—that is, hat—if you had asked
for it."

"And suppose I asked for it now ? "

"Oh, you wouldn't; look, it has eight buttons," rejoined
Nid in a tone of mock pathos that augured well for her
success on the stage.

"Oh, and you don't bestow gloves on your champions with
over two. Is that so ? "

Nid nodded. "Queen Guinevere and her ladies, I believe,
only bestowed mittens, and those woollen ones. I don't
believe much in those old chivalry myths."

"What a shocking little pagan you are!" replied Morant,
laughing. "Your opinions would be scouted in society,
where we believe in old pictures, old furniture, old books, old
china, in short, everything that savours of antiquity. Have
you a fancy for going on the stage ? "

"Yes, I should like to test my abilities in that way. What
ambitious girl, brought up as I have been, would not? I
don't mean in this sort of theatre ; but where does a woman
find the world so immediately at her feet as a successful
actress ? The sovereignty of the queen of the stage is, according to the little I know, more gratifying to the vanity of
a woman than that of the real queens of the world."

Herbert Morant stared amazed. How could this child of sixteen have arrived at this worldly knowledge ?

At last he said,

" These, Miss Foxborough, are not your own thoughts. You are quoting your mother, surely."

" No! but you are right, those are not my own ideas ; they are my father's. I have heard him talk on the subject so often I am scarce likely to forget his arguments. Still, though I know it would please him to see me a great success on the stage, yet I know I can do just as I like about it."

" And you mean to try it ? "

" Perhaps. I don't know. Of course, I have been to a great extent trained for it. A pity so much good instruction should be thrown away, don't you think so ? " said Nid, with an interrogative upraising of her pretty brows.

" It is not for me to advise, but it struck me, Mrs. Foxborough did not much favour the idea," replied Morant; " but surely there is somebody bowing to you," and he called Nid's attention to a gentleman in the stalls, who was evidently striving to attract her attention.

" Mr. Cudemore," said the girl quietly, as she acknowledged his bow; " he is a friend of papa's. I don't quite know what he is, but either a theatrical agent or provincial manager, or something of that kind."

A dark, slight, wiry man, with a decidedly Jewish cast of countenance, Mr. Cudemore was somewhat striking-looking, and that was probably the reason why he had attracted Morant's attention. It was not that he was remarkably ugly, far from it—he was rather the reverse ; but the keen, dark eyes, the slightly curved nose, and the thin compressed lips, gave a cruel, hawk-like expression to his countenance. He showed very white, regular teeth when he smiled, and he was both lavish of smiles, and amazingly silky in manner, but a physiognomist would have suspected a touch of the tiger under all this purring, and been quite prepared to find him cruel, rapacious, and vindictive, and they would have been right. Clever and unscrupulous, he lived upon the weaknesses of his fellow-creatures, and had derived much profit from theatrical speculations. His plan was to advance money to people desirous of opening theatres ; he would accommodate rising actors or dramatists, but the borrowers invariably found the bond carried terrible interest, and that Cudemore exacted it to the uttermost farthing, while as a rule he took very good care to protect himself against much possibility of loss. In short, the man, though he usually termed himself a theatrical agent, was in reality a theatrical money-lender, and many a successful artist had groaned for some years under the lien Mr. Cudemore held over his salary, obtained before he had made a name, and when money was hard to come by, as it is usually in our early days, let our calling be what it may. A man this destined to have much influence on the lives of the pair now looking so nonchalantly at him from that stage-box at the Syringa.

However, Herbert Morant troubled himself but little about Mr. Cudemore just then. Turning to his companion, " Do you come here very often ? " he asked.

"No ; nor does mamma either. She only comes about twice a week, except when she is in the bill : then she comes every night, and I come very often. I like to hear her sing, and I love to see the reception she gets. She is a great favourite, Mr. Morant."

" I know she is, for though I never was here before, I have heard her elsewhere. What a very fine hall it is ! "

" Is it not ? and it's all papa's doing," rejoined Nid, with some little justifiable pride.

At this moment Mrs. Foxborough entered the box.

" Well, Mr. Morant, I trust you have been fairly amused. These trapeze people are clever, are they not ? As soon as they are finished I think, Nid, we will be off. I should like to get away before the crowd comes out, and the brougham is at the stage door.

" I am quite ready, mamma," replied the girl, rising.

" Come, then.   Good night, Mr. Morant."

But Herbert Morant insisted on seeing the ladies to their carriage, and when they shook hands Mrs. Foxborough said they should always be glad to see him at Tapton Cottage, and Nid smiled an endorsement of the invitation

CHAPTER III.

HERE were days lang syne when the Municipal Council of Baumborough had droned and dozed and wrangled over paving and lighting rates, but such debating as that had been long relegated to the past, and discussion now was as lively, acrimonious, and personal as it is apt to be at St. Stephen's. The member for Pickleton Ward would express his opinion of "the little job"; the member for the Stannagate was seeking to impose upon the Council in terms more forcible than polite. The member for the Stannagate might have no motive of the kind in the matter he wished to carry, but the member for Pickleton Ward had determined to denounce it as a job, as giving more scope for that fiery and scathing eloquence which he was conscious of possessing. Local politics ran high in Baumborough, and its citizens, marching with the times, had of late years found their tongues, and were enamoured of the sound of their own sweet voices. Some of the seniors were wont to recall times when there was considerably less verbiage about their proceedings, and considerably more business got through at a sitting, and to hint that all these formalities had come into vogue with the present Town Clerk; for there was no denying now that the Baumborough Municipal Council imitated the great Legislative Council of the nation as closely as might be, and members were constantly moving and dividing over amendments, and indulging in vituperation and motions for adjournment, and, in fact, showed a happy appetite for the science of obstruction as invented by their betters, most creditable to their intelligence. Whatever they might have done in former days, nobody could say proposed changes or improvements were not amply ventilated now; the erection of an additional lamp-post or a new pump constituting quite sufficient matter for floods of speechifying and much patriotic invective.

That such a scheme as the building of a theatre should occasion much commotion and stormy debate amid an excitable body like the Town Council of Baumborough may easily be imagined; not a city father of the lot but had much to say both for or against the affair, and seemed most determinedly bent, too, upon saying it; and the less he knew of the subject the more he seemed to have to say. The Parliament was about equally divided concerning it. While the member for the Stannagate pronounced that it would afford much intellectual pleasure to the inhabitants of Baumborough and its neighbourhood, besides being a steady, if modest, augmentation of revenue, the member for Pickleton Ward denounced the whole thing as the most bare-faced, flagrant piece of jobbery that had occurred within his memory. It was not wanted, it could never be made to pay, it would require an additional rate, and a very heavy rate too, to sustain this white elephant that some weak-minded members had been gulled into giving their support to. The day on which the decision was to be finally arrived at had at last come, and it was known that both parties meant to put forth all their strength, and it was announced that Mr. Stanger, the member for Pickleton Ward, would come out uncommonly strong, and deliver a regular flagellation to the unfortunate Brocklebank, the member for the Stannagate, the leading supporter of the scheme; for in his position as Town Clerk, John Fossdyke took care never to lead the movement of which he was the inspiration; he pulled the strings, had much to say to the ultimate vote, spoke sparingly, and gave the leader he selected his brief on these occasions; but he kept himself far more in the background than his real power and position warranted. The consequence of this was that the majority of the Council had no idea of how very much he had to say to the decisions they came to.

Mr. Fossdyke was there to-day, calmly prepared for the battle. He had his plans and estimates all ready to lay before the Council; had conferred long and earnestly with Mr. Brocklebank, whom he had selected to bring the scheme forward; and, as he told his friend Dr. Ingleby, was determined to carry his point.

" I am not quite clear that Baumborough wants a theatre," rejoined the doctor; "and I don't suppose Baumborough can tell till it's got one. It's the old story of Sam Slick. People can get along without a clock who've never had one, but let them once get used to having one in the house, and they can't do without it. Of course I shall back you, but it will be a close fight."

" It will be a fight, but I shall win, and if I don't win this time I shall fight it over and over again until I do succeed," said Mr. Fossdyke.

The meeting commenced, and the Town Clerk, having briefly observed that he had procured the plan and estimates for the building in accordance with the directions given him by the Council at their last meeting, placed them on the table and sat down. In an instant Mr. Brocklebank was on his feet, and commenced a flowery speech, in which all the cut-and-dried arguments in favour of the stage were recapitulated —"how it held the mirror of truth and nature up to mankind, and in depicting the consequences of yielding to unbridled passions it preached as impressive a warning as could be delivered from the pulpit; how it afforded elevated and intellectual amusement, which tended to make men, ay, and women too, better and wiser; how that in thus interesting the lower classes you were weaning them from the public-

houses, and awaking them, if he might be allowed to say so,
to a higher intelligence. Should a town like Baumborough,
the rapid increase of which was one of the many marvels of
our great and glorious country, be the only town of similar
population without a Thespian Temple? Gentlemen," continued the orator, warming to his work, "the theatre has
been a prominent feature in all great civilizations. Any
Roman town of the slightest importance boasted its theatre.
Panem et circenses was the universal cry of that turbulent
capital—that grand people, gentlemen, holding that the intellectual food of the play-house was as necessary as the very
staple of life itself. (Hear, hear, and cheers from the Brocklebank faction, mingled with an ironical ' Oh, oh,' from Mr.
Stanger.) Commercially, there can be no doubt about its
being a great success. Mr. Fossdyke proposes that we should
borrow six thousand pounds on the security of our rates, with
which to erect and decorate the building, and the estimate,
as you see, is well inside that. The corner of the Market-
place, which he has selected as a site, is already the property
of the town. We shall have no difficulty in borrowing the
sum at a trifle over four per cent., or, I am assured, in letting
the theatre at a rent that will return us six per cent. for our
money. If at the expiration of three years the theatre is the
great success which I have no doubt it will be, we may look
forward to raising the rent, or undertaking the concern ourselves; in the first case, it may be safely assumed we shall
turn ten per cent. on our capital, and in the latter, that is,
if we elect to take the thing into our own hands, twenty.
The arguments I have laid before you, gentlemen, are in my
opinion conclusive as an improvement to the town, as a
vehicle of culture, or as a mere commercial speculation, it is
incumbent on Baumborough to have a theatre" (an audible
bosh! from Mr. Stanger); "and in conclusion, I might add
that nobody is more likely to be extensively benefited by it
than the member for Pickleton Ward, the elevation of whose
English is much to be desired."

"I said bosh, sir," exclaimed Mr. Stanger, springing angrily to his feet. "I believe that to be a good dictionary word, and eminently descriptive of the farrago of nonsense to which we have just listened."

Cries of "Order" and "gutter English" from Mr. Brocklebank.

"Mr. Mayor," continued the now thoroughly exasperated Stanger, "I venture to request the attention of the honourable gentlemen present for a few minutes while I expose the tissue of lies" (Cries of "Order, order"), "I mean to say, sir, fallacies that the member for Stannagate has just spoken. To begin with, he talks the usual 'bosh'—I repeat 'bosh'; it may be gutter English, but it is tolerably well understood English—about the elevation of the masses, culture, &c. But, sir, a theatre means simply a show that will pay; and a manager that knows his work gives the public what pulls 'em in and draws their money. As for preaching an impressive lesson, an improving lesson, I have always been given to understand the play of 'Jack Sheppard' induced many youths to take up burglary as a trade." ("Monstrous, ridiculous, absurd," from Mr. Brocklebank.) "If ridiculous, why did the Lord Chamberlain prohibit the piece? Answer me that!" and Mr. Stanger brought his fist down on the table with a vehemence that made the inkstands dance. "I believe 'George Barnwell' had no salutary effect, and that 'Dick Turpin' was demoralizing" ("Pooh, a mere circus piece," from the Brocklebank faction); "and who, I ask, gentlemen, is to guarantee this theatre won't be a circus? Drury Lane has been a circus," and once more the inkstands jigged in response to Mr. Stanger's fist. "Commercially, I tell you, the whole affair is a sham. The town can't support a theatre, and it will never return the bare interest on the original debt, let alone a profit. And now, gentlemen, I come to the windiest part of this very windy gentleman's speech. He has favoured us with some classical reminiscences. I had not the good fortune of a university education, which he doubtless had." (Ironical cheers from the Stanger party, who were well aware the member for Stannagate got his education at Baumborough Grammar School.) " I can't quote Latin like my gifted friend, but am free to confess that, as far as I recollect, the old Roman mob war-cry he quoted might be freely translated prog and circuses. Gentlemen, do you contemplate keeping your poor in idleness and running this theatre for their amusement, or do you not ? If you don't I move, as an amendment to the motion of the member for Stannagate, that it be consigned to the like obscurity from which its proposer sprung."

Shouts of "Order, order," "Go on," "Hooray," and excuses, &c.

" Mr. Mayor," stuttered Brocklebank, purple with wrath, and rising to his feet, "I protest——"

" Spoke, spoke, divide, divide," chorussed the meeting generally.

" Mr. Mayor," suddenly exclaimed Dr. Ingleby, in those quiet, resonant, even tones, to which the turbulent meeting were well accustomed, "divested of acrimony and embellishments, this question seems to me to be in a nutshell—first, does Baumborough require a theatre, or does it not ? In my humble opinion, it ought to have one. Secondly, can the Municipal Council supply that requirement ? to which again I answer decidedly. I fancy the concern will always return a fair interest for our outlay, and we don't look to more on improvements ; " and here the doctor dropped quietly back into his seat.

" I have only one word to add," observed John Fossdyke, rising in his turn, " and that is to thoroughly endorse all my friend Dr. Ingleby has said, with this slight addenda, that I firmly believe it will be speedily found to prove a most paying investment."

" Might I ask, sir," inquired Mr. Totterdell (he had carried his point and achieved a seat on the Council), " whether Mr. Fossdyke has any previous experience of theatrical matters to warrant our belief in his opinion ? "

The Town Clerk's brow darkened, but he remained mute to the appeal.

"The question seems to me out of order," said the Mayor, "unless Mr. Fossdyke wishes to explain himself upon that point."

"I never give explanation to impertinent curiosity," rejoined the Town Clerk, curtly.

"I think, gentlemen, the sooner we come to a decision the better," said the Mayor; "there seems to be a bitterness imported into the question which I am at a loss to account for."

A good stock speech this of the Mayor's, and one which he had occasion to deliver on most occasions, inasmuch as discussion in the parliament of Baumborough meant, to its councillors generally, the releasing of much bile and personality, and the present meeting would have been characterized by its members as lively, but kept well within the bounds of decorum; and now came the decision—a close thing, as Dr. Ingleby had predicted, but the Brocklebank party were successful, and the building of a theatre was carried.

Very jubilant looked John Fossdyke as he rose in response to the Mayor's invitation to enter into the details of how he proposed to raise the funds for the carrying out of his new hobby, for that this was a hobby of the Town Clerk's was well known to every man in the room. Men are wont to look exultant when they carry their point, and yet there are often times when defeat would profit them more. Victory has wrecked many a throne and many a ministry; it is not sometimes till the battle is over that we find out what success has cost us, and the sight of the bill makes men ofttimes curse the hour they threw themselves into the fray. Triumphant is John Fossdyke just now, but he little dreams how speedily his account will be submitted to him for settlement.

He rises jauntily, and explains that for a prosperous town like Baumborough, with no liabilities worth mentioning, to borrow money on its rates at very moderate interest is the simplest and easiest of financial operations. He himself can, without difficulty, in the course of a few days, find people who will gladly advance the money required at four, or, at the outside, four and a half per cent.; indeed, he observes, the sole delay about the business will be occasioned—and here John Fossdyke favours the meeting with a jocular smile —in the haggling over the interest. "In short, gentlemen, it will probably take a few days for us to argue out a matter of £30 or so, and I think you may depend upon my attending carefully to your interests."

"But, Mr. Mayor, I would respectfully ask to submit one question to the meeting," bleated Mr. Totterdell. "I see by the half-yearly reports we have a sum of £5,400 lying at mortgage at four and a half per cent. on those new buildings connected with the railway. Would it not be more advisable to call that in than to borrow money?"

"Yes, Mr. Totterdell, that is quite a subject for the consideration of the meeting. Perhaps it *would* be better to invest that money in a theatre than to raise money for the purpose."

Again did John Fossdyke's brow darken as, with some little irritation palpable in his tones, he replied that notice had to be given about the calling in of mortgages, and that implied time. It was impossible that money could be available for some months, and he trusted now the theatre was decided upon, that it would be built and open ere that. He was an advocate for carrying things out at once, and not being a year before a resolution was acted on. Now all this was nothing to the member for Pickleton Ward; but Mr. Stanger, always restless and irritable under defeat, thought he saw some possibility of annoying his opponents, at all events John Fossdyke, by advocating Mr. Totterdell's proposal. He was on his legs in an instant.

"If," he said, "a mortgage requires notice to call in, a theatre requires time to build, nor is it customary to pay the contractor till the contract is completed. The contractor may demand an advance on work done, no doubt, but our credit is good enough with the local banks for such short accommodation as that implies. I most emphatically support Mr. Totterdell's suggestion, and beg that he will make a motion to that effect."

" Would Mr. Totterdell make a motion ? " Would he not —or half-a-dozen of them at the slightest encouragement. He got rosy red with excitement ; he fussed and plumed himself like the elderly turkey-cock he was, and he gobble, gobble, gobbled, and clucked as he got up to put his first resolution to the Council. This was the dream of his life, and he felt at last he was a factor in the government of his country. Baumborough might rejoice in a caucus some day, and he be the manipulator of it. Who could tell ? In the meantime no neophyte at St. Stephen's, whose maiden speech had the approbation of the Prime Minister, could have felt more thoroughly devoted to the man who had fully recognized his ability. Henceforth Mr. Totterdell was bound to the wheels of Mr. Stanger's chariot, and would throw in his lot with that gentleman.

There was much desultory discussion about Mr. Totterdell's motion ; and although, as far as he dared put himself forward, John Fossdyke strongly opposed it, neither Brocklebank nor his friends could see the slightest objection to such an arrangement, and it was consequently carried by a considerable majority. There were two men who walked away from the meeting of the Baumborough parliament that day who had both carried their points, and who were both destined speedily to regret such triumph. The one exulted much in his victory ; the other was already conscious that it was Quatre Bras before Waterloo. Mr. Totterdell was jubilant over the success of his motion ; but John Fossdyke wished grimly he had never advocated the building of a theatre in Baumborough

CHAPTER IV.

"MONEY NEVER WAS SCARCER."

MRS. FOXBOROUGH was sitting quietly in her drawing-room chatting with Nid, about a week after the latter's adventure in the Regent's Park, when a cab pulled up with a sharp jerk at the door, speedily followed by a sonorous application of the knocker. Mrs. Foxborough started. "That's your father, Nid!" she exclaimed; and dashing out of the room, found herself immediately enfolded in the arms of a dark, stalwart, florid-complexioned man, who kissed her with unmistakable warmth.

"Nid, darling," he continued, releasing his wife to embrace his daughter. "No need to ask how you are, child. You look more blooming and bonny every time I come back."

"You have no business to go away, papa," pouted Nid. "You can't imagine what ailments I suffer from in your absence."

"I have business, that's just what takes me away," laughed James Foxborough; "but I suppose, my dear, you can give me something to eat, for I am outrageously hungry."

"Of course; just go and sit down and talk to Nid for a few minutes, and I'll see about it at once. You sha'n't have long to wait."

That James Foxborough should appear suddenly and without warning in his home occasioned no surprise; it was his

way, he hated letter-writing, was a very bad correspondent,
and seldom gave intimation of his return till his hand was on
the knocker.   Even his wife was often in complete ignorance
of his whereabouts for weeks. She was used to it, and though
she occasionally declared she might as well have married a
ship captain, never worried her spouse about his shortcomings
in the epistolary way. By the expiration of Nid's narrative
of her misadventure, and how Sir Lancelot had come to her
rescue, a story which seemed to interest her father considerably, Mrs. Foxborough announced that refreshments were
ready for the traveller, and the three adjourned to the dining-
room.

"And has he called since to inquire after the distressed
damsel whom he succoured?"

"Indeed, he has," replied Mrs. Foxborough, "half-a-dozen
times, and we have got quite to like him. Nid, who was in
a great state of mind at first that her hero should not be up
to her standard of masculine beauty, has got reconciled to
his red hair at last, I believe."

"It isn't very red you know, mamma," said the girl,
"and I declare he's not half bad-looking."

"Morant, Herbert Morant. I've a hazy idea I know
something about some Morants.   I must ask."

"Don't flatter yourself that you are going to discover he is
heir to a large fortune, because he says he's not; and though
I'm sure he's awfully clever, he don't seem quite to know
how to turn his abilities to account," continued Nid.   "It is
embarrassing, that, you know, papa; I really should not
know myself whether to embark in tragedy or comedy."

"Tragedy, child, with your figure," cried her father,
laughing.

"I won't be laughed at," cried the girl, with a petulant
shrug of her shoulders. "I'm not so very small as all that,
and I'm not done growing yet—I presume I'm big enough
for Juliet, any way."

"Never mind, darling, it will be time enough to think of

that a year or two hence. Have you seen or heard anything of Cudemore lately, Nydia? I want to see him if he is in town."

"Yes; he was at the Syringa about three weeks since, and has called here twice since. Once we were out, and once we saw him. I don't care much about him myself, Jim; but, of course, I know he is a business friend of yours, and therefore I am always civil; still I don't want him hanging round here."

"I shouldn't think he's very likely to trouble you in that way," replied Foxborough.

"I don't know," replied his wife, significantly.

"He really is a nuisance, papa; and Mr. Morant, who met him the last time he was here, denounced him as an awful—an awful, what was it? Oh yes, I know—cad."

"Well, it is necessary that I should see him on a little matter of business. In the meanwhile, how is the Syringa doing?"

"Very well indeed. I don't say we haven't done better, but we can't complain. I'll just get the books and run over them with you. The receipts are well ahead of the outgoings."

"If you two are going to talk business, I shall run away till you have done," cried Nid.

"Do, my dear," replied her mother. "We sha'n't be very long, but your father and I must have a business talk, and perhaps the sooner it's over the better. You don't want Cudemore to find you money, do you?" she inquired, anxiously, as Nid left the room.

"That's just it," replied her husband.

"Oh, dear, James! You know what a terrible price he always makes us pay for it. I was in hopes now we were at last clear, that we should never have to go to him again. Besides, look at the books, there's a real good balance at the bank. Leave me £500 to go on with, and you can take the rest. I must have something in hand in case of a bad time at the Syringa—the salary list is so large."

"It's not near enough, Nydia; I want a good deal more than that."

" Why, surely you can't have had such a disastrous campaign as that. I don't know where you've been exactly; I never do know, but——"

" Tut, tut," he interrupted, " this is a different thing altogether. I am suddenly called upon to find money for a speculation I embarked in some years ago."

"But raise it somewhere else, Jim. I have particular reasons for wishing you not to get deep in Cudemore's books just now."

" Why particularly just now ? " with a look of no little surprise. " It's bad any time, I grant you; but why worse now ? "

" Because, you see, Nid is fast becoming a woman, and I feel pretty sure that Mr. Cudemore admires her."

" Why, she's a mere child yet, and as for Cudemore, he's old enough to be her father," exclaimed Foxborough, in utter bewilderment.

" Nid wants only a few days of seventeen, and Mr. Cudemore, though much older than her, is only some five or six-and-thirty after all. I don't think he would consider himself a bit too old to marry her."

" I don't suppose such an idea has ever entered his head. You women always think that the world is in a conspiracy to rob you of your daughters as soon as they become marriageable."

" We are better judges than you, Jim, believe me," retorted Mrs. Foxborough, smiling. " You men never suspect a wedding, though the whole preliminaries go on under your nose, until you're asked to the breakfast. Once more, I say, I am very sorry that you must have recourse to Mr. Cudemore, but if you must there's no use saying anything more about it."

" You're a sensible woman, Nydia ; and I'd take your advice in a minute if I could, but I must have the money at once, and I do not see my way as to finding it without Cudemore's help. He'll advance it, I dare say, on the security of the Syringa, though no doubt I shall have to pay stiffish interest."

Mrs. Foxborough sighed. It was not quite two years ago since they had cleared off the last mortgage on the Syringa, and the music-hall had at last become to them a really lucrative property. Previously they had had to be content with scarce a moiety of the actual profits, Mr. Cudemore and one or two others sharing very considerably in the success of the enterprise. It seemed a pity, Mrs. Foxborough thought, not to keep so flourishing a concern in their own hands, and though she was fain to admit that the capital which had enabled them to build and open the Syringa had been acquired by these country speculations of her husband, yet she did wish he would abandon them now, live quietly at home with her, and devote his whole energies to the management of the music-hall. True, she could and did rule that establishment most successfully herself, but she wished to have her husband always with her. These enforced separations were all very well when they were battling with this world in their early days, but now they had established a business that would keep them comfortably, and enable them to provide for Nid; what more did they want? She was tired of this perpetual grass widowhood; what reason now was there for its continuance? All this did Mrs. Foxborough urge, by no means for the first time, on her husband; but he replied that it was not so easy to withdraw from some of the speculations he had embarked in as she imagined.

"I am engaged, Nydia, in other things than country theatrical companies; and though, darling, I would like nothing better than to do as you say, and have done with them all, it is just now as impossible as it is to do without having recourse to Cudemore."

"I can only say once more, Jim, I'm awfully sorry; but you know best. How long am I to have you with me this time?"

"Very few days, I am sorry to say. Don't look so disappointed. I shall settle down and become the most humdrum of husbands before long, I dare say."

"Have you two done all your sums ? " laughed Nid, as she entered the room. " When mamma gets to her books, as she calls those awful-looking ledgers, I always run away. Do you know she threatened to teach me housekeeping the other day, and I felt just as I did before I fell sick of the measles."

"It is a thing you will most likely find the want of some day," replied her mother.

" Oh no ! oh no ! if *he* is not rich enough to keep a house-keeper *he'll* have to do the books himself," said Nid. "I can't add up, and I know they cheat me dreadfully in my change at the shops."

" Under which circumstances," observed her father, "unless *he* happens to be wealthy I shall send him about his business."

" That responsibility would rest with me, sir," replied Nid, with a mock courtesy. "Your posing as the tyrannical and despotic father would make even the elephants at the Zoological over the way trumpet with indignation."

At this moment there was a sharp knock at the door.

"A little late for a visitor," exclaimed Mrs. Foxborough. " I wonder who it is ? "

" Nonsense," said Nid, "it is Mr. Morant, of course ; and placing herself at the door, she threw herself into a theatrical attitude, and as it opened exclaimed, melodramatically, " Papa, my preserver ! "

If ever a young lady looked a little nonplussed it was Nid, as Mr. Cudemore quietly entered the room, and bowing low in answer to her exclamation, rejoined, " Delighted, I am sure, to hear it, Miss Foxborough, although quite unaware I had been so fortunate. How do do, Foxborough," he continued, turning to the manager, and bowing to his wife. " I heard incidentally at the Syringa that you were back, and came up just to shake hands with you."

Mr. Cudemore had an astonishing knack of hearing things **incidentally.**

"Ah! I had no idea they even knew of my arrival, but any way you are just the man I want to see. Tell them, Nydia, to put the tray in my den, and when you have said ' How do you do ' to the ladies we will adjourn there for a cigar."

That under these circumstances Mr. Cudemore's respects to the ladies was a thing speedily accomplished may be readily conceived, and in something like ten minutes he and his host were seated in a snug room at the back of the house, employed in the congenial task of selecting a cigar from one or two open boxes.

"These if you like 'em pretty full-flavoured, but try those small pale fellows if you like 'em mild, and now what will you take to drink? There's the usual triumv'rate, brandy, gin, and whisky, and seltzer behind you. Help yourself."

"Where have you been? Did you do pretty well on tour?" inquired Mr. Cudemore, as he lit a cigar.

"Never mind that; I want to talk to you about something else."

"Money?" asked Cudemore, with a slight elevation of the eyebrows. "Ah!" he continued, in answer to the other's nod of assent, "I thought so. When people want a quiet talk with me it's always on that topic. Money never was scarcer than it is just now."

"That, according to my experience, is its normal state," replied Foxborough, quietly, "more especially whenever I want to borrow any."

"Do you want much?" inquired the money-lender, languidly, for Mr. Cudemore was not at all of the old conventional type, but rather affected the languid man of fashion, though his dark eyes watched his companion with a glance keen as a hawk.

"Yes, a good bit. I want £6,000."

"That'll take some finding. What do you want it for?"

"That's my affair, and no business of the lender. The security is."

"Ah, yes, the security, what about that?" said Cudemore, softly.

"Well, the same as before—the Syringa—the plant there is worth the money pretty well, and then there's the building, with, as you know, a pretty long lease to run, as they gave me a fresh one when I undertook to erect the present house. However, you know all about it; you've had it in pledge before."

"Yes; but not for quite so heavy a sum, my friend."

"No; but you were not the sole mortgagee, then. You will be this time. There's no lien whatever on the Hall."

"If that's the case, I'll see what I can do," replied Cudemore, slowly. "You don't want this money immediately, I suppose?"

"Well, no, not quite; in a month or six weeks will do."

"Very good; I'll see about it; but you'll have to pay more than five per cent. I don't think the security will be considered quite good enough to do it at conventional prices."

"It should be. The security's good enough, and you know it," returned the manager.

"It may be, but people are whimmy on these points, and I doubt finding a client except at a tempting price. You might die or go broke, and then there might be a difficulty about getting a good man to carry on the concern; and where's the interest to come from if the Syringa shuts up?"

"They could always foreclose and recover their capital," retorted Foxborough.

"Oh, I don't know, nothing is so fluctuating in value as theatrical property. However, I'll do the best I can for you. No, nothing more, thank you; it's time I was off. Good night," and Mr. Cudemore took his departure.

"A point or two in my game," muttered that worthy, as he strolled homewards. "I wonder what Jim Foxborough wants with £6,000."

CHAPTER V.

M R. TOTTERDELL, having achieved, if not quite the object of his ambition, yet a provincial imitation of it, felt that it behoved him to be busy. Was he not the elect of the Town Council of Baumborough, and had not the eminent Mr. Stanger approved of his maiden effort at legislation? New brooms are proverbial for their investigation of nooks and corners. Mr. Totterdell was an idle man, and, it may be remembered, possessed with an insatiable spirit of curiosity concerning his neighbours, assiduously inquiring into the working of local rates; and the financial affairs of the Town Council enabled him to pick up information in a manner that might almost bear comparison with Dame Eleanor Spearing in Hood's famous "Tale of a Trumpet." The man was fast becoming a positive plague to Baumborough.

Nothing, perhaps, puzzled Mr. Totterdell more at the time than John Fossdyke's extraordinary indifference to the erection of the theatre. He had been the chief promoter of the scheme; he had taken a prominent part in carrying it through the Town Council, and now he seemed utterly indifferent as to its completion. He took no interest in its building, for it was by this time begun, and was progressing rapidly. He never went near it, and if appealed to and reminded of his professed knowledge of things theatrical, replied, "I know nothing of the construction of theatres; such things are best left to the architect." He had no doubt it would be an improvement thoroughly appreciated by Baumborough when they got it; in the meantime the unfortunate contractor was suffering quite sufficient impediment and annoyance already from the interference of fussy busybodies without his becoming an additional clog on his endeavours; and with this parting shot at Mr. Totterdell, who had gradually attained the position of his *bête noir*, the Town Clerk closed further discussion.

John Fossdyke was by no means the only man who began to regret the election of Mr. Totterdell to the Town Council. Baumborough was probably no whit more corrupt than its neighbours, nor even than that great windy Town Council of the nation which it so assiduously copied; but as every one knows, there is considerable give and take in all such assemblies, and an amicable understanding "that you wink at my little job and I wink at yours" is the unwritten law of all parliaments, local or national. But what was to be done with a man who, instead of promoting schemes of his own, spent his whole time in stripping the drapery off those of his fellows? Promote what you may, and it immediately becomes your business to demonstrate to the public that it will fill their pockets, that it will, if it succeeds, undoubtedly fill yours is an incident that it would be egotism to dwell upon. Mr. Totterdell, in his laudable desire for information and the doing of his duty as a Town Councillor, was always exposing this particular phase of his brethren's legislation; not intentionally, but nothing can lead to such mischief sooner than fatuous questioning in these matters. Even Mr. Stanger had been led, in a moment of exasperation at some unexpected sidelight being suddenly cast upon some pet project of his own, to stigmatize Mr. Totterdell as "a mere malignant interrogator that had lately crept into their

midst." Still, though abandoned of the great Stanger, Mr.
Totterdell was not without a small following. There are
always some people left out in the cold at all distributions
of the loaves and fishes, and these are keenly alive to criticism
of their more fortunate brethren.

"It is a most extraordinary thing, Mary, that your husband
should run away in this manner," said Mr. Totterdell, comfortably ensconced in his pet easy-chair in his goddaughter's
drawing-room at Dyke. "This theatre was his own pet
hobby, and now, instead of stopping to look after it, he goes
off nobody knows where. I have to do everything; the
architect is very pig-headed, and will insist upon having his
own way. Fossdyke knows I don't understand everything
about theatres, and yet he leaves everything to me. They
are all alike, the whole Council, even Stanger gets abusive
the minute one tries to make oneself useful; called me a
malignant something or other yesterday because I asked a
question connected with the paving and lighting rate. He's
a director of the Gas Company, you know, and I thought
was just the man to tell me."

"Rumour says the Gas Company have got a preposterously
high contract, and are making a very good thing out of the
lighting of Baumborough," said Miss Hyde, who was present,
and appeared to possess a considerable sense of the ludicrous.

"And how was I to get at that fact without inquiring?
How does one get at any fact without using one's tongue?"
rejoined Mr. Totterdell, testily. "Providence gave us tongues
for the purpose of asking questions. I suppose you will
admit that?"

"Well, I never heard that laid down as their special feature
in our organization," rejoined Bessie, laughing, "though I'll
admit that is a use some of us are apt to principally put them
to."

"You may depend upon it, when you become a public
man," and Mr. Totterdell rolled this out in unctuous tones,
as if the eyes of Europe were upon him, "there is nothing

like looking into things. Now there's your husband, Mary. a good man of business, no doubt, but he was about to make the mistake of levying an extra rate to pay for this theatre till I pointed out how much better it would be to use the money we had out at mortgage."

"I don't think my husband quite agreed with you on that point," rejoined Mrs. Fossdyke. "He said something about the imprudence of trespassing on your reserve fund."

This was rather a mild way of putting John Fossdyke's comments on Mr. Totterdell's proposal. He had stigmatized that gentleman to his wife as a doddering, inquisitive, fussy, mischief-making old idiot.

"Fiddle-de-dee, I am quite as much a business man as John ; but this is just what it is—no sooner do the Town Council find they have got a hard-working, business man among them, than they leave him to pull the whole coach. Nobody ever comes near this theatre but me. I've half a mind to resign, and be pestered with it no longer," and Mr. Totterdell looked round at the two ladies a little inquisitively to see how they received this mendacious statement.

He would no more have voluntarily resigned his seat in the Council than his life, and had a dim suspicion that his hearers were perfectly aware of that fact.

At this moment the door opened, and the footman announced "Mr. Soames, ma'am!"

"Now what on earth can that young brewer want here again?" ejaculated Mr. Totterdell.

Mrs. Fossdyke cast a mischievous glance at Bessie and burst out laughing, somewhat to the discomposure of the young lady, who coloured, bit her lips, and made a slight deprecatory motion of her hand as Philip Soames entered the room. A tall, dark, good-looking young fellow, and upon this occasion attired in flannels and white shoes, Phil looked the picture of a young athlete, and at boating, cricket, or lawn-tennis Phil Soames could hold his own very fairly. He had gone through the usual course of the offspring of the plutocracy now-a-days, been sent to Eton to make acquaintance with the sprouting nobility, graduated at Cambridge, and finally, after some one or two continental excursions, been called upon to take his place in the firm. There was not an atom of nonsense about Phil Soames; he and his got their living by beer, and the young one had never had any false shame about the mash-tub. There was a university story about Phil, often quoted in his favour.

It was at some late supper-party, of which the majority of the company were of the aristocratic order, when some eldest scion of a ducal family rather twitted him with his father's avocation.

"All right, Skendleby," he rejoined, laughing, "bear in mind the world grows more democratic daily, and it is quite possible the time will come when it can do without dukes, but there's no fear of its trying to get on without brewers. Hops, sir, will be to the fore when strawberry leaves are considerably at a discount."

If Phil Soames' path in life had been left entirely to his own discretion it was odds he had elected otherwise, but he was a shrewd, sensible young man, and when it was put plainly to him that he ought to prepare to take his father's place in the very thriving concern the brewery was, Phil at once responded to the call, and went in with a will, as he said, to learn his trade.

" I have come, Mrs. Fossdyke, to persuade you to honour the cricket-field with your presence, to remind you and Miss Hyde that Baumborough has been bearded by Bunbury, that we shall have a band playing all the afternoon, and tea properly set forth at the canonical hour. All Baumborough ladies are bound to share our triumph, or weep o'er our defeat. Don't you think so, Miss Hyde?"

"I think we are bound to crown you with bays if triumphant, which in these days means applaud till our gloves split. But if beaten, Monsieur, don't come to us for pity; and," she continued, speaking, "I'll not believe such a thing could

be. Don't you remember your grand victory over the
Bunbury men last year? Well, we are coming down to
see you play another such innings, are we not, Mrs.
Fossdyke?"

"Yes, Bessie, I think if Mr. Soames will give us some
tea as he promises, it will be a very pleasant way of passing
the afternoon."

Phil Soames murmured a grateful assent, which was undoubtedly genuine. The recalling of our former triumphs by
a pretty woman is one of the most insidious forms of feminine
flattery, and one which, accompanied by a triumphant smile,
as if they participated in the glory of the day, invariably
knocks over the male creature. It ought to be held unlawful,
and deemed as unfair as shooting a hare on its seat. So it
was settled that the whole party should come and take tea
on the cricket-ground, and witness, it was to be hoped, the
triumph of the Baumborough eleven, under the captaincy of
Phil Soames, having extorted which promise that young
gentleman took his departure.

Mrs. Fossdyke had for some time noticed Mr. Soames's
growing admiration for Bessie, and, to say the truth, was
very well satisfied with it, and had encouraged it unostenta-
tiously not a little. She had come to regard the girl almost
as her own daughter, as also had her husband. Who had
they to leave their money to but her, for neither of them had
any near relatives, nor did they care much about the few they
had. Mrs. Fossdyke thought it would be a very suitable
match, and though she could not but foresee it was quite
possible the Soameses might not like it, yet she fancied Phil
was a young man likely to insist on his own way in a point
of this kind. She gave the young man credit for plenty of
determination and strength of character, and in this she did
him only justice. The point she had so far overlooked was,
that Bessie was not Miss Fossdyke but Miss Hyde, and it was
her godfather's perpetual vague inquisitiveness as to " where
did she come from" that first made her remember that

5

question would naturally be asked by the Soames family in the event of any engagement between Phil and Bessie.

She questioned the girl, who adhered to her original story that she had been brought up by her aunt, and that when she grew up she had found that home uncomfortable. When questioned about her parents, Bessie grew strangely reticent. She believed her father was dead, and declined to say anything about her mother; further than she had a mother alive, Mrs. Fossdyke could elicit nothing.

Thanks to her godfather's insatiable curiosity, Mrs. Fossdyke found herself for the first time in her life face to face with a mystery—nay, more, as she dwelt upon the fact she pictured herself surrounded by mystery. The situation had its charm; to a woman who had so far led a humdrum life there was an astonishing salt given to existence by the very idea. Her imagination speedily supposed an occult connection between her husband's continual absences and Bessie Hyde—John had introduced her into the house. Was Bessie his daughter by a former wife or, more possibly, still living mistress? The girl admitted she had a mother alive, but declared that she had never known her father, and believed him to be dead. This staggered Mrs. Fossdyke. She was a clear-headed, good, plain, common-sense woman. She might not be clever, but was better calculated to get on in this world than many that are. She reflected that she had always found Bessie Hyde eminently truthful, and the girl never wavered nor hesitated in her account of her father. About her mother she refused to talk, and as to what station in life she might be in, Mrs. Fossdyke could learn nothing. Still, though after turning it over carefully in her own mind the good lady discarded this first solution of the riddle, the question yet remained as to where did she come from, and what was the business that occasioned these mysterious absences of her husband, and there was little fear that these problems were likely to escape her mind while Mr. Totterdell remained a constant visitor at Dyke.

The Baumborough cricket ground was a pretty sight this afternoon, thronged as it was with the townspeople and neighbourhood. It was very different from the great annual picnics at Lord's on the occasions of the University or Public School matches. Most of the ladies here knew something of the game, had relatives or friends engaged in it, for Baumborough was situated in the hop counties, in which cricket had its birth, and is at this present more understanded of the people than it is in the north. Was it not a Maid of Kent who invented round-hand bowling in accordance with the dictates of nature, unfavourable in women, to the underhand method, and laudably desirous of curbing the conceit of her brothers? There were four marquees at one end of the ground. Two of these were dedicated to the club and their guests, and the other two were open to the public; but all four seemed flowing with milk and honey. Two bands alternately rattled off gay, lively music, the one that of the Channelshire Yeomanry from Canterton, the other that of "The Baumborough Own."

"I'm alluding, of course, to the local volunteers," as the old burlesque song says.

It was altogether a very pretty sight when Mrs. Fossdyke and Bessie, accompanied by Mr. Totterdell, made their appearance upon the ground. It was an annual match, and whether Baumborough or Bunbury were the better men was a subject of considerable interest to the dwellers therein. This year the first trial of strength had taken place at Bunbury, and, after a fiercely-contested game, had terminated in favour of the home team. That Baumborough should be keen to wipe off this defeat was but natural, and Baumborough could urge with justice that she had not been enabled to exhibit her real strength in the first contest. Mr. Soames had been prevented playing, for instance, in consequence of a strained wrist, and both as a bat and wicket-keeper he was an irreplaceable loss to his side. Bunbury had just been disposed of as Mrs. Fossdyke and her companions arrived upon the ground, for a stubborn and somewhat unexpectedly protracted second innings, leaving their adversaries 153 to win. It was not a disheartening score altogether, but it was one that took a good deal of putting together among county elevens. Baumborough had begun so well, had got rid of two or three of their adversaries' best men at such a comparatively cheap rate, that they had felt rather astounded at the stand made by the tail of the Bunbury team. It is so at times, a good bat or two get set, and rather beat the bowling, and the last wickets knock up runs in an almost unaccountable fashion. But now it is Baumborough's turn, and Phil Soames sends to the wickets Tom Dumps, the most imperturbable sticker, and a Mr. Herring, a careful bat, one who can hit a bit when he gets fairly in. As for the redoubtable Dumps, he has been known to pass an afternoon at the wicket without adding twenty runs to the score. He is the sort of bat bowlers despise and hate. He never takes liberties, never goes out of his ground, and never hits; he guards his stumps, and now and again pokes one successfully away for a single; but he is nevertheless a very useful man at the start, always difficult to get rid of, and calculated to weary the attack of the enemy. Dogged, passive resistance is wont to aggravate, and inert defence to be the most exasperating of opposition, and the adversaries of Baumborough were always no little pleased to get rid of Tom Dumps.

"We learn from Horace, Homer sometimes nods," and upon this occasion the renowned Dumps was also caught napping, for before he had blocked, played, or poked some half-score balls, one ran up his bat, and dropped an easy catch into the hands of point. There was no slight dismay in the Baumborough camp at this unexpected casualty, but when Mr. Herring speedily followed suit, and also succumbed to the enemy's bowling, Phil Soames saw that demoralization was fast setting in amongst his followers. They were beginning to apprehend there must be something more than met the eye in the Bunbury bowling; and in cricket, as in

war, the establishment of a funk is fatal. Soames was equal
to the occasion. He saw, like a great commander, that the
time had come when it behoved him to place himself in front
of the battle, and, with a few courteous words of apology,
established Mrs. Fossdyke and Bessie in the ladies' tent, and
seizing his bat, went forth to do or die for Baumborough.

Phil Soames's arrival at the wicket threw quite a new
aspect on the game. He played a few balls easily, but quietly,
just to get his eye in, and then he began to hit freely. His
partner acquired confidence from the way his captain
" slipped into " the bowling, and runs came fast ; and when
Phil had to mourn his companion's departure, the aspect of
the game was entirely changed. The telegraph board showed
68 runs for three wickets, and the Baumborough Captain's
record was " 35 not out." Further, his men had recovered
confidence, and stood up to their adversaries' attack with
plenty of reliance on themselves.

Mr. Totterdell meanwhile was making himself a most
insufferable nuisance in the tent. It is not easy to explain
cricket to any one who does not understand it, and that was
just Mr. Totterdell's position. He wanted to know why a
man was out? why one man went in before another? He
wanted to know all about the financial state of the club, for
ever since his memorable hit about raising the money for
the theatre, Mr. Totterdell imagined he had much genius for
finances, and panted to reform all existing institutions in
Baumborough on this head ; had, indeed, been particularly
anxious in respect to the calling in of that mortgage he had
suggested to the Municipal Council, but the clerks in John
Fossdyke's office declined to give him any information in the
absence of their principal, while two or three cronies to whom
he mentioned it opined that the Town Clerk was best left to
do the town's business. Gradually people steal away from
Mr. Totterdell's vicinity. Those who, in their good nature,
had attempted to appease his thirst for knowledge, felt aghast
at the incubus they had saddled themselves with, and, exe-

crating their weakness, passed over to the other side the marquee, or out into the sunshine. Mrs. Fossdyke alone remains near her godfather.

The game is getting now highly exciting; after a well-played and most useful innings to his side, a good many of whom he has seen succumb during his stay at the wickets, Phil Soames fell a victim to a smart bit of fielding of the Bunbury men while rashly endeavouring to steal a somewhat risky run. Quite an ovation meets him as he walks back to the marquee, which the seventy-four to his name on the telegraph board thoroughly justifies. Baumborough have now fifteen runs to get, and three wickets still to be disposed of.

"Pray accept our congratulations, Mr. Soames," exclaimed Bessie Hyde, with a radiant smile, as she extended her hand. "You came nobly to the rescue at a time when things were looking very sad for us. We shall beat them now, don't you think so?"

"We can only hope so. It will probably be a very close thing. We have only one man we can rely on much for the runs left; but have you had some tea?"

"Oh dear, yes; I have been well taken care of, thank you."

"Then come for a stroll with me. Now the sun is low, it is pleasanter outside than in the tent."

They accordingly stepped forth amongst the throng that were promenading about this end of the cricket-field, and Soames had to stop more than once to receive congratulations from his enthusiastic fellow-townsmen on his successful innings.

"Let us get a little out of the crowd, Miss Hyde. I am no doubt as conceited as most people, but I am ashamed to be complimented any more before you. I expect you to laugh at me. As if no fellow ever put up seventy runs before."

"Ah," laughed Bessie, "I am afraid the vanity peeps out in that very speech. It is not so much that you got seventy-four runs, but that you got them for Baumborough when she needed them sorely."

"I stand properly rebuked," he replied, with an amused smile. "What a terrible analyzer of human motives you are! I feel almost afraid of you. Don't you find it rather trying seeing so much of Mr. Totterdell? I declare I never call at Dyke without finding him, and if he makes himself half as unpleasant there as he does in other places, you must have a hard time of it. I can't think how Fossdyke stands it. I don't wonder he is a good deal away."

"I am afraid Mr. Totterdell is doing unwittingly a great deal of mischief at Dyke," replied the girl, gravely.

"How so?"

"Mr. Fossdyke dislikes him, to begin with; in the next place, he is always inquiring into Mr. Fossdyke's affairs, and Mr. Fossdyke naturally resents that. Most men would."

"Certainly; but I don't see he is doing much mischief in that. He is committing an impertinence," said Phil, "for which John Fossdyke is just the man to snub him handsomely."

"No, but he has infected Mrs. Fossdyke with his own ungovernable curiosity, and she now has taken to questioning her husband about his business affairs. I assure you Mr. Totterdell has made Dyke so uncomfortable that I am very much afraid I must leave it."

"You leave Dyke—nonsense, Miss Hyde—why how can this affect you?"

"That I cannot tell you, but it does."

They walked on for some little time in silence. Phil Soames was under no delusion with regard to his feelings for Bessie. He knew that he loved her frankly and honestly, and had quite made up his mind to marry her if he could. If he had not as yet asked her to be his wife it was from no uncertainty of purpose on his part, but simply because he was afraid what her answer might be. She liked him well enough, no doubt, danced a good deal with him, and was always well content to have him assigned as her cavalier at dinner-party or picnic, but he'd a shrewd suspicion Miss Hyde

would look for rather more in a partner for life than a
partner in a ball-room or at lawn tennis. It must be borne
in mind that Baumborough was not aware of Miss Hyde's
exact position at Dyke. They looked upon her as a niece or
some relation of Mr. Fossdyke, now recognized as his adopted
daughter, and accepted her as such. Baumborough, no
doubt, in the first instance, had regarded Bessie as "a poor
relative," and rather a dependant, but the way she had
always been treated by the Fossdykes had speedily made them
adopt the other view. Neither the Town Clerk nor his wife
had ever announced Bessie's exact status in their house, but
had left Baumborough to draw its own deductions, and
Baumborough was certainly justified by appearances in the
conclusion it had come to ; but of course the result was that
Miss Hyde was regarded as a young lady who would probably
bring her husband a good bit of money, not perhaps at the
time, but in years to come. A pretty girl with these prospects
is not wont to want wooers, and therefore Bessie stood in a
very different position in Phil Soames's eyes to what she held
in reality. He doubted whether he had made sufficient
progress in the girl's good graces to risk asking her to be his
wife, and thought a premature avowal of his love might be
fatal to his hopes. His remark, when he did open his lips,
was by no means of a sentimental character.

"The confounded old idiot," he muttered, half aloud.

"You mean Mr. Totterdell, I presume," said Bessie.
"He certainly is not discreet, and things went on more
pleasantly at Dyke before his arrival in Baumborough,
undoubtedly."

"Why on earth does not John Fossdyke kick him out of
the house ? " asked Phil.

"He could hardly shut the door in the face of his wife's
godfather ; and you might as well hint to a rhinoceros that
he was not wanted as to Mr. Totterdell."

"I'd make him understand it, though, if I were Fossdyke ;
but never mind him. Why must **you** go ? "

"I have told you that Dyke has become so uncomfortable; I cannot tell you more."

"When do you mean going?" asked Phil, persistently.

"Oh, I can't say exactly; besides, it really can't concern you, Mr. Soames," replied Miss Hyde, somewhat coquettishly.

"You know very well it concerns me very deeply; you know, Bessie."

"Stop," interrupted the girl. "I declare we have forgotten all about the cricket. What does that cheer mean? Is that victory for Baumborough?"

Phil glanced for a moment at the telegraph board.

"Yes," he replied, "we have won by two wickets. But never mind that just now. I have something to say to you, something that I have wanted to say to you for some time."

"No, not now, please. I really must go and look after Mrs. Fossdyke," exclaimed Bessie, hurriedly; and she turned abruptly to walk in the direction of the tents, but almost immediately felt her wrist clasped gently, but firmly.

"I have gone too far, or not far enough," said Phil, in low tones. "You must hear me out now, Bessie."

They had gained in their stroll the opposite side of the cricket-ground to the marquees, and that, never much patronized by the lookers-on, was now entirely deserted.

"Stay one moment," said the girl, quietly, releasing her wrist, and fronting him; "listen to me before you speak. You think I am a relative of Mr. Fossdyke, and his adopted daughter, probably heiress to his property. Is it not so?"

He bowed his head in assent.

"I am nothing of the kind; I am no relation to him whatever. I am Mrs. Fossdyke's paid companion, at a salary of eighty pounds a year, though she has never allowed me to realize the position. Now, Mr. Soames, perhaps you will take me across the ground to *my mistress*," and the girl drew herself up defiantly.

"Yes, when I have said what I have got to say. What

you have told me astonishes me somewhat, but surely, Bessie, you don't think so meanly of me as to think it could make the slightest difference. You know I love you. Bessie, will you be my wife?" and as he finished he once more possessed himself of her hand.

She dropped her eyes, and for a few minutes he could see the colour come and go in her cheeks, and once she essayed vainly to speak. He could not understand her emotion, and when she at length found her voice, it came hard and mechanically, and she spoke like one repeating a lesson.

"I thank you deeply for the honour you have done me, but I cannot marry you, Mr. Soames."

"Why not?" he asked curtly, and in his excitement he crushed the hand he held almost savagely in his own. She uttered a slight cry and he released her. "Is it that you cannot love me?"

"No," she replied, as her voice shook and the tears gathered in her eyes, "it is not that. I could love you. God help me, I do love you, Philip, but I cannot be your wife."

"But why not? You own you love me. In a worldly point of view I am well able to take care of you, and honestly hope to win the consent of the Fossdykes as well as your friends to our marriage. I love you for your own sweet self. What reason can there be that you should send me away miserable?"

"I cannot tell you. I only know that I can never marry any one until he knows all about me; and I have not the courage to tell my story to you."

"Bessie, my darling, this is sheer nonsense. That you can have done anything in your young life that is bitter shame to you I'll not believe. You are shrinking from a phantom horror of your own imagining."

"No, indeed I am not. Please, please, Philip, take me across to Mrs. Fossdyke. See, people are beginning to leave the ground."

" Upon one condition, that you promise to tell me why you cannot marry me within the next three days."

" No, I cannot promise that, indeed I cannot."

" Well, will you promise me this, not to give me my answer decidedly till the expiration of that time ? "

Bessie hesitated for a minute or so, and then replied—

" Yes, if you wish it ; but it is not fair to you. I feel I shall only have to repeat that I can never be your wife, Philip."

She said the last words slowly and almost mournfully, and seemed to linger in almost caressing manner over the utterance of her lover's name.

" Bessie, if you love me truly, I'll not believe that you will give me the same answer three days hence."

She only shook her head sadly as they quickened their steps towards the now well-nigh deserted marquees.

" Why, my dear Bessie, I thought you were lost," exclaimed Mrs. Fossdyke ; " I have sent messengers in all directions in search of you. We can take credit for one thing, Mr. Soames, we really are pretty well the last to withdraw from the field."

" Very kind of you to come and so crown our hard-won victory, Mrs. Fossdyke," said Phil hastily, in order to cover his fair companion's confusion, but the young lady knew better than to compromise herself by making any excuses.

" Now, what on earth could that young brewer have had to say to Miss Hyde all this time," muttered Mr. Totterdell. " I never found him talkative myself."

CHAPTER VI.

MR. CUDEMORE AT HOME.

MR. CUDEMORE occupied a small house in Spring Gardens, the ground floor of which he had turned into offices. On the first he had a dining-room, opening into a larger apartment, fitted up as half smoking-room, half library, while above he had his bedroom and dressing-room. He is lounging at the window of this non-descript apartment on the first floor this afternoon, engaged in earnest conversation with a slight, fashionably-dressed man, who seems more interested in the flower in his button-hole than Mr. Cudemore's discourse. Only he looked so indifferent he might have been deemed one of Mr. Cudemore's clients; but people who are engaged in borrowing money seem usually more absorbed in the business in hand. Mr. Sturton was the well-known Bond-street tailor, who had found it expedient to do no little business with Mr. Cudemore. Sometimes he wanted that gentleman's opinion about bills he had received in the course of legitimate business; sometimes he wanted to get some he considered doubtful discounted, and Cudemore could very often get that done at a considerable sacrifice among his brethren, who will at times speculate in such commodities, if they can pick them up at a low rate, on the chance of their coming in some day, when more legitimate traders decline to have anything to say to such paper. Further, Mr. Sturton at times advanced money to his customers through the medium of Cudemore. He never affected to do such a thing himself, but when he had every reason to believe they were men of substance, would say, if they confided their troubles to him, that he believed Mr. Cudemore, of Spring Gardens, was a liberal gentleman in that line.

Professing amongst his friends the most democratic opinions, Mr. Sturton had a sneaking regard for his aristocratic patrons, and measured a marquis with an unctuous admiration most edifying to witness. He further affected a languid interest in the turf, about which he knew nothing, and cared less; but he thought it the proper thing to do, and one of his aspirations was to be as fashionable as his customers. It was of him that the following anecdote was narrated :—

Lady R., well known over the Leicestershire grass country, once entered his shop, accompanied by her liege lord, to give an order.

"I think I had the pleasure of seeing your ladyship at the opera last night," remarked Mr. Sturton, in his most dulcet tones.

"Good gracious, Dick! what does the man mean?" exclaimed the sporting countess. "Please tell him I've come to order a habit."

Poor Mr. Sturton, he perhaps never was more completely extinguished, and his talk waxed more fiercely Radical than ever; and though numbering many members of the House of Lords on his books, yet he vehemently demanded the extinction of the Hereditary Chamber.

"The security is excellent, I can vouch for. However, of course I'll make that all clear to you. I have got so much money out just now that I can't quite manage this business alone, and I am particularly anxious to help Foxborough."

"Why?" lisped Mr. Sturton.

He might affect a languid, lisping manner, but he was quite as keen a man of business as the money-lender.

"Well, it don't matter to you. I want you to find half this money at ten per cent.—not quite such interest as we have had, but then the security's better, and I'll buy you out again at the end of six months."

"I should rather like to know your object in being particularly anxious to help Foxborough. That he is a friend, and that you rather like him, is, you know, as well as I do, no argument in money-lending, which trade consists in obtaining the highest possible interest at the lowest possible risk."

"You needn't teach me my business," returned Cudemore; "I'm not quite a fool in it, as you must admit by this time. I have my reason for wishing to have some hold over James Foxborough. I could fancy your finding money for Lady Jane or Lord Augustus with a similar view. What would that be to me? Nothing. What concerns me is, is it safe and good enough to risk coin in? I tell you—nay, have shown you—this is; what more do you want? If it isn't good enough for you, it will be, no doubt, for somebody else," and Mr. Cudemore threw himself back into his chair, as a man whose argument is spent.

"Now it is no use going on like that," rejoined the other, in his usual languid fashion. "Of course I am curious to know your special interest in making this loan; but there is no necessity I should. Show me the security, is all I say, and I'll find my share of the money. I suppose that's sufficient," and Mr. Sturton looked with keen glance at his companion. He had no wish to quarrel with the money-lender, had many excellent reasons indeed for not doing so. "Now what about the bill of young Morant's—is that good? I suppose you have made inquiries?"

"Yes, that's good enough. I fancy we might go a little further with him if he wants it. What is it for?"

"Part payment of his account. He was hard up for ready money, a common complaint among my customers, as you know."

" Men don't quite expect to pay your prices, Sturton, and not get credit. Like the betting-ring, if you've only capital your business is sure to be profitable in the long run."

" Yes; only, like the bookmakers, our bad debts beat us at times," retorted Mr. Sturton, a little sharply. " However, I suppose we have nothing more to talk about. You'll want this money pretty soon ? " he observed, as he rose to depart.

" At once. Jim Foxborough is coming here to see me almost immediately about it. I told them to show him into the office if you had not left."

" Well, I am off now. You can depend on me for the coin in the course of two or three days. Adoo ! " and with this Mr. Sturton leisurely disappeared from the apartment.

" Now for Foxborough, I must impose terms upon him that won't be exactly in the bond ; but when a man wants money badly he's apt to assent to a good deal he wouldn't otherwise. Six thousand pounds, too, is not quite so easy to borrow, even when your security is pretty good. I wonder what he wants it for : he always has been a close man about his affairs, bar the Syringa, and that I was too much in to be kept in the dark about," soliloquized the money-lender. " He may have hit upon something of the same sort down at Birmingham or Leeds, promising to turn out as good a spec. as the Syringa. Crafty beggar, don't mean to have me in it this time, and perhaps he's about right," and Cudemore indulged in a dry chuckle, as he reflected over the money he had made out of the Syringa. What with advancing a few hundreds on loan at usurious interest, and taking a share in the venture, which it afterwards cost Foxborough a pretty penny to get back into his own hands, Cudemore had done uncommonly well over that business.

A tap at the door, and the money-lender's clerk announced that Mr. Foxborough was in the office.

" Show him up in five minutes, Cooper," rejoined Mr. Cudemore, as usual.

Mr. Cudemore's system was peculiar. His offices consisted of three rooms communicating. The outer and smaller one was tenanted by the office boy, the second served for the two clerks, the younger of whom was, though, a boy of preternatural acuteness; while the inner sanctuary was reserved for the money-lender himself. A second door enabled him, if he pleased, to leave the room, and gain the stairs leading to the rooms overhead. If he was in the office the visitor was requested to wait in the clerk's room; if not, he was ushered into Mr. Cudemore's sanctum, and left to wait there. All known clients were after a little delay shown up to the first floor, but the unknown were invariably interviewed to commence with in the office, the money-lender descending from above for that purpose, "like a hawk upon a wild duck," as an imaginative victim once described it, if he did not happen to be in his own private den. The five minutes' wait was often very much prolonged with a new or a shaky client, especially with a new one. "It don't do to have 'em thinking I sit here dying to lend money," argued that gentleman; "the sooner they understand the difficulty of borrowing it, the sooner they get reconciled to forty per cent., and acquire a taste for rare wines, fancy pictures, and other things that accompany the last agonies." Except with very big fish be in no hurry to strike, was the money-lender's maxim, and he was doing a pretty thriving trade.

"Mr. Foxborough, sir," said the clerk, once more opening the door; and that gentleman entered the room, to which this was by no means his first visit.

Mr. Cudemore shook hands cordially with his visitor, and immediately proffered a cigar and a glass of amontillado.

"Unless you prefer a brandy and seltzer," he added, thoughtfully. "Your business looks like coming all right, but we must have a talk over it; you see you want it so quickly."

"Getting the money to go into a speculation a month after the chance has gone by is not of much use," rejoined Jim Foxborough, sententiously.

" Ah, it's so urgent as that, is it? You must think it a very good thing to be so sweet upon it ? "

"Perhaps I do. It looks like it, or I shouldn't be so anxious to borrow money for it. It'll pay me pretty well, I fancy; but remember what it may be is no business of yours, nor have I any intention of telling you."

" Well, as you say, it is no business of mine further than that natural curiosity about our fellows' concerns that becomes a habit of my trade. You might want a few thousands more, you see, my dear friend," and Mr. Cudemore looked inquiringly at his visitor. " We might even find that, if one knew what it was for——"

"Never fear, I sha'n't come to you for them, even if I should. You might not think the security good enough, you know. When can I have this money ? "

" Oh, in a few days, if we can arrange one other trifling matter," rejoined Mr. Cudemore, slowly. " The fact is," he continued, and assuming an air of *bonhommie*, which did not sit particularly well upon him, " I am getting on, Foxborough, although I can still claim to be a young man."

The proprietor of the Syringa nodded.

" It is getting time, in short, that I settled down; in fact, married."

" Well, fire away," rejoined Foxborough, " I'm not your guardian. You don't want my consent, nor, d—n me, I should think, any one else's."

" Excuse me, but you can't marry a girl in this country without her consent, at all events."

" No, providing she's twenty-one; except, I'm told, in fashionable circles, and the higher bred they are the less, I hear, they have to say to it. However, Cudemore, I don't suppose you have set your affections on—

    'A nobleman's daughter—a lady of rank !' "

sang Mr. Foxborough, ribaldly chanting a well-known music-hall song of the day.

    6

" I'm talking to you in earnest," said the money-lender,
sternly ; " and the sooner you understand that the better it
will be for both of us."

Foxborough immediately assumed a more decorous manner.
The idea of Cudemore's marriage had rather tickled him, but
he now remembered men didn't like to be joked on the point,
and that " ridiculing the noblest feelings of our nature," was
always an admittedly good text to go into a passion upon and
use strong and fervid oratory.

" I beg your pardon, Cudemore," he exclaimed, " but the
old fox that has lost his tail must have his joke at the young
one who persists in entering the trap. I sincerely trust you
will be happy, and allow me to be one of the wedding
party."

He had utterly forgotten his wife's warning on this point,
had, in fact, deemed it so ridiculous that he had na more idea
of what Cudemore was driving at than the veriest stranger
could have had.

" Your absence could be scarcely spared on the occasion,"
replied the money-lender, a little huskily, for he recognized
that his visitor had as yet no idea of what he meant. " I
want your interest with Miss Foxborough in my behalf, and
your permission to make her my wife."

" You want to marry Nid ? Why, she's a child. Preposterous ! impossible ! absurd ! "

" I don't see anything absurd about it," replied Mr.
Cudemore, tartly ; for even money-lenders when smitten of
the tender passion are as sensitive as other men. " Many
girls marry young, and as for disparity of age, the fifteen
years between us is no more than exists in hundreds of cases,
and very often there is a great deal more ! "

" Why, the child's only fifteen or so," exclaimed Jim
Foxborough in all honesty, for that Nid was grown up nearly
and turned of seventeen had escaped his notice, as it has that
of many another father immersed in business which took him
much from home.

" She's in her eighteenth year, I have her mother's word for it, and I'm in my thirty-fourth," rejoined Mr. Cudemore.

" Shouldn't have fancied you'd ever see thirty-eight again," retorted Mr. Foxborough, with undue discretion, for the money-lender might have been anything between thirty and forty almost.

" It is just possible I may find the arrangement of the loan not to be managed if we can't come to some terms on this matter," returned Cudemore, grimly.

" And by G-d, sir ! " exclaimed Foxborough, " if you think Nid is to be thrown in as a bonus on the transaction you very much mistake me. I'd sooner bust up and go to prison than consent to such an iniquitous agreement. I'll not pretend but that this money is of great moment to me," he continued, mastering his passion ; " that the speculation I want it for is—is a thing, in fact, it is of urgent necessity ; but it is possible, no doubt, to raise the funds elsewhere, and I tell you again, sooner than trade my daughter away as if she was a slave-girl I'll do without it altogether."

Mr. Cudemore might be a little ruffled, but the training of his profession had demonstrated to him long ago the absurdity of losing his temper. He could not, therefore, fail to mark the incoherence of Jim Foxborough's speech. To quarrel with him was the last thing he intended. He had set his heart, as men of his age do at times, on marrying a scarcely emancipated school-girl. A rupture with her father was not likely to assist his wishes, and, moreover, this proposed loan was a safe, comfortable ten per cent. investment, with sundry legal charges of which Mr. Cudemore might count upon appropriating the lion's share, for he had qualified as a solicitor, though he never practised out of his own special business.

" I don't see," he said at length, " that you have any call to get violent because I want to marry your daughter. Miss Foxborough is a sweet, pretty girl, and good, I believe, as she's pretty. She's grown up, though you mayn't see it ; will have plenty of sweethearts before long, no doubt, and that I should want to be first in the field was mere common prudence on my part. I can give her a real good home. She may have her carriage, and need have no occasion to cut things fine in either her milliners' bills or her housekeeping. I don't know, as far as position goes, there's much to choose between you and me. I don't want to marry her against her inclination. I only want your good wishes for my success, that's all."

Jim Foxborough knew very well that was not a bit what the money-lender had meant, but it sounded all very plausible put in this manner, and then again he was in somewhat urgent need of this money.

"I cannot say I wish it," he replied, after a few moments' consideration. "I don't think her mother wishes it, and I don't believe the child herself has ever thought about it. I don't think you are a suitable husband for Nid. Hear me out," he continued, seeing the other was about to interrupt him. "I know you've got money, and can give her a good home and all that, but still I doubt her being happy with you. You've no tastes in common."

"Excuse me, Miss Foxborough's tastes are artistic, so are mine."

The proprietor of the Syringa stared for a moment in sheer amazement at the audacious speaker. At last he rejoined drily :

"Well, I should hardly have thought them so. I have no intention of interfering with Nid's choice when she is old enough to know her own mind. At present I undoubtedly don't consider her so. It will be time enough to talk about this a year or two hence, if you still wish it. Now, about the money?" and Foxborough threw himself back, and strove to affect an indifference to Cudemore's reply, which no man endeavouring to borrow money ever successfully achieved.

The money-lender felt he had failed signally in his scheme so far, but he was much too shrewd not to see that to come to a rupture with Foxborough was certainly not the way to improve his chance of marrying Foxborough's daughter. It was his interest to find the money from every point of view, and the pursuit of his own interests Mr. Cudemore never neglected. Naturally, he replied the money should be forth-coming.

CHAPTER VII.

"NID'S ADVICE."

ERBERT MORANT has suddenly awakened to the fact that he has made a confounded fool of himself. The fact dawned upon him as he lay in bed sipping his matutinal cup of tea one summer morning in Morpeth Terrace, and was brought home to his intelligence by the perusal of sundry blue-looking epistles that had just arrived, and which all contained more or less urgent appeals for money, the culminating shock being a polite intimation from Mr. Sturton that his bill at ninety days' sight for £100 would fall due on the following day, and he trusted would be duly met at the expiration of the ordinary three days' grace.

Mr. Morant had been cursed, as he himself said, "with a small independence, just enough to induce a man to do nothing, and not quite enough to live upon." He was not particularly extravagant, but he did what his associates did, and that among young men, in the heyday of youth, with excellent spirits and unimpaired digestion, meant a good deal. He assisted at most that was going on in town, and do it as you will, that runs into money. The consequence was, he was always spending more than he had. This had already twice necessitated dips into his limited capital, followed, of course, by a corresponding reduction of income, and it was now becoming clear to him that a third call upon his principal was imminent. It was disgusting very, just too as he had begun to think how nice it would be to settle down and marry Nid Foxborough.

" This must be looked into and put a stop to at once," he exclaimed, as he sprang out of bed and into his bath, and for the next few minutes there might have been heard a wondrous splashing and sluicing, mixed with muttered objurgations and sublime resolutions.

" Cursed fool, life chucked away, give it up, make a clean slate of it, suppose there'll bo enough left to buy bread and cheese ; I'll take up a trade, by the Lord, and stick to it ; must have the pull any way, you can't spend money while you are trying to make it."

It has been before pointed out that Mr. Herbert Morant was somewhat eccentric, and that, moreover, his slight eccentricities were not only tolerated, but contributed no little to his popularity. If there was one person with whom Herbert Morant was a special favourite, it was Mrs. Marriott, the housekeeper of the chambers in Morpeth Terrace, in a set of which Morant had resided ever since he left the university some five or six years ago. She regarded him as quite the pick of all her gentlemen, chiefly perhaps because out of the half-dozen or so tenants none ever bantered her as Herbert Morant did.

His toilet completed, he rang the bell for breakfast, and told the servant who brought it he wished to speak to Mrs. Marriott at her earliest convenience, and that lady's advent speedily followed.

"Ah ! good morning, Mrs. Marriott," he exclaimed, " I have sent for you to say that we are once more on the verge of a crisis—financial crisis, of course. I have experienced more than one since I have enjoyed the comfort of being under your charge."

" Lor', sir, I'm sure I hope it isn't very bad," rejoined the housekeeper, who had rather vague notions of what Mr. Morant called his crises.

" Mrs. Marriott, I must request no feminine frivolity," said Herbert, impressively. " I have instructed you in your duties during crises ; I presume you haven't forgotten them—the strictest economy, mind. I can afford nothing that costs ready money, except washing and candles. It's a mercy I can do without coals this warm weather. Your book, mind, must be absolutely an affair to be settled in Queen's heads——"

" And with regard to other things, sir, I suppose they're to go on as usual ? "

" Quite so, Mrs. Marriott. Anything that goes down in a book you will obtain as usual. We must not disturb the mysterious currents of trade, nor derange any fellow-creature's system of double entry. You understand, Mrs. Marriott ? "

" Yes," replied the housekeeper, laughing ; " but you know, sir, it makes no real difference. You said yourself last time it all came to the same thing at the end of the quarter."

" You don't understand these things, Marriott. I am acting on the soundest financial principles. When there is a run upon bullion the Bank of England always raises the rate of discount, which is tantamount to declining to part with ready money except under severe pressure. That's the principle ; we must exist like the snipes this quarter, on lengthy bills. Also remember I am never at home, or laid up with confluent smallpox. Great men like editors, and gentlemen in difficulties, are always hard to interview. Were you ever in gaol, Mrs. Marriott ? "

" Lord, sir, what a question ! " said the housekeeper, rather indignantly.

" Pooh ! I don't mean as a victim ; I mean as a consoler."

" Well, sir, I don't know whoever could have told you, but when Marriott got into difficulties and was ' took,' I used sometimes to go and see him," whispered the widow. " I sometimes think that it was his anxieties that killed him."

Perhaps they had, for the deceased Marriott's, a retired butler who had gravitated into the public line, chief anxiety latterly had been the attainment of as much brandy and water as possible.

" Mrs. Marriott, when they have cast me into a dungeon with gyves upon my wrists, I shall expect you to visit me as somebody in history, whose name I don't precisely recollect, used to visit somebody else whose patronymic at this minute I can't exactly remember."

With which Christy Minstrel jest Mr. Morant dismissed his housekeeper, and lighting a cigar, sat down to reflect upon his position. He had had his joke with Mrs. Marriott, but there was some method in his madness. The housekeeper did not understand a good deal of his chaff, but she thoroughly comprehended the main drift of it, to wit, that money was scarce, and that lunches and dinners in chambers when ordered were to be based on economical principles. Still, this sort of saving is not much use to a man in a big money scrape, and as a rule men never live so well as just before bankruptcy. I think it is in Disraeli's ' Young Duke' that the Marquis and his wife, having tried economy for a year and found it a failure, once more announce expense as no object. The saving seemed so utterly inadequate to the effacement of the difficulties as not to be worth going on with. Herbert Morant was no fool, and was quite as well aware of this as that continued reckless living only increased them. What was he to do ?—as for paying his debts there would be little difficulty about that, but it involved further sacrifice of capital, and this would be to leave him with a very shrunken income. A man who had failed to make both ends meet on five hundred a year was hardly likely to get along on little more than half that sum.

There could be no doubt about it, he must do something. If it had not been for Nid it is odds he would have decided on emigration—realizing his capital, and trying his luck in Australia or New Zealand; but he could not make up his mind to lose all hope of winning Nid for his wife. His visits had been frequent to the cottage by the Regent's Park of

late ; and though he saw but little of the master of the house,
Mrs. Foxborough always received him quite graciously, and
Nid with the sunniest of smiles. She tyrannized over him in
the prettiest way, was always giving him petty commissions,
such as procuring her a song, some flowers, a new book, or
else " the correct version of a little bit of theatrical gossip,"
and Herbert Morant kissed his silken chain of servitude
metaphorically, and exulted that he was bound to the wheels
of the child enchantress's chariot. He wished to marry this
girl, and had fair reason to suppose that neither she herself
nor her mother would be averse to such a proposal on his
part—true, she was very young, only sweet seventeen, but
girls have been " wooed and married and a'" at that age
many times. Now, what was he to do ? If he had embarked
in any profession when he first came to London, and stuck
to it, he would have now been probably making an income
that, joined to what he had of his own, would have enabled
him to offer any girl a modest home. He had made a fool of
himself, but it was no use tearing his hair over that ; the
question was, what was he to set his hand to ? At twenty-
eight a man can hardly be said not to have a career still
before him.

He smoked on, and still the problem seemed no nearer of
solution.

" Confound it !" he exclaimed, " dear old Phil Soames used
to say at Cambridge—' A man with average ability and education, if he has only energy, can always get his living.
Don't you believe he can't—it's only want of determination
that prevents him. He goes about asking for something to
do, instead of telling people what he wants to do, and asking
them to give him a start.' Hang it—what is it I want to do ?
and I can only answer vaguely something to get a living out
of. Dear old Phil, I wonder where he is now. He used to
talk so plucky about getting his living, but I fancy his bread
was pretty well buttered all the same, and he has not had
much occasion to trouble himself on that score. Heigho, I

don't get on with this cursed conundrum—How I'm to
make a respectable living—it's the toughest double acrostic
ever was tackled. I think I'll go up to the cottage and talk
it over with Mrs. Foxborough. She's a shrewd, practical
woman."

Arrived at the cottage, he was shown into the pretty
drawing-room, which he found tenanted by Nid only.

" Mamma's out," she said, as she greeted him with a smile,
" so you will have to put up with me for the present."

" That is a fate most men would resign themselves to with
much satisfaction; but I do want to see your mother all the
same."

" Nothing easier; you will only have to wait a little. I
don't suppose it will be very long before she is in. It has
one drawback, for you will be expected to entertain me."

" I can't say I feel much like entertaining anybody; the
fact is, I have got into a scrape, Nid."

" I am awfully sorry ; but do—do you think you ought to
call me Nid ? " asked the girl, with a demure hesitation irre-
sistibly coquettish.

" Certainly ; doesn't everybody who knows you really well
call you Nid ? Didn't your godfathers and godmothers on
your baptism give you this name ? " replied Morant.

" No, sir; they did not. I was christened Nydia Foxborough ; but what are these ? " she continued, as Herbert
extracted from his pockets a small parcel and an envelope.

" That is the broken fan you gave me, I hope now duly
repaired ; and that is the box for Covent Garden next Friday.
Your mother promised to take you if I succeeded in getting a
box, and I triumphed."

" Oh, how good of you ! Ah, yes, Mr. Morant, I think I
must be Nid to you."

" You mercenary little lady ! was there ever such a case
of bribery seen, I wonder ? "

" Don't laugh at me—how dare you ? What girl in her
teens wouldn't overlook being called by her Christian name

in a man who brought her an opera box ? But what is the scrape you have got into ?—nothing very bad, is it ? "

" No ; I have only been spending more money than I ought."

" Why get this opera box, then ? It is very kind of you, but surely it is only spending more money again."

If Nid had never known what it was to want money, she was not used to lavish expenditure either. Her mother was an excellent manager, and made their income go a long way while living comfortably, but Nid was not unaccustomed to hear the expression, " they couldn't afford it."

" Oh, that makes no difference, and it will give you a pleasure, and I should never count loss much in that case. It isn't the money part of the scrape. I can pay my way out of that ; but the thing is I must really get to work and do something for my living."

" Surely, there's no great hardship in that," rejoined the girl, who was wont to see most, both of the women and men, with whom she came in contact earn their bread, and who looked forward to doing it herself in another year or two.

" No, certainly not ; but you will hardly believe it, Nid, that, great hulking fellow as I am, upon my word I don't know how to set about it. There was a dear old friend of mine who used always to say that any man with tolerable brains, a fair education, and energy, could earn a decent living."

" Would you think it very presumptuous in me if I offered you advice ? " said Nid, timidly.

" No. What is it ? "

" I think if I were you I would consult that friend."

" Eureka ! You don't know what that is, but it's equivalent to the very thing in this case. What a clever little girl it is ! Look here, Nid, I'll follow your advice, and you shall keep my secret. It would be very sweet to think that I owed my start in life to you, darling."

" Mr. Morant ! "

" Well, I allow I hadn't the right to call you that yet; but I hope to have some of these days. Ask your mother if I may come to your box at Covent Garden on Friday. I shall not wait to see her now—I found such a shrewd adviser in her place."

" Come and dine with us, and escort us properly. The brougham has a back seat, and I'll see mamma sends you an invitation."

"Thanks; that will be delightful. Good-bye, and God bless you, darling," added Herbert as he shook hands, and this time Nid only laughed as she held up a chiding fore-finger.

If there was not an engagement between these young people, they had, at all events, arrived at a tacit under-standing.

CHAPTER VIII.

"DISCORD AT DYKE."

T is all very well, John, but it is not fair to keep your wife in total ignorance of everything," exclaimed Mrs. Fossdyke upon the evening of her husband's return, as they sat in the drawing-room at Dyke, indulging in a *tête-à-tête* after Miss Hyde, pleading a bad headache, had retired to bed. "You go away, I don't know where, and refuse to tell me anything about your proceedings when you return."

"You know very well, Mary, I never discuss business subjects with you, nor very much with any one else. I have played my hand alone all my life."

"But remember it was my money gave you your first real start in life, and I do trust——"

"You're entitled to remind me of it for the remainder of my existence. Listen to what I say. I never did, and never mean to, talk over my affairs with you. I got you to understand that once, and you were quite content, and never troubled your head. We were excellent friends in those days. Now that meddling mischief-monger, old Totterdell, has poisoned your understanding, and you're simply an incarnation of suspicion. The doddering old idiot has been to my office while I was away, questioning my clerks about some of my business. You don't suppose I mean to stand that. Of

course my people were much too well trained to tell him anything; but the next time he comes here I shall tell him to
go, and if he can't take that as a hint—and he is not good at
taking hints—I shall kick him down the front doorsteps and
see if he comprehends that."

" John, you couldn't ! My godfather ! How dare you talk
so ? He is an old man, too, recollect. All Baumborough
would cry shame on you."

"Don't you believe it ! Totterdell has made himself so
obnoxious of late from his perpetual inquisitiveness and
gossiping that I think Baumborough is more likely to express
astonishment I hadn't done it long before; but he is, as you
say, an old man, and therefore safe from anything of that
sort. Still, mark me, I'll have him about Dyke no more, and
the sooner you make that clear to his understanding the
better. If you don't, I shall, and it will be probably a little
more coarsely conveyed to him."

" I'll not have my relatives debarred my house," retorted
Mrs. Fossdyke, with a stamp of her foot, and an angry toss
of her head ; " more mine than yours, I've little doubt, if we
could only look into how it was paid for."

" I'm not going to argue with an angry woman."

" I never was calmer in my life," screamed Mrs. Fossdyke.
" If there is any loss of temper it is on your side, I'm sorry
to say, John. Talk about kicking relatives down the front
doorsteps, indeed ! "

" He is not a relative, and I've told you I'm not going to
kick him."

" I detest nagging, it's unmanly. Now perhaps, Mr.
Fossdyke, you will explain to me all about Miss Hyde."

" I've told you already that there is nothing to explain
further than has been explained. Bessie can go whence she
came if it is your wish, in fact, no doubt will if, prompted by
your imbecile godfather, you make things unpleasant to
her."

" I don't; it is you who make things unpleasant by half-confidences and abuse of my relations." And Mrs. Fossdyke sniffed defiantly.

"As I told you before, he is not a relation."

"Oh, no, perhaps not in the eye of the law; but I should hope there are moral principles which guide us in reference to the ties of kinship."

"If you'd some moral principles that guided you in the paths of common sense, Mary, it would be a comfort," retorted John Fossdyke, angrily.

"I may be a fool—quite as big a fool as my unfortunate godfather; but I'm not an idiot either, John," retorted Mrs. Fossdyke, now perfectly white with anger. "Again I ask you, Who is Miss Hyde?"

And now it began to dawn upon John Fossdyke that he was likely to get the worst of this quarrel, for he was very fond indeed of Bessie, loving her as his own daughter, which she was not, whatever suspicions might have arisen in the brain of Town Councillor Totterdell or the wife of his bosom; but he foresaw that Mrs. Fossdyke's jealousy was aroused concerning the girl, and that it would probably overwhelm the regard in which she had held her. The calling her ostentatiously Miss Hyde, instead of the more endearing Bessie, was significant of the brewing of the tempest, and in his heart the Town Clerk muttered maledictions against Totterdell the inquisitive, heavy, if low.

"Well, Mr. Fossdyke," resumed the lady, lighting her bedroom candle, with no little parade, "I ask you once more, Who is Miss Hyde?"

"You had better ask her, Mary?"

"Oh, you needn't think I haven't done that, but she declines to tell me anything about herself; says her father is dead, that her mother is still alive, but she refused to say anything further. You can tell me something about her mother, I make very little doubt."

"Go to bed, woman," rejoined her husband, sternly. "You little know what you are talking about. If ever you

gain the knowledge you crave, it may be the worse for you.
Go to bed, I say, and check the scurrilous tongue of you."

For a few moments Mrs. Fossdyke was awed by her
husband's manner, then recovering herself, she exclaimed,
" It is quite evident you do know all about her. I have only
to say I must refuse to tolerate a young person whose antecedents are involved in such questionable mystery any longer
under my roof."

"It isn't your roof," thundered John Fossdyke, now
thoroughly aroused, "and it is for me to say who shall
shelter beneath it. I begin to comprehend how men are in-
censed to raise their hand against a woman, and how a
century ago a country squire might have recourse to the
stirrup-leather."

The lady became aware of a look in the face of her lord
she had never seen before, and though a high-spirited woman,
she shrank before it, and retired without even hurling that
Parthian gibe so loved of her sex.

John Fossdyke knew that this was but a barren victory.
He might decree what he pleased, yet if his wife chose she
could easily make Bessie's further residence at Dyke impossible. Not only as mistress of the house could she make
Bessie's position intolerable, but if she suddenly discoun-
tenanced her, and said markedly that Miss Hyde was a
protégée of her husband's, and lived with them not because
she (Mrs. Fossdyke) wished it, but because Mr. Fossdyke
ordered it, there would be a pretty wagging of tongues in
Baumborough, and Bessie was like to have little character
left, poor girl, before many weeks were over. He could
picture it all—Bessie's astonishment at the first rebuff, her
agony at finding herself shunned by those who once made so
much of her, while Mrs. Fossdyke posed as a cross between
an outraged woman and a Christian martyr, and finally the
Town Clerk cursed the wife of his bosom as he thought of
what she might be capable in her wrath.

And yet she was by no means a bad-hearted woman, nor

7

yet a bad-tempered one ; a little wearing it may be at times on the subject of her family and the dower she had brought her husband ; her present unhealthy state of mind had been brought about slowly but entirely by Mr. Totterdell. His inquisitiveness and conjectures had first sown suspicion in her mind. She had gradually brooded over things, stimulated all the time by her godfather's perpetual questions and speculations, till she had constructed a very pretty little romance for herself, to wit, that Bessie Hyde was John Fossdyke's illegitimate child, and that her mother was still living somewhere under his protection. No wonder the good lady's temper grew a little crisp at her assumed discovery. That Miss Hyde seemed dull and out of spirits John Fossdyke thought only natural. She had welcomed him warmly, but somewhat sadly, on his arrival, and had, as beforesaid, pleaded headache and retired early. That Mrs. Fossdyke had commenced making Dyke impossible to her was evident to the Town Clerk, but in this he did his wife injustice ; further than severe cross-examination as to her birth and parents Bessie had no cause to complain. The mistress of Dyke kept all her wrath for her husband.

But Bessie had her troubles. She had promised to give Philip Soames an answer to that question he had asked in the cricket-field in three days. The three days had elapsed and the answer had been given, and Bessie was sore at heart she had given it. She had told him that she could not be his wife without telling him her secret, and she had told him she could not make up her mind to do that. Philip had pleaded his best, and the girl loved him very dearly.

" Listen, my darling," he had said, " I'll not believe that you ever committed any ill ; only tell me that you come to me with no stain upon your name, and that no one can point the finger of scorn at you, and I'll ask for no more. Keep this terrible bugbear to yourself as long as you list, and one day we shall laugh at it together, believe me."

But Bessie had hung her head and declined to give the

desired assurance, and Philip Soames had taken her in his
arms, pressed his lips solemnly on her brow, and walked
sadly away into the night; and Bessie had gone up to her
room, had a great cry, and wondered if she could have felt
more miserable if she had confided that woeful secret to her
lover. He might have declined to take her, as, indeed, she
had compelled him to do now; but he would have pitied her,
and Bessie felt proudly that, think what he might, her story
would never have passed Philip Soames's lips. Then she
thought she would consult Mr. Fossdyke when he came back.
Why had he not been at home, that she might have consulted him during those three days? It was too late now.
Like the sped arrow, the word spoken never comes back, and
she had said Philip Soames nay, and received his farewell
kiss. She must leave Dyke, she thought. She could not
endure to meet her lover constantly, and he knowing there
was a story of shame connected with her. She would feel
now as if all Baumborough knew it. While the altercation
was going on in the drawing-room between John Fossdyke
and his wife, Bessie had in the quiet of her chamber made up
her mind as to what she would do. She would confide to
Mr. Fossdyke all that had passed between her and Philip
Soames, and then she would quit Dyke and look out for
another situation. That she should ever be as happy as she
had been at Dyke was not likely, but she would prefer anything to going back to live with her aunt. Thanks to John
Fossdyke's liberality, she had money in hand to maintain
herself easily for the next few months, and surely before that
time expired she would have found something to do.

Now the Town Clerk was just as desirous of a private con-
ference with Bessie as she was with him, and after breakfast
the next morning he, perfectly regardless of his wife's snort
of indignation at the proposal, said quietly,—

" Come into the garden for ten minutes, Bessie; I have
something to say to you."

" And I to you, Mr. Fossdyke," replied the girl, as she
stepped out of the window on to the pleasaunce.

"Which of us shall commence?" asked the Town Clerk, as, having gained the rosary, they seated themselves on a bench.

"I think I had better listen to you first," replied Miss Hyde.

"Very good. What I have got to say is soon said. You will believe me when I tell you how sincerely sorry I am to have to say it, but I see no alternative. I think, Bessie, you must leave Dyke. Mrs. Fossdyke has been so worked upon by that miserable old fool Totterdell, that she has constructed a mystery in her mind about you which makes your further stay here impossible for me. What the exact maggot she has in her brain may be I don't really know, but from her present temper I fancy you also would find remaining with her equally impracticable. Has she been making things unpleasant to you as yet?"

"No, indeed; further than that she has manifested great curiosity about my antecedents," replied Bessie, hanging her head, "she has been kind as ever."

"And now what is it that you have got to say to me?" asked John Fossdyke.

"That for a reason of my own I also think it is best I should leave Dyke. Mr. Fossdyke," continued the girl earnestly, while the blood surged to her temples, "you know all about me, and I only know how good you have been to me. Since you have been away Mr. Soames has asked me to marry him."

"My dear child, I am delighted to hear it. He's not only a good match from a worldly point of view, but there's not a finer, more straightforward young fellow anywhere within hail of Baumborough; any girl might be proud to have won his love."

"But—but," replied Bessie, as the tears gathered in her eyes, "you know I could not say yes."

"Good heaven! girl, you don't mean to say you have said no to the best *parti* in the neighbourhood?"

" How could I do otherwise, unless I had the courage to tell him my luckless history? You know, Mr. Fossdyke, I could not do that."

" I am not at all clear about that. You have been twitted with your birth by an acidulated puritanical aunt, from the moment you grew old enough to understand it. I also have recommended you to keep silence on the subject, and pointed out that it would be always against your getting any such situation; not, I trust, as you hold here, but as you meant seeking when I suggested your coming to us, and then your sweet cousins, no doubt, were always casting it in your teeth. Now, answer me these two questions, How much did you tell Philip Soames?—for of course you told him something—and do you think he loves you in genuine earnest?"

" I told him," replied Bessie, " my real position here; that I was neither relation nor adopted daughter of yours, whatever Baumborough might think, but simply Mrs. Fossdyke's paid companion."

" Ha! and what did he say to that?"

" That it made no difference; that he was ready to take me for myself; but I told him that it could never be."

" There, Bessie, my dear, I don't quite agree with you. If you like Philip Soames well enough, I think it will be. I don't imagine your antecedents will, from my knowledge of his character, have much weight with him. You are quite right, he must know your whole story first; and if—as I believe he will—he again asks you to marry him, your fate will be in your own hands. It will be my business to let Soames know your secret."

" I really am tired of all this mystery," exclaimed the voice of Mrs. Fossdyke, who, attended by Mr. Totterdell, had advanced noiselessly over the soft turf, and caught her husband's concluding words. " If there is a secret connected with Miss Hyde, then I claim to be informed of it at once. I should fancy I am a much more proper person to be entrusted with it than Mr. Soames."

As for Mr. Totterdell, his face depicted the most lively curiosity, while his ears were evidently literally agape for intelligence.

"Who did he say she was, Mary?" he asked, breathlessly, glancing at Bessie.

But John Fossdyke rose in his wrath, with that look on his face that his wife had never witnessed till the previous night.

"Who Miss Hyde is matters little to you, as from this time I trust you will abstain from ever darkening my doorstep again; your mischievous tongue and insatiable curiosity have already caused plenty of unpleasantness in Baumborough. You occupy yourself prying into my private affairs, and I tolerate that from no man. Go, and let me see no more of you at Dyke."

"Yes, sir, I shall go," retorted Mr. Totterdell, "and I shall not return; but if you think, John Fossdyke, your losing your temper is going to stop people talking, you are very much mistaken. I assure you all Baumborough are wanting to know who Miss Hyde is," and with this parting salvo the old gentleman took his departure.

"As for you, Mary," continued John Fossdyke, sternly, "you need trouble yourself no more about secrets or mysteries. Bessie will leave us in about a week. I have just arranged it with her," and so saying, he turned abruptly and walked back to the house.

As for Mrs. Fossdyke, instead of, as might have been expected, pouring forth the vials of her wrath upon Miss Hyde's head, she sat down upon the bench and indulged in a good cry at the idea of her departure; even going so far in her penitence as to admit that had it not been for her godfather, she would never even have dreamt of there being any mystery about Bessie.

CHAPTER IX.

"WHAT A TEASE YOU ARE, HERBERT."

HEN Mrs. Foxborough heard her daughter's account of Herbert Morant's visit, she looked somewhat serious. Nid had not told all the particulars of that visit, and her mother knew very well that she had not. Mrs. Foxborough quite understood, from the way the girl told her story, that there had been definite love-passages between her and Herbert Morant; and Mrs. Foxborough now asked herself whether it had been wise on her part, not merely to allow, but to encourage the intimacy between them. She in her own heart was decidedly averse to Nid's appearing on the stage. What she desired for her daughter was that she should marry a gentleman in easy circumstances, and never have anything to do with the profession. She would have scorned the idea of endeavouring to entrap Herbert Morant; in her eyes Nid was good enough for any scion of the peerage, but she liked the young fellow, she thought Nid also had a *penchant* that way. And, well, if they should happen to fancy one another, Morant was just the son-in-law she should welcome with much satisfaction. But this account of his impecuniosity was a startling surprise for Mrs. Foxborough. She had no idea but what Morant was a man in easy circumstances. A rich man, no; but a man who could take very

good care of her child if she gave her into his hands.   Mrs.
Foxborough thought now, if Nid married him, the girl would
have to begin at once to take her share of bringing grist to
the mill ; and then Mrs. Foxborough had grim reminiscences
of many a case in her own experience in which the wife had
made the income, while the husband contented himself with
spending three-fourths of it.   She was much too clever a
woman to say anything to Nid, but she bitterly regretted that
she had allowed Morant to attain so intimate a footing in the
house.   As for her erratic lord and master, he was once more
off on one of his country tours ; but even had he not been, it
is doubtful whether Mrs. Foxborough would have deemed
this quite a case for consulting him about.

She yielded, of course, to Nid's petition, and allowed that
young lady to send off a note of invitation to dinner for Friday
night, but she puzzled her brain meanwhile no little as to
how she should manage to place Herbert Morant on that
distant footing that she was now extremely desirous to see
him upon.   She was worldly and vigilant, as keenly alive to
a detrimental match as any Belgravian mother, when it came
to the disposal of her treasure.   Of no gentle birth herself,
she had mixed enough in fair society to attain refined manners
and to appreciate them.   That Nid should marry a *bonâ fide*
gentleman was an article of faith with her ; but then he must
undoubtedly have enough money to support a wife.   Morant
had answered all these qualifications, she thought, and now
he had unexpectedly broken down in a very essential one.
And while we scheme and plot in our little way, the gods
give another shake to the kaleidoscope we call life, which
produces quite a fresh arrangement of the pieces, and produces corresponding perplexity in our minds as to what is the
goal we are desirous of arriving at.

Herbert Morant, meanwhile, was simply delighted with
the so far success of Nid's idea, and sanguine after his manner
as to the result.   Philip Soames had not only answered his
letter, but answered it in the most satisfactory way.

"Not only," he said, "do I still stick to my old theory that there's work to be had by any man with average brains and energy, but I can find it for you. Come down and stay with me for a fortnight, and talk it over. I shall be delighted to see you, old man, if nothing else comes of it; but if you are really in earnest something else will. Given you're good to put your neck into the collar, I'll guarantee you're earning your corn. Anyway, come and hear what I have to say. It's a dullish place, no doubt, but it's all new to you. I'll do you decently, and, bar finding fault with the malt, you can please yourself on all points. Sneering at our *brose* is insulting the family scutcheon, and you'll run the risk of being mashed in one of our own tubs. We bear with no deriding of beer in our stronghold. Once more, my dear Herbert, I say come; if you're half the man you were at Cambridge, I'll show you an opening which may be a good deal what you choose to make it.

"Ever yours,
"Phil Soames.

"*Mallington House, Baumborough.*"

Mr. Morant was jubilant over this letter. He was not only bored with the tread-mill of fashion, up which his feet incessantly trod, but in his love for Nid he had an incentive for work such as he had long required. He felt too that he had it in him. He had worked hard enough at times in the getting up of all sorts of amusements, such as balls, private theatricals, cricket-matches, picnics, &c.—why should he not expend all this energy in something remunerative? Yes, office hours would, of course, at first come irksome. It would be a deuce of a bore getting up at half-past eight, or thereabouts, and going to bed at midnight would no doubt have a humdrum flavour about it to start with. But there were some of his acquaintances in the Guards who he knew had often to meet terribly early engagements, and yet these things never seemed to disturb the equanimity of those light-hearted warriors amid the small hours. He supposed it was easy to educate yourself, and to get along upon about four hours sleep. We are all creatures of habit, and lying in bed till twelve is simply chronic indolence. No, in the future, like "Young Phillip, the falconer," of the old ballad, he meant to be "up with the dawn," and then he burst out laughing as he thought of young Dimsdale's rendering of the old saw the night before last at a late supper party—

> "Early to bed and early to rise
> Shows a man can be a fool if he tries."

Mr. Morant arrived in excellent time at Tapton Cottage; but if he had counted upon the chance of a *tête-à-tête* with Nid he was mistaken, for he found Mrs. Foxborough alone in the drawing-room when he entered. That lady welcomed him warmly, thanked him for sending the box, and murmuring something about dinner being ready directly, motioned him to a seat.

"I am going to bid you good-bye for a bit after to-night, Mrs. Foxborough," said Herbert. "I am going into the country."

"Ah, for some shooting," rejoined his hostess. "I don't know much about such things, but is not this the month you commence to kill partridges?"

"No, I am going away with far higher views than mere amusement," rejoined Morant, in somewhat grandiloquent fashion. He had a misty idea that there was something heroic in earning his own living. "I am going into the country to discuss my future career with an old friend."

"I am sure I wish you every success most heartily, Mr. Morant. I fancy you will do well in whatever you set your hand to. I was sorry to hear from Nid that it had become necessary, not but that I think it all for your good. Still, I am afraid it means that you have lost money in some way, which is always rather disheartening."

"No, Mrs. Foxborough; I have lost no money, but I have

spent it. You see before you a reformed character, bubbling over with virtuous resolutions."

"Let me see him quick," cried Nid, as she advanced into the room, "before he has bubbled over and there is no virtuous resolution left."

"Nid, my darling!" said her mother, reprovingly.

"You are right, Miss Foxborough; 'methinks he doth protest too much.' Nevertheless, my fair confederate, your advice has been taken, the oracle has spoken. I am going to rise in future at half-past eight, to retire to bed early; in fact, to become a regular business man and leading citizen."

"And what is to be the business, and where?" asked Nid, as they walked in to dinner.

"Upon my honour, I don't know, but it must be immensely facilitated by early rising; don't you think so, Mrs. Foxborough? Let me manage that chicken for you. I assure you I spent this morning in the study of alarum clocks. I never yet slept with one of those fiendish instruments of torture in the room. It must be a perfect acoustic shower-bath when it goes off."

"But, mind, you will have to get up when it calls you, and not behave like that bad-tempered man at Cambridge you told me about who only threw his boots at them, and broke twenty-seven one term," laughed Nid.

"Ah! poor Tom Rawlinson. I am afraid I am a little like him. He was always going to begin reading, but he got plucked for his 'smalls,' and faded away from academic groves in spite of all his resolutions and mechanical contrivances."

"Ah, Mr. Morant, but you are not going to share the fate of Mr. Rawlinson, and be what do you call it? I don't know what it means in the least, but presume it means failure in some shape," exclaimed Mrs. Foxborough. "Here's success to the new undertaking, whatever it be, and best wishes." And so saying, the hostess raised her glass to her lips with a cheery smile. "And now, Nid, run and get your cloak, and tell Ellen to bring me mine; the brougham will be round directly."

No sooner had her daughter left the room than Mrs. Foxborough, with her accustomed frankness, came to the point.

"You are going away, Mr. Morant," she said, "and have no sincerer well-wisher than I am. When you come back I must ask you to visit us rather more sparingly. You doubtless mean nothing, but you pay my little girl a good deal of attention. She has seen nothing of the world as yet, and I don't want the child made a fool of. Girls of her age, especially with her somewhat romantic temperament, are quite apt to mistake good-natured courtesy for something more, and I do you the justice to think you would wish that no more than I should."

"If I pay your daughter attention, Mrs. Foxborough, it is with the deliberate intent of winning her for my wife if I can; so pray don't think of my visiting here in any other sense. If I have said nothing to you as yet, well, I am not quite sure that I have made progress enough with Nid to justify my doing so."

These lovers, these lovers—can they ever be relied on to tell the exact truth? To each other, of course not, for the glamour of their passion colours all their speech; they mean it at the time, but it rarely lasts for all time. Herbert Morant was hardly speaking to the best of his belief when he professed to doubt his progress with Nid.

"We won't discuss that for the present, Mr. Morant. By your own confession you cannot afford to marry as yet, and therefore it would be hardly fair on so young a girl as Nid to hamper her with an engagement. Don't get angry at the word hamper—I use it advisedly. You can both well afford to wait; and though I don't want you to come too often, pray don't think you are 'boycotted.' Succeed in your new career, and show me you can maintain a wife, and if Nid can make up her mind you will have no enemy in me. Now, Mr. Morant, we understand each other, and there's my hand."

Herbert pressed his hostess's hand and uttered some incoherent words of gratitude, in the midst of which the door opened, and in walked the subject of their conversation.

"Really, Mr. Morant, if it wasn't with mamma, who can do no wrong, I should say I had interrupted a love scene," exclaimed Nid.

"I am not at all sure you haven't," rejoined her mother, laughing; "but quick, Ellen, give me my cloak; it is high time we were off."

"What were you and mamma having such a confabulation about?" asked Nid, between the acts of the Trovatore.

"Shall I tell you? She was giving her consent to my marriage whenever I had acquired sufficient means to maintain a wife."

Nid coloured, and became absorbed in contemplation of the house, sweeping it with her glasses as if in anxious search of some much-valued acquaintance.

"The trouble will be getting some one else's consent afterwards," continued Herbert. "Do you think I have any chance, Nid?"

"How should I know?" rejoined the girl pettishly, over her shoulder. She knew very well what he meant. She regarded herself as tacitly engaged to him, but yet she was a little flustered at the idea of being asked to marry him in downright plain English. She was very young, bear in mind.

"Who should know better, darling? I don't want to ask your mother this, Nid. Have I a chance?"

Still no answer, and Miss Foxborough apparently more intent upon seeking that valued acquaintance than ever.

"You won't see me again for some time, dearest. Say, at least, you shall be glad to see me back."

Suddenly Nid dropped her opera glasses, a little hand stole

into Morant's, and a murmured "What a tease you are, Herbert," fell upon his ear.

It was not a very direct answer to his question, but he seemed quite content, and till the fall of the curtain, Mrs. Foxborough was, sad to say, left entirely to her own meditations.

CHAPTER X.

MR. FOSSDYKE speedily found that his prognostications were fulfilled. Mr. Totterdell, formerly exasperating merely from fatuous curiosity, had now become actively malignant. He trotted about giving a somewhat garbled account of the way he had been turned out of Dyke, " merely because I expressed, what all Baumborough expresses, some wish to know who Miss Hyde really is : " and then Mr. Totterdell went on to insinuate that if there was not something wrong there would surely be no reason to make a mystery about her. He hoped his poor goddaughter, when she did discover the truth, might find it still possible to get on with her husband. He wished to insinuate nothing, but the skeleton in the cupboard was almost certain to be discovered sooner or later, and want of perfect confidence between man and wife had been productive of domestic unhappiness from time out of mind.

Only din things sufficiently into people's heads, and they will end by believing anything. They always argue that there must be some truth in it; it may not be all true, but there is foundation of some sort for the story, and before a week was passed there were not wanting those in Baumborough who looked askew at Miss Hyde. Moreover, Totterdell's pertinacious inquiries into the financial affairs of the

Council, attributable chiefly to his irritation at having been
sharply snubbed in Fossdyke's office, began to beget a slight
distrust of the Town Clerk. Once more it was buzzed about
that the tradespeople had always trouble in getting their
money from John Fossdyke, and a vague suspicion was
abroad that he was in monetary difficulties. True, his friends
argued that it was impossible; look at the emoluments he
held, his business was pretty good, he had got money with
his wife, and some of the farmers around Baumborough quite
guffawed at the idea when it reached their ears. "Lawyer
Fossdyke want money! Why, that bangs all, he's always
some to lend, man, to any one with decent security." Still,
spite of all this, there were some members of the Municipal
Council who held it would not be an injudicious thing to take
strict stock of their affairs, to look into their investments as
well as their books.

John Fossdyke met all this not altogether without annoyance, but certainly with unblenching front. His accounts,
he said, were ready for the Town Council whenever they
chose to demand them, and he should be happy to tender
ample explanation on any point that might not seem perfectly
clear to them; but he was not going to submit to cross-
examination by a fussy busybody simply because he happened
to be elected to the Corporation—an individual, moreover,
whose scandalous tongue had compelled him to close his
doors against him. If John Fossdyke was not having altogether a rosy time, neither was Mr. Totterdell. Both the
Town Clerk and Miss Hyde were popular in Baumborough,
and a very large portion of the community took their parts
with considerable vehemence. Mr. Totterdell, on the contrary, was very much the reverse; and even those who for
one motive or another ranged themselves on his side, manifested no little contempt for their mischief-making leader.
Another thing, too, that had been a veritable staggerer for
Mr. Totterdell, was the sudden defection of his goddaughter.
That gentleman, the afternoon he left Dyke, white with

indignation at being morally kicked out of the house, flattered himself that Mrs. Fossdyke would take up the cudgels in his behalf, and deafen all Baumborough with the story of her wrongs. Mary Fossdyke did nothing of the kind; she might abuse or find fault with her husband herself, but, like many another woman, she had no idea of allowing any one else that privilege in her presence. Then again, she was honestly a little penitent about Bessie, and the idea of her going made the good lady very unhappy. She took the girl about with her everywhere, and made more of Miss Hyde publicly than ever. Some few might look askance, but Mrs. Fossdyke carried too many guns for this outside circle. She was of the very cream of Baumborough society, and not to be cowed by Mr. Totterdell's adherents. Indeed, that gentleman would very willingly have dropped the whole business of inquiry into the books of the Town Clerk if he could, but he had associates who insisted upon his seeing the thing out. Men who start agitations or popular cries can never estimate where the craze may carry them, and when Mr. Totterdell in his petulance allowed himself to indulge in innuendo against John Fossdyke he little dreamt what would come of it.

Very angry and very sad was Philip Soames when these rumours first reached his ears. They came to him, as might be expected, in exaggerated shape. He heard that Miss Hyde had turned out to be John Fossdyke's illegitimate daughter, that there had been a tremendous scene at Dyke upon Mrs. Fossdyke's making the discovery, she having been all along under the delusion that the young lady was her husband's niece, that there had been a terrible quarrel, which had been temporarily patched up, the Town Clerk and his wife having agreed to keep their differences at all events to themselves, that Mrs. Fossdyke was going about everywhere with Miss Hyde just to throw dust in people's eyes, but she had stipulated Miss Hyde should be sent away at the end of the month. Further, that the Town Clerk was said to be in

8

money difficulties, and the Municipal Council would probably deprive him of his appointment.

Phil Soames was a sensible young man, and did not take all he heard for gospel, but he could not but recall his last interview with Bessie, and wonder to himself was this her secret. It was quite possible she might view the stain upon her birth in such exaggerated fashion as to deem it a bar to entering a respectable family as a daughter. It was hard to believe that a bright, handsome, straightforward girl such as Bessie Hyde could have any shameful story of her own to tell ; but that she might have been brought up to consider her illegitimacy placed her under a ban was easy of understanding. Phil Soames went grimly about his work in a manner very different from his wont ; he stuck to it, if anything, more pertinaciously than ever, but the spring seemed out of him. He laboured more like a machine, very different from the gay, light-hearted manner that was habitual to him. His love for Bessie Hyde was no passing fancy, and Mr. Philip Soames was very tenacious about what he took in hand, be it what it might. But he felt powerless in this instance. He could not discover what he had to combat ; unless he could prevail upon Miss Hyde to tell him her story, he was helpless.

Mr. Fossdyke, too, after his absence from home, found so many things that required his attention that he was deeply immersed in business, and so never found time somehow to see Phil Soames and confide to him Bessie's history. The girl constantly wondered whether he had done so, but, as may be easily understood, was shy of reminding him of their conversation. As for Mrs. Fossdyke, she had studiously avoided all reference to delicate subjects since the scene in the rosary, and though her husband not only recognized, but had told her so, how well she had done her wifely duty in confronting all the scandal Mr. Totterdell had set rolling, yet he had been no more communicative to her than to Phil Soames ; so that relations in the Dyke family still lacked confidence and cordiality all round in great measure. One thing specially noticeable, as many remembered afterwards, was, that John Fossdyke seemed out of spirits, and somewhat irritable, all the time. And yet one of the schemes he had set his heart on had arrived at maturity, for the Baumborough Theatre was a thing accomplished, and the opening night, under the patronage of the Mayor and Municipal Council, announced in gigantic posters all through the length and breadth of the town. If Baumborough had doubted whether it wanted a theatre at one time, it had no sort of uncertainty but that was one of its requirements now—in fact, Baumborough was all agog for the eventful evening, and quite marvelled how it had managed to endure life so long without a dramatic temple. Everybody was going, not only the upper social stratum, but all the tradespeople and the shopmen had announced their intention of being present. A lessee of substance had been procured, and he had made satisfactory arrangements with an excellent provincial company to take Baumborough in their tour, and the theatre was accordingly announced to open with a Robertsonian comedy.

It was curiously illustrative of the old axiom, that he who bears the brunt of the battle does not always get the credit of winning the fight, for the bigger half of Baumborough were under a hazy impression that the erection of the theatre was due chiefly to the unflagging exertions of Mr. Totterdell. It was true he told every one so, and there is no doubt if you persistently tell people a consistent story of yourself, the majority will in the end believe you. He had been the bane of the contractor's life, with his endless questions and impossible suggestions, for he had been perpetually in and out all the time the building was in hand, while John Fossdyke, without whom the thing never would have come to pass, had seldom gone near it. Mr. Totterdell was now buzzing about like a hilarious bluebottle, rubbing his hands and saying he had devoted a good deal of time to it, to say nothing of taking a good deal of trouble; but he did think—yes, he might venture to say—Baumborough would pronounce it a very bright, pretty little house when they saw it. And people believed this old impostor, who in reality had vexed the souls of those entrusted with the work, and even in some cases slightly hindered it.

But the evening came, and the market-place of Baumborough resounded with the rattle of wheels; vehicles of all descriptions rolled over its stones, private carriages from round about and the suburbs of the town, hack flies hired from the principal inns, even the hotel omnibuses were in requisition, and the ladies of Baumborough, in silk and satin, flounce and furbelow, thronged into the stalls and boxes. It was a full house—stalls, pit, dress circle, upper boxes, and gallery were crowded; and during the overture Baumborough had plenty to do in admiring the really pretty little theatre it had acquired, and in exchanging salutes. The Mayor was there with all his family, beaming in all the glory of a stage box. The Town Council generally were scattered about, including not only Mr. Totterdell, more than ever convinced that this gaily-lighted festive amphitheatre was all his creation, but even Stanger, its whilom fierce opponent; but Stanger, the representative of Pickleton Ward, was a sound, practical man, who said he combated theories, but always accepted accomplished facts.

John Fossdyke, with his wife and Miss Hyde, were there in the stage box opposite the Mayor's. Mr. Philip Soames was there, moodily meditating whether it would be out of place to go round between the acts and say "how do you do?" to Mrs. Fossdyke. Several of the clergy were there, who, without being engaged in that incongruous absurdity, "the Stage and Church Guild," could see no harm in the innocent amusement the English stage as a rule affords. There are plenty of extremists of all creeds in these days, alas! who, by their puritanical dogmas, are teaching men rapidly to profess no creed at all, and cannot be made to see the harm done to all religion by their rabid intolerance.

The curtain rises on that old favourite play, "Ours," and the audience greet the garden scene at once with a good-humoured burst of applause. A play that always goes, if played, and yet makes us sometimes wonder why it should, the grand effect of the second act culminating in a lady making a pudding in the third. It certainly was Mrs. Bancroft who was the original compounder of that pudding, and that goes for a good deal. Her business has become, of course, traditional. The piece went as well as ever, the company were capable, and the audience were delighted. Seated next to Mr. Totterdell was a dark-complexioned gentleman, attired in the orthodox sables, who exercised that gentleman immensely. He was apparently a stranger, at all events Mr. Totterdell had never seen him before, and any enigma of this kind had the mysterious fascination that double acrostics have upon some people.

"Monstrous pretty little theatre," remarked the stranger, at the end of the first act. "I suppose all your leading notables are here to-night—the Mayor that, I presume, judging by his chain of office, and, God bless me——"and here the stranger suddenly paused, and looking rapidly round in another direction than the stage, inquired who that gentleman was in an upper box.

"That, sir, is a brother member of mine on the Municipal Council, Mr. Brocklebank, perhaps, next to myself, the chief promoter of the theatre you have done me the honour to admire. It cost me a good deal of time and trouble; there were prejudices to be overcome, but to-night's triumph repays me for all. My name, sir, is Totterdell—a name you will find tolerably well known in Baumborough. May I ask to whom I have the pleasure of speaking?"

"My name! Ah, yes! my name! My name is Viator, and I am staying in the neighbourhood."

"Vyater—a very singular name; sounds as if you were of foreign extraction."

"Yes, of what is designated nomad Italian origin, I fancy. But who is that gentleman in the O. P. stage box?"

"Might I ask what you mean by that?" inquired Totterdell.

"Why, you told me you mainly got up the theatre, so I naturally supposed you understood theatrical slang. The O. P. side means opposite the prompt side, and the prompter is always on the stage left."

"Ah, you mean in the box opposite the Mayor—that is John Fossdyke, our Town Clerk. A bumptious, bad-tempered man, that I intend to have turned out of the place before long. He don't know his place," continued Totterdell, with increasing acerbity. "He does not seem to understand, sir, that he is the servant of the Council, and when servants don't comprehend their situations we discharge them;" and when Mr. Totterdell got so earnest in his language, a reproving hush ran round the adjacent pit and stalls, for the curtain had just risen on the second act.

"John Fossdyke," said the stranger, in a low tone; "would you mind spelling it for me?"

Mr. Totterdell, in a much subdued voice, at once complied with the request.

"Grand dramatic effect that," observed the stranger, as the curtain fell on the measured tramp of the soldiery on their way to the East, at the conclusion of the second act. "Mr. Fossdyke been settled long in Baumborough?"

"Gracious, yes, many years; but what makes you interested about that?"

"Can hardly say that," replied the stranger, with much *nonchalance.* "I have some idea I knew a Fossdyke somewhat early in life. Bless you, I can't even recollect where. School with him, perhaps. Can't say where I met him, exactly; not that I mean to say that your Baumborough Fossdyke is my Fossdyke. Not even sure whether mine was a Fossdyke or a Mossdyke. Met him on business, perhaps."

"Just so; quite likely. What did you say your business was, Mr. Vyater?" inquired Mr. Totterdell, eagerly.

"I don't know that I said anything about my business," answered the other, with an amused smile.

"You seem to know a good deal about theatricals. Are you connected with the profession in any way?"

"Well, I might be, and then again I might be connected with coals," rejoined the stranger, laughing. "Yes, I do know a little about theatricals; considering I dabble in them a good deal, I ought to. You've gratified my curiosity, so I'll gratify yours. My business here was to see your new theatre and calculate whether I could get anything out of it on some future occasion."

"And you're much gratified, of course?" remarked Totterdell, pompously.

"Hum! If I've seen ' Ours' once I should think I've seen it thirty times. It's done well here, but I've seen it done better. You've a big house to-night; but if you're a fisherman you'll understand what I mean when I say this is the first cast of the net in a new swim. It's a chance whether you will catch as many fish again. No, I've reckoned you up; you're worth a fifty-pound note, for a two days' spec, might run to a little more."

"Nonsense, sir; why I look forward to a regular theatre, open nearly all the year round."

"Bosh," responded the stranger, blandly, if not politely. "Your lessee's no such fool as that; he knows if he tried that game the shutters would be up for good after the first year. Stock companies, as a rule, my good sir, are amongst the institutions of the past."

Bosh! to a Town Councillor! Mr. Totterdell felt this was revolutionary, an upheaval of things, prophetic of woe to the nation. The word bosh might possibly be used by one Town Councillor to another. The great Stanger, indeed, upon one memorable occasion, had recourse to the somewhat offensive word, but it was not to be permitted of the outside public. However, before he could clothe the rebuke that rose to his lips in words of sufficient severity, the curtain rose upon the third act

"Now, my friend," said the unabashed stranger, "you'll understand there's a good deal in the making of a pudding. If it wasn't cleverly compounded this act wouldn't pull through."

Philip Soames, after a stern argument with himself, had at last determined that common politeness required he should go round and pay his respects to Mrs. Fossdyke. After chatting a bit with that lady and her husband, he lingered a little at the back of the box with Miss Hyde.

"Am I to take your answer of the other day as final, Bessie?" he whispered.

"I am afraid so, Philip," she replied, softly. "Unless, indeed—but that, I fancy, is unlikely."

"Unless what?" he asked, brusquely.

"Unless Mr. Fossdyke speaks to you about me. If he should you will at all events know why I feel I am bound, in justice to yourself, Philip, to say no when I would gladly say yes. I make no secret that I love you, but I cannot marry you."

"Mr. Fossdyke speak to me!" he replied. "What about? Is it likely?"

"No; I don't know; I should think not. Please don't ask me anything more, Philip."

"I won't now, nor will I till I have had a talk with Mr. Fossdyke; if he does not speak to me I mean to speak to him, Bessie. Good night," and, having pressed her hand warmly, Philip Soames withdrew to witness the third act of "Ours."

John Fossdyke looked gloomily on at this, as indeed he had at the whole representation. Considering how energetic he had been about promoting the erection of the building, it was singular how little interest he took in the play. He never left his box, and said but little to either his wife or Bessie; but gazed at the stage in a moody, pre-occupied fashion, as a man might who was there from a sense of duty, but who, far from being either interested or amused, was

scarce conscious of the pageant passing before his eyes.
More than once the stranger eyed him keenly, and at last
said in a low voice—

"I suppose Mr. Foss—Fossdyke thinks from his official
position that he's bound to attend when the Mayor and
Council patronize the show, or else he gives me the idea of
rather disapproving of theatricals, or at all events being
somewhat bored with them."

"There you make a mistake," returned Totterdell. "He
was one of the advocates of the scheme, but he turned out
a bit of a humbug."

"How so?"

"Why, he said he understood a good deal about theatricals, but the minute the thing was in hand and fairly began,
he never came near the place. No, sir, the whole superintending of the building was left to me, and a pretty life I led
the contractors I can tell you."

In justice to Mr. Totterdell, it must be admitted that the
contractors would have subscribed to this opinion.

"Oh, they want looking after, those fellows," rejoined the
stranger, carelessly. "Fossdyke any family? Is that his
daughter, for instance, in the box with him?"

"No, that's Miss Hyde; a mystery, no one in Baumborough
knows who she is, and when I say she isn't his daughter she
may be for all I know. I don't say she is, but she may be.
She may be anybody, indeed."

"Quite so. Nice-looking girl, anyhow," replied the
stranger.

"She's a very flippant young woman," retorted Totterdell,
quickly, who had his suspicions that Bessie sometimes rather
laughed at him. "Lor'!" he continued, "it quite makes
one shiver," as the simulated whistle of the wild Crimean
snowstorm from the stage smote upon their ear, and Sergeant
Brown enters the hut accompanied by a rush of snow-
flakes.

"Great effect from a well-toned whistle and a winnowing

machine at the wing, isn't it? So they don't know who Miss Hyde is, eh?"

"No. You seem to take rather an interest in Fossdyke's family, Mr. Vyater. By-the-by, how do you spell your name?"

"Depends upon what branch of the family you belong to," rejoined the stranger. "As a speller I'm always variable; it isn't my strong point."

"And you are stopping?" asked Mr. Totterdell.

"Bless you, I hope not. I'm like an eight days' clock, I never stop unless I'm run down. I'm always on the move, here, there, and everywhere. 'I'm always on the move, sir,' as the old song says."

Mr. Totterdell said no more; it had suddenly occurred to him that this stranger was as flippant as Miss Hyde, and no more disposed to give an account of himself. Mr. Totterdell distrusted people who were not prepared to unfold their lives and pursuits, at all events so far as he was concerned, and he both feared and reprobated that favourite pastime of the present day called "chaff." He was conscious of much inability to take part in that amusement, and that when cast amongst it he was like the blind man in the game of blind man's buff, the recipient of many tweaks, buffets, and pinches, and with no recollection of having caught any one.

The comedy came to a conclusion amidst tumultuous applause, all the performers were "called," and then came a pause before the after-piece, during which the Mayor and a few of the leading citizens went behind the scenes to congratulate the manager. It was not to be supposed that fussy, pompous Mr. Totterdell, who had finally convinced himself that he was the founder of the Theatre Royal, Baumborough, would neglect this ceremony. But although he had haunted the building during its growth, Mr. Totterdell was a novice behind the scenes. He lost his way, got his toes trod on by carpenters and scene-shifters, and finally was brought up "all standing" in speechless astonishment at coming across the flippant stranger engaged in conversation with a lady whom he at once recognized as the portrayer of "Mary Netley" in the comedy.

"If you are looking for the manager's room it's there to the left. Here, one of you fellows, just show this gentleman to Mr. Sampson's room, will you, please," said the stranger, airily.

"Who is he? Who the devil is he?" muttered Totterdell as he followed his guide. "I'll ask Sampson; he's sure to know."

But in that Mr. Totterdell was mistaken, the manager had a somewhat numerous levee, and consequently but little time to give to any one individual. He could naturally give no answer as to who a man was whom he didn't see, and had very insufficient time to have described to him. Mr. Totterdell emerged from Mr. Sampson's sanctum no whit the wiser, only to find the stranger still discoursing volubly with some other members of the company, and the old gentleman's curiosity began to attain white heat concerning whom he might be.

John Fossdyke had not been amongst those who had "gone round" to congratulate Mr. Sampson, and to drink success to the Baumborough Theatre, for the champagne corks were flying in the manager's room; that wine, as is well known, being rather a speciality of all theatrical enterprises. The Town Clerk certainly justified the stranger's criticism, and looked as if, though some sense of duty constrained him to be there, his thoughts were miles away. He looked round the house very little, and gazed at the stage in a dreamy, abstracted manner that attracted his wife's attention. She could not understand her restless energetic husband in this absent and apathetic state, and at last said to him, "Are you ill, John? If so, perhaps we had better go home at once."

"No, nothing is the matter. I have a bit of a headache, but I will see it out. We must, Mary; the carriage won't turn up till the performance is over, remember."

In the meantime the stranger had once more resumed his
seat at Mr. Totterdell's side, and that gentleman determined
once more to try a little cross-examination.

"You seem tolerably at home behind the scenes, sir," he
remarked.

"Yes," rejoined the other, carelessly, "the back of the
floats is no novelty to me; but," he continued, laughing,
"considering you built the theatre, it struck me you weren't
very good at finding your way about, you seemed regularly
dumbfoozled."

Mr. Totterdell swelled like an outraged turkey-cock. Was
this the way to address a Town Councillor? And he had
given the stranger clearly to understand that he held that
dignified office. He did not exactly know what dumbfoozled
might mean, but nobody could regard the being told they
looked dumbfoozled as complimentary.

"Well, I can't afford to see this farce out, good though it
is," and as he spoke, the stranger rose, drew a silk muffler
out of the pocket of his overcoat, which had been hanging
over the back of his stall, and as he did so, a piece of paper,
evidently drawn out with the muffler, fluttered to the ground.
Mr. Totterdell was fascinated; his eyes had caught the fall of
the paper; could he but obtain it he would very likely get at
what he was so anxious to know, namely, who the stranger
was. It was a blank envelope, that much Mr. Totterdell
could see already. The stranger was most provokingly
deliberate about muffling his throat and getting into his
overcoat; but at last, all unconscious of his loss, he bade
Mr. Totterdell a courteous good-night and left the theatre.
Mr. Totterdell waited a few minutes to be quite sure of his
departure, gazed furtively around to see if he was observed
—no, all eyes were on the stage—and then pounced upon
the envelope. It was open and unaddressed; and from the
interior Mr. Totterdell extracted a theatrical bill. It was
the programme of the Syringa Music Hall; lessee, Mr.
Foxborough; and once again Mr. Totterdell felt that the

acquisition of knowledge of our fellows is sometimes an arduous and difficult pursuit.

But the curtain comes down at last amidst a storm of applause, in response to which it again rises, and " God save the Queen " is sung by the whole company. This was hardly a success, the orchestra and the leading lady who took the solos not being altogether in accord about the key while the company generally seemed each to have their own version of the National Anthem, and adhere to it with contemptuous disregard of their companions. Still, as the audience made their way to their respective homes, they agreed that the Baumborough Theatre was a great success. Mr. Totterdell only felt discontented. The mysterious stranger weighed upon his mind. Who the deuce was he? The music-hall bill that Mr. Totterdell had so eagerly pounced upon even that gentleman was fain to confess told nothing ; people of all classes went to such places of amusement, and though Mr. Totterdell had never heard of the particular hall in question, he made no doubt it was much of a muchness with other places of the kind. No, there was nothing to be made out of that, yet Mr. Totterdell literally yearned to know who the stranger might be.

Breakfast at Dyke was at an early hour, and the post-bag generally arrived in the middle of that meal. John Fossdyke opened it as usual next morning, and distributed the letters, and then began leisurely to run through his own. Suddenly an ejaculation escaped him, and it was plain to Bessie and Mrs. Fossdyke, who looked towards him at the half cry, that the letter he was reading moved him terribly. For a moment his face blanched to his very lips and his mouth quivered—the hand that held the letter shook, and Mrs. Fossdyke, springing from her chair, exclaimed, " Good heavens! John, what is the matter ? "

The Town Clerk mastered himself by a supreme effort, and rejoined in husky tones, " Nothing, Mary, nothing now ; please don't fidget."

"But you have heard bad news of some sort?"

"Yes, I have heard bad news. Now, do sit down, and don't make a fuss. I must go over to Bunbury this afternoon, and may not be back, in fact, shall probably not get back to-night."

"But, John, it is only an hour's rail to Bunbury; surely you can get through your business and come home by the last train. You look so ill, I shall feel dreadfully uneasy if you don't come back."

Miss Hyde looked anxious, although she forebore to speak.

"No, I don't think it likely I shall be able to get back to-night. Tell Robert to put up a few things in my bag and bring it down to the office. Good-bye, Mary; good-bye, Bessie; " and John Fossdyke kissed his wife with unusual gravity, and went his way.

CHAPTER XI.

" A DINNER AT THE HOPLINE.

UNBURY was a pretty, old-fashioned little town, distant some thirty miles from Baumborough, with which it had direct communication by rail. Bunbury rather turned up its nose at Baumborough, although double its size, as an essentially modern production, for Bunbury had been the resort of the cream of society a hundred years ago, when Baumborough, albeit in existence, was of very small account. Bunbury lay in a hole, but boasted a Spa, a delightful old-world promenade fringed with trees, and shops under shady arcades, and assembly rooms, which enjoyed a prestige of the past. Inhabitants of Bunbury who accosted you told you of all sorts of royalties and celebrities who had disported themselves in minuet and country dance upon those boards, while the pump-room had in its day enjoyed a celebrity only second to Bath. It was a delicious, dreamy old town for an overworked man to come to; the quaint old red-brick houses and that delightful drowsy old promenade, with its benches, whereon to sit and listen to the everlasting German band, a good one be it understood, was just the perfection of utter indolence. The country all round, too, was charming with its luxuriance of wood interspersed by occasional glorious patches of moorland, and made Bunbury a place much in vogue with London men who wanted a few days' rest, for it was no great distance from the metropolis, and the communication easy.

Bunbury, built in a hole, or perhaps I should say at the foot of a hill, had gradually spread up the ascent, the sides of which were now studded with villas and hotels, and it is with one of these last we have now to do. The "Hopbine" had been one of the very first hostelries built, as the towns-people would say, "up hill." It was an old-fashioned house, and though with a capital name, and very good quiet country connection, was completely eclipsed by its more magnificent neighbours. Still its *habitués* were wont to assert that there was a good deal more comfort to be got out of the unpreten-tious Hopbine than out of its more gorgeous competitors, and that old Joe Marlinson had better stuff in his cellars than any one else in Bunbury. The landlord was a bit of a character. He had a fairish sum of money laid by, at all events enough to make him independent, and though courteous over to his regular customers, or to any one he reckoned a gentleman, he could be unmistakably awkward to those who did not come up to what he considered the Hopbine standard, for the old man was fussily convinced that the Hopbine was the leading inn in Bunbury, and that no real gentry ever went to those new-fangled hotels. Joe Marlinson, who looked like a respectable old butler in appearance, and dressed in a somewhat bygone fashion, still held to the venerable term inn, and alluded to "those hotels" with undisguised con-tempt. The Hopbine paid its way doubtless, but worked as it was under Joe Marlinson's rule, it was a house no man could get much of a living out of. Old Marlinson worked it more for pleasure than profit, and were you not a gentleman in his practised eyes, he would as soon be rid of you as not. He didn't care so much about what a customer spent as what he was—he was always saying the old house should never lose caste in his day. It had never entertained any but quality, and it never should while he lived. It always had been the inn of the country gentlemen round Bunbury, and he wasn't going to keep a house for riff-raff.

One Saturday afternoon there arrived at the Hopbine a gentleman from London, who desired a bedroom and sitting-room from that day till Monday. Although he had engaged a sitting-room, he elected to dine in the coffee-room. Having finished his dinner, he desired the waiter to get him an evening paper, without thinking that this merely meant his seeing the first edition of the *Globe*, which he had read coming down in the train. When he became aware of his mistake, he exclaimed, " Pooh, waiter, I have seen this. Get me something else. Haven't you a local paper ? "

The waiter produced the *Bunbury Chronicle*, after which the stranger proceeded to meditate and sip his coffee. At last he once more called the waiter and said, " I see there's a new theatre open at Baumborough on Monday, I suppose I can get back if I go to it ? "

" Oh, yes, sir ; train leaves Baumborough at 11.40, arrives at Bunbury 12.35—just suits, sir."

" All right, then, let 'em know at the bar; I'll stay over Monday night. And now, where's the smoking-room ? "

" Beg pardon, sir, but we haven't a regular smoke-room. You can smoke here, sir, after nine o'clock, and it only wants half an hour. Anything more, sir ?

"No ; might prove a little too much for the establishment if I gave any more orders just now. I'll stroll outside with my cigar."

The gentleman of No. 11, for want of a better designation the Hopbine was compelled to christen him by the number of his room, led a quiet, inoffensive life all Sunday and Monday. He read, wrote, and smoked a good deal in his sitting-room, but as he received neither letters nor telegrams, the Hopbine remained in complete ignorance of No. 11's actual status in this world, which a little annoyed Mr. Marlinson. Still his guest was quiet and inoffensive, giving himself neither airs nor the house trouble, and though Joe Marlinson's mind misgave him No. 11 was not a genuine gentleman, still he thought he might pass in these democratic days. On the

9

Monday No. 11 dined early, and went to attend the Baumborough Theatre. He returned that night, and the next morning gave notice in the bar that he should remain another day, ordered dinner for two in his own sitting-room, and said he expected a gentleman to dine with him, who might probably want a bed. That afternoon the gentleman arrived, and a good deal to the astonishment of the house, turned out to be Mr. Fossdyke, the well-known Town Clerk and solicitor of Baumborough. Mr. Fossdyke asked for No. 11 as Mr. Foxborough, and for the first time Joe Marlinson and his myrmidons became aware of No. 11's name.

The two gentlemen sat down to as good a dinner as the Hopbine could serve up, for No. 11 had particularly remarked in ordering it that he would leave it chiefly to the cook, but let there be grouse, and let it be a good dinner. He had conferred with Mr. Marlinson on the subject of wines, and not a little ruffled that worthy's bristles by receiving his almost confidential mention of some very old port with a deprecating smile, and observing—

" A grand wine, no doubt, the wine of a past generation, who had time to nurse their gout when they got it—somewhat obsolete in these days of hurry and dyspepsia. No, my good friend, the driest champagne you have in the cellar for dinner and a good sound claret afterwards. That I think will do, and if you have any belief in your champagne, don't over ice it, mind."

Old Marlinson was not a little nettled by this cool customer. The offering to produce that treasured old port at all was, he considered, a piece of condescension on his part to a stranger, and that it should not have been greatly appreciated ruffled the old man not a little. He had small opinion of men who neither drank old ale nor old port. A very antiquated landlord indeed was mine host of the Hopbine. He got out the required wines, and indignantly intended leaving their preparation and distribution to the head waiter, instead of bringing in the first bottle of port after dinner as was his custom ; but upon seeing that Mr. Fossdyke was the guest, he changed his mind and resolved to have an eye on things. Mr. Fossdyke was a man of position and repute round the country-side. Not county family exactly, though Mr. Fossdyke through his wife claimed connection with more than one of them, but a bustling, energetic man much respected and looked up to. In short, old Joe Marlinson thought it by no means inconsistent with his dignity to just pay the compliment of pouring out a glass of wine to a man of Mr. Fossdyke's calibre.

It struck the waiter, and also the landlord, who contrived to be in the room when Mr. Fossdyke arrived, that there was no great amount of geniality in the greeting of the two men, nor, good though the dinner was, did they seem to thaw under the influence of toothsome soup and side-dish, or sparkling wine. Their talk seemed somewhat constrained, and not of the gay, bordering on boisterous, nature that is apt to characterize the meeting of two old chums in a *tête-à-tête* dinner. Especially did it strike old Joe Marlinson that Mr. Fossdyke seemed out of spirits, and though he gulped down bumpers of champagne, his appetite seemed very indifferent. There was an irritability about him, too, which Marlinson, who knew him well, had never seen before. Dinner ended, the host with no little pomposity put a bottle of his best claret on the table and then withdrew. It was apparently approved, for another bottle and yet another followed, and it was on nearing the door with this last, in that stealthy way characteristic of waiters, that Thomas, the official in question, caught Mr. Fossdyke's voice raised in anger, and as he entered the room heard the stranger reply in cold, rasping tones, " The game is in my hands, and those are my terms." The words struck him as rather peculiar, but presuming it to be some business dispute, he did not think very much of it. The *séance* between the two men was late ; brandies and soda followed the claret, and though Mr. Fossdyke was not reputed a wine-bibber, he certainly was by no means abstemious this night.

The Hopbine was an early house, and Bunbury might certainly claim to be an early place. It was only here and there that the unhallowed click of the billiard balls could be heard even after eleven. Bunbury was Arcadian in its habits, blessed, doubtless, with all the petty spites and malice we shall recognize in that visionary land when we get there. At a few minutes after eleven, Thomas the waiter inquired if No. 11 would require anything more before the bar closed, and being answered in the negative, wished the gentlemen good-night, and was about to leave the room, when the stranger called him back, said that he must leave by the 8.30 train for London next morning, requested that his bill might be ready, and himself called accordingly—that is, a good hour before. Thomas carried out these orders, gave due notice in the bar, and having done that betook himself to bed.

Mr. Foxborough responded promptly to the chambermaid's appeal next morning. He was ready in good time, swallowed a cup of tea, bolted an egg, paid his bill, including the preceding night's dinner, and departed to the station in the hotel omnibus, an institution which, much against his grain, Joe Marlinson had found himself compelled to adopt. Mr. Fossdyke was late next morning, very late; but though Marlinson knew the Town Clerk very well it was the first time he had ever stayed at the Hopbine, and consequently they knew nothing of his habits. Upon the few occasions that John Fossdyke had slept in Bunbury he had stayed at the house of a friend, but it was rarely when business called him there that he did not manage to get back to Baumborough at night. Still, though he had given no orders, the head chambermaid thought she might take it on her own responsibility to knock at his door at ten, a late hour for Bunbury, but there was no reply; and that damsel, knowing from the depths of her experience that men sometimes were long sleeping off their wine, and having gathered from Thomas that No. 11's little dinner had been prolific in the matter of drink, troubled her head no more until about

twelve, when she again tapped at the door. That is the discomfort of these semi-civilized districts ; in our provincial
hotels, as in America, they won't let you sleep. In London
or Paris I don't suppose they would disturb you for two or
three days ; they understand the cosmopolitan citizen in
those places, who is very uncertain in his getting up and
lying down. However, again that chambermaid met no
response, and again she went away on the fidget. No
uneasiness, bear in mind, with regard to the health of John
Fossdyke, but she liked to see her rooms done by midday or
thereabouts, and Mr. Fossdyke was upsetting the whole of
her routine by his persistent slumbers. It is astonishing how
interfering with their routine exasperates people, and that
men should ever invite one to breakfast is cause of enmity in
the minds of many ; there are those, remember, who would
always prefer attending a friend's funeral to his breakfast.
The one is a final solemnity, the other capable of ghastly
repetition. Those breakfasts of Rogers make one shiver to
read about. A sarcasm with your French roll, and your
cutlet served up in an epigram at your own expense.

But in the meantime we are forgetting John Fossdyke.
Two o'clock came, and still the Town Clerk made no sign.
That a man could slumber to that hour in the day was beside
the Hopbino experience. The chambermaid knocked once
more, and this time as a person having authority, who would
not longer be denied; but still there was no response nor
sound to be heard from within the chamber. The woman
got uneasy, and resolved to acquaint her master. Mr.
Marlinson opened his eyes wide when he heard of the state
of things. He in particular, of specially early habits, could
understand no man taking such prolonged and unnatural
rest. Mr. Fossdyke might have had a fit; the chambermaid
was instructed to batter the door once more, and, failing to
get reply, to immediately report the same to Mr. Marlinson.

The woman did as she was bid, but speedily returned to
say that she could get no answer whatever from Mr. Foss-

dyke's chamber, and her face showed clearly that she feared something amiss. Old Marlinson himself thought the thing looked serious, and at once ascended the stairs, and after delivering himself of a storm of knocks, enough to have awakened the seven sleepers, without response, he turned the handle.

"It's no use, sir," said the chambermaid; "it's locked. I tried it myself before I came to you."

But the lock was only such as is on ordinary bedroom doors, there was no bolt, and at the instigation of his master the boots, with a vigorous kick or two, speedily burst it open. The blinds were drawn close, and the glimmer of daylight that penetrated the apartment did not at first permit eyes blinded with the full flood of sunlight to see what was within the room; but already a great awe fell upon them; and the unbroken stillness told them they were in the presence of a terrible tragedy. Quickly old Marlinson entered the room and drew up the blind from the nearest window, and then a scream from the chambermaid broke the silence. Half-dressed under the window at the other side of the room lay John Fossdyke, a smile almost on his face, but with a quaint, old-fashioned dagger buried in his heart. A chair and the writing-table which stood in the window were both upset, but otherwise there was no sign of a severe struggle, neither was there much blood. The weapon, the obvious cause of death, had been left in the wound, and prevented any great effusion of blood. The shirt-front was a little stained, that was all.

For a few seconds old Joe Marlinson stood stupefied. Murder is happily not customary in hotels, and the present tragedy was quite outside the old man's experience. The boots, a practical man, was the first to recall him to a sense of the situation.

"I suppose, sir," he said, after raising the dead man's head for a moment, and then becoming conscious of the inability of any one in this world to do aught for him, once

more gently allowing it to rest upon the floor—" I had best
fetch the police and send for a doctor."

" Fetch the police!   Yes," repeated old Marlinson, rousing
himself—" yes, and a doctor, and in the meantime close
this room ; and mind," he said, turning to the chambermaid,
" nobody is to enter it.   Draw a table, or something, across
the door, as the lock is broke," and then the old gentleman
went down to his snuggery and pondered what he should do
next.

The result of his cogitations was that evening Dr. Ingleby
received a telegram—

" Something very serious happened to Mr. Fossdyke ; please
come over by first train.

" From Joseph Marlinson, Hopbine Hotel, Bunbury."

CHAPTER XII.

HIEF-INSPECTOR THRESHER, head of the Bunbury police force, was a shrewd energetic officer, and no sooner was the intelligence of the murder at the Hopbine conveyed to him than he at once started for that hostelry. When he arrived he found Dr. Duncome, a good old-fashioned leading physician of the town, already in the room, with Joe Marlinson, the boots, William Gibbons, and Eliza Salter, the head chambermaid. Dr. Duncome's examination was short and conclusive; there could be no doubt but what Mr. Fossdyke was dead, and had been, in the doctor's opinion, dead for some hours. He withdrew the dagger gently from the breast, thereby occasioning some slight additional effusion of blood, and solemnly informed his auditors that, which no one of them had ever doubted, was the cause of death, and then handed the weapon over to the inspector. It was a queer little Eastern dagger such as one might pick up easily in Cairo, Constantinople, Algiers, or, for the matter of that, even in London. The sort of weapon that tourists are rather given to purchase, turning them into drawing-room toys or paper-knives. "It has pierced the heart, so far as I can judge without the post mortem, which will of course follow, and that naturally would cause death almost instantaneously," continued the doctor, and there his part in the business for the present ended; but it was of course far otherwise with the inspector.

He naturally had to hear whatever information the inmates of the house had to give, and was speedily in possession of the story of Mr. Foxborough's arrival there on the Saturday, how he stayed on and went to the opening of the Baumborough Theatre on Monday, how the deceased gentleman arrived to dine with him on the Tuesday night, how high words had been heard to pass between them, and how early upon Wednesday morning Mr. Foxborough settled his bill and departed. Mr. Marlinson, the boots, and the chambermaid were unanimous in their opinion that No. 11 was the probable perpetrator of the crime ; and as Inspector Thresher continued to sift all the evidence he could collect, he was fain to admit it was difficult to point with suspicion to any one else. A further examination of the dead man's chamber showed his watch and purse untouched on the dressing-table, nor did it seem likely that any property had been taken from his room. Plunder, then, clearly was not the motive of the murder. On the other hand, he had come over on purpose to meet this Mr. Foxborough. That there had been little cordiality between them was borne witness to by both the landlord and waiter; in fact, in the opinion of both of those the manner of the two men towards each other had been markedly constrained, and very different from what might have been expected under the circumstances. Further, there were the high words which the waiter had heard, and the rather remarkable expression which Mr. Foxborough had made use of—" The game is in my hands, and those are my terms." And yet these words hardly justified the conclusion that their utterer would rise in the dead of the night and slay his guest. Another thing, too, that seemed to indicate John Fossdyke had been foully murdered was that the key of the room was gone. If it was a case of suicide the key would have been probably in the lock, but at all events would have been found within the room. The doctor had said that, as far as he could judge from the rapid examination of the body he had made, it was possible that Mr. Fossdyke was self-murdered, though he did not for one moment believe such to be the case. Further questioning of the boots elicited the fact that Mr. Foxborough had taken a ticket for London. He, William Gibbons, the boots, had gone down with the omnibus to the station, as he constantly did, seen Mr. Foxborough into the train, and put his portmanteau into the carriage with him; it was a small portmanteau, such as gentlemen put up their things in for a few days' visit. It was the through morning train to town, patronized chiefly by the business men living at Bunbury, and stopped nowhere between that place and London.

Having further ascertained that Mr. Marlinson had telegraphed to Dr. Ingleby, at Baumborough, Inspector Thresher, after a little reflection, thought that the best thing he could do was to communicate in the same way with Scotland Yard, as the apprehension of Mr. Foxborough must undoubtedly devolve upon the London police. By this time, as may be supposed, the news of the murder had spread through all Bunbury and created a profound sensation, for the Town Clerk was known to most of the leading citizens, more or less; and there is something thrilling when one we have known comes to a tragical ending in our midst. People congregated in knots on the promenade, and discussed the details of the murder as far as they had yet transpired in subdued voices, and those who could recall having seen the mysterious stranger were in great request and eagerly questioned. As for William Gibbons, he was quite overwhelmed with pints of ale and his own popularity. As a rule Bunbury was not wont to exhibit much solicitude about the thirst of William, but at present they seemed in a conspiracy to quench it if practicable, and it may be here remarked that William, when it came to sound ale, would have bothered a garden-engine on that score.

Joe Marlinson had turned remarkably sulky over the whole

affair, refused to talk about it, and was evidently in high
dudgeon that anybody should have had the presumption to
commit such a terrible crime in an old well-established
county-house like the Hopbine. Regret for poor John
Fossdyke seemed to be submerged in the old man by the
indignation occasioned by the tragedy having occurred at the
Hopbine. Listening to his angry muttering one could
almost believe that there were inns kept expressly in which
to make away with one's fellow-creatures, and once again
was reminded that from time immemorial the absurdly gro-
tesque is running close alongside the saddest catastrophes.
The evening brought two men to Bunbury, who arrived there
from opposite directions. The first was Dr. Ingleby, who
had heard the whole story of the murder of his old friend
while waiting for the train upon Baumborough platform from
Phil Soames, who in his turn had learnt it from the guard
who had come by the previous train from Bunbury, and who
had charge of a retriever for that gentleman; the meeting of
which animal indeed was the cause of Phil's presence at the
station.

"I haven't time to think much about it," exclaimed Dr.
Ingleby. "I must go on to the Hopbine, though I shall
come back by the next train. From what you tell me my
presence there is useless, and I shall be more wanted at
Dyke. But, Phil, you must do something for me. Mrs.
Fossdyke must not be left to learn these awful tidings by
chance, and now the news is once in Baumborough, no one
can say when it will reach her. You must go out to Dyke
and break it. No pleasant task I'm setting you, my boy, but
I've known you from a child, and I know you're true grit.
I think, perhaps, if you broke it first to Miss Hyde it would be
best. She's a steady, sensible girl that, and I have an idea
would come out in an emergency like this. Good-bye, and
use your own discretion as to how; but, mind, it must be
told. Here's the train."

"Good-bye, and trust me to do my best, doctor," rejoined

Phil; "though, God knows, it's a terrible task you've set me."

Arrived at Bunbury, Dr. Ingleby drove straight to the Hopbine, where he was cordially received by old Marlinson.

"Course I knew you'd come, doctor, and I dare say heard the awful news before you got here. It's dreadful to think of poor Lawyer Fossdyke being murdered at all, but that the infernal scoundrel should have the audacity to lure him to the Hopbine, of all places in the world, beats me. Ordered the best of everything in the house, too, and turned up his nose at my old port. I ought to have known he was no fit company for the Hopbine by that."

"Never mind that just now, Marlinson. I want to take a last look at my old friend, and then I must hurry back to Baumborough. Remember, that those near and dear to him have to hear all about this, and it will be a dreadful blow to them. Poor Mrs. Fossdyke was wonderfully attached to her husband, and will feel it bitterly."

"Come this way, sir. I allow no one into the room, according with Mr. Thresher's orders. He lays a good deal of stress on the London men whom he expects down seeing it exactly as he found it," and taking a candle, Marlinson led the way.

The room was just as it had been when first burst into, with the exception that the dead man had been lifted from the floor, laid reverently upon the bed, and covered with a sheet. Dr. Ingleby drew back the cloth from over the face, and gazed sadly upon the features of his unfortunate friend, placed his fingers mechanically on the heart, and then peered down upon the small, clear cut through which a man's life had welled. He knew John Fossdyke was dead; it was evident to his practised eye that that stab had killed him. What motive could John Fossdyke's murderer have had?

"From what I'm told, you knew Mr. Fossdyke well, and can perhaps, therefore, clear up at once the first important fact in the case, Dr. Ingleby," said a voice at his elbow.

which made him start, and then he became aware of two other figures in the room, and turned sharply to survey them. One he at once recognized as Inspector Thresher, chief of the Bunbury police force—the other, and it was he that had spoken, was a little wiry, grizzle-haired man, clean-shaved, and dressed in most ordinary fashion, with a pair of restless, bright hazel eyes, that seemed wandering in all directions.

"I'm Silas Usher, Criminal Investigation Department, Scotland Yard," continued the little grey man, "and I'm in charge of this murder. I have heard the rough particulars from my friend, Inspector Thresher, and must be back in town by the night train. I'm always open about what I'm driving at; odd that you'll say for a man of my profession, but I find nothing pays better. I tell people I want to know the way to Ramsgate say, having told them who I am. Well, this is the result—those who are straight, give me all the information they can, those who are not, imagine at once I want to go to Margate, and are, therefore, profuse also in their information with regard to the road to Ramsgate."

It is superfluous to observe that Sergeant Silas Usher by no means conducted his inquiries with this primitive simplicity. He was indeed one of the most astute officers in the force, having strongly pronounced that first great faculty of the detective policeman, rapid inductive reasoning.

"And what, Mr. Usher, is the question you wish to ask me?" inquired Dr. Ingleby.

"This, sir. I want you to see the dagger with which Mr. Fossdyke was slain, and tell me whether you recognize it as his."

"You see, sometimes," added Mr. Usher, "when we are called in this way the first thing to ascertain is whether there has been a murder committed at all. Lots of times when people are missing their friends rush to the conclusion they are murdered, and it very soon turns out they are all alive, though not doing exactly what they ought. In a case like this my experience tells me the first cry will be murder naturally; but there is a great probability of its being suicide. Still, what looks like clearing that question up is the weapon that caused death. I have seen it down at Thresher's place, and it is peculiar. I don't mean to say there never was another like it, but they would be decidedly rarely met with. Some of Mr. Fossdyke's relatives and friends must know if he owned such a dagger. If he did it may be fairly presumed a case of suicide; if, on the other hand, no one ever saw such a weapon in his possession, it is fair to argue the other way, and presume it is murder, and the peculiarity of the weapon is a strong clue to the ultimate finding of the murderer."

" Well, I've not seen it yet," rejoined Dr. Ingleby.

"I know, sir," interrupted Mr. Usher; "but you will just look in at Thresher's place on the way to the train. Can't delay you two minutes, mere question whether you recognize that dagger as the property of the deceased or not. Of course your answer in the negative would not be final, but if some of his friends recognize it I should very much doubt there being any murder at all about the business."

Once more did Dr. Ingleby turn and look sorrowfully at the features of his energetic and somewhat combative friend, whose determination and fluent tongue would never trouble men more; then gently drawing the sheet over the face, he announced himself in readiness to accompany Sergeant Usher to the police office. Upon being shown the dagger he at once said that he had never seen it before. He had been very intimate with the deceased, and had been a constant visitor to his house, but he had never set eyes upon the weapon in question. He was quite sure if he had ever seen it he couldn't have forgotten it.

"This Mr. Foxborough, may I ask if you ever saw or heard of him?"

"I not only never saw him, but have no recollection of ever hearing such a name in my life," replied Dr. Ingleby; "but it is fair to tell you that Mr. Fossdyke had business connections with many people of whom neither his family nor friends knew anything. He was a man reticent in business matters, as men of his profession are bound to be. Nobody employs a gabbling solicitor."

"Thank you, sir; that's all I want to know at present. Our people, whom I have informed by telegraph, will, what we call, reckon up all the Foxboroughs in London in the next forty-eight hours. I am taking up a tolerably accurate verbal picture of the one who was here, but the key to the whole thing, I fancy, is not to be found in Bunbury."

"Not to be found here," ejaculated Inspector Thresher; "why, you have got witnesses to identify, and all the rest, in the town. You've only got to find the man."

"That's just it, my good friend, and the clue to his whereabouts don't seem to be in Bunbury."

Dr. Ingleby looked hard at the speaker as he said quietly—

"I should have thought you would have traced him from this place most readily."

"Perhaps you are right," replied Sergeant Usher; "but I'm a pig-headed sort of man, who can only reckon up matters my own way. But it's time I was off to the station, and you also, sir."

The two accordingly made their way to the railway, and after the two policemen had seen Dr. Ingleby off to Baumborough, Inspector Thresher bade farewell to his professional brother as the up-train for London ran into the station.

"You'll be down again for the inquest, of course?" remarked Thresher, as he shook hands.

"Yes; but I tell you candidly I don't think we shall make much out of that; but there's no saying. Good-bye."

CHAPTER XIII.

T was with a heavy heart that Phil Soames made the best of his way to Dyke in accordance with his promise to Dr. Ingleby. He was sincerely sorry for John Fossdyke, whom he had known before he, Phil, emerged from his teens, and had always liked. There had been something attractive to a young fellow in the Town Clerk's restless energy and go; in the keen way in which he threw himself into the promotion of all amusement for Baumborough. He had been the heart and soul at one time of that very cricket club of which Phil Soames was now the captain; not that Mr. Fossdyke had ever played, but he had been a first-rate secretary, arranged matches, &c., and really made the club; had put them on a sound financial footing, and raised their cricketing status fifty per cent. in the county. Then again, this was a terrible story to have to tell a wife; and Phil Soames, who knew the *ménage* well, and was a shrewd observer, believed that though the Fossdykes might tiff a bit, the lady really loved her husband at bottom. However, as Dr. Ingleby had said, the story had to be told, and that quickly, and Phil Soames was not of the sort that blench when called on to face awkward work.

He rang the bell and looked at his watch when he arrived at Dyke. It was a little awkward, it was just about the time the ladies would be adjusting their toilettes for dinner. When the door opened, he said at once to the man-servant who opened it, "I must see Miss Hyde at once, Robert. I'll step into the study and wait there. Tell Miss Hyde I am here, if you can see her alone, but say a person from Baumborough wants to see her if you can't. Not a word to any one else. I am the bearer of bad news, which you'll all know in half an hour."

Marvelling greatly, Robert left to do his errand, and found Miss Hyde and Mrs. Fossdyke just leaving the drawing-room to dress. Bessie, on learning the message, followed him at once; and Mrs. Fossdyke, supposing that the person from Baumborough was a tradesman of some sort, went upstairs to her room.

"Philip!" exclaimed Miss Hyde, as she entered the study, even before the confidential Robert was out of hearing, so astounded was she at the appearance of Mr. Soames in this fashion, "What does this mean?"

"Sit down, please," he replied, after he had shaken hands. "Yes, in that big chair will be best. I have come over to break some terrible tidings to you. Mr. Fossdyke has met with a very severe accident."

"On the railway?" asked the girl, leaning forward as the colour died out of her cheeks. "Is it—is it dangerous?"

"Yes, Bessie, I am very much afraid fatal," he replied, gently. "Of course there is hope while there is life," and then he dropped his eyes, unable longer to confront the eager, frightened gaze that met his own.

"There is no hope, Philip—none. I can read it in your face —he is dead, or dying. Which? tell me which, in pity's name."

"Dead," he rejoined, in a low voice.

"It is very terrible," she murmured; "what will his poor wife do? She loved him, Philip, indeed she did, though they might not seem to quite hit it off at times. And, oh, how good they have both been to me," and Bessie bowed her head, and sobbed audibly.

10

Soames let the girl's tears have full play; he felt that his task was but as yet only half accomplished, and felt dreadfully nervous about the telling how John Fossdyke really came to his end.

"I am better now," she said at length; "tell me where it happened, and how? Of course I must break this to Mrs. Fossdyke, and she will naturally desire to know all particulars."

"Can you be very brave, Bessie? Can you bear to hear that there is something peculiarly sad about Mr. Fossdyke's death. It was no railway accident."

The girl's eyes dilated as she stared in expectant bewilderment at Soames.

"Nerve yourself," he continued; "remember we must look to you to support and comfort Mrs. Fossdyke under her trial."

"I understand," she said, faintly, "go on, please, quick."

"Mr. Fossdyke has been murdered," rejoined Soames, in slow, measured tones; "stabbed to the heart in his bed at Bunbury."

Bessie threw up her hands before her face as if blinded.

"Murdered," she said, in a low voice. "Good heavens! have they any suspicions as to who is the assassin, and what his motive?"

"His motive! No; but there is strong presumption that a Mr. Foxborough, who invited him——"

"Oh, my God!" exclaimed the girl, as she fell back in her chair, blanched and all but senseless. She looked so like swooning that Phil was about to ring for assistance, when a rapid gesture of her hand stayed him.

"It only wanted this," she murmured, and then she apparently became unconscious.

For a second or two Soames once more fingered the bell, then glancing round the room he rushed at a vase of flowers; quick as thought the blossoms lay scattered on the carpet, and half of the water in which they had stood was dashed

into the fainting girl's face ; then soaking his handkerchief
in the remainder he proceeded to daub her temples after the
only conventional fashion understood by male creatures.
With a quick gasp or two she came round in a few minutes.

" Keep quiet, and don't try to talk yet," said Phil, authori-
tatively. " Shall I ring, or would you rather I did not ? "

A slight but emphatic shake of the head answered the
question.

That the news of John Fossdyke's murder should upset
Miss Hyde was only natural. She was a plucky girl, and
had fought bravely against the shock to her nerves, no doubt ;
but what puzzled Phil Soames was her ejaculation just before
she swooned—"It only wanted this ! " What could she
mean ? It must be remembered that the mystery which she
declared rendered her marriage with him impossible was ever
in the young man's mind. Did her exclamation in any way
relate to that? He was still pondering on this when Bessie,
having in some measure recovered herself, said : " Of course
I must tell Mrs. Fossdyke ; and now, Philip, I think you had
better go. It will be a terrible night for us both ; and when
you get back to Baumborough tell Dr. Ingleby to look in
about ten or so, if he can."

" Certainly I will, but he has gone over to Bunbury, and
can scarcely be back so soon as that. I shall meet him at
the station, and feel sure he means coming out before he goes
to bed. It was he who sent me here to break it."

"He's always so thoughtful," replied Bessie, and as she
spoke the door opened, and in came Mrs. Fossdyke.

" Well, upon my word," she exclaimed, laughing. " How
do you do, Mr. Soames ? and so, Bessie, this is the person
from Baumborough; really, Philip, I could never have believed in your obtaining entrance into my house under such
remarkably false colours. What am I to think ?—explain,
young people, explain. Am I to ask him to dinner, Bessie,
or not ? "

It was so evident to the pair that, far from having the

slightest inkling of the truth, Mrs. Fossdyke merely suspected
them of having come to the understanding which she had
set her heart upon, that they both looked so distressed the
good lady could not but notice it.

"What is the matter with you both? Have you been
quarrelling? What is it? You both look as if you had
come to infinite grief."

To hear the poor woman thus jesting at what was in store
for her was more than Phil Soames could bear. "No dinner
to-night, thanks, Mrs. Fossdyke; good-night. Good-night,
Bessie—Miss Hyde I mean. God bless you," and with this
somewhat incoherent speech—he took his departure.

No man could have been more curiously moved by the
death of a fellow-creature than was Mr. Totterdell when he
first heard of the murder of John Fossdyke. He was a fussy,
garrulous, and inquisitive old man, and had lately proved
himself a rancorous old man to boot with regard to the luckless Town Clerk. He had fiercely resented the being literally
turned out of Dyke, but to do him justice his enmity was not
of that unsparing, malignant kind that refused to be buried
in the grave. He was unfeignedly sorry for the past, and
deeply regretted that ever he should have moved for an inquisition into the financial affairs of the town. He had
lamented before that his wrath had moved him to that step,
it was subject of still bitterer lamentation now. But as the
details of the murder reached Baumborough, there stole
across Mr. Totterdell a little glow of satisfaction that he had
in his writing-table drawer that bill of the Syringa Music
Hall, and was not only one of those who had actually held
converse with the murderer, but was able to point out to the
police where he might be found. Conscious of possessing
this information, Mr. Totterdell positively swelled with importance. To a man of his disposition being the repository
of the clue to a great crime was delicious. He (Totterdell)
at all events now must come prominently before the public.
His name would be in all the papers, and to one of his incal-

culable vanity this went for a good deal. To be pointed out
as *the* Mr. Totterdell who led to the solution of the great
Bunbury murder was fame. Questionable that perhaps, but
for the time being it would undoubtedly be notoriety, a sub-
stitute that amply suffices most people in these days. Then
Mr. Totterdell remembered how he had actually pointed out
John Fossdyke to his supposed murderer, and began to suffer
agonies of remorse ; but again it occurred to him that it was
the stranger who had demanded who the Town Clerk might
be, and that had he refused the required information his
interlocutor would have experienced no difficulty in obtaining
it from some one else ; so he became more tranquil on this
point. But to whom to disburthen himself of the mighty
secret within his breast troubled him much. Another thing,
too, which gave a singular titillation both to Mr. Totterdell's
nerves and vanity, was the idea that he had sat next a
veritable murderer at the theatre only twenty-four hours
before he committed his crime. Of this he made no secret ;
indeed, dilated on the subject all over Baumborough. Mr.
Totterdell never tired of describing the stranger nor impro-
vising the discourse that took place between them, and that
conversation so lengthened in proportion to the number of
times that Mr. Totterdell recapitulated the story that it appeared impossible that either he or the stranger could have
heard anything of the play.

Now there was one singular fact about all this easily
accounted for if you bear in mind Mr. Totterdell's prevailing
characteristics, insatiable curiosity combined, remember, with
incalculable vanity, prompting him to obtain notoriety at all
hazards. The result was that, freely as he talked of having
met him in front of the house, he was perfectly mute about
having come across Mr. Foxborough behind the scenes. He
could, he thought, give all the information concerning the
stranger the police could possibly require, and was jealous
that any one else should intrude themselves on his platform.
He proposed to pose as the main witness in the great Bun-

bury murder case—a mere matter of notoriety! Quite so,
but men have risked their lives for nothing else time out of
mind, notably in the year of grace 1882 concerning crossing
the Channel in balloons.

When Dr. Ingleby, having returned from Bunbury, got out
to Dyke, he found that he was most decidedly wanted. His
old friend, Mrs. Fossdyke, was perfectly stunned by the news,
and past anything but making one wild wail of remorse for
what she was pleased to term her late unwifely behaviour.
She reproached herself bitterly about her last quarrel with
her husband, and wept piteously over some misty idea that
she had in some sort contributed to the catastrophe. But
what did surprise Dr. Ingleby was the excessive prostration
of Miss Hyde. The girl struggled bravely against it, but her
unutterable woe was as unmistakable as it was difficult to
account for. Granted she had lost a very dear friend, still it
was hard to understand a tolerably self-contained young lady
like Miss Hyde being so completely upset by it. She did her
best—she struggled hard to console and comfort poor Mrs.
Fossdyke, but Dr. Ingleby was fain to confess that she seemed
more in need of comforting herself. A case this in which
there was little to be done for either sufferer. Words of consolation at such times seem commonplace, and medical aid
is superfluous.

But the next day Dr. Ingleby was astonished by the appari-
tion of Sergeant Silas Usher in his surgery—that he entered
unannounced it is almost unnecessary to say. Silas Usher
usually turned up without any official announcement. He
had a way of appearing at people's sides in a stealthy, ghost-
like fashion positively appalling, and his very name caused
terror to the tip-top professors of the art of burglary. It was
related how one of the great artists in that line had been
utterly paralyzed in his last exploit by having whispered into
his ears as he was clearing out a countess's jewel-box, and
greedily gloating over a diamond bracelet,—

"Very pretty, Bill Simmonds, ain't it? but it won't fit you

anything like as well as these," and before the astonished robber could collect his faculties the handcuffs snapped round his wrists, and his retirement from a world he had for some time adorned was an accomplished fact.

"I have just run down, sir, to make a few inquiries in Baumborough, and you're the man I want in the first instance. I don't want to intrude on the family at Dyke, of course, but it is essential I should get answers from them to these two questions: Did they ever know a Mr. Foxborough, or hear of him? and did they ever see this in Mr. Fossdyke's possession?" and Sergeant Usher produced the fatal weapon which had been found in John Fossdyke's breast.

A slight shiver ran through Dr. Ingleby's frame, not at the sight of the weapon, for his medical training had steeled his nerves to all that sort of thing, but he did think it would be a gruesome task to show that ghastly toy to the mourners at Dyke.

"Now don't you run away, doctor, with the idea that I'm a man of no feeling," exclaimed the sergeant, who saw at a glance what was passing through Dr. Ingleby's mind. "Nobody understands the susceptibilities more than I do, and, bless you, nobody humours them more. Now these are important questions, and answers to 'em quite invaluable. But, of course, you'll introduce this," he continued, tapping the dagger, "as a paper knife found in a half-cut novel which Mr. Foxborough left inadvertently behind him. It is to spare all unpleasantness I come to you. Introduce me as what seems best to yourself, but you shall make the inquiries. I only want to be present when they are made, but I think you had best admit at once I'm a police agent. As I told you before, I'm in charge of this murder, and it's a matter of professional pride to bring it home to some one."

"You seem pretty indifferent whom you hang," rejoined Dr. Ingleby, sharply.

"Nothing of the kind, sir," replied Sergeant Usher, "but it is a sort of reproach to my professional reputation not to pick up the perpetrator of a big crime like this. More especially because it seems so simple. Who but Mr. Foxborough could have committed this murder? I told you, sir, I am always candid myself on principle, but we must have the links in the chain complete, and that is the reason I am compelled to disturb the ladies at Dyke, almost in the first agonies of their grief."

"To-morrow, I might, Sergeant Usher, but as the medical adviser of the family, I emphatically say Mrs. Fossdyke and Miss Hyde are too thoroughly crushed by this blow for you to see them to-day. There are probably one or two more points you would like to question them over, and on the whole you will benefit by the delay."

Silas Usher mused for a little, and then said, "Well, it may be so. I, of course, am very anxious to know what induced Mr. Fossdyke to go over to Bunbury. We know Foxborough came here on Monday night. He probably met the deceased and asked him to dine, which, from motives we have as yet no clue to, Mr. Fossdyke accepted; but from the witnesses at the Hopbine, it does not appear to have been simply a dinner between two old friends. If the invitation was given verbally it is very likely that some one heard it given. At all events there must be people in Baumborough who noticed this stranger. If, which may be possible, the man wrote, there's a chance that the ladies at Dyke know something about it, and that the letter is not as yet destroyed. You see, doctor, if you can get hold of a man's handwriting— and this Foxborough was undoubtedly an educated man—or if you can get hold of an accurate description of him, you are pretty much upon his track."

"All of which makes it quite clear to me that you won't altogether waste a day in Baumborough, Sergeant Usher. At all events, I'll not sanction you going out to Dyke to-day."

"It may be you're right, sir," rejoined the detective. "Anyhow, it seems I have got to pass the day here, and therefore I must just make the best of it. I'll call in to-morrow, doctor, to see what you can do for me. Good morning."

That Sergeant Usher went about seeking information would not at all describe that worthy's proceedings; he simply pervaded the town, he had something to say to every one, and it was highly creditable to his versatility and universal knowledge that the people with whom he conversed differed largely about the little grey man's calling. The ostler at the King's Arms, where Mr. Usher was located, had no doubt whatever that he was somehow connected with horses. At the principal stationer's they put him down as having something to do with theatricals, while other people differed as to whether it was corn or cattle the little gentleman at the King's Arms had come down to buy. But that in the course of three or four hours' gossiping with everybody he came across, Sergeant Usher had arrived at the fact that Mr. Foxborough had sat next Mr. Totterdell in the stalls upon the opening night of the theatre, and that nobody in Baumborough knew so much about the whole affair as that gentleman may easily be conceived. Clearly Mr. Totterdell was the man the sergeant wanted, and to ascertain where Mr. Totterdell lived was, of course, easy. Who he was had been fully explained also—his connection with Mrs. Fossdyke, his quarrel with her husband, &c. All such local gossip is easily picked up in an incredibly short time in a country town by such a practised hand as Sergeant Usher; and further, the detective had got a very fair inkling of what manner of man Mr. Totterdell was.

The fussy Town Councillor dwelt in a prim-looking house standing in an equally prim-looking garden, situated in the outskirts of the town, and thither towards the afternoon Sergeant Usher made his way. He was in exceeding good humour with himself, for he considered he had done a very fair morning's work, although most of his informants had been fain to admit they had not noticed the stranger themselves; while even those that professed to have remarked him were so vague and vacillating in their description that the shrewd Sergeant Usher speedily came to the conclusion that " they thought they'd seen him," was about what their testimony really amounted to, but they were all clear and confident that Mr. Totterdell had conversed with the stranger, and could describe his personal appearance, manner, &c. ; indeed, it was he who had been asked to point out Mr. Fossdyke by this Mr. Foxborough.

Mr. Totterdell was at home, and the sergeant was at once shown into his presence. " Mr. Silas Usher," he repeated, reading the name written on an envelope, which had been sent into him. " May I ask what your business is with me ? "

" I thought maybe, sir, the name might have told you. Silas Usher is pretty well known at Scotland Yard, and you might have come across the name in biggish murder cases before now."

" Of course, of course," exclaimed Mr. Totterdell, wriggling in his chair, after his custom, when excited about anything. " Pray sit down, Mr. Usher."

He had been turning over in his mind with whom he was to disburden himself of the mighty secret hidden in his breast, and here was the very man he wanted come to his door.

" I have every reason to believe, Mr. Totterdell, that you can give me some very important information, and as this murder is put in my charge, I come to learn all you have to tell me concerning it."

" And you couldn't have come to any one in Baumborough who can tell you half so much about it. I was an intimate friend of the poor fellow that's gone, you know, godfather to his wife and all that sort of thing, and though he behaved very badly and ungratefully to me at last, I bore him no malice."

What poor John Fossdyke had to be grateful about was not quite so clear.

" Dear me," continued the old impostor, " I little thought

when I slaved so to get up the Baumborough Theatre that I was, so to speak, digging John Fossdyke's grave, but that was his fault; he never was open with any one. If he had only been candid, Mr. Usher; if he had only been candid——"

"Ah! Mr. Totterdell, then he never mentioned Fox-borough's name to you?"

"No, nor to any one else, or I must have heard of it. I hear everything that goes on in Baumborough."

"And you actually sat next this man in the theatre on Monday night," interposed the sergeant rather hurriedly, for he already saw that the newly-elected Town Councillor was not one of those who narrate their story briefly.

"That was just what I was going to tell you," rejoined Mr. Totterdell, testily, "only you interrupted me. Yes, I sat near the miscreant at the theatre; a dark-complexioned man, dressed in evening clothes, as unlike a murderer as could be," and the old gentleman paused, and looked at the sergeant as much as to say, "What do you think of that?"

Mr. Usher vouchsafed no opinion, his professional know-ledge told him that men of all classes had taken their fellows' lives at times.

"Well," continued Mr. Totterdell, "the villain was very affable. Said he was in the theatrical line himself. He asked who two or three people were, amongst others John Fossdyke."

"Give any reason?" interposed the sergeant, in a curt rat-trap sort of way that made the old gentleman start.

"Yes, he said he thought he had met him somewhere, had been at school with him, perhaps, but he didn't seem to recognize the name at all. He thought I said Mossdyke, and when I repeated Fossdyke, asked me to spell it, which I did. Then he asked me if Miss Hyde was his daughter, and I told him no, that she was one of our great mysteries, that no one knew exactly who she was. We don't, you know; it's very curious that, Mr. Usher. Baumborough cannot get at who she is exactly."

"And, of course, sir, you had no idea of what this stranger's name was?"

"Well, I had and I hadn't. It so happens I am in possession of a singular piece of evidence, which, though it told nothing then, is valuable now, as it tells you where to find James Foxborough."

"James!" exclaimed the sergeant. You vo got at his Christian name then, Mr. Totterdell?"

"Yes," exclaimed the old gentleman, with an asthmatic chuckle, as he got out of his chair, and went across to the writing-table. "When," he continued, as he opened a drawer, "the stranger got up to leave he pulled a silk muffler out of his pocket to put round his throat, and as he did so he dropped this," and Mr. Totterdell held up the music-hall bill he had picked up in the theatre. "Look at it."

"Syringa Music Hall! Yes, I know the place well; but any one might go there; this don't tell us much. Ha! Lessee, Mr. James Foxborough. Yes, stupid of me not to remember it before. I know all about it now. Wife, handsome woman, sings rather well. I don't think I ever saw Foxborough. Can't have done. I never forget any one I've once seen. You can keep that, Mr. Totterdell, it's a valuable clue, but excuse my observing it's no evidence. It is open to any one to have a Syringa bill in his coat-pocket."

The old gentleman gasped with indignation. He had held that bill to be a most damning piece of testimony.

"You see," continued the sergeant, who saw what was passing through Mr. Totterdell's mind, "beyond that it recalled to my mind that James Foxborough is lessee of the Syringa, a fact some of our people in town are sure to have remembered, that bill tells us nothing. I've no doubt a man calling himself Foxborough sat next you in the stalls on Monday night, and when we apprehend James Foxborough you will know at a glance whether that's the man."

"Undoubtedly," returned Mr. Totterdell, somewhat reviving as it dawned upon him that after all he was destined to play the *rôle* of a leading witness.

"Well, sir, I don't think I need trespass any longer on your valuable time. I'm a candid man myself, Mr. Totterdell, and I have no doubt that—thanks to the valuable clue you have placed in my hands—we shall soon know all about James Foxborough, and where to find him when we want him. Good-day, sir."

"If his time is valuable he loses a mint of money per annum," muttered Sergeant Usher, as he walked away. "Such a long-winded old chump at telling a story one don't often see, thank goodness. Now, if this is James Foxborough of the Syringa, what on earth could be his quarrel with Mr. Fossdyke? That is a thing has to be got at in some sort. Secondly, it all looks too plain sailing. Men don't take rooms at hotels in the country in their own name, ask their enemy to dinner, murder him, and return quietly to town by the first train in the morning; and yet that's what this comes to. Outside my experience that is a long way. No; it looks so simple that I'd bet it turns out a complicated case. I suppose I'd best go out to Dyke to-morrow, if the doctor will let me, and ask the ladies two or three questions, though I don't suppose much will come of it."

The next morning Sergeant Usher wended his way to Dr. Ingleby's, to learn if it was possible for him to ask those two or three questions of Mrs. Fossdyke and Miss Hyde that he was so anxious to put.

"I have been out to see them already, and have arranged that, painful though it be, it shall be done. But I must manage this business in my own way. The interview must be as brief as you can possibly make it. The questions will have to be put by me, and I have guaranteed you shall not open your lips, although you are to be present. They understand who you are, and that they are answering my questions for your benefit."

At first Sergeant Usher looked somewhat disappointed, then brightening up a bit, said, "It won't take five minutes, doctor. There are only three questions, but I want as distinct answers to them as possible, please. I had better write them down."

"Do, while I order the trap. There are writing things."

A few minutes later and Dr. Ingleby and the sergeant were driving towards Dyke. On their arrival they were at once shown into the drawing-room, where the two ladies were waiting to receive them. They welcomed Dr. Ingleby with a faint smile, and acknowledged Sergeant Usher's bow with a slight bend of the head.

"My dear Mrs. Fossdyke, we sha'n't worry you for more than a few minutes, but in the interests of justice I am going to ask you three questions. First, did you ever see this fanciful toy before?" and he exhibited the weapon that had bereft John Fossdyke of life.

A decided negative from both ladies.

"Secondly, did your husband to your knowledge know anything of a Mr. Foxborough?"

"I never heard of such a person," replied Mrs. Fossdyke, briefly.

"I never knew a Mr. Foxborough," faltered Miss Hyde, with visible emotion.

"Lastly, are you aware what induced your husband to go over to Bunbury on Tuesday?"

"Certainly," replied Mrs. Fossdyke, "he went in consequence of a letter which he received by the morning post, and by which he was evidently much put out. We both noticed it, Bessie, did we not?"

Miss Hyde bent her head in token of assent.

"So much so," continued Mrs. Fossdyke, "that I asked him if he was ill, and afterwards urged him not to stay the night at Bunbury, but come home to dinner. Oh, why, why did he not follow my advice?" and the good lady's tears flowed afresh.

"There, there, my dear friend," said the doctor, sooth-ingly, "we need trouble you no more. Good-bye for the present—good-bye, Miss Hyde. I shall be up again in the evening."

Sergeant Usher had already glided noiselessly out of the room in accordance with his covenant.

"Well," said the doctor, as he joined him in the hall, "I trust you have learnt all you want to know."

"Not quite," rejoined Sergeant Usher. "I want to know when Miss Hyde heard of Mr. Foxborough."

"Why, she said she never had."

"Excuse me, she said she had never seen him, and I believe her; but from the way she said it I have a strong idea she's heard of him."

"That idea never would have entered my head."

"I dare say not, doctor. You're not accustomed to weigh people's words as I am," replied Sergeant Usher, as they got into the trap.

"Were you satisfied with the result of your questions?" asked Dr. Ingleby, after a few moments, during which his companion seemed plunged in a brown study.

"I'd give a hundred pounds for that letter," quoth Sergeant Usher, moodily.

CHAPTER XIV.

CLUB GOSSIP.

HERBERT MORANT, with his things neatly packed, including that valuable clock with an alarum, is casting a cursory eye round his rooms to make sure that nothing is forgotten, when there is a tap at the door, followed by the entrance of Mrs. Marriott with a telegram. It was from Phil Soames, and ran as follows :—" Sorry to put you off, but cannot receive you at present; particulars by post." Mr. Morant read the telegram attentively, and then observed in a moralizing mood, " This is in accordance with the ordering of things by a perverse providence. No sooner do I plant the ladder that tends to fortune and turn to collect my effects than the malignant fairy whose glass the butler neglected to fill on the occasion of the festival of my christening, cuts up rough and kicks it down. Phil Soames," continued the ever sanguine Morant, " told me the ball was at my foot; they always do tell you that, but what's the use when you're not good at the game, and don't understand a drop-kick. But old Phil, I know him so well, he'd have kicked off the ball, and I should have nothing to do but to run after it. Well, there's nothing for it but to await the arrival of the post, and in the meantime man must dine, and in the case of a fellow holding my ' high resolve,' improve his mind afterwards, but whether that shall be done by the pursuit of whist, billiards, or dramatic representation accident must determine."

The next morning brought Mr. Morant a letter from Soames. It was as follows:—

"Dear Herbert,—I am sorry to put you off, but the sad tragedy that has befallen Baumborough must be my excuse. It has cast a temporary gloom over the whole town, and many of us who knew and loved John Fossdyke feel it deeply. I have known him for the last fourteen years, from a boy, in short. He was a great friend of all my family, and we were inexpressibly grieved when the news came of his sad fate. As soon as we have a little got over the shock you must come as arranged. For the present adieu.

"Ever yours,
"Philip Soames."

"P.S.—The papers will give you all the details of the Bunbury murder, and spare me the pain of relating them."

To say that Mr. Morant sat up in bed after reading this epistle would faintly characterize that young gentleman's movements. He bounced out of bed and dashed into his sitting-room in search of the morning paper. A great murder always exercises a curious fascination upon the public, and that fascination is increased when we are connected, however faintly, with the crime. Mr. Morant's intimate friend on this occasion had been an intimate friend of the murdered man. But Herbert Morant is destined to find himself more intimately connected with the crime than that; another minute and the columns of the *Standard* will disclose to him that the supposed murderer is the father of the girl he wishes to marry.

Morant tore the paper open, glanced his eye rapidly over its pages, and for a little failed to discover what he sought.

"Ha! here it is," he exclaimed, as "Mysterious Murder at Bunbury" met his gaze, and he proceeded to peruse the

11

account with no little interest. The murder had taken place on the Tuesday night presumably, though it was not till Wednesday afternoon that it had been discovered. It was now Friday morning, so the papers by this had obtained very detailed accounts of the crime, and the writer for the *Standard* had told his story in very dramatic fashion. But when after reading all the preliminaries with which we are already acquainted, Morant came to this pithy line, " On the Tuesday the friend of No. 11 appeared in the person of John Fossdyke, a gentleman well known in Bunbury, and asked for Mr. Foxborough," he dropped the paper with a cry of horror; then he took heart. Foxborough might not be a common name, but there were doubtless more Foxboroughs than one in the world. He picked the paper up and read on : the particulars of the murder were told clearly and faithfully; but the last paragraph bore a later date than the remainder of the report, and had evidently been transmitted by telegraph. " I have just heard that evidence has been discovered this day in Baumborough which would appear to indicate that Mr. James Foxborough, the well-known lessee of the Syringa Music Hall, is the Mr. Foxborough who was staying at the Hopbine."

Once more he dropped the paper, and remained staring into vacancy. Was it possible that the man he knew, Nid's father, could have risen in the night and deliberately slain his guest ? It was too horrible. A more deliberate murder, apparently, had never been committed, and whatever the motive might have been, it was as yet perfectly unfathomable. Not the slightest suggestion was made by the correspondent of the paper as to the cause of the crime, and the more he thought of it the more bewildered Herbert Morant became. He read that account over and over again in the intervals of dressing; the ghastly story had a weird fascination for him. He felt already growing upon him that morbid feeling, which makes all other things seem tame in comparison with the solution of a mystery of this kind. There are always a small proportion of imaginative people who are held spell-bound by the contemplation of a great crime. For the time being they think of nothing else, they read all the papers for fear the slightest detail should escape them, they build ingenious theories concerning the affair with more or less cleverness in proportion to their reasoning capabilities, and the proportion of educated people who understand what is actually evidence is surprisingly small.

His breakfast finished, Herbert Morant went down to his club. He wanted to see what the other papers might have to say about it; to hear what mankind were saying about this Bunbury murder. The papers varied little in their accounts, some of course were rather more meagre than others, but the leading journals were all pretty much in accordance with the story he had at first read. With humanity it was different. Not only had men much to say and said it, but they improvised knowledge and enumerated theories which made poor Herbert stand aghast.

"Good Lord, sir, there's not much to be astonished at," said old Sir Cranbury Pye, a wicked old man, who had been about town for half a century or thereabouts. "Know all about that fellow Foxborough, real name Ikey Solomon, begun life in the prize ring, in the last days of that noble institution, clever light-weight, but couldn't be trusted, more often on the cross than the square. When that pillar of the constitution, the P. R., came to an end, Ikey started a silver hell at the East-end, got on, and went round the races, Brighton, Doncaster, you know, a little chicken *hot*, as well as cold chicken for supper; found that game rather drying up, so went into the music-hall line, and started the Syringa. Good little chap, Ikey, don't know whether he stuck the other fellow, not proved yet anyhow, but don't suppose Ikey would stick at murder, as a matter of business any more than he would at crossing a fight or *quëering* a flat:" the whole of which farrago was listened to and accepted by some of the younger members of "the Theatiné" with much reverence and interest, Sir Cranbury having no more knowledge of James Foxborough than he had of the Emperor of China.

" Never read a more conclusive case in my life," grunted old Major Borrobosh ; " poor fellow didn't want watch or money, of course. Papers of some kind ; deeds very likely. What did they quarrel about ? Something of that sort, of course—this fellow Fossdyke, you see, wouldn't give 'em up. Foxborough goes at night to steal 'em, means having 'em somehow—the other fellow wakes. Foxborough gives him a dig in the ribs with his dagger, bones the papers, locks the door, and slopes next morning, plain as a pikestaff. What say, hey ? Premeditated, hey ? No, no, not premeditated ——"

" Look here, you fellows needn't go bellowing it about, you know," said Lacquers, " but I heard all about it from a fellow who has got a friend who corresponds with a chap down at Baumborough. The fellow Foxborough had a daughter who went as nursery governess to John Fossdyke. Fossdyke brought her to grief, and her father killed Fossdyke out of revenge. That's the real story of the affair."

Pleasant all this for poor Herbert Morant, whose chivalrous disposition led him strongly to stand up for his new friends, but he hadn't knocked about London the last half-dozen years without acquiring some knowledge of the world, and that warned him the confronting of the club gossip was like tilting at windmills in these days. Even in the old duelling days, and credited with wielding a deadly pistol, to curb the tongues of one of our great monachal caravansaries was hopeless. To attempt it in these times would be ridiculous. Then the young man could but acknowledge to himself that he knew next to nothing of Foxborough. Of Mrs. Foxborough and Nid, yes, that was different ; but Herbert was aware that consummate scoundrels before now have been blessed with charming feminine belongings. He felt very miserable as he walked out of the Theatinê ; true, he believed very little of all these rumours he had heard, but there was no getting away from the fact that James Foxborough stood in imminent danger of being charged with murder, and, guilty or not guilty, that must occasion infinite agony to the girl he loved and her mother ; and Herbert was very fond of Mrs. Fox-borough as well as Nid, although not quite in the same pro-portion. At last it occurred to Herbert he would walk out to Tapton Cottage, and inquire after its inmates—if possible, see them. It would show, at all events, both his sympathy and disbelief in the charge, and having come to this resolu-tion he stepped out manfully, and without further vacillation, in the direction of Regent's Park.

That the papers should so soon have got at the connection between James Foxborough and the Syringa was due chiefly to Mr. Totterdell. That garrulous old gentleman, having once parted with his hardly-kept secret, thought it was as well to derive as much enjoyment as possible from it, and to that end confidentially showed the music-hall bill, and con-fided the story of how he came by it to every friend or ac-quaintance he came across. To Mr. Totterdell Baumborough owed the knowledge that the eminent Sergeant Usher had spent a day in their midst, and, according to Mr. Totterdell, the sergeant had admitted that but for his assistance he would not yet have been on the track of the murderer.

As he neared Tapton Cottage, Herbert Morant's feet im-perceptibly lagged. It was not that he faltered for one moment in his purpose; he longed to express his deep sym-pathy with them in their anguish, his utter disbelief in Mr. Foxborough being capable of the atrocious crime ascribed to him ; but what was he to say to those stricken women ? Words are so weak, and come so unreadily to our lips on these occasions of bitter sorrow, especially, perhaps, to men. However, if his pace had slackened, Morant had still held steadily on, and consequently was now within a few yards of the cottage. Suddenly his eye fell mechanically upon a shabbily-dressed man, who was lounging slowly along on the other side of the road, at a pace that implied, at all events,

time was no object to him.   Morant took little notice of him ;
the man had merely attracted his gaze, not caught his attention,
and all street-strollers, or, as the French would term them,
flaneurs, know what that distinction is.   With a nervous hand
Morant knocked, and the answering damsel he noticed was not
the parlour-maid who usually officiated in that respect.   She
was a servant he knew though, well enough, being Mrs. Foxborough's own maid ; and in answer to his inquiry she replied
that her mistress was at home, but saw no one.   The girl's
face was grave enough, and she seemed to think there was no
more to be said.

"But, Jenny," pleaded Morant, "I think she would see
me ; at all events, take my name in, like a good girl ; " and
mindful of sundry *douceurs* that had fallen to her lot since
Mr. Morant had become a visitor at Tapton Cottage, she
thought, well perhaps missis might make an exception in his
favour ; at all events, if he would wait she would go and see.

After some delay Jenny returned with the information that
Mrs. Foxborough would see Mr. Morant, and marshalled him
to the drawing-room forthwith.

Mrs. Foxborough came forward to greet him with head
erect, and a dignity of manner he had never seen in her
before.

"You have heard of course, Mr. Morant," she said, extending her hand, "of the shame that has come upon us?
Shame !   What am I saying !   Scandalous, scurrilous accusation, that will bring more shame upon those that make it.
But you have heard the infamous charge launched at my
husband ?   This it is to live in a free country, and enjoy the
benefits of civilization ; where a ribald press can even state
such slander as this without fear of pains and penalties."

"Mrs. Foxborough, I only heard of this terrible charge
this morning, and have come out at once to assure you of my
utter disbelief in it, and to ask if there is any possible use I
can be to you——"

"Ah ! I thought you would stand by us, Mr. Morant,"

she replied, in slightly softened tones. "You have met my dear husband, and know that he was incapable of wilfully injuring any human being, much more of such a crime as this——"

"It is impossible, of course ; but where is he ? Does he know of the horrible allegation against him. Surely he ought to be informed of it at once—to come forward and confute it at once," replied Morant, hurriedly. "I don't go by what the papers say, but surely if he did ask this Mr. Fossdyke to dine with him at the Hopbine, he had best come forward and tell his plain story of the business."

"I never heard him mention the name of Fossdyke in my life," replied Mrs. Foxborough, as she sank into a chair.

"Then it is very possible that he is not the Mr. Foxborough who stayed at the Hopbine. Have you written to him ? "

"No, I cannot. I don't know exactly where he is. We never correspond much when he is away. The last letter I had from him was from a place called Slackford."

"Great heavens ! Why, that is no great distance from Bunbury."

"Indeed! But what has that to do with it ?" retorted Mrs. Foxborough, rearing her head proudly.

"I don't know ; nothing, I suppose," rejoined Herbert, no little discomposed.

"No ; it is perhaps a little unfortunate that I do not know his address, but it can matter very little. The papers must ere this have told him of the infamy they have dared to lay to his door, and I am expecting a telegram every moment to say that he is at Bunbury."

"Ah, that would be most satisfactory. How does Nid bear it ?"

"Well, poor child, it was impossible to keep it from her, or else I would have done ; but I reflected she was sure to learn it in the course of two or three days, and thought she'd best hear it from me. Indeed, it was quite a chance she did not see it in the paper before I did. She's terribly knocked

down. There is very little of the Roman maiden about Nid,
I fear," said Mrs. Foxborough, with a faint smile.

"May I see her?"

"No, I think not to-day. My doors are closed to every
one, but I mean to make an exception in your favour, Mr.
Morant. You have offered to serve me. I wonder whether
you will undertake the first thing I ask you to do for me."

"Certainly, Mrs. Foxborough," exclaimed the young man,
eagerly.

"Well, listen. The inquest commenced to-day, and will, I
am told, extend over to-morrow. Will you go down and bring
me a faithful account of the proceedings?" and even proud
and plucky Mrs. Foxborough's lips trembled a little as she
spoke.

"They have summoned Ellen. You saw she did not open
the door for you. What they can want with her I have no
idea. And more, Mr. Morant, we are a marked house. We
are under surveillance. A spy lurks opposite our gate night
and day to watch who comes and goes. You may not have
noticed him, but he was there; and it is quite possible that
you also may find yourself dogged on account of your visit
here."

"It'll perhaps be bad for the dogger if I do," replied
Morant, with no little savage elation at the idea of taking it
out of some one. "I will do your errand willingly, Mrs.
Foxborough, and be off to Bunbury by to-night's train. I
even thank you for trusting me with it, not so much as a
mark of your friendship as for the relief it is that I am doing
something to aid you in this terrible trial. Give my love to
Nid, and now I'll wish you good-bye, trusting to bring you
back good news from Bunbury to-morrow night." As Herbert
Morant left the cottage he became conscious of that same
lounging individual upon whom his eye had before mechanically rested, now apparently leisurely pursuing his way towards the West-end, and at once awoke to the fact that this
man was keeping watch and ward over Mrs. Foxborough's

house. At first he thought the man's intention was to follow him, and Morant only waited to convince himself of this, to turn pretty fiercely upon his attendant, but ere they had gone three hundred yards the shabbily-dressed one turned back again, and it was clear that watching Tapton Cottage was his sole business.

As Herbert Morant walked home, he could not but reflect that the accumulation of evidence against Mr. Foxborough certainly was awkward. That he should be in the neighbourhood of Bunbury, as confessedly by his wife he was at the time of the murder, that somebody of his name should have invited the unfortunate Fossdyke to dinner at the Hopbine, and that he, Foxborough, was still not to be heard of, constituted an unfortunate concatenation of facts that might suffice to cast suspicion upon any one so circumstanced. Of course, he would see the papers, and then naturally would appear at the inquest and give an account of himself, and there would be an end of the whole business as far as he was concerned. But Morant could not help reflecting gravely, how very easy it may be for a man to fall under the shadow of crime, when circumstances could so array themselves against one as they had against James Foxborough.

CHAPTER XV.

"MURDER ON THE MIND."

ERY curious are the ripples cast upon life's stream by a great crime; as the circles thrown upon the stream by the sudden plunge of the big stone you have thrown in widen and get gradually fainter, so does the suddenly-snatched life, especially if one amongst the middle or higher classes, move men more or less as their connection with the dead man was small or great; whether they move in the more immediate radius or the outer circles of the sped man's existence, so are they affected by his untimely end.

Philip Soames was within the inner radius, and so much affected by the Bunbury murder as to be quite incapable of paying ordinary attention to business. The dead man and his wife had not only, as before said, been very dear friends of his family for a long while, but he had taken it into his head to connect Bessie's secret somehow with the catastrophe. What connection the two could have even Phil could hazard no opinion about; but he could not forget the expression that escaped her when he broke the murder of John Fossdyke to her. "It only wanted this," she had murmured, half unconsciously. Also she had asked him at the theatre if Mr. Fossdyke had said anything about her to him. He utterly discredited the scandalous tattle which Mr. Totterdell had circulated concerning Miss Hyde in Baumborough, and it

was well for that familiar old gentleman that he was as old
as inquisitive, or else it was quite likely he might have met
rough chastisement at Phil's hands; but he had come to the
conclusion that Mr. Fossdyke knew something of Miss Hyde
previous to her appearance in Baumborough, something more
a good deal than Bessie had acknowledged to. Looking back
coolly over the past, Philip called to mind that Miss Hyde
had undoubtedly made her *début* among them as Mrs. Fossdyke's companion; that her brightness, good looks, and the
way the Fossdykes treated her, had made people forget this,
and gradually suppose her a relation. He further remembered
that neither Mr. nor Mrs. Fossdyke had ever endorsed this
assumption. He was firmly convinced, as men are at times,
that with the investigation of this murder would also be disclosed this secret of Bessie's which so distressed her, and
which he verily believed to be a mere bugbear; that there
was something about the girl's relatives or antecedents to
which she attached a disgrace, in all probability much over-
estimated, he thought probable; but that any disgrace attached to Bessie on her own account he would have scorned
to believe. The consequence was that Phil Soames listened
to every scrap of gossip, and read the different versions of the
event in the papers with feverish interest.

And the reading, although this was in the first forty-eight
hours since the discovery of the crime, already waxed considerable; this was a murder that had attracted the papers,
and had also excited the public. The local position of the
murdered man, the status of the supposed murderer; and,
moreover, the extraordinary audacity of the affair, if Mr.
Foxborough really was the murderer. To ask an excessively
well-known man to dine at a first-class hotel, stab him during
the night-time, pay the bill, and quietly depart by the first
train in the morning, was a cynicism of crime that made
people shiver. Under such circumstances what life was safe?
Another thing which still more inflamed public curiosity
concerning the business was that, despite the usual stereo-

typed phrase "that the police are understood to be in possession of a clue to the whereabouts of the supposed criminal," it was quite patent that they had as yet laid no hand upon him, and some outspoken sceptical journals, which maintained their footing chiefly by taking up bold and rather startling views about most things, did not hesitate to avow that they had failed to discover the slightest trace of him. Be that as it might, it was quite clear that Mr. Foxborough had not as yet come to the front, loudly protesting his innocence, as might be looked for in an innocent man.

It was true there were a far smaller but more logical section of the public who agreed it looked very much more like suicide than murder; only to meet with the vehement retort from their excited fellows: "If it's not murder, where is Foxborough? Why doesn't he come forward and tell his story like a man?" To which the logical minority contending for suicide retorted, of course, he would come forward at the proper time, which would be at the inquest.

These last arguments *pro* and *con* were in men's mouths and not in the papers, not but what plenty of rhetoricians would have been glad to see them there had time or editors permitted.

Another atom of humanity, who, although he has never seen John Fossdyke, yet finds himself involved in the swirl occasioned by his tumultuous plunge into the waters of Lethe, is Mr. Sturton, the eminent Bond Street tailor. He, it may be remembered, assisted Mr. Cudemore to provide money for the presumed murderer's necessities on the security of the Syringa Music Hall. It is no anxiety about his money, it is the curious fascination cast over people by an extraordinary murder, intensified tenfold if connected indirectly even with one of the actors in the tragedy. Mr. Sturton almost felt compelled to apologize for taking interest in such a plebeian murder; grand democrat though he was, and useless as in his speech he professed the House of Peers to be, in his heart he grovelled at a coronet. And yet these objects of his reverence tried him hard at times. One of his noble customers only lately in ordering a suit of clothes had expressed his approbation of a certain material.

" You'll find it charming, my lord," said Mr. Sturton. " I can answer for it, because I have tried it myself."

" You ! " replied the ruthless young Baron. " You have ! damme, show me something else; you don't suppose I want to dress like my tailor, do you ? "

Candour compels me to add that that young nobleman would have been infinitely better dressed if he had. But Mr. Sturton was more impressed that night than ever with the necessity of disestablishing the House of Lords. Still he also has caught the epidemic, the fascination of crime, and hurries down to Bunbury to be present at the inquest.

All Baumborough and Bunbury have caught the infection and talk of nothing else, every rumour is listened to with feverish impatience, the railway bookstall is stripped of the evening papers in less than half an hour, and the proprietor writes for a double supply for the morrow. All London trains are waylaid as they pass through to know if they bring any news about the murder, and the question on all men's lips in those parts is, " Have they taken Foxborough ? " Still though the papers all concur in representing him as unheard of so far, whatever information the police may have they keep strictly to themselves. Mr. Totterdell, as might be supposed, is a sight to behold; he haunts the station and buys papers with utter recklessness; he reads them, he recapitulates every rumour, and he pretends to be in possession of the most astounding information if he were only permitted to divulge it. He writes letter after letter of suggestions to Sergeant Usher at Scotland Yard, and is no whit discouraged at getting no replies. I am afraid at this time he might have been not inaptly described as going about with his mouth full of lies and his pockets full of halfpence; these latter for the purchase of journals.

The first day of the inquest is over, and, as was generally

understood, only the preliminaries were got through, such as viewing the body, the identification of the deceased, &c.; the real interest was to centre on the second day's proceedings, when some important evidence would be probably produced, and all Baumborough had made up its mind to be present. Another person too who took an absorbing interest in the proceedings, as may well be supposed, was Dr. Ingleby. He had been one of the deceased's most intimate friends, and was the first to become acquainted with the tragic death that had befallen him. It was only natural that he should be influenced by the weird fascination of this mysterious crime, for, granting it was conclusively proved that James Foxborough was the criminal, where had the two men met, and what deadly quarrel was there between them to provoke Foxborough to commit such a cold-blooded murder? Another thing, too, calculated to excite any person's curiosity, was a short conversation he (the doctor) had held with Sergeant Usher on their return from Dyke.

"Now, Dr. Ingleby," said the detective, "I am not going beating about the bush with you. I'm naturally a candid man."

The doctor's eye twinkled.

"Well," continued Sergeant Usher, with a chuckle quite as candid as is good for people, "but you can keep your mouth shut, and I can't do without your help. First, I want to ask you a question. Did you ever hear a rumour of Mr. Fossdyke having an intrigue with any woman either before or since his marriage?"

"Certainly not! Why?"

"You see this murder looks uncommon like a piece of bitter revenge. What do you know about Miss Hyde, sir? I heard in the town there was a mystery about her."

"She came here as Mrs. Fossdyke's companion, and I don't believe there is any mystery about her at all. That old fool Totterdell set that story afloat, simply because the girl declined to recite her biography to him."

"Now, doctor, I want you to move the ladies at Dyke to search high and low for that letter."

"The letter which took poor Fossdyke to Bunbury?"

"Just so. I have an idea that letter might change the whole aspect of the case. I take it Mr. Fossdyke knew the writing and the writer, and if the handwriting is that of James Foxborough it will begin to look excessively awkward for that gentleman. If he is innocent, he will most likely give himself up after the inquest, and in any case we shall hear of him in two or three days, I fancy; but, mark me, Dr. Ingleby, if by any chance it should turn out that James Foxborough is not guilty, then the murderer is a real artist, and has left a blind track and not a trace of his own footsteps. He will be difficult to lay hold of. Good-bye, sir, for the present. I may see you at the inquest perhaps," and so saying Sergeant Usher took his departure.

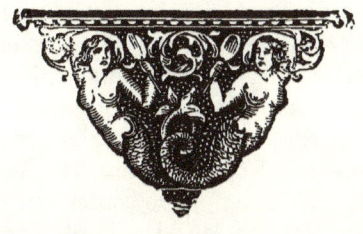

CHAPTER XVI.

THE INQUEST.

THERE was a bustle in the streets of Bunbury, such as might betoken a market day, and yet it was neither the buying nor the selling of corn or vegetables, neither the chaffering for fruit nor poultry, that had thronged Bunbury on this occasion. To learn how a man came by his end was the matter that brought most people into the town this bright autumn morning. The people surged about the railway station, eddied about the streets, but sooner or later flowed up the hill and gravitated towards the Hopbine, where the inquest was being held. Getting into the room had been hopeless half an hour after the coroner had taken his seat, but we all know how persistently a crowd will hang about locked doors with some indefinite idea of seeing or learning something. Old Joe Marlinson sits in the bar-parlour almost speechless with indignation. A crowd permeate the Hopbine, whom Mr. Marlinson in his wrath designates as " scum "; they order spirits and water in jocund and plentiful fashion, laugh at the head-waiter's remonstrance anent their smoking in the coffee-room, and not only smoke there, but about all the lower part of the hotel generally: they lunch freely, and seem to look upon the whole thing in the light of " a bean feast " or some such festivity, instead of the investigation of a presumed murder.

Old Marlinson is in a state of mind bordering on distraction. He devoutly trusts James Foxborough will be captured and endure the extreme penalty of the law; not so much for the crime he is supposed to have committed, but for his disgusting presumption in having selected the Hopbine in which to accomplish his purpose. The old man has appealed to Inspector Thresher to clear the house, and given a confused opinion in support of his application that they were all drunk and disorderly, and that he wanted no riff-raff at the Hopbine. In vain did the inspector laughingly observe, if they weren't all county families, they were a good-humoured, orderly crowd enough, that there was a certain amount of license allowable on these occasions, that the Hopbine was, after all, a house of call, and could not refuse to serve guests in canonical hours, and that it was right good for trade.

"House of call," gasped old Marlinson, "well I'm dashed! —the Hopbine a house of call just like any hedge alehouse,— well I'm d——d. Clear the house, Thresher, clear the house," and he continued at intervals to call upon the good-natured inspector to "clear the house" with the same obstinate incongruity as "Mrs. F.'s aunt" demanded Arthur Clenman's ejection through the window.

The big room upstairs in which the inquest was sitting was as full as it was allowed to be, for the coroner had long ago given stringent orders against further admission thereto. The preliminaries had been got over as narrated in the last chapter the day before, and the medical testimony had been then taken. Both Drs. Duncome and Ingleby were clear and consistent in their testimony that John Fossdyke met his death from the dagger-wound in his chest, they had neither of them the slightest doubt the blade had pierced the heart, and death must have been almost instantaneous; that it was possible the wound was self-inflicted they both concurred, but about its probability they differed. Dr. Duncome gave his opinion that it was probable Mr. Fossdyke had himself dealt the blow that killed him. Dr. Ingleby, on the contrary,

12

while not denying that it was quite possible it was so, pointed out that in the case of a man stabbing himself the wound would usually have a downward direction, as it would be natural to him to deal the blow overhand. In this case the wound ran slightly upwards, as a man might deliver it with a foil or in a duel with swords. To him it appeared that the wound was the result of a lunge rather than a stab. He did not deny that it might have been self-inflicted, but he considered that it was improbable. Dr. Ingleby's testimony had of course thrown a strong suspicion of "wilful murder" around the case, and the excitement concerning the second day's inquiry was very great. It was rumoured, as it so often is rumoured under these circumstances, that startling disclosures would be made in the course of the day, that some extremely trenchant evidence would be come by, that a lady had been brought down from London who could throw most important light upon the case, &c. It was quite clear that this second day of the inquiry would be of much interest.

Phil Soames, with face grave and stern, is there in company with Dr. Ingleby, to see what the result of the day may be. Hardly has the former taken his seat when he feels a hand upon his shoulder, and a voice familiar in days gone by, exclaim—"How are you, Phil?" He turns, and recognizing Morant, wrings his hand heartily as he asks, "Good heavens, Herbert! what brought you here?"

"It's odd, Phil, very," replies the latter quietly, as he sat down beside his old university chum, "but I have as deep an interest in this case as you. If the murdered man was a dear friend of yours, the supposed murderer is a friend of mine. I don't know so very much about him, but with his wife and daughter I am very intimate, and you may easily imagine the terrible state of mind they are in about the whole business. I no more believe Foxborough capable of such a crime than I do you: that appearances look horribly against him I'll admit, but I fully expect to see him turn up to-day and explain everything."

"I trust he may," replied Soames; "but Thresher, the head of the police here, gave me to understand just now, that the accumulated evidence against Foxborough is terribly strong. It is a mysterious case, and at present incomprehensible. My own idea is that some old quarrel existed between the pair, and also some money transactions which has been the reason of their meeting, that the old feud was renewed, and maddened by wine and probably having had the worst of the altercation with poor Fossdyke, in a moment of passion Foxborough slew him."

"Good heavens, Phil, according to what I have read the man was stabbed in his sleep!"

"That that was not the case, my friend Dr. Ingleby can vouch for. Allow me to introduce you."

The two gentlemen bowed.

"No," said Dr. Ingleby, " poor Fossdyke was not murdered in his sleep; he was out of bed and in his shirt and trousers, and, moreover, the bed had never been slept in. My theory, Mr. Morant, is that he was killed in the sitting-room adjoining, and carried to the bedroom after he was dead; but we shall hear what Inspector Thresher has got to bring before us to-day."

"You are conclusive, Dr. Ingleby, as to its being murder then, and not a case of suicide?" said Morant.

"Yes, I am, and I have told you my theory of the whole crime; but please remember that though I can set forth arguments against its being self-murder, and though the evidence will show you clearly that Fossdyke was never slain in his bed, yet I am bound to say my idea that he was killed in the sitting-room is utterly unwarranted by any evidence as yet produced."

And now the coroner re-opens the inquiry, and the jury shuffle into their places. A well-known solicitor of much experience in criminal cases has been sent down to watch the case for the Crown, and the first witness on the day's list is Eliza Salter, the chambermaid. She recapitulates the evidence she has already given as to her unavailing attempts to rouse Mr. Fossdyke, how as the day wore on she gently turned the door-handle with a view of peeping into the room, thinking something might have befallen him, and found the door locked ; then she called her master, and after once more knocking very loudly, William Gibbons, the boots, by Mr. Marlinson's orders, broke the door open, and they found the deceased gentleman lying on the floor with a curious dagger planted in his breast. The writing-table in the room and the chair were upset; the bed had evidently not been occupied.

Mr. Trail, the gentleman watching the case on behalf of the crown, obtained permission from the Coroner to put a few questions to the witness, and elicited the following facts : —Mr. Fossdyke was attired in his shirt and trousers, yes, and boots ; he had dressed for dinner, and when discovered had his neckcloth on also.   He had taken off nothing but his coat.   The waistcoat had certainly not been pierced by the dagger, but it was a low-cut dress waistcoat, and the stab was dealt outside it, nearly in the centre of the chest.   The key was not in the lock, nor had they been able to find it as yet, though the room had been searched closely.

Mr. Trail had enjoyed a quarter of an hour's conversation with Sergeant Usher, who had suggested the points that in his opinion required clearing up.

Mr. Marlinson followed and gave corroborative evidence to Eliza Salter, the chambermaid.   Further questioned by Mr. Trail, he said that every bedroom in the Hopbine had a key to it invariably kept in the inside of the door.   Mr. Fossdyke's room being locked was conclusive evidence that the key had been in the lock as it should be, but what had become of the key he could not say.   Inspector Thresher had given him to understand that the discovery of this key was a matter of importance.   Couldn't see it mattered much himself, but all the same he had given orders it was to be found if possible. Search high, search low, they could find nothing of that key.

Here the witness expressed himself in an excited and somewhat incoherent speech to the effect that this was a pretty
thing to happen in a first-class hotel, that some people ought
to feel ashamed of themselves, winding up with a request to
the coroner to clear the house ; after which he was led gently
away by Inspector Thresher, murmuring repeated blessings
upon the assembly generally, and spent the remainder of the
afternoon in confidentially cursing and tasting the liqueurs
at the back of the bar-parlour. Dr. Ingleby had not failed
to notice that though Inspector Thresher, of the Bunbury
police, apparently controlled the production of evidence, he
now and again referred to a quiet little grey man, who seemed
almost to deprecate being noticed at all, and whom probably
few other people regarded, much less recognized, as Sergeant
Usher.

The next witness was William Gibbons, the boots. William
proved what is termed rather a flippant witness. He had in
his humble way that misty idea that accident had given him
that opportunity of distinguishing himself which was perme-
ating the brain of Mr. Totterdell. William Gibbons had little
doubt in his own mind that the whole key to the mystery lay
with him, and that when his testimony had been taken there
would be merely the trifling addenda of arresting and hanging
Foxborough to follow. He deposed how he had called Mr.
Foxborough on Wednesday, the 4th of September, about
seven o'clock. Mr. Foxborough had arrived at the Hopbine
on Saturday, August 31st, had gone over to Baumborough on
Monday, September 2nd, had received Mr. Fossdyke to dinner
on Tuesday the 3rd, and left on the following day. He called
Mr. Foxborough at the time mentioned by his own order, as
he wished to catch the 8.30 train for town, which was a
through train, and stopped nowhere between Bunbury and
London. He saw Mr. Foxborough off by that train, and put
his portmanteau into the carriage with him. In the afternoon he was called by his master to break open Mr. Fossdyke's door, had heard from Eliza Salter previously how late

that gentleman was sleeping; how she could get no answer to her knocks, and how she went so far as to say she thought "something must have happened to him, a fit or such like," continued the witness, "which it had; when we get the door open the poor gentleman was lying on his back with a fanciful dagger buried in his chest, that was the fit he had, poor soul, and it's my opinion, gentlemen, that a more slimy, cold-blooded viper——"

Mr. Gibbons was sharply pulled up by the coroner, who informed him they should not require his opinion, simply his account of what he had seen, and that he appeared to have already narrated all he knew from personal observation.

Further questioned by Mr. Trail, William Gibbons said they had none of them known Mr. Foxborough's name until Mr. Fossdyke had asked for him by it. He had himself thought there was something suspicious in a guest keeping his name dark. In all his experience, and as——

Here once more the coroner ruthlessly interposed, and curtly informed Mr. Gibbons they required neither his thoughts nor the results of his experience, and that unless Mr. Trail had any further question to ask him he might retire.

Mr. Trail having declined to attempt the extraction of further evidence from the redoubtable William, that worthy withdrew murmuring, "If this was the way these here murders was sifted, if the opinions of sensible men who had, so to speak, been in a way almost in it, weren't to be thought of any account, how did any crowners or juries or blessed peelers think they was going to get at the rights of things?"

"I wouldn't for the world, Phil, say a word against the poor fellow that's gone, but it really seems to me there is next to no evidence of murder," whispered Morant. "Dr. Ingleby says that his opinion is theory only."

"Yes, but not with regard to the wound; that he holds decidedly was not self-inflicted. Still so far there is not much to implicate Foxborough beyond this: If it is murder, and not Foxborough, who on earth can it be ? "

Thomas Jenkinson, the waiter, was now brought forward by Inspector Thresher. He bore witness to the arrival of No. 11 on the Saturday, to his sudden interest in the opening of the Baumborough Theatre, how on his return from there on Monday he announced that he had a friend coming to dine with him next day ; how the following morning he gave rather elaborate directions about this dinner to Mr. Marlinson, and how eventually Mr. Fossdyke arrived, and asked for No. 11 under the name of Foxborough ; they had not known his name at the Hopbine previously. Further questioned by Mr. Trail, Jenkinson said the two gentlemen drank a good deal of wine, but were neither of them the least the worse for liquor when he left them. Took up a tray according to order at half-past ten with a small decanter of brandy and four bottles of seltzer. Two bottles of the seltzer only were drunk, but all the brandy was gone when the chambermaid brought it down the next morning. Heard the voices of both gentlemen raised as if in dispute as he brought up the tray, and as he entered the room heard Mr. Foxborough say, "The game is in my hands, and they are my terms," or words to that effect. The gentlemen stopped talking the minute they saw him. Had never seen Mr. Fossdyke before, and should not have known who he was, but was told by his master and Salter, who both, it appeared, knew him.

The next witness was Inspector Thresher, whose evidence was brief and business-like. He simply testified to having been sent for by Marlinson, and finding Mr. Fossdyke stabbed through the heart, and stone dead, as described by three of the previous witnesses. He at once took charge of the room and everything in it, and telegraphed a brief account of the affair to Scotland Yard. The unfortunate gentleman's rings, watch, and some ten pounds odd, consisting of a five-pound note, gold, and silver, lay on the dressing-table. He knew Mr. Fossdyke perfectly ; he was often over in Bunbury for a day or so; but usually got back to Baumborough to sleep.

And now, wheezing and puffing with excitement, Mr. Totterdell appears. He is a splendid specimen of that very aggravating species, the discursive witness ; convinced too at this present that the eyes of England are upon him, and will continue on him for no little time, for the evidence he is about to give before the coroner will but whet the curiosity of the public for the disclosures he will be likely to make at the trial, when everything he wishes to tell is drawn from him by the acute questioning of counsel. Mr. Totterdell is happily oblivious of that other side of tendering important evidence— namely, the being turned inside out by a sharp cross-examiner, a process that usually gives a witness of his description a literal approximation to what a cockchafer's feelings must be with a pin through him. No buzz left in him, but as deadly gnawing at the vitals as ever Prometheus endured on his rock.

Now, the coroner—who thoroughly understood his work, and was a tolerably firm, decisive man to boot, generally kept his jury in excellent order for instance, and promptly put a stop to irrelevant tendencies in Marlinsons or Bill Gibbonses —had this one weakness, he couldn't quite harden his heart to cut a gentleman short in similar fashion. Mr. Totterdell, Town Councillor of Baumborough, in his eyes, claimed indulgence not to be granted to witnesses of more plebeian positions, and that worthy gentleman commenced his evidence with a little homily concerning his regret that he and the lamented deceased had not of late been on intimate terms. Nobody regretted it more than he did, but it was not his fault ; it all arose from that fatal reticence that was the blot in poor Fossdyke's character ; and here Mr. Totterdell looked around, as if to point out to the spectators the flood of light he was letting in upon the case.

The coroner, who had been fidgeting in his chair for some minutes, took advantage of the pause to say, " You must pardon my remarking, Mr. Totterdell, that all this has nothing to do with the inquiry, and that I must request you to confine your evidence as to what you may know of Mr. Foxborough."

" I am beginning my story, sir, from the first ; it is not probable that any one can throw such light upon this awful crime as myself, and I must request——" continued Mr. Totterdell.

" You're perfectly right, Mr. Coroner," struck in Mr. Trail ; " as watching the case for the Crown I have no hesitation in pointing out, first, that the witness's evidence so far is utterly irrelevant to the matter in hand ; and, in the second place, I am requested to say that these details are likely to be peculiarly painful to the deceased's family."

" As I said before, Mr. Totterdell," remarked the coroner, " I must beg you to restrict your evidence to your personal knowledge of Mr. Foxborough for the present, and what took place between you at Baumborough. If you have nothing to tell us on this point we will not detain you any longer."

If the coroner had studied for weeks how to extinguish the discursive Totterdell he could have set upon nothing so effectual. The bare idea that his evidence might be dispensed with gave that gentleman a cold shiver. It was in a much more submissive manner that he rejoined, " I was only anxious to make things as clear as possible, and am sorry that the truth should be offensive to my goddaughter, Mrs. Fossdyke ; but if, sir, in a preliminary inquiry like this, you desire condensed evidence, of course I can give you a sketch of what I have to tell."

" Preliminary inquiry," " Sketch of what he had to tell" —these two phrases put the coroner on his mettle. He had no idea of his court being looked at in that light, and the impertinence of suggesting that an outline of evidence was sufficient for his inquiry, made that official modify his views about treating Mr. Totterdell with much consideration not a little.

"I have only to say, Mr. Totterdell, that this investigation cannot go on for ever," he remarked, sharply. "If you have anything to tell us, perhaps you will be kind enough to do so at once without further rambling; if not I will hear the next witness."

The fear of not being allowed to tell his story at once coerced Mr. Totterdell into telling it as far as in him lay without amplifications, and, supported by Mr. Trail, the coroner determined to pull the garrulous old gentleman up sharply if he attempted any such wild digression as he had commenced with; but to narrate what we know or have seen succinctly is only given to the few, and men of the Totterdell stamp can no more help being diffuse on an occasion of this kind than they can help breathing. The clear, concise account, so prized by lawyers, scientific inquirers, medical men, &c.—all, in short, who wish to arrive at facts as quickly as may be—is not possible to many from whom they are compelled to collect evidence. Mr. Totterdell, in vague, wandering fashion, disclosed how he had made the acquaintance of the stranger at the opening of the Baumborough theatre, his curiosity about who people were, his especial curiosity with regard to the deceased, how the stranger had even requested him to spell the name of Fossdyke, how he had asked who Miss Hyde was, and here Mr. Totterdell would have been wildly discursive if the coroner had not intervened. Pulled up abruptly on this point, the old gentleman narrated, with sundry shrugs and grimaces, how he had picked up the music-hall bill, and so arrived at the stranger's name, "and thus," he added, looking round for applause and posing as if receiving the freedom of the city in a gold box, "was enabled to give valuable information to the police and be of inestimable service to my country." And neither the goose that saved the Capitol, nor the first Stuart discovering the Gunpowder Plot, ever looked half so sagacious as Mr. Totterdell at this juncture. Nobody in the room had listened more closely to Mr. Totterdell's evidence than Sergeant

Usher; indeed, although keeping himself sedulously in the background, not even Mr. Trail was keeping a keener watch over the case.

" Pretty conclusive, that, I should say," remarked Inspector Thresher, as he crossed over to where the sergeant was seated.

" He told all he knew, and was very anxious to tell a deal more he didn't. What a wasteful creature of time it is. It was well the coroner responded so quickly to Mr. Trail, just to curb him up a bit."

" What does this next witness know about it ? "

" Well, to tell you the plain truth, Thresher, that's just what I am a little curious to see," rejoined the sergeant.

" I can't see how a young woman from London can throw much light on it."

" Lord ! there's no knowing," rejoined the sergeant, quietly. " It's astonishing the light I've seen thrown upon things by young women in my time."

Ellen Maitland, a nice-looking, quietly-dressed girl, here stepped forward and answered to her name. She seemed very nervous, and was obviously much distressed. She was parlour-maid, she said, to Mrs. Foxborough, at Tapton Cottage, Regent's Park. Did not know what she had been summoned here for. Had heard of the murder, but knew nothing whatever of Mr. Fossdyke. Had never seen or even heard of him till the last two days. Her master was much away from home; had last seen him about a week ago at Tapton Cottage. Knew that he was suspected of this crime, but felt sure that he had nothing to do with it.

The coroner looked a little impatiently at Inspector Thresher, as much as to say, " Producing witnesses like this is simply frittering away the time of the court." Inspector Thresher on his part looked round for Sergeant Usher, who in reality was responsible for Ellen Maitland's appearance, but that worthy was nowhere to be seen. The coroner signified that he had no further occasion for the witness; and she was about to leave the table, when Mr. Trail suddenly rose and said, "With your permission, Mr. Coroner, I have a question or two to put to this young woman."

The coroner signified his assent.

Then almost with the dexterity of a conjurer, Mr. Trail produced that quaint Eastern dagger that has played so prominent a part in the history of this crime, and turning abruptly on Ellen Maitland asked—"Had she ever seen that before?"

The girl half uttered a low cry of dismay, for she had read enough in the papers to know what that weapon was. She hesitated for a moment, and then faltered forth a reluctant "Yes."

"Where had she seen it?"

"At Tapton Cottage. It was sometimes in the drawing-room, but more generally in Mr. Foxborough's own room."

"Good heavens, Phil!" whispered Herbert Morant, "I know that dagger well. I've played with it often. Its nominal use was that of a paper-cutter, but a knick-knack more described its status than any other term."

"I am sorry for you," returned Soames, as he gripped his friend's hand. "I begin to fear your trouble is like to prove worse than mine own."

"What do you think?" asked Herbert, in an awe-struck whisper.

"Hush," replied Phil. "I only know that things are looking very ugly for Mr. Foxborough. Where can he be? It is almost preposterous to suppose in these days he can possibly be ignorant of the awful indictment against him; of the awful crime with which he is charged."

"It will be terrible news for me to take back to London," murmured Morant in tremulous tones.

"It looks bad," rejoined Phil, "but we haven't heard it out yet."

"Do you know," resumed Mr. Trail, "whether Mr. Foxborough took this away with him when he last left London?"

The witness could not say, not to her knowledge at all events.

" When did you first miss it ? "

" I have never missed it. I didn't notice that it had disappeared."

" Then for all you know positively," observed Mr. Trail, " that dagger might be actually in Tapton Cottage at this moment ? "

" It might," but the witness remembered that she had not seen it lately; "if that was not the same dagger it was the very ditto of it."

Mr. Trail then intimated that he had no other questions to put and Inspector Thresher informed the coroner that he had no further evidence to produce. Poor Ellen Maitland retired in a somewhat tearful state, produced by the fear that she had somehow worked woe to her mistress, for whom she had the greatest admiration and respect. And then the coroner proceeded to sum up. He commented first on the medical testimony, which, as he pointed out, was at variance, whereas Dr. Duncome rather inclined to believe it was a case of suicide, Dr. Ingleby was strongly of opinion that the wound was not self-inflicted. It was quite clear that, whoever No. 11 might be, the deceased recognized him under the name of Foxborough, and asked for him by that appellation. The evidence of Mr. Totterdell was as yet of small account, as he could not identify the stranger as James Foxborough, the dropped music-hall bill of course going for nothing; but, if in consequence of their verdict Foxborough should be apprehended, then Mr. Totterdell's evidence as to his identity or not with the stranger at the theatre would be of the highest importance. He was only calling the attention of the jury to the more salient points of the evidence, and the testimony of the last witness perhaps tended more to implicate Foxborough than anything else. Ellen Maitland identified the weapon with which the crime had been committed as her master's property. The motive for this murder, if murder

you consider it, was so far unapparent, but that is by no
means uncommon in crimes of this description. The facts
were briefly these: " Mr. Fossdyke comes to the Hopbine to
dine with a strange gentleman, whom he before the landlord
and waiter recognized as Mr. Foxborough; they undoubtedly
have some dispute in the course of the evening. Mr. Foxborough leaves the first thing next morning, and has not
since been heard of, while in the afternoon his guest is found
stabbed through the heart, and the somewhat peculiar weapon
with which the crime was accomplished is proved to be the
property of the still absent Foxborough. Of course, gentlemen, you may find it suicide, but in the event of your finding
it murder, I would submit to your consideration whether
you are not justified in returning a verdict of wilful murder
against James Foxborough."

There was a brief consultation amongst the jury, and then
the foreman intimated to the coroner that they had arrived
at a conclusion, and, in response to the customary interrogatory on his part, the foreman returned, on behalf of himself
and brethren, a verdict of " Wilful murder against James
Foxborough."

The verdict was quite in accordance with popular expecta-
tion, and yet the day's proceedings had influenced some of
the lookers-on in a way they little expected. Mr. Sturton,
for instance, now that a verdict of wilful murder was actually
recorded against the missing Foxborough, was perturbed in
his mind about that loan of £6,000 of which he found
the major part not a fortnight ago. It is not that he is
anxious about his money, that he knows is well secured, but
he is not clear whether it is not his duty to communicate
with the police, and let them know how well furnished with
funds the fugitive is. He has as much horror of being mixed
up in a case of this kind as Mr. Totterdell has pride, and yet
he would fain, as a law-abiding citizen, do his duty to the
State; still he thinks, as he wends his way to the station,
there is no necessity for immediate action. It will be time

enough to communicate with Scotland Yard a day or two hence.

"It's of course useless asking you to come back with me, Herbert," said Soames, "but remember, in a week or two, when we have a little got over all this trouble, I shall expect you to pay me your deferred visit."

"I am only too anxious to do so, but I must go back to-night. You were saying it was a cruel task the having to break the sad tidings of her husband's death to Mrs. Fossdyke, but think, Phil, the story I have got to tell when I reach London—to tell these unfortunate ladies what a coroner's inquest has branded their husband and father."

"It's hard—cruel hard," replied Soames, as he gripped his friend's hand. "God send you well through it, old man."

"One moment, Dr. Ingleby," said a voice in his ear, as he was about to follow Phil into the Bunbury train, "but have you made out anything about that letter?"

"No, I am sorry to tell you that so far all search for it has proved fruitless; you still attach great importance to its discovery?"

"I told you that, sir," replied Sergeant Usher, "I told you that letter was worth a hundred pounds a few days ago. Well, sir, I tell you it's worth two hundred now," and with that mysterious commentary on the result of the day's proceedings the sergeant disappeared.

CHAPTER XVII.

ERGEANT USHER occupies a second floor in Spring Gardens. It is handy to the Yard and to a good many other places which are in the ordinary routine of the sergeant's business ; railway stations like Charing Cross and Victoria within easy distance, Marylebone, Bow Street, and Westminster police courts specially come-atable, to say nothing of the Seven Dials, Drury Lane, Short's Gardens, Bedfordbury, and the slums of Westminster, all, so to speak, being under the sergeant's own eye. Mr. Usher is a bachelor ; he has a mean opinion of the other sex, probably consequent on bad treatment received at the hands of one of them, although he professes it to be founded on professional experience. A profound believer Mr. Usher in the theory of *cherchez la femme.* A woman, he contends, is at the bottom of most crimes, and when puzzled by an intricate case the sergeant invariably takes it that a woman, as yet undis-covered, is the probable motive-factor.

" Having no fair partner to share his home, the sergeant is constrained in a great measure to do for himself," and a defter bachelor is seldom come across. Having let himself into his lodgings with his latch-key, after his usually noiseless fashion, on his return from Bunbury, the sergeant proceeded to light the fire, throw off his boots, and then in the easy *déshabillé* of slippers and shirt sleeves, looked in the cupboard for a gridiron and a couple of chops; those obtained, and the fire by this having sufficiently burnt up, Mr. Usher proceeded first to broil his chops, and then to consume them with the adjuncts of bread, pickles, &c., all furnished by the same inexhaustible cupboard. Leaving the clearing up to the charwoman next morning, Mr. Usher next produced a bottle of whiskey, put the kettle on the fire, and having lit a long clay pipe, sat down to smoke and ruminate over this Bunbury case as far as he had carried it.

"It is a queer business this," he muttered to himself, "and it certainly begins to look awkward for Foxborough, and yet, after all, the strongest evidence against him is himself. If he is not guilty, where is he? and, Usher, my friend, I don't mind owning to you in confidence, that's 'a rum 'un.' If anybody had told me a man like James Foxborough could openly leave Bunbury for London, be wanted within twelve hours, and have apparently vanished into space, I'd have called him a noddy; but we can't find a trace of him from the time he left Bunbury platform. Until that girl recognized the dagger to-day, I was beginning to suspect we were in search of the wrong Foxborough; and yet, if that is so, why does not James Foxborough come forward? Every one's talking about this murder; he must have heard he's accused of it, and to prove an *alibi* if he was not the man at Bunbury must be as simple as falling off a log. It's perhaps a little early to speak, but it strikes me as somewhat odd that the theatrical agents seem all abroad about him as the manager of touring country companies; they seem to know nothing about him in that line, and yet any man who has anything to do with that sort of business is pretty well known right through the profession.

"No, this murder—and I feel pretty clear now that it is a murder—is, as Mr. Squeers said of natur', 'a rum 'un.' The why of it and the where of it? for it is not at all clear to me that Fossdyke was killed in his bedroom. I'm candid, very;

13

but I did not let on to Dr. Ingleby that my theory coincided with his, and that the man was stabbed in the sitting-room. I reckoned up that room, too, but could make nothing out of it; the leaving the dagger in the wound, whether done by accident or design, of course stopped the effusion of blood; still it is curious there were no traces whatever of it. Shrewd man, old Ingleby; his theory about the direction of the wound had stuff in it." And here Mr. Usher refilled his pipe and mixed himself a jorum of hot whiskey and water.

Staring into the glowing coals, and puffing forth heavy clouds of smoke, the sergeant resumed his argument:

" There's that letter, the key to the whole business I'd lay my life if I could but come by it, but that's not likely now; Fossdyke probably destroyed it. Miss Hyde, now—I shouldn't wonder if that girl could throw some light upon the affair if she chose. She had heard and knew something of James Foxborough before the murder, I'd bet my life, but she's not the young woman to commit herself, I fancy. Once we lay hold of Foxborough, and he is identified with the man at the Hopbine, it is simple enough, but as things stand at present no jury would find him guilty of murder, in my opinion. To think him so, and find him so, are two different things in the mind of a juror, and in this case he'd be right. The evidence, if awkward, is not conclusive as yet. But how are we to get at Foxborough?—privately I own I'm beat. Watching the house in the Regent's Park neighbourhood is no good—he has never been near it yet, and is not likely to make for that now. I'll see the watch is taken off to-morrow—it's useless, and leaving the nest unguarded might perchance ensnare our bird. A man like Foxborough would be well supplied with money and brains, and with them a man ought to beat all Scotland Yard in London. If we don't come upon James Foxborough in a few days I shall begin to feel pretty confident that he is the man we want, but as yet I've not quite made up my mind about it. Nice old man about a town that Totterdell. Shouldn't wonder if he don't cause a murder or so before he dies. A daft, diffuse gabbler like that sets people pretty wild at times, and leads to the cutting of the wrong throat. Rough, rough, very rough—just like turkeys—we never kill the old gobbler who makes all the cackle, but some of his unfortunate followers who are weak enough to listen to him ; " and with this profound moral reflection, Sergeant Usher knocked the ashes out of his pipe, finished his whiskey and water, and took himself off to bed.

That a coroner's jury had returned a verdict of " Wilful murder against James Foxborough " did not go for much in the eyes of Sergeant Usher ; people were neither hung nor sentenced on the direction of a coroner's jury, and a conviction that had not that result was a mere blank cartridge affair compared to a regular battle in the sergeant's eyes. This man was an enthusiast in his vocation—he was not one whit bloodthirsty, he had no craving for any extreme sentence against the unfortunate he had brought face to face with the gallows, but he was keen for a conviction. It was the pride of a logician who desires to see his carefully thought-out argument endorsed. He was like that famous historical dog—the pointer who in a game-abounding country did his *devoir* so nobly, but whose miserable employer missed shot after shot and brought nothing to hand. How that animal at last put its tail between its legs, roused the welkin (whatever that may be) with its howl, and fled disgusted to its kennel, is it not recorded in the " Lies about Dogs," lately published by the Society of " Animated Fiction ? "

Sergeant Usher was much like that noble and hardly-tried pointer ; when juries refused to " run straight " and convict the quarry he had marked down and brought to their notice, the gallant officer also betook himself to his private apartments in deep dudgeon, not, as I have already said, from any fierce thirst for his victim's annihilation, but that his carefully worked-out chain of reasoning should be deemed inconclusive was gall and wormwood. Was it not Hazlitt who said in reference to the tumultuous ending of some stormy disputation, " The blow was nothing, and you'll admit I had the best of the argument " ? That was Sergeant Usher's case exactly ; if you refused to put faith in his inductive theory he was disgusted, but to do him justice no man ever was more sceptical of evidence or sifted it closer, and if that done he had satisfied himself, that he was unmistakably annoyed if others did not arrive at a similar conclusion.

The Press and the public meanwhile have no little to say about the lethargy and inefficiency of the police. No allowance is made for the difficulty of tracking a culprit who has once gained the shelter of this gigantic warren of London with its multiplicity of burrows. The hunted deer is usually safe when he gains the herd, and that is pretty much the case of the criminal who has once reached the metropolis, always premising two things, that he has command of money, and is no recognized unit of the Bedouins of Babylon, in which latter case he suffers under the great disadvantage of his haunts, habits, and person being known to the police in the first place, and the chance of being *realized* by his comrades in the second, that is, betrayed for the reward. Still the public, and the Press as the echo of the public thought, are ever feverishly anxious for the apprehension of the hero of a sensational crime, and no journal has yet even hinted that has taken place.

The sergeant next morning awoke clear and cool-headed as ever. Having dressed and finished his breakfast he sat down to carefully study the report of the inquest in the morning paper, and as he smoked his pipe and thought over this he slowly arrived at a definite conclusion. Placing the arrest of Foxborough on one side, where was there any probability of obtaining a clue to the true story of this crime ? Was it to be discovered in Tapton Cottage ? He thought not ; if Foxborough was the murderer he fancied his wife and daughter were in complete ignorance of any motive that could have possibly led to it. No, it was not to Tapton Cottage that he must look for information. He could hardly expect to derive assistance from them in any case, but the sergeant came to the conclusion that they could tell him little even if they would. There were four channels he reckoned from which it was possible inspiration might spring. First and foremost, that letter, which had taken John Fossdyke to Bunbury, could it but be come by; secondly, he had a strong idea that Miss Hyde could tell something about James Foxborough if she would; thirdly, he could not help imagining that those rooms of the Hopbine must be able to tell something if closely interrogated. He was haunted with the idea that they had not as yet been thoroughly investigated, and yet he himself had examined them narrowly ; and, lastly, he had a vague idea that the wearisome creature Totterdell, as Mr. Usher mentally dubbed him, might have something of importance to tell, could one but get at it ; only to be arrived at, thinks the sergeant, by listening to some hours of blethering and by much judicious questioning.

It therefore became quite evident to Sergeant Usher that Baumborough must be his head-quarters for the present. The apprehension of Foxborough he must leave to his brethren as far as London went, but the niceties of the case he feels convinced are only to be worked out through the four channels indicated, and he is fain to confess that they seem to promise but little information. Still, the sergeant has unravelled skeins tangled as this in his time, when the key of the puzzle looked quite as unattainable. He possesses the chief qualities of a scientific investigator, patience—coolness, and a natural faculty for inductive reasoning ; and though admitting to himself that things do not look promising, resolves to start for Baumborough as soon as he has conferred with his chiefs in Scotland Yard. Sergeant Usher's arrangements are speedily made, and that evening sees him once more in Baumborough. One of the first visits he pays is to Dr. Ingleby. He is admitted at once, but the doctor receives him with a shake of the head.

"You have come in the vain hope that that letter might

have been discovered, but I am sorry to say it has not, and I tell you fairly, that I think there is little or no chance of coming upon it now. All likely places have been closely overhauled without a sign of it. Mrs. Fossdyke and Miss Hyde, although neither of them read it over, were both positive it was quite a short note and agree in thinking it was probably destroyed. From the account of the scene at the breakfast-table," continued Dr. Ingleby, "I have no doubt you are quite right in the estimate you put upon that note. It was a good deal more than an invitation to dinner, no doubt; men are not agitated in the way poor Fossdyke is described to have been by notes of that kind. I presume that if he had it about him it would have been found at the Hopbine."

"His clothes and effects, you see, sir, were searched by Inspector Thresher before I got there; and bear in mind, it was not till I went over to Dyke with you that I ever heard of that letter. I looked the room pretty carefully over, but it is true it was more with a view to discovering some trace of a struggle or obtaining some evidence bearing on the actual perpetration of the crime. It is possible, of course, he may have had the letter about him, but I can't think Thresher would have overlooked it. He may not be a practised officer like myself at these inquiries, but his search would be thorough, and he would be quite able to judge of the importance of such a document if he had found it. Not likely, I'm afraid, we shall come across it now, but mark me, doctor, that letter would have thrown a good deal of light upon this case, which is at present as queer a puzzle as ever I had set me."

"Yes," rejoined Dr. Ingleby, musingly. "What the connection was between the two men is at present a complete mystery. Still, I recollect hearing Totterdell, when we had considerable discussion about the erection of the Baumborough Theatre, say that he had heard Fossdyke claim to having had much experience of theatrical matters in

his younger days; indeed he asked him a question something
to the effect at the Council one day."

"Ah!" ejaculated the sergeant.

"However, Fossdyke brusquely declined to answer him.
They didn't hit it off very well, as you know?"

"No; thank you very much for that hint, sir. It would
quite probably be the bond between them;" and although
the open-hearted sergeant did not think that there was any
necessity for informing Dr. Ingleby of his intention, he then
and there determined to attempt the solution of the mystery
by tracing back John Fossdyke's early career.

"One thing more. Would it be possible for me to have a
talk with Miss Hyde?"

"No; not at present. Besides, what can you want with
her?" inquired the doctor, in no little astonishment.

"Well, I am convinced she knows something of James
Foxborough. Will you question her about him for me?
She has said she has never seen him, but she has knowledge
of him in some shape."

"I have no objection to do that, letting her know before-
hand that it is for your information, mind."

"Quite so; quite so; and now I'll say good-night. I'll call
in before leaving Baumborough to-morrow and hear anything
you may have to tell me. Once more, good-night, sir;" and
so saying Sergeant Usher vanished in the darkness.

He busied himself about Baumborough in that sort of
desultory fashion in which the sergeant always pursued his
inquiries. He seemed the veriest lounger about, ready to
gossip with anybody upon any subject, or even to drink with
any one; but though free enough in the matter of paying for
other people's liquor, it was little Mr. Usher consumed
himself. Similarly, though he was addicted apparently to
holding the most idle converse, yet both eye and ear were
ever on the alert; and let him discourse about trade, politics,
horse-racing, the weather, or, in a town like Baumborough,
about the price of corn or oxen, the talk invariably gravitated

towards the murder. Mr. Usher had no objection to advance some vague view of his own upon the subject, but noted keenly what other people might say. That there was much winnowing of chaff inevitable in such investigation no one knew better than Mr. Usher. No one had a keener eye for that grain of evidence or information when he crossed it than the sergeant, but he had talked through many a long day and deemed the words of his fellow-men idle.

Mr. Usher had laid down his programme and intended to adhere rigidly to it; he was by no means sanguine, but the four channels from which he conceived inspiration with regard to the crime might come he resolved should be honestly dredged. The recovery of the letter seemed hopeless; he had picked up nothing more of any use to him in the town; he had only to see whether Dr. Ingleby had been more successful at Dyke, and then he was off to Bunbury to spend a night or so at the Hopbine. An afternoon with Mr. Totterdell he reserved to the last. Detective officers are human, and may be pardoned for hesitating to resort to desperate endeavours in their vocation until extremity compels.

"Well, sir, have you any tidings for me?" asked the sergeant, as he entered Dr. Ingleby's library late in the afternoon.

"Yes, in one sense; but what you will I fancy term none. I questioned Miss Hyde on the subject of James Foxborough. She admits she knows him by name, and as the proprietor of the Syringa Music Hall perfectly well, but says she never saw him in her life, and cannot connect him in any way with Mr. Fossdyke. She further declares her knowledge of Mr. Foxborough can have no bearing on this case and would be excessively painful for her to explain."

"There is no more then to be said, sir. I rather fancy I should be a better judge than Miss Hyde of how far her knowledge of James Foxborough might tend to connect him with the deceased, but of course if the young lady does not wish to tell what she knows, there is nothing so far to justify our annoying her. I'm off, so we'll say good-bye."

" Good-bye, Sergeant Usher," replied the doctor, a little crisply. He rather liked the sergeant, but he was indignant that he should imagine Miss Hyde would keep back anything that could possibly tend to throw light upon the catastrophe they were all lamenting.

"Good sort, the doctor," murmured Mr. Usher, when he found himself in the street. "Not worth a cent. in my business, though ; lets his feelings run away with him, as if sifting evidence and feelings could possibly go together. That Miss Hyde could throw a deal of light on the business, I'll bet my life, if she could be persuaded to speak out. She has nothing to do with it, nor is she aware that what she can testify bears in the slightest degree on the affair, but I am convinced it does. Now a real, good overhaul of the rooms at the Hop-bine, and then—then, I suppose, a long afternoon with that wearisome creature Totterdell will have to be got through. The only way to get at what the likes of him has to say is simply to let him talk and give him time."

*   *   *   *   *   *

That night an elderly gentleman pulled up at the door of the Hopbine and demanded rooms. He was a gentleman apparently of the old school, small in stature, formal in manner, as well as slightly irritable. A curious combination, that even awed Mr. Marlinson when he came in contact with him. Formal and polite in the first instance, but unmistak-ably waspish when he didn't get his own way, and he proved hard to satisfy in the matter of rooms. They must be on the first floor he asserted, and to those allotted to him he ex-pressed the strongest aversion. At length Mr. Marlinson said boldly he should regret very much not being able to accommodate the gentleman, but that unless those rooms suited him he had no others vacant on that floor, except a set just at present out of use. If the gentleman ever looked at a paper he had no doubt read of the awful calamity that had befallen the Hopbine, and here Mr. Marlinson paused to give the stranger an opportunity of condoling with him.

"You mean," said the old gentleman, "the set in which the murder was committed. But I have no superstitions; interviewed, tried, and hung too many murderers in India to have any compunctions about apartments because some little difference of opinion was quietly disposed of in them. No, no, my good friend, in all my experience it's the dead men alone you can rely upon not turning up again. Give them long spells of imprisonment and still the scoundrels come before you again, but once dead they are done with and bother you no more. Let's see the rooms."

"He ain't a sticker at trifles apparently," muttered Mr. Marlinson; but at the same time it flashed across him what an excellent person the old gentleman would be to sit in judgment on James Foxborough, wherever he should be laid hands on. The new-comer professed himself perfectly satisfied with these rooms, ordered a snug little dinner and a fire in the sitting-room, remarking that long residence in India was apt to make one somewhat chilly when once more encountering the climate of one's native land. It was a raw evening, and a blaze in the grate was unmistakably cheerful, and Sergeant Usher, for, of course, the *ci-devant* Indian judge was that functionary, his dinner satisfactorily disposed of, thought as he sat sipping his port and cracking his walnuts that the Hopbine was a very comfortable and well-conducted house. He had metamorphosed himself so as to have an unrestricted investigation of the rooms, not sanguine about obtaining a result by any means, but he wished to look these rooms over and pick up what he might in the hotel without taking the Hopbine into his confidence. He had not even let Inspector Thresher know of his presence, but determined to work out this business by himself. It might be, perhaps, the swagger of a well-known London officer, or it might be genuine disbelief in his professional colleague, but certain it is that the sergeant was not prepared to give much credence to Inspector Thresher in this business.

No sooner did he have the room to himself than Mr. Usher commenced his course of investigation. He had questioned the waiter no little during dinner concerning the murder, and Jenkinson, after the manner of his class, was only too delighted to tell his story, and readily led into the relation of all the minor details. Not an article in the room but was closely scrutinized, and to aid him in his task the sergeant drew from his breast-pocket a strong magnifying-glass. Through this, and even going down on his knees for the purpose, he carefully examined the carpet and also the furniture, but no tell-tale stain supported the theory of both Dr. Ingleby and himself, that it was in that room John Fossdyke came by his death. Neither on carpet nor furniture could Mr. Usher's well-trained eyes detect the sign of a struggle nor the deep-hued spots he sought. The theory might be just, but there was nothing whatever to corroborate it.

Mr. Usher sat down, lit his pipe, ordered some spirits and water, and proceeded to reflect over the affair generally.

If Fossdyke was killed here, he said to himself, either by accident or design, it was an uncommonly well-managed assassination. Not a trace of it is to be found. If he was killed in the bedroom, how did it come about? or is it, despite Dr. Ingleby's opinion, a mere ordinary case of suicide? No, I don't believe it is a matter of self-murder; that the quarrel should arise here, and Foxborough in his anger slay him, is intelligible enough, but that he should have followed him to his bedroom and killed him without creating a disturbance seems almost incredible. In his sleep, yes, but Mr. Fossdyke evidently met his death before he had undressed, before he had hardly begun to throw his clothes off. I've no craving to see ghosts, but if John Fossdyke's spirit would give me a wrinkle to-night I'd be obliged to it, and I don't think I'd be too much agitated to take down the evidence.

However, the sergeant's sleep proved as dreamless as a healthy man's after a moderate modicum of grog and tobacco should do. No inspiration came to him from the world of shadows, and as he sprang out of bed next day he exclaimed, " The sitting-room won't speak ; I wonder whether this room will disclose the secret of that September evening. The key of the door, for instance, if it was suicide, where is it ? If it is murder, it may be anywhere ; but if the former, it must be here," and Mr. Usher began an eager and searching investigation of the apartment. It was one of the best bedrooms in the Hopbine, and so somewhat extensively furnished. Not an inch of the old-fashioned mahogany wardrobe did the sergeant leave unexplored ; he turned out the drawers, pulling them out and looking behind them, seeking principally for this missing key. The man had been found dead, stabbed to death in his room, there was no necessity to prove that—but whether it was his own doing or another's was matter of grave inquiry, and to this fact the sergeant was now confining himself, not altogether incapable of noting anything that might bear upon the case, but concentrating himself, as great scientific discoverers usually do, for the time upon the one point. He searched the drawers of the dressing-table, he moved the washing-stand, he moved the bed, he felt the carpet all over with his hands and bare feet, he withdrew the gaudy-cut paper device that masked the fireplace, disclosing some few crumpled scraps of paper behind it, but no key. He peered up the chimney, and even felt on either side of the flue, but he discovered nothing. He opened the window, examined the sill, and took the bearings of the flower-bed below. Possibly the dead man might have thrown the key from thence if he were self-slain. Mr. Usher had best consult the flower-bed on that subject, for that seems to be his last chance of arriving at the discovery he aims at.

But the sergeant, like many other people in earnest, searching for one truth discovers another—that it is a cold, raw, damp morning, and that between an open window, scant clothing, and an unsuccessful quest, besides the chill of dis-appointment, he has contracted physical shivers. He rings the bell and orders the chambermaid to light a fire and bring him a cup of tea. He a little staggered Eliza Salter by the request, fires in September being an unheard-of thing in bed-rooms in an old conservative house like the Hopbine, which rather held that there were seasons for fires and seasons for fanciful papers on the hearth, not to be interfered with by trifling variations in the weather. Still the eccentricities of travellers were wondrous, and of returned Anglo-Indians anything might be expected, and Bunbury had considerable experience of these, the pretty little town being much affected by these whilom shakers of the pagoda tree.

Eliza soon returns with both tea and kindling, and having placed the former on the table, proceeds to clear out the grate previous to laying the fire. Mr. Usher idly watches her, and with his mind still absorbed on the mystery of the key, stares vacantly at the few scraps of paper the chambermaid has raked out and which still lie within the fender. Eliza quietly continues her work, puts a match to the kindling, and is about to thrust the above-mentioned paper scraps into the grate to assist the new-born fire when she is startled out of all equilibrium by the crotchety old Indian with the asthmatical cough (for such had Mr. Usher appeared to her) suddenly exclaiming : " Stop, for your life, girl ! Let me see every scrap of that paper before you burn it."

He was but just in time, and as the sergeant often said afterwards, when alluding to the Bunbury murder case, " I can't tell to this minute what put the notion into my head."

The chambermaid pauses, gathers the four or five scraps of paper together, and hands them over to that peremptory old Indian.

An impatient pshaw, and the sergeant contemptuously throws back to Eliza Salter a couple of old washing-bills, records of guests long departed ; but as he flattens out the third piece of crumpled paper, he cannot restrain from a slight start, and ejaculating with bated breath, " By heavens! it's the letter."

Yes, there it was, unmistakably enough, the note that had brought John Fossdyke to the Hopbine. A scrap of paper worth two hundred pounds, according to the finder's own appraisement, cast carelessly at the back of the grate, as a man might ordinarily be supposed to do when dressing for the feast to which such letter invited him, kept up to that time in order there should be no mistake about time or date.

Infallible key to the mystery had Mr. Usher pronounced this could it be come by, of which he had abandoned all hope; and now he has got it and reads it, the sergeant is fain to confess that it is not quite so big a clue as he anticipated. A mere scrap of a note; any ordinary invitation to dinner conveyed as much, and it was with a puzzled expression that Mr. Usher—the chambermaid having departed—for the sixth or seventh time read over the following :—

　　　　　　　　　　　　　　　" Hopline, Septr. 3rd.

"DEAR FOSSDYKE,

　　　" Dine with me here to-morrow at 7.30. I have something rather serious to communicate to you concerning our last conversation. Circumstances have improved my business position regarding it considerably. I feel sure you will not fail me when you see that I am

　　　　　　　　　　" Ever sincerely yours,
　　　　　　　　　　　　" JAMES FOXBOROUGH.

" Bunbury, Monday night."

And once more did the sergeant come to the conclusion that letter was " a rum 'un." Valuable, no doubt, and likely, probably, to lead up to something in the future, but it was rather hard to see " the how " of that just now. Meanwhile Mr. Usher determined to keep the finding of that letter entirely to himself. Nobody but Eliza Salter had been present when the discovery was made, and she had not in the least connected the strange gentleman with the murder further than he was mighty anxious concerning it. An opinion in which a comparison of notes with Jenkinson, the waiter, confirmed her.

CHAPTER XVIII.

THE SERGEANT PUZZLED.

IT was difficult to make much out of that letter no doubt. Sergeant Usher, great as had been his exultation at its recovery, was compelled to own himself disappointed at its contents. He twisted and tossed it over in his mind again and again while he dressed, but was fain to confess he as yet saw no key to the enigma in that careless, laconic epistle. Still no one knew better than the sergeant how easy is the rendering of a cipher when you have once come at the initial letters ; a mysterious epistle at present, but containing three or four points which yet might throw much light on the affair when he once learnt to read between the lines. That he is possessor of this letter is a fact Sergeant Usher concludes to keep entirely to himself for a little, but in this that intelligent officer considerably overreached himself.

Eliza Salter might not be an out-of-the-way clever girl, but a keen eye for surreptitious *billet-doux* is part and parcel of a soubrette's training, if ever she may hope to thrive in her vocation. Lady's-maid or chambermaid, if she don't understand deft passing of notes and taking of gold pieces, she is basely ignorant of her calling. Thunderstruck by the peremptory order of the old Indian to hand those scraps of paper to him, it was scarcely to be supposed that she did not observe, busy as she might affect to be over the fire, that the old gentleman was obviously interested by one that he retained. Your astute man is often upset by an inferior adversary, whom he has held too cheap. It is years ago since I saw one of the best billiard-markers in London beaten by an adversary to whom he had given three-fourths of the game, and never troubled himself about, till his reckless opponent bet him a sovereign on the result. Then that marker laid down to it, but too late, luck, and the free style of the play produced on a neophyte by a bottle of old port proved too much for him, and the amateur won easy. How many millions that marker wanted to play it over again for I forget, but the winner knew better than that, and confined himself to chaffing his antagonist on what he perfectly comprehended was a most fluky victory.

From people coming to see the rooms in which the murder had been committed, the murder had become the epidemic one might say of the Hopbine. Salter confided to Jenkinson that the old gentleman had found an important paper; then she confidentially apprised Gibbons, the boots, of the same; then she demanded sympathy from her auditors on her having had courage to light the fire, and so gradually paved the way to proclaim herself heroine of this important discovery, though of what this discovery consisted she was entirely ignorant. In due time the affair came to old Joe Marlinson's ears, and once more was the worthy landlord exercised past conception. It couldn't perhaps lead to another murder being perpetrated at the Hopbine, but that another inquest would be held, Joe Marlinson thought quite possible.

"I am going to have it, I tell you, Salter; it's your business to burn up odds and ends of that sort, and not let old Indian vultures come hopping about snaking things like badly-brought-up magpies. Look here, Jenkinson, I mean just snuffing this business out at once. I ain't going to have the Hopbine converted into a criminal court if I know it. When that old magpie rings for his breakfast, I'll just go up

14

and let him have a bit of my mind. He's no more right to
steal waste paper out of the grate than he has tidies off the
chairs, or napkins off the dinner-table. I'll not stand it;
blame me if I do. Don't you forget, Jenkinson, I'll see to
his rolls and coffee being hot enough. These retired Indians,
as they are called, are very intrusive in my opinion."

Despite his own curiosity, Jenkinson was constrained to
bow to his master's orders, and when the strange gentleman's
breakfast was ready, duly acquainted his master with the
fact. It was with much pomposity that Mr. Marlinson placed
the quaint old Queen Anne silver coffee-pot on the table.
The Hopbine was not a little proud of its old plate and its
old wine, and had fair reason in both cases. The returned
Oriental seemed very oblivious of Mr. Marlinson's presence;
"Couldn't have paid less attention to an under-waiter," as
that gentleman remarked afterwards when narrating the
story.

"That will do, you can put things down, and go," observed
Sergeant Usher, still puzzling over that letter, and getting
fidgety at the way his attendant buzzed about the room.

"You'll excuse me, sir, but I've got just a trifle to say first.
We don't like criminal inquiries and inquests, and such
things, at the Hopbine. I happen to be its proprietor—that
is to say, the landlord. I suppose you understand common
sense, I don't mean common law, because that's expecting a
good deal of any one, but what you find in the Hopbine
belongs to the Hopbine, mind, whether it's pillow-cases,
spoons, or scraps of paper. I'm told you've taken possession
of a bit of paper. I am not going to put up with that, as a
matter of simple kindling I wouldn't make a fuss about it,
but if that's going to bring more judges, juries, and inquests
and riff-raff, I tell you I don't mean standing it. Now just
give me the bit of paper, and we will see it burnt all comfortable."

The sergeant had listened to this speech with no little
amusement, and as a humorist could not resist the tempta-

tion of giving the autocratic landlord of the Hopbine a slight shock.

"Look here, Joe Marlinson," he said, rising, and utterly dropping his asthmatic cough and old-fashioned courtly manner, "I'm Sergeant Usher of the Criminal Investigation Department. You've seen me before, though you don't quite tumble to me now. I do pretty much as I like wherever my duty calls upon me to go. I've got all I want out of the Hopbine, and a deal more than I expected, and shall be off by the twelve train; but don't you talk any more nonsense about what may be taken out of the house, and what may not be done, to me. You've one thing to be grateful for——" and here the sergeant paused for interrogation.

But old Joe was past that. With eyes starting out of his head, and a mouth eminently adapted for fly-catching, he stood awaiting what further surprise was in store for him.

"I'm not fool enough," continued Mr. Usher, "to suppose I can muzzle a whole hotel. I'm going at twelve, and you may be thankful I don't take you and most of your people with me, just to ensure your not talking about what you don't understand."

"Me! You threaten to take me to prison!" gasped Marlinson.

Mr. Usher had reckoned up the landlord of the Hopbine on his previous visit thereto, and it was with an amused smile he replied—

"No! don't I tell you I sha'n't; but if you will have these sort of things done in your house, you know——"

"There it is—that's the way they go on," exclaimed Marlinson, excitedly. "One might suppose I'd asked the scoundrel to come down here throat-cutting—that my advertisements ran, 'To be done away with on the premises.' I wish I was dead. I wish the old place was burnt down. Once I've seen Foxborough hung I'll never draw cork nor hand plate again. Now, sir, I'm ready. You come here as an old Indian judge, and turn out to be a thief-catcher. I mean a manslayer; no,

I mean a man-catcher. No, I don't know what I mean, or who anybody is, or where anybody goes to. Where's Foxborough ? Is it Jenkinson ? Is Eliza Salter a disguised countess or female poisoner ? Go it, put on the handcuffs ! I know nothing about it, but no matter, I'm ready : take me, take anything else you fancy ! "

"This comes of quenching excitement and irritation with noyeau, curaçoa, and kümmel," muttered the sergeant. "Too much taking done already, as far as he's concerned."

"Nonsense, Mr. Marlinson. You've had the mischance to have a man killed in your house. A temporary annoyance, no doubt, but still you may safely say about over now. You will be troubled no more, probably, except to give evidence on the trial, and you know very well not the faintest suspicion ever attached to any one of your people."

"I'm worried out of my life. People come here, and no matter where you put 'em, you can't convince 'em it isn't the room in which the murder took place, and if you do succeed in doing that then they want to see the room where the murder was committed at once. I tell you what it is, sergeant, I've come to well-nigh telling them, at times, there was no murder on the bill of fare to-night, but no one can say what will be served up for supper. I knew poor Mr. Fossdyke well, and many a dinner he's ate in this house; but that, as far as my memory serves, was both the first and last bed ever he engaged. I'll never get right, Mr. Usher, till the trial's done. I can't sleep and I can't rest, and I can't do without more drink than is good for me."

And here Mr. Marlinson sat down, leaned his head upon his hand, and appeared the very picture of dejection.

"Now, look here, Mr. Marlinson," said the sergeant, clapping him on the shoulder, a sign of encouragement to which the landlord of the Hopbine responded to by hastily holding forth his hands. "Nonsense ! what a noddy you're making of yourself. I neither want to arrest nor place the bracelets on you," answered Mr. Usher, in response to this gesture. "I'm off to town, as I said before, by the midday train. I've found something of importance here, I don't mind admitting. I'm a candid, outspoken man myself, never seeing any good come of mysteries, and as all the hotel knows it, I don't object to acknowledging it's a letter of some consequence. If I don't tell you more, it's only to save you knowing. This will be all over Baumborough before evening; all over London by to-morrow morning. Everybody will come to you; they will say Mr. Marlinson knows all about it. And you can reply, 'Right you are, I do. Sergeant Usher confided the whole thing to me, but, mark you, it was in strict confidence, and my lips are sealed.' Now, Marlinson, we understand each other. Good-bye, and God bless you. Send up the bill, please. I'll just put up my traps and then I'm off."

Joe Marlinson descended to his sanctum, the bar parlour, much mollified. Facts as personified by Sergeant Usher had proved too strong for him, but it had been a soothing of his ruffled plumes to think he was the sole confidant of that eminent officer concerning the latest discovery bearing on the great Bunbury murder, and it was not till many hours after the sergeant's departure that old Joe thoroughly became cognizant of the fact that he had been told nothing.

Candid very was Mr. Usher, but his candour a little resembled the razors of the old story that were made not to shave but to sell. Sergeant Usher on his way to London turns the letter over and over again in his mind. He has as yet made nothing out of it, but is still firmly convinced the key to the enigma is in his breast pocket—a key in cipher, it is true, key of which cipher has yet to be come by; but that in the eyes of this experienced tracker of crime is a mere question of time and detail. A few weeks and he will show who committed this murder, and why. What perplexed him more than anything was the complete disappearance of Foxborough; that they should not be able to lay hands upon him was nothing, but after leaving Bunbury Station he seemed to have vanished from the face of the earth.

Evening papers must be sold, the public in these times likes its news highly spiced, or, to use a phrase of the day, is greedy of "intensified intelligence." Consequently the special editions found it necessary to continually furnish problematic reports about Foxborough; rumours of his arrest being imminent, wild details of his life and so on flowed freely from Fleet Street, that great emporium of all our latest information, and in the race of competition it is small cause for wonder that Fleet Street at times gets a little loose in its latest intelligence. Concerning the antecedents of Mr. Foxborough, it was undoubtedly at variance, as also with regard to what had become of him, and the public were served up nightly with what the public dearly love—fresh and well-spiced food for speculation; the Theatiné Club being by no means sole monopolist of romantic history concerning the fugitive.

That terrible endorser of a man's criminality, a reward of two hundred pounds for the apprehension of James Foxborough, now covers the walls, especially in the vicinity of police stations, and looms prominent in the papers. To have a price set upon one's head may be difficult to realize for most of us, but it cannot be calculated to induce faith in our fellow-creatures. It is reverting to those primitive times when the discovery of any one or anything on his trail made man decidedly uncomfortable, to the days when he was as often hunted as hunting, when the selection of the fittest was still undetermined, and whether our supposed ancestors, the anthropoid apes, or the bigger cats, such as tigers, &c., became lords of the world doubtful; our superior intelligence to this hour being in great measure marked by our superior capabilities of destruction.

The more Sergeant Usher thought over that letter the more resolved he was to keep it to himself, as far as possible, for the present. That it would not only be all over Bunbury but probably be in the papers, that important documentary evidence had been discovered at the Hopbine, was to be looked for, but the sergeant felt pretty confident that except himself and Foxborough there was no living soul aware of the contents of that note. There was one fact about it desirable to establish as quickly as possible, and that was its being in the fugitive's handwriting, and the sergeant felt a little puzzled as to where to go to establish that identification. He was, however, a man accustomed to settle such problems rapidly, and a day or two after his return to town betook himself to the Syringa Music Hall, and asked to see Mrs. Foxborough. Not only was the sergeant, of course, perfectly aware that a wife could give no evidence against her husband, but he was also essentially a considerate man in his vocation ; ruthless, it might be, to the professed criminal, but in cases like the present always anxious to spare the feelings of the unfortunate's relatives as much as might be. The espionage kept over Tapton Cottage by his subordinates had made him conversant with Mrs. Foxborough's present habits.

He knew that she went to the Syringa no more than was absolutely necessary for looking after the business details of that establishment, and that her visit invariably took place in the morning, still he asked for Mrs. Foxborough to make quite certain she was not there. Informed of that fact, he demanded to see Mr. Slant, the stage-manager, and was forthwith informed out of hand that gentleman was engaged, and could see nobody.

"Just so, my flippant young friend," rejoined the sergeant, drily ; " but take that note round to him, and you'll find he'll see me, and mind if he don't get it pretty sharp, and happens to hear by post I called this evening, he'll see you, my chick, to-morrow, and you'll find the interview more lively than agreeable."

The quiet consciousness of power with which the sergeant delivered his speech somewhat overawed the young gentleman in the ticket-office, and he condescended to despatch a myrmi-

don with the note.   It contained nothing but the sergeant's
official card—

SERGEANT SILAS USHER,
Criminal Investigation Department,
Scotland Yard,

with pencilled at the bottom, "desires to see you as soon as
possible." Mr. Slant knows that the law is not to be
coquetted with, and is, moreover, smitten with that curiosity
respecting the Bunbury murder which has already laid such
violent hold upon the public. "Ask the gentleman to step
this way at once," is his prompt response. He welcomes Mr.
Usher cordially; to stand well with police officials is matter
of policy with all places of public entertainment, but essentially when your license depends on that incomprehensible
body the Middlesex magistrates, the why or wherefore of
whose decisions defy forecast or scrutiny.

"Take a chair, Mr. Usher. You've come no doubt about
something connected with this terrible business down at
Bunbury with which our 'boss' is unhappily mixed up.
Kind-hearted man, Mr. Usher, and I can't believe it of him,
although we didn't see much of him here."

This was mere looseness of expression on Mr. Slant's
part, and was not to be taken as laying down the argument
that attendance at music-halls strengthens one against an
infringement of the sixth commandment.

"It's cut up the Mistress terrible; a bright, cheerful woman
she is naturally, with a merry word and good-natured smile
for every one; kind-hearted, too, with any of them here as
gets into trouble, and we've lazy limmers amongst us who
impose on her not a little, and would more, business woman
as she is, if I didn't interfere a bit. But what is it you
want?"

"Do you know James Foxborough's signature when you
see it?" inquired the sergeant, curtly.

"Certainly, I have seen it many times, although the
cheques are more often signed by Mrs. Foxborough. They

bank at the London and Westminster; whether they've separate accounts or not I can't say."

"Very good, now," said Mr. Usher, taking an envelope from his breast-pocket, and producing therefrom a paper peculiarly folded and laying it on the table; "is that James Foxborough's signature?"

Nothing of the epistle but the subscriber's name was visible.

Mr. Slant looked at it for an instant and then replied, "I should say undoubtedly not."

"Feel pretty positive, I suppose?" observed the sergeant with a slight interrogatory elevation of his eyebrows.

"Yes," replied the stage manager, "I don't believe that to be signed by James Foxborough. Take it to the London and Westminster Bank and see what they think of it. Is that a document of supposed importance?"

"Dear me, no," rejoined candid Mr. Usher, "no bearing upon the case. I should fancy none whatever; might have had, though, undoubtedly if it had been proved genuine. It's a mere plan, tI dare say. Bless you, we always encounter bits of fun on these occasions, more from mere mischief than any attempt of the accused's friend to mislead us. Good-night, Mr. Slant. I hope this unfortunate affair has not interfered with the fortunes of the Syringa."

"It seems a cruel thing to say, sergeant, but it's a fact all the same. We've never done such business. The murder seems to have been the most tremendous advertisement we ever had. What the deuce they come for it's impossible to say. They can hardly expect Foxborough, with £200 offered for his apprehension, to appear, and it is not very likely his wife, poor thing, would do so either under the circumstances; but they come, Mr. Usher, as if," continued the stage-manager, dropping his voice, "we were doing the murder here nightly."

"I can quite understand it. Mark me," repeated the sergeant, "in a big criminal case we could always let the whole court off in stalls at two guineas a-piece easy. Yes, we've put down cock-fighting and prize-fighting, but the taste

exists, only it takes another form of gratifying itself. Good-
night."

The bull at the stake, the captive before the lion, the
murderer at bay in the dock, there is much similarity in all
these, and Imperial London, despite all our brag of civilization,
seems to have much the tastes of Imperial Rome. Sergeant
Usher, as he wended his way to Spring Gardens, was lost in
deepest cogitation. He had treated Mr. Slant's non-recog-
nition of James Foxborough's signature as a thing of no
consequence, and for which he was quite prepared; but, in
reality, he had never been much more astonished. That
this identical note was what took Fossdyke to Bunbury he'd
no doubt. If Foxborough did not write it, who on earth
did? Was there somebody else mixed up in the business?
It evidently was going to be, as he had first suspected, a
more complicated affair than it appeared. He would submit
that signature to the London and Westminster Bank, but he
had little doubt that Mr. Slant's opinion would be confirmed.

CHAPTER XIX.

JOHN FOSSDYKE'S AFFAIRS

HOW are you, doctor ? " said Phil Soames, as he made his way into the familiar sanctum to which he had been a privileged intruder for many a year.

"Ah, Phil!" exclaimed Dr. Ingleby, looking up from a mass of papers with which he was apparently wrestling, "I am very glad to see you. I suppose there is no fresh news about this terrible business?"

"None. Foxborough is either lying concealed in London, or has fled the country, I should imagine. At all events there is no news of him whatever. The police seem baffled at present. Turn me out if I am interrupting you."

"Not a bit; glad to see you, whatever brings you."

"Well, I called chiefly to ask after poor Mrs. Fossdyke and Miss Hyde. Of course I've left my card and inquired at Dyke; but I have seen nobody, and you, probably, have seen them."

"Yes," replied the doctor, "and Mrs. Fossdyke, now that she has got over the first shock, bears it better than I antici-pated. Miss Hyde, I think, seems the more thoroughly upset of the two. By the way, I used to fancy, Phil, you were a little sweet in that quarter," and here Dr. Ingleby eyed his companion somewhat keenly.

"I not only was but am," replied the young man, doggedly.

" Ah, then, perhaps, it is just as well you should hear what I have to tell you. Bessie Hyde is a sweet girl, and much too good to be made a fool of."

" You needn't tell me that," interrupted Phil, somewhat roughly.

" Ah, but you probably have mistaken ideas regarding her. Firstly, that she is the adopted daughter of the Fossdykes."

"I am under no mistaken impression of that nature," rejoined Phil, slowly. "I asked her to marry me some time back. She was very careful to disabuse my mind on that point then, and told me she was nothing but Mrs. Fossdyke s paid companion."

" And what, pray, was the result of that conversation ? "

" She declined the honour," replied Phil, " saying there were unsurmountable obstacles, that unless she could tell me the story of her past life, it was impossible ; that she had not the courage to do that ; and, finally, though she didn't exactly say so, gave me to understand poor Fossdyke was acquainted with her whole history."

" Curious," said Dr. Ingleby, as he called to mind Sergeant Usher's dictum, that Miss Hyde could probably throw light upon this mysterious affair if she would tell what she knew about James Foxborough, little as she might think it. " Still, Phil, there is one thing more you had better know. You may fancy that Miss Hyde, although not nominally an adopted daughter, is likely to succeed eventually to the bulk of what John Fossdyke has left ? "

" I have never thought about it," replied Philip, quietly.

" Well, it will come rather as a surprise to Baumborough, but as one of his executors I have of course been looking into his affairs now the funeral is over, and it looks to me very much as if he has left very little indeed behind him. I can't understand it, and we haven't quite got to the bottom of things yet, but it looks to me as if even the biggest half of Mrs. Fossdyke's fortune has disappeared. I am afraid she will be found to have been left very poorly off. That she will have to give up Dyke, and either sell it or let it, is I think certain."

"You do amaze me," rejoined Soames. "Not that it makes the slightest difference to me. I mean to marry Bessie if I can, and don't expect her to bring me anything, but I am very sorry indeed for Mrs. Fossdyke; giving up Dyke will come very hard upon her. Do you think I might venture to call?"

"Yes, do, it will do them good; rouse them up a bit, especially Miss Hyde. You evidently don't deem her answer conclusive, and putting money considerations on one side, you will be a lucky fellow, Phil, if you win her. She's a special favourite of mine."

"I have got her mysterious past to get at first. I don't believe the bugbear she torments herself with to be of the slightest consequence in reality; but to discover it is the difficulty. I shall say good-bye for the present, and walk out to Dyke."

Arrived there at the expiration of half an hour, Philip sent in his name, and hoped the ladies would see him. Poor Mrs. Fossdyke looked very sad in her sombre draperies, and evidently felt her loss acutely; the remembrance that she had not been quite as good a wife to him who was gone as she might have been of late was a subject of bitter regret, and she thought ruefully over that passage of arms on the subject of Bessie Hyde, which had been in truth the severest quarrel of her married life. She had done her best to make up for it, but felt her husband had never been quite the same man afterwards. He had always worn an absent, preoccupied look, as if worried with business cares or difficulties. Her penitence for that momentary abandoning of herself to her godfather's insidious counsel had made her marvellously tender to Bessie ever since. Fond of the girl she had always been, and it was nothing but curiosity concerning her antecedents, fanned into a flame by the irrepressible Totterdell, that had led her to play the part she had. Since her husband's death she and Bessie sorrowed for him together, and the girl had become inexpressibly dear to her.

She rose with a faint smile to welcome Philip.

"You were always such a favourite with dear John," she said, as they shook hands. " It would have been hard to lose him at any time, but that he should come to such a violent death is too dreadful."

" I am sure the whole town and country sympathize with you in your terrible trial, Mrs. Fossdyke, and the most heartfelt regret and pity is everywhere expressed for your poor husband's sad fate," replied Phil; and then he turned and greeted Miss Hyde.

Bessie looked very pale, and her lip shook a little as she faltered forth her welcome.

Then Mrs. Fossdyke began to tell Philip of her plans for the future. "I mean to go away," she said, " in about a fortnight, to some quiet seaside place—change will be good for both of us; everything here reminds us of all we have gone through lately, and him who has gone. I have never dared to look into the study since that evening when I came and found you with Bessie, and little dreamt what you had come over to break to us."

" Saddest errand ever I was sent upon, but I deemed it best you should not be left to learn such awful intelligence by accident; and news of that kind spreads like wild-fire."

" Both you and Dr. Ingleby were everything that was kind and considerate; indeed, everybody has been that."

" I hope we have all done what little we could, but then it is so little. I trust they may not trouble you much on the trial, but it is possible, Mrs. Fossdyke, remember, that your evidence will be deemed necessary. I mention this now so that you may accustom yourself to the idea."

"They have apprehended Mr. Foxborough?" then asked Bessie, anxiously.

" No," replied Soames; " so far, I believe, the police have no trace of him whatever."

" I could almost hope they might not find him," now observed Mrs. Fossdyke, in a low voice, " nothing can give me
my John back again, and I confess I dread the idea of
appearing in a court of law."

" You may rest quite assured that you will be spared all
possible pain, and be treated with the greatest consideration,
and you also, Miss Hyde."

" They cannot possibly want to question me," exclaimed
Bessie. " I can tell them nothing."

" It is quite open to question whether they will require
either of you ; at all events, the criminal is not caught as
yet," said Soames, rising. " Will you walk with me as far
as the gate, Miss Hyde ? A little fresh air would do you
good, I'm sure."

For a few seconds Bessie hesitated, and poor Mrs. Fossdyke
faltered out, " You've nothing dreadful to tell to-night surely,
Mr. Soames ? If so, let me hear it at once."

" Nothing, I assure you. I can say all I have to say here
if Miss Hyde wishes."

" I will walk with you to the gate," interposed Bessie,
hastily. " I'll run and get my hat."

Phil Soames wished Mrs. Fossdyke good-bye, and in
another minute he and Miss Hyde were strolling slowly down
the drive. Bessie looked very handsome in her dark robes ;
mourning suits a brunette invariably, and the trouble of the
last few days had thrown a languor around her brilliant
beauty that was infinitely bewitching.

" I want to know if you are still resolute not to tell me
what it is stands between us ? You pretty well know poor
Fossdyke meant to have done so. Be generous, Bessie ; I
love you so dearly that I ought to be allowed to judge
whether the obstacle you talk of is insurmountable."

" More so, Philip, than ever," replied the girl, turning
away her head.

" Do you mean that poor Fossdyke's death has still further
increased the impediment ? "

"Yes. Philip, you must think of me no more. I have walked down here with you on purpose to say this in common justice to you, to again thank you for the honour you **have** done me, and to tell you that though I acknowledge you have won my heart, my giving myself to you is now more impossible than ever ! "

" Will you let Mrs. Fossdyke be judge ? "

" Great heavens, no ! She of all women must never know my story now."

" Would you let Dr. Ingleby judge between us ? "

"No ! I tell you, Philip, we must part. Good-bye and God bless you," and with a quick little nod, Bessie turned abruptly and sped back to the house.

CHAPTER XX.

ERBERT MORANT snatched something to eat after the inquest was concluded, and made his way to London by the same train as Sergeant Usher. He had noticed him at the Hopbine, and again on the platform, but had no idea of who he was. Phil Soames didn't know the detective by sight, neither did Ellen Maitland, and with the exception of Dr. Ingleby, to whom Phil had introduced him, those were the sole acquaintances that Herbert had in Baumborough; the doctor in his worldly wisdom thought it best to make no parade of his acquaintance with Mr. Usher, and raised himself considerably in the sergeant's estimation by such laudable reticence.

Arrived in town, Morant took Ellen under his charge, put her into a cab, and, jumping in beside her, drove out to Tapton Cottage. Mrs. Foxborough herself opened the door to them, and though she carried herself bravely, there was a slight quiver about the mouth and fidgety nervousness in her manner that betrayed her extreme anxiety. She was a proud, passionate woman, with all the immense self-controlled power that such women invariably possess up to a certain point, but who, when the barrier of their pride once breaks down, are reckless of all considerations but their own wild impulses.

" Go down, Ellen, at once, and get something to eat, I'm

15

sure, poor girl, it's been a hard day for you as for us. No, don't protest, and don't cry. I know very well you wouldn't say one syllable against me or mine if you could help it. Go now."

"But, Missus," said the girl, half sobbing, "they made me say I'd seen the dagger before. I was obliged to do it; indeed I was."

Mrs. Foxborough gave a slight start, but mastering herself by a strong effort said, quietly, "You were obliged to tell the truth, Ellen, of course. I'll hear your story to-morrow. Go, now, get your supper and then be off to bed as soon as they will let you."

Mrs. Foxborough knew too well that the cook and her own maid had to have their curiosity satisfied before Ellen would be permitted to seek her chamber.

"Now, Mr. Morant," she continued, "come into the drawing-room and tell us all. I say us, for Nid insists upon knowing everything. She says suspense is the least endurable form of agony, and I think she is perhaps right; at all events it is useless to keep her in ignorance, poor child, any longer. She claims her right to share our great sorrow, and as I cannot spare it her, I feel I have no longer the right to refuse. I tell you that, Mr. Morant, in order that you may feel no reticence in speaking before her."

As she finished they entered the drawing-room, and Nid springing from a low chair by the table, exclaimed eagerly, "Oh! Herbert, what have you to tell us? Mamma wouldn't let me come to the door with her, but I am to hear everything, everything."

"Mr. Morant has been told that, darling. Sit down and try to bear his tidings as bravely as you can," replied Mrs. Foxborough.

"I bring no good news for you, I am sorry to say, but rest satisfied, I am going to tell you the whole truth—it would be useless to do otherwise, for every paper will contain the whole story to-morrow morning, and the later evening ones have

most of it to-night. It is a verdict against your husband to
its fullest extent ; but mind, though the evidence was perhaps
enough to warrant that to a coroner's jury, the facts against
him are curiously slight."

Mrs. Foxborough leant against the mantelpiece as a slight
shiver ran through her frame, but her head kept its habitual
proud pose, and she looked Morant steadily in the face. As
for Nid, she cowered in her chair, listening to the narrative
with flushed cheeks and tearful lashes, looking like a crushed
flower in her abandon.

" Your husband's extraordinary absence ! The fact that
he asked Mr. Fossdyke to dinner, and was recognized by him
under the name of Foxborough, and—and——"

Here for the life of him Herbert could not master a choking
sensation in his throat, as he looked upon the two sorely-
tried women before him.

" Go on, quick," exclaimed Mrs. Foxborough, in a low tone.

" And," continued Herbert, " the singular coincidence that
the weapon with which Fossdyke was slain was either that
dagger which I've often played with in this very room, or its
exact counterpart, constitutes the whole evidence against
him."

" That Eastern poignard, the one he used as a paper knife,
why if it isn't here it must be in James's own room," cried
Mrs. Foxborough, as she glanced nervously round the tables.
" Quick, Nid, get a light, child, and let's find it."

" Stop, please, for one moment," cried Morant. " Ellen
was obliged to confess she did not remember seeing it the
last week or so, though she could not say that she had missed
it ; but she, like me, recognized the dagger produced. Dear
Mrs. Foxborough, this has been a cruel, trying day to you.
Take my advice, and endeavour to get a good night's rest,
and search for that dagger to-morrow."

" A good night's rest," she rejoined, almost contemptuously,
" do you suppose I have known that since this horrible charge
against my husband was first bruited abroad?"

" I fear not," he murmured, struck even as she spoke with
the ravages the last few days had worked in her handsome
face.

" No, nor do you suppose I can sleep to-night till I have
sought the house through for that miserable toy. I should
be false to my dear husband if I failed in anything that might
aid him in his need. Good-night, Mr. Morant, you have
been a loyal friend to us this day ; " and Mrs. Foxborough
extended her hand. " Come and see us again soon."

" Good-night," replied Herbert, clasping it warmly ; and
then turning to Nid, who had risen to bid him farewell, he
folded her suddenly in his arms and imprinted a warm kiss
upon her lips. " I claim her for weal and woe, Mrs. Foxborough," he said, apologetically, " and shall never believe,
let them prove what they will, that if Fossdyke unfortunately
did meet his fate at your husband's hands, it was anything
other than the result of a sudden and quite unpremeditated
quarrel."

" Bless you for that, Mr. Morant," exclaimed 'Mrs. Foxborough, as her face flushed with pleasure at the young man's
loyal suggestion. " Nid is not likely to think worse of you
for the way you stand by us in our troubles. Once more,
good-night," and with another pressure of the hand from his
hostess, and a kiss blown to him by Nid, Herbert Morant
was dismissed.

He mused a good deal as he made his way home over this
incomprehensible murder. There were plenty of others fascinated by the attractions of a great crime, who, though
having nothing but an abstract interest in it, were quite as
much absorbed in speculation concerning it as Morant could
be. His remark to Mrs. Foxborough was significant that his
faith was in some measure shaken in Foxborough's innocence.
It would have been noted by a close observer that though
Morant still staunchly refused to admit that the luckless
lessee of the Syringa was a murderer, he conceded the fact
that he might have been guilty of manslaughter. To his mind

that dagger was conclusive evidence ; he knew the toy so well, he had fiddled with it too often in the drawing-room at Tapton Cottage to feel any doubt about its identity, and how could it be in the hands of any one else but Foxborough, and was it not conclusively shown that Foxborough was the man who had asked John Fossdyke to dinner, and with whom he had dined ?

Morant, though he had been called to the Bar, had never studied law nor that preliminary the law of evidence. His conclusions were precisely those to which a considerable portion of the public had equally arrived, although a numerous section held to the theory of truculent, deliberate, cold-blooded assassination. In cases of this kind the culprit is tried nightly at the clubs according to the evidence in the evening papers, and though "the sports of the Coliseum" would be deemed accursed of modern society, yet gambling on a man's life has always its votaries, and there is usually some wagering on the verdict when a great criminal is on his trial.

Then Morant's thoughts took another turn, and he thought how pretty Nid had looked in her blushes and confusion at his sudden embrace, and he vowed, happen what might, he'd be staunch to the girl, let what may be her father's fate ; even if he had the misfortune to be shriven at the foot of the leaf-less tree. What a terrible business this murder was ! Here was poor old Phil Soames all upset ; not only were Herbert's *fiancée* and her mother suffering agonies reflecting to some extent upon him, but all his schemes for a start in the world were left in abeyance, and yet Herbert knew that starting late in life, as he was, there was no time to be lost in beginning. His love for Nid had transformed this man. For the first time in his life he was anxious to be up and doing ; he, who had always pitied the getting up and derided the doing of most people—and undoubtedly it was the lot of many of his associates who rose early to do so of compulsion and to very little purpose—was most anxious to buckle to hard work on his own account. But he was bound to wait ; without

Phil Soames' advice he could not see in what direction to make a start, and there was one consolation in the meantime, that Mrs. Foxborough and Nid really did at present require his advice and assistance in some measure. They had told him they should be always glad to see him in their troubles, and there was no doubt that he could bring them intelligence it would be difficult for them in their retirement to come by. That a man desperately in love, and also moved to the sincerest pity for the family of the lady of his adoration in their sorrow, should feel it his duty to console and comfort may be easily understood, and so despite that inward prompting that it behoved him to bend his neck to the yoke without more delay, Herbert Morant reconciled himself to the decrees of fate, and resolved to take care as far as he could of Nid and her mother for the present.

During the next week the papers were rife with reports of the usual imbecilities that invariably follow upon the commission of a great crime. Provincial constables arrest harmless individuals moving about in pursuance of their usual avocations upon no grounds whatever but that they are strangers, and that in the eyes of the rural police their ways, like those of the heathen Chinee, are peculiar. The average number of good-for-nothing inebriates becoming dimly conscious that they have forfeited all right of existence, in moments of deep despondency give themselves up as the murderer of John Fossdyke, and having had sobriety shaken into them by enforced abstinence and ammonia, whiningly plead drunken ignorance of what they had been talking about. Scotland Yard is inundated with senseless letters, and new-comers in suburban neighbourhoods find the neighbourhood's eye emphatically upon them. Scotland Yard, as personified by Sergeant Usher, keeps its own counsel, and that illustrious individual in bursts of unwonted candour confides to himself that " it's a rum 'un."

Every day does Herbert make his way out to Tapton Cottage, and that there he is warmly welcomed by Mrs. Foxborough and Nid may be easily imagined. That he is looked upon as engaged to the latter now, is matter of course, even Mrs. Foxborough no longer affects to treat it as an arrangement of the future, whatever the marriage may be; but Herbert cannot help noticing how this terrible suspense is telling on Mrs. Foxborough. The defiant handsome face begins to look sadly worn, and even a silver thread or two is visible in the rich chestnut tresses. Not much to be wondered at, when one remembers this woman loves her husband very dearly, and sees no way of rebutting the terrible crime laid to his charge. She has had no word of him for weeks; that is nothing, she is used to that. She has often before been as long without hearing from him, but then this is different. If alive and in England, it is impossible he can be ignorant of the terrible accusation against him of that dreadful verdict— Wilful murder. Absurd in these days of papers perpetual, of telegrams, and of instantaneous diffusion of news, real, false, or mixed, what might be termed half-and-half or embellished facts; absurd to suppose a man could possibly be ignorant of such a charge hanging over him, and gradually Mrs. Foxborough, who scoffed at any idea of her husband's guilt, had arrived at the conclusion that he also had come to an untimely end. She pretended to give no explanation of the Bunbury tragedy, but she remarked sadly to Herbert, "If my husband were alive he would come forward at once to confute this miserable accusation, I tell you. Well, if that is not so, how is it the police cannot find him? I feel certain that he is dead. I cannot tell you why—one can never account for a presentiment, but I feel that he is dead. How? where? why? I can no more attempt to explain than who it was that killed poor Mr. Foasdyke, but that all this will be unfolded in due course I entertain no doubt."

"I am getting dreadfully unhappy about mamma," said Nid, one afternoon, when Mrs. Foxborough had retired to her own room, and left the young people in undisputed possession of the drawing-room. "She suffers terribly. She keeps up and wears a plucky face and undaunted front to the world generally, but oh! Herbert, she breaks down terribly at night! I hear her pacing up and down her room like a wild thing, and the other night I stole down upon her. She turned upon me quite fierce, asked what I was doing up at that hour, and ordered me peremptorily to bed. But I wasn't going to have that, you know; and so I just dashed at her, got my arms round her neck, and in two minutes we were both crying our eyes out.

"Of course, Herbert, as a mere man, you can't understand what that is, to us women. The relief, the luxury it is! Bad for both of us it is, of course. I love my poor father very dearly, but, Herbert, you have taught me to understand how a wife loves her husband, and I know now what my love for my father is as compared with mother's. I feel ashamed of it. Yes, sir, literally ashamed at this minute to think what you are to me when my father, who I dearly love, is under such a terrible accusation. I never saw much of him, no doubt. I've been at school a good deal, you see; and then since my emancipation, father has been a good bit away; but, whenever he was here, no father could have been kinder. Nothing was ever too good for mother and me. If I hadn't a chariot and four and robes of gold brocade, it was because mother curbed his too lavish hand. I can never believe him guilty of what they allege, Herbert; but, as I said before, the whole thing is killing mother. Can't you see it in her face?"

"Only too well, Nid, dearest; it's sad to see the work the last two or three weeks have wrought in your mother's handsome face, but what are we to do? You know well, and I think Mrs. Foxborough does also, there is nothing within my power that I would not do to aid her in this her hour of trial; but, Nid, we are helpless, we can at present but wait the course of events."

"No, I suppose we can do no more, but I am sure, Herbert, that anything that can be done you will do," whispered Nid, with all that grand belief in her lover incidental to girls in the first stage of love's young dream. As married women, sad to say, they have not that magnificent belief in our omniscience and capabilities; they have discovered we are pretty much as foolish as our neighbours, get into quite our average of scrapes, and show no peculiar aptitude for getting out of the most part of them ; extricating ourselves for the most part in most prosaic and commonplace fashion.

"Good-bye, Nid, dearest," said Morant, as he once more clasped his betrothed to his breast. "I shall, of course, come out every day, if it is only to tell you that there is no news, and that as far as the public are concerned is just what is the state of the case at present. Whether the police know more I can't say, but your mother's theory that her husband, like John Fossdyke, has been foully dealt with, would I fancy rather startle them, and yet if your father is alive it seems unaccountable they cannot hear of him."

Nid's reply was brief, and of the kind interesting only to the recipient.

CHAPTER XXI.

MR. STURTON IS CONSCIENCE STRICKEN.

E have already seen that Mr. Sturton was entangled in the mysterious fascination that is apt to surround a great crime. It had taken him down to Bunbury so that he might be present at the inquest, and from that time he had experienced a feverish anxiety to hear of James Foxborough's arrest, not that he had any violent animosity to the criminal, but that he was morbidly desirous of seeing the riddle of this murder unravelled. Although he had through Cudemore lent money to Foxborough, he had never seen him, and Mr. Sturton was at the present much disturbed in his mind about this very loan. It was not that he was anxious about his money ; he had very fair security for that, but he debated very much with himself, whether it was not his duty to acquaint the police with the fact of Foxborough being in possession of so large a sum of money.

The days slipped by, and still the papers contained no clue to what they had tacitly agreed to call the Bunbury mystery. The public had certainly got no further intelligence since the inquest, and the general belief was that Foxborough had effected his escape from the country, and fled either to America or Spain. The whole affair seemed at a dead lock, and with the exception, perhaps, of Sergeant Usher, nobody had much idea that the culprit would ever be brought to justice. The sergeant was, as we know, in possession of a little bit of evidence about which the world knew nothing, and pondering over that note in his lodgings in Spring Gardens Mr. Usher muttered more than once, " Whenever I can read this aright I shall know all about the Bunbury murder. It might be Arabic or Chinese for all I can make of it at present, but just as one learns foreign languages after a bit, so I shall understand this note. One thing is clear already, if Foxborough was the murderer he had a con- federate."

Mr. Sturton at last made up his mind to communicate with the police, but previous to doing so thought it might be as well to talk the thing over with Mr. Cudemore. He had a suspicion that gentleman would be very much opposed ¦to either the police or any one else being acquainted with his money-lending transactions; still Mr. Sturton, for all his languid and somewhat affected manner, was quite capable of taking his own line, and was little likely to be overruled by Cudemore, whom he always treated as a subordinate ; finding him capital at times, throwing business into his way no doubt, but always assuming the position of the big capitalist. Cudemore, indeed, like many ostensible money-lenders, was dependent in considerable measure upon bigger men than him- self, and Mr. Sturton was his great patron. Very handy indeed also to Scotland Yard for the reporting of his little bit of in- telligence was Mr. Cudemore's residence, reflected Mr. Sturton.

The thing had to be discussed with that gentleman as a matter of detail, but that he would communicate with the police, Mr. Sturton had quite made up his mind. That the famous Sergeant Usher was living within a few doors of Mr. Cudemore, and habitually had his meals at the Wellington Restaurant, would have startled Mr. Sturton not a little. Still more would it have surprised Mr. Cudemore that his junior clerk was aware of this fact, that he habitually lunched at the same restaurant, and spent his whole time staring at the eminent detective. Of course Sergeant Usher knew all about him, the clerk ; he did that from sheer habit. To what he called "reckon up" all those with whom he came in contact had become second nature to him, and therefore with no earthly motive he had learnt all about Mr. Cudemore's clerk. In similar fashion he, with no particular reason, had acquired a general knowledge of Mr. Cudemore and his pursuits ; quite promiscuously, be it understood. It was information picked up in the way that a man trained to take note of everything that takes place around him would almost imperceptibly acquire of any one living in his vicinity. Of course he had put a question here and there. Men like Sergeant Usher cannot for the life of them resist doing that. They have, and they're very little account in their profession unless they do have, an insatiable thirst for information about every one. They should always regard it as possible they may want to know all about a man, and Sergeant Usher pursued an inquiry of this description mechanically, and without any definite aim. Still it would have astonished Mr. Cudemore not a little to know that one of the crack detectives of "The Yard" was living within a few doors of him, and had more than a general idea of his (Cudemore's) business. There was nothing about Mr. Cudemore's business that might cause him to fear the interposition of the police, and yet at the same time they were just the sort of transactions that men desired secrecy about. Men driven to borrow money don't, as a rule, wish the fact advertised ; there is a touch of the Spartan boy with the fox beneath his cloak about the process, they prefer to bleed inwardly, and that the hemorrhage is severe and exhausting, let those who have painfully gone through the ordeal testify.

Mr. Sturton, upon presenting himself in Spring Gardens, is speedily ushered upstairs. The clerks know him, and are quite aware that he is a visitor by no means to be kept waiting. They have, perhaps, rather hazy ideas of what his actual relations with their master may be, but they know Mr. Cudemore is always at home to Mr. Sturton.

The great sartorial artist salutes his confederate in his usual affected languid manner, correctly copied from one of his most *blasé* customers, who generally orders his coats, &c., by the half-score, and whose superb *nonchalance* is the subject of Mr. Sturton's unbounded admiration.

"Delighted to see you," exclaimed Mr. Cudemore, as he shook hands, and then proceeded to roll an easy-chair to the fire for the accommodation of his guest. "I suppose it is business of some sort to which I am indebted for the pleasure of seeing you?"

"Well, yes, it is. I want to have a talk with you about that money we advanced to James Foxborough. You see, we're so to speak mixed up in this Bunbury murder."

"Good heavens! Don't talk in that way," rejoined Cudemore. "We can't be held responsible for the future career of every man we lend money to. Besides, as I always told you, the security is good enough, and if you don't like it I can manage to take up your share of the loan."

"Not at all, that's not it," interposed Mr. Sturton. "I know the Syringa Music Hall is to be found, although Foxborough isn't, and what is more, I don't think he ever will be now. I take it he's got clean out of the country. But I think we ought to let the police know that he is in possession of that big sum of money."

"I object to that altogether," exclaimed Cudemore, vehemently. "No money-lender makes a confidant of the police; besides, what is the use of it? According to your own view the man has fled the country. It won't further the ends of justice or in the least contribute to his apprehension to publish the fact that his pockets are full of money. Besides, ours is a profession," he continued, with a sneer, "that does good by stealth. The advances we make at heavy percentage we don't publish on the housetops; in fact it is a calling we don't usually talk about. As for you, I should have imagined that you had every reason for not letting the world know that you traded on its necessities."

" You are right, Cudemore," rejoined the other, " I don't particularly want the public to know that I do a quiet and tolerably lucrative business here with you. Sending a man the money to pay yourself don't sound a profitable transaction to the uninitiated, but let him only have tolerable prospects, and it's a very tidy game. But, remember this, it doesn't at all follow my name is to appear. The information may be of use to the police, or it may not; at all events, there is no reason for making the thing public."

" And don't you think the police will want to know why you didn't come forward with your information before ? " retorted Cudemore, spitefully. " They well may, as it is past my comprehension. If you are bent upon advertising your-self as a money-lender, and in connection with the Bunbury murder, it seems singular that you should have put it off for so long."

" I tell you there's no necessity whatever for the appear-ance of our names," replied Mr. Sturton, quietly. " Anyway, I have made up my mind to give that much information to the police, and it is for them to make use of it if they can."

" I tell you, again, that I strongly object to your doing so," exclaimed Cudemore, vehemently. " Look here, if this is a matter of money, I'll, as I said before, find your share of the loan in a few days. It will be then altogether my affair, and you will be absolved from all conscientious scruples."

" I tell you that it is nothing of that sort, once more. I am not in the least uneasy about my money, but I consider the police ought to be informed of Foxborough having this sum in his possession, and I intend they shall."

" And once more I protest against your doing anything of the sort. You've no right to compromise me," said Mr Cudemore, irritably.

" All right, I won't; I'll make it appear that I found the money in conjunction with others, and who the others are need not transpire. I can't for the life of me see what you are raising such a pother about."

"I tell you I don't want the police interfering with my private affairs," rejoined Mr. Cudemore, doggedly.

"I'll argue the thing no longer, but remember I shall do what I have made up my mind to do as soon as I leave these rooms."

Mr. Cudemore shot a most malignant glance at his companion, a glance that augured ill for Mr. Sturton's well-being, should it ever depend on the money-lender's good wishes, but he made no further reply. He knew from experience that Sturton was placidly immovable when he had once determined on anything. He would discuss it in his usual languid fashion as long as you liked, but invariably remained of precisely the same opinion. He was a man of much quiet tenacity of purpose, and, a thing Cudemore had yet to learn, opposition only strengthened him in his determination whatever it might be.

"So young Morant paid up. I never expected that of him. I thought he was certain to renew."

"No, the young gentleman has fallen in love and turned over a fresh leaf; he's paid off his tradesmen and done with all transactions involving stamped paper. The fool thinks that having spent the best part of what money he had, the remainder will go further if there are two people to keep instead of one."

"Why, who does he want to marry?" asked Sturton.

"Miss Foxborough."

"But that is a marriage I think will probably not come off, as I understand," said Mr. Sturton, carelessly, "you are interested in preventing it. Well," he continued, rising, "I wish you every success, and, in the meantime, good-bye."

"And are you going across to Scotland Yard?"

"Undoubtedly, but don't disturb yourself, your name will not appear," and so saying Mr. Sturton took his departure.

True to his word, the Bond-street maestro made his way across to the police head-quarters, and briefly explained his errand. He was requested to sit down and wait a few minutes while they sent for the officer in charge of the case. Sergeant Usher was speedily on the spot, and no little pleased at the idea of receiving any fresh information bearing upon the Bunbury mystery. He was perhaps the one officer who was still confident of unravelling the tangle. Utterly non-plussed just at present he would admit, but he stuck to it he had a clue whenever he had learnt how to use it. He felt he had got the signal-book, but had yet to learn how to read the flags.

He listened attentively to Mr. Sturton's statement, merely remarking that it was singular that Mr. Foxborough should borrow so large a sum without having some definite object in view. Did Mr. Sturton know at all for what purpose it was required? No. Curious, six thousand pounds is a good deal of money to raise to carry about as pocket-money. He was very much obliged to Mr. Sturton for the information, which might very possibly turn out of great value. Mr. Sturton's name in the papers? Certainly not. This fact would rest between them; indeed, far from wishing to publish it he, Sergeant Usher, would have asked Mr. Sturton as a particular favour not to mention it to any one, and so the sergeant politely bowed his visitor out, and went home to ruminate on this last bit of information.

CHAPTER XXII.

ERGEANT USHER did not commit himself much before Mr. Sturton, but when he got back to his own fireside he sat down and smoked a perfect succession of meditative pipes over this new feature in the case. What on earth had Foxborough wanted so large a sum of money as that for ? Was it that having raised all the money he could command he then went in to wreak his vengeance on the man with whom he had an implacable feud, and, his victim done to death, made his way precipitately to the nearest sea-port, and from thence to foreign parts ? No, Mr. Usher was not inclined to accept that solution of the case, and another thing that puzzled the sergeant not a little was the curious fact that, except at the Syringa, Mr. Foxborough seemed unknown in theatrical circles, and the sergeant had been very diligent in his inquiries on that point. Mr. Usher was puzzled as to what direction he should now make research in. At last it flashed across him that some further evidence as to Foxborough's personality was to be come by in Baum-borough ; there must be somebody else besides Mr. Totterdell who had noticed the stranger at the theatre. In country places, where every one is well known by sight, a stranger would invariably attract attention. He had been unlucky before in not getting hold of the right people. Moreover, the

16

sergeant reflected that he had not as yet, to use his own
expression, "turned Mr. Totterdell inside out," and he had
a hazy idea that there was something to be got out of that
garrulous old gentleman, if one could but get at it. That
Mr. Totterdell would maunder away a whole afternoon before
blurting out the one fact worth knowing which he had to tell,
the sergeant thought was likely, but he had experienced that
sort of witness before, and knew that there was nothing for
it but patience and—yes, he had one other receipt which he
had found efficacious in similar cases—namely, to affect
incredulity. It was apt to make a weariful witness protest
so much, that you did at last get at the one grain of evidence
he had to give worth noting.

There was another important fact in the case now, according
to Sergeant Usher's judgment ; he had come to the conclusion
that Foxborough had a confederate, and it was possible
that it was the confederate, and not Foxborough, who had
sat next Mr. Totterdell at the theatre. At all events,
Foxborough had got somebody to write that note, and it was
singular that the reward offered for the murderer's apprehension had not induced this person to come forward. The
handwriting was unmistakably a man's, and yet people conversant with James Foxborough's handwriting were quite
positive it was not his. The sergeant with those ideas once
more ran down to Baumborough and commenced his inquiries.
He talked as before with everybody he came across in easy
and affable fashion, invariably turning the conversation before
long on the great Bunbury mystery, but indefatigably as he
gossiped for two days he failed to pick up one particle of
information that might be turned to account. He had, it is
true, got hold of one or two people who had positively noticed
the stranger, not vaguely thinking that they saw him, but
describing him definitely as a dark gentleman, of medium
height, attired in evening costume. Still, this amounted to
nothing. Foxborough was a dark-complexioned man by all
accounts, and therefore there was no reason to dispute the

original theory that he was the man who had been present at the theatre.

On the third day the sergeant proceeded to call upon Mr. Totterdell, and prepared himself for a tolerably long conversation. That gentleman, upon receiving his card, was only too delighted to admit him. Mr. Totterdell, in good truth, had been very much depressed about the turn things had taken lately. He had pressed for an inquiry into the financial affairs of the town, and this had turned out perfectly groundless. The Town Clerk was rumoured to have left but little behind him, still his books were all in regular order, and there was no warrant for supposing that, whatever he might have done with his own, he had ever made ducks and drakes of the public money. It is customary to speak tenderly of the dead, and when a man makes so tragic an end of it as John Fossdyke, pity makes folks recall his good qualities only. Baumborough forgot the Town Clerk's aggressive and domineering manner, and remembered only the many improvements that he had promoted in their midst. Baumborough further called to mind that it was Mr. Totterdell, who in spiteful fashion had moved for an inquiry into its financial condition, and that his object in so doing had been principally to annoy John Fossdyke, who had very properly turned him out of his house as a meddlesome mischief-maker. Mr. Totterdell had succeeded in making himself, by dint of his insatiable curiosity and strong propensity to babble, exceedingly unpopular, and this last move had placed him in very bad odour with his fellow-citizens. It was true he would gladly have withdrawn his motion, but some of John Fossdyke's enemies—and he was much too self-assertive a man not to have made several—took good care the matter should not be allowed to drop. His untimely death it had been of course impossible to foresee, and the motion made in Mr. Totterdell's name bore, if loosely looked at, the aspect of a malignant attempt to blacken a dead man's fame. People declined to hear Mr. Totterdell's explanation, and that

he had moved for the inquiry out of mere malice and consequent on his quarrel with the luckless Town Clerk he was
unable to deny. Mr. Tottordell had an idea that if he could
appear as a prominent witness against Foxborough, and contribute not a little to his conviction, that Baumborough would
condone his offending and take him once more into favour.
That his present unpopularity was due to his inquisitive and
meddlesome disposition, and not to the unfortunate circumstance of his having moved for that inquiry, never occurred
to him. We are seldom conscious of our besetting sins, and,
as a rule, men never plead guilty to tattling and curiosity;
rather despising those vices, we are little likely to acknowledge to a weakness concerning them.

" Ah ! Mr. Usher,"exclaimed Mr. Totterdell, as the sergeant
quietly entered his drawing-room, " delighted to see you;
knew you'd have to come to me again. That old fool of a
coroner, you of course saw, deliberately suppressed my
evidence. I hope it was only ignorance ; but how are the
perpetrators of crimes like this to be arrived at if the chief
evidence about them is to be deliberately sat upon ? You
were there, Mr. Usher, and saw the coroner, abetted by Mr.
Trail, deliberately squash my evidence. I had no opportunity of stating one-half of what I know.

"That's just where it is, sir. I said if they'd only let Mr.
Totterdell tell his story in his own way we should get at the
rights of things, but it's just like these muddle-headed country
officials, they are so anxious to display their little bit of authority that they can't help interfering just to show they have
the right to."

" Quite so, Mr. Usher, and if I had told my story things
might bear a different aspect now. Foxborough might be in
custody perhaps."

" Well, I don't mind telling you in confidence. I'm always
straight and above-board with the people in the case, but it
is to go no further, mind : that it's getting just a question
whether he ever will be in custody. He is either about the

deepest card ever I came across, or rather can't come across, or else what they're saying about Baumborough is true."

"Saying about Baumborough," interposed Mr. Totterdell, greedily. "What are they saying in the town ; nothing about me, eh ? "

"Well, that's just where it is, sir; they're a gossiping, good-for-nothing set, and they seem to be mighty spiteful against you."

"Too true, sergeant, too true, they are ; and all because I endeavour to do my duty ; but what is it they say ? "

"They declare you never saw Mr. Foxborough at all, that you either dreamt it or saw some traveller passing through who happened to drop a Syringa bill, and you imagined the rest."

"Ah, they say that," cried Totterdell, his face flushed with anger. "Wait till the trial comes off, and see what they have to say then."

"Getting open to question, as I said before, whether there will be a trial. It don't require much gumption," continued the sergeant, "to understand that you can't have a trial without somebody to try."

"Nonsense," stammered Mr. Totterdell : "you don't mean to say there is no chance of the scoundrel's apprehension."

"Well, I am coming to the opinion of Baumborough that you didn't see Foxborough. Your opinion that you did is only based on that music-hall bill, you know, and that amounts to nothing."

"But," exclaimed Mr. Totterdell, vehemently, "I am not the only person who recognized him, or rather who spoke to him."

The sergeant pricked up his ears, but all he said was, "Well, I can't find any one else that had any talk with him in all Baumborough."

"Perhaps not," retorted Mr. Totterdell, triumphantly, "but all the world doesn't reside in Baumborough. Foxborough went behind the scenes ; I saw him there myself, and they all seemed to know him."

" Oh," said the sergeant, convinced now that he had about turned Mr. Totterdell out, " he went behind the scenes, did he? Would you, sir, as a particular favour, try to recollect who ' all' may mean. Who individually did he speak to ? " Now here Mr. Totterdell broke down in ignominious fashion. He at first said every one—then, well, not exactly every one ; and finally, dexterously manipulated by Sergeant Usher, he was brought to confess that he had only seen the presumed Foxborough speak to the lady who had played Mary Netley in " Ours," he had forgotten her name.

But this was a fact tangible and important in the sergeant's eyes. It would be simple enough to find out who the lady was, and also where she was now engaged. A professional lady is generally easy to discover. But the sergeant was once more a little staggered ; this fact was all in favour of its being Foxborough himself, and if so the accomplice had confined himself to writing the note, and had nothing more to do with the matter. Foxborough would of course be likely to know theatrical people, although the sergeant had not been able to make out so far that he was known amongst them.

" Well, Mr. Totterdell," observed the sergeant, who was by this time most thoroughly conversant with the old gentleman's anxiety to appear as a witness, " this may turn out rather important for you; if we can only manage to find this young lady, you see, she will corroborate your evidence, and then the chain will be getting complete."

" Didn't I say so before? If the coroner had only allowed me to tell my story at Bunbury you'd have found this young lady before now."

" If you had only produced the most important fact in your wallet at the inquest, Mr. Totterdell, we might probably have arrested the murderer before this," replied the sergeant, curtly.

" You don't mean you can't find this young lady? The manager of the theatre, I dare say, can give you her name."

" Oh I'll have her name, and find her in four-and-twenty hours, but it is not likely to lead to finding Foxborough now."

" You surely don't mean that he has fled the country?" asked Mr. Totterdell, anxiously.

" All I mean, sir, is that if people would afford the police all the information in their power instead of half of it, it would be more conducive to the ends of justice."

And leaving Mr. Totterdell to digest this observation the sergeant bowed himself out.

To ascertain that the leading lady at the opening of the Baumborough Theatre had been a Miss Lightcomb required, of course, only two minutes' conversation with the manager of that establishment, and a reference to the *Era* quickly revealed the fact that she was at present fulfilling an engagement at the Margate Theatre, and thither Sergeant Usher betook himself without loss of time.

Pretty Miss Lightcomb was not a little surprised at an abrupt visit from a stranger, and a little perturbed when her visitor announced his professional position. Dexterously questioned by Sergeant Usher she said that of course she had read all about the Bunbury murder, but what could she know about it? She had never even been in Bunbury, nor had she to her knowledge ever seen Mr. Fossdyke. Of course she was aware that he had been present at the opening of the theatre, but she did not know him by sight, nor could one always distinguish people in front even if you did. Had she spoken to James Foxborough behind the scenes that night? Most certainly not. She had never even seen Mr. Foxborough in her life. Could hardly say she ever knew him by name before this terrible murder brought his name so prominently before the public. Could scarcely say who she had seen that night, there were a good many gentlemen came round, pretty well all strangers to her; many of them said something complimentary about her acting of Mary Netley; there was champagne and other refreshments going on in the manager's room, and most of the gentlemen were on their way there.

No! she had been on the stage the last seven years, and she had never heard of Mr. Foxborough in connection with the country business. All her engagements had been in the country; she had never succeeded in getting on the London boards.

"Then, Miss Lightcomb," said the sergeant, at last, "it is fair to presume that you have a pretty considerable acquaintance with country managers?"

"Certainly I know personally a great many of them. I have fulfilled engagements all over England, besides taking a turn in Edinburgh and Glasgow, but I never heard of any company conducted by Mr. Foxborough. It is possible he had a stage name, you know; it is a common enough custom in our profession."

"Quite so, but I don't fancy he ever appeared himself; he merely managed a touring company. Ah, well, I need trouble you no further, Miss Lightcomb, at present; it is curious you shouldn't have heard of Mr. Foxborough. Good morning!"

"And it is curious," continued the sergeant to himself when he got outside the modest lodgings in which the actress resided, "I can't find anybody who ever has met Foxborough in his vocation, while, if ever there was a profession in which a man was well before the public, it is the theatrical. That he is lessee of the Syringa is certain, but about his other stage speculations nobody seems to know anything. It is a very interesting case, and Foxborough is about the most shadowy customer ever I was in quest of. He doesn't write his own letters, and doesn't apparently practise his own profession; but he commits one of the coolest, most audacious murders ever known, and disappears. I wonder whether that talkative old fool Totterdell is addicted to drink or opium. He must have seen some one though who did drop that music-hall bill and whom he fancied he saw behind the scenes afterwards. If he had only let one know that he had seen the man in the stalls speaking to Miss Lightcomb at the time, it is probable that the girl might have called to mind who did speak to her; still, as she said most of them were strangers to her, perhaps the very man I want might have been one of those."

Once more Sergeant Usher found himself driven back to his old conclusion, that it was " a rum 'un." However, there was nothing more to be done in Margate, and Miss Lightcomb had apparently nothing to tell, and yet the sergeant was impressed with the idea that, just like Mr. Totterdell, she would give a valuable bit of information could he but get it out of her. He did not think for one moment she was wilfully keeping back anything, but simply that for the want of the key-note he had been unable to arrive at what he wanted. All the questions he could think of that bore upon the matter he had put, and the actress had answered them frankly and freely; but Mr. Usher was aware that in the detection of crime you may walk round and round a thing and not see it; examine people who could and are quite willing to tell you what you want to know, and yet not arrive at that fact. Some trifling matter that appears to have nothing to do with the case is just the one missing link in a chain of circumstantial evidence that the police are in search of, and the possessor of that knowledge has no conception of its importance.

Sergeant Usher determined to go back to Baumborough. Nothing had come of his last discovery there, but it was possible diligent investigation might lead to something yet, and no chess player was ever more absorbed in an intricate problem than Sergeant Usher in the elucidation of the Bunbury mystery. Should anything suggest that crucial question to which he believed Miss Lightcomb possessed the answer, she was always to be found without difficulty.

Nothing in these high-pressure days attains the dignity of more than a nine days' wonder, and it could not be supposed that Baumborough could sustain its interest about John Fossdyke's untimely end any longer. His assassin had

apparently beat the police, and the tragedy seemed destined
to be one of those semi-revealed crimes of which we have
only too many. But there were some few people in the town
who still had strong interest in the solution of the riddle.
Mr. Totterdell, for reasons already stated, deemed that it
would put him straight with divers of his fellow-citizens, who
now unmistakably gave him the cold shoulder, could the
criminal but be apprehended. Philip Soames had a strong
idea that if ever the story of the Bunbury mystery should be
unfolded he should arrive at Bessie's secret, and Dr. Ingleby
held a similar view. Soames had called often at Dyke of
late and always been received with the greatest cordiality by
Mrs. Fossdyke. The widow had returned from her excursion
to the seaside, and Dr. Ingleby had made known to her the
alteration in her circumstances. Curiously enough she was
by no means distressed at the idea of leaving Dyke. On the
contrary, she said she should never like the place again, and
remarked that she should have left it under any circumstances.
She talked matters over freely with the young man, and told
him she should take a small house in Baumborough. Even
had her means permitted it, what did she want with a place
like Dyke? She should live a good deal in retirement henceforth; glad to see her old friends, of course, but after such a
blow as had befallen her it was not likely a woman would
ever mix much with the world again. As for Miss Hyde, she
always welcomed Philip with a sweet smile and frank clasp of
the hand, but she never suffered herself to be alone with him.
She had decidedly refused to accompany him either for a
turn round the garden or as far as the gate upon the one or
two occasions that he had begged that favour of her, giving
him to understand distinctly that all was over between them,
and Philip began to get despondent about ever carrying his
point. There is no winning a girl's confidence if you can
never secure a *tête-à-tête* with her. Folk don't, as a rule, un-
bosom themselves in public, albeit that insufferable bore who
always will inflict his domestic economy, from the price of

his wife's last dress to what he pays for his washing, is ever manifest in the land. Still these are hardly to be called confidences ; distasteful revelations is I fancy what many of the victims would describe them. Philip Soames determined at last to have a quiet talk over his love affair with Dr. Ingleby. He cannot help thinking the doctor can force Bessie's hand if he will but try, and Philip is fain to confess he can make nothing of it himself, hard as he has striven. Were Foxborough only arrested he thinks the trial might throw some side-light that would reveal to him the cause of Bessie's scruples ; for that they were mere scruples Philip was convinced. Full of this design he took his road to the doctor's one morning and made his way into the study.

"Well, Philip, what brings you here so early ? Glad to see you at any time, as you know, but you don't often honour me so soon as this."

" Well, I have come to ask your help as an old friend. I told you how I stand with Miss Hyde, and I'm in real earnest about marrying that girl ; but I'm at a dead lock. If she simply said me nay, well, I should be bound to take my answer with the best grace I could muster ; but she owns she loves me, yet declares there are insurmountable obstacles to our marrying. Now if I could arrive at the obstacles I should probably not think much of them, but I can't. I want you to try if you cannot extort a confession."

" This is rather an awkward task you seek to impose upon me, Phil. Miss Hyde has always been a special favourite of mine, and I flatter myself I stand pretty high in her good graces, but I don't know how she would take such interference on my part. She's a girl that, mark me, can hold her own, and knows how to check what she may deem an unjustifiable liberty."

" I acknowledge all you say, my dear doctor, and I wouldn't urge you to do this save for two things. Bessie has owned she loved me, and I am sure she is acting, though most conscientiously, ' for my sake,' to use her own words, yet under a misconception. I know, my dear old friend, I am to some extent exposing you to a rebuff; but you know Bessie, and must feel assured that if she will not make confession to you her refusal will be courteously couched."

"I know all that, Phil, still I have a strong dislike to seeking a confidence. If people bring you their troubles, well, one must do the best one can for them, but when they prefer to suffer in silence it seems gratuitous impertinence to endeavour to discover what they so obviously wish to conceal."

"I admit all that, but I am asking you to run some mischance of that nature for my sake," cried Phil. "My life's happiness is at stake, and though it may appear presumption to say so, I think perhaps Bessie's also. I am bound to leave no stone unturned, nor any friend who I think may aid me unsolicited for help under such circumstances. I think you can aid me, and I know you will when you have thought it over."

"I fancy I shall be so rash," replied the doctor. "Give me a minute to think about it."

"You shall have ten, if you like," replied Phil, smiling, "because I know you mean saying yes at the end of them."

The doctor thought it over and then said—

"I'll do my best for you. I'll see Miss Hyde, and if I can induce her to tell me her story——"

"Gentleman to see you, sir," exclaimed the voice of the doctor's servant, and as the man spoke Dr. Ingleby became aware of the presence of Sergeant Usher.

"Beg pardon, sir, but your young man gave me to understand you were disengaged, or else I wouldn't have intruded. Can't say I regret it, as I just arrived in time to hear you say you would try to make Miss Hyde tell you her story. That's just where it is, if we could only induce people to speak out at once what a lot of things would be put straight, and what an amount of miscarriage of justice would be prevented. I don't say it's wilful perversity, because it ain't; it's human infirmity, that's what it is; it's people's utter incapacity to tell all they know about anything. Here's Mr. Totterdell, for instance, tells me the day before yesterday a little circumstance that if I'd known two months ago would have been worth any money in the case. Well, off I go to see the party alluded to, and of course they've forgot the very thing they were wanted to remember. It's aggravating, very; it's as if we were engaged in a regular game of hunt the slipper with the British public, only the British public are not hiding the slipper intentionally."

Philip Soames had stared with amazement and no slight indignation at this little grey, voluble man, as he delivered the above tirade, and Dr. Ingleby saw that explanation was imperative.

" My dear Phil," he exclaimed, " allow me to make you known to Sergeant Usher of the Criminal Investigation Department, Scotland Yard. As for making you known to him, that I fancy is superfluous. I have little doubt there are few of the leading townspeople here with whom the sergeant is unacquainted by this."

The sergeant made a respectful bow and admitted he had the pleasure of knowing Mr. Soames by sight.

But the young man was by no means mollified.

"I don't understand the unnecessary dragging of Miss Hyde's name into the case," he exclaimed, haughtily. " You must be aware she can know nothing about it. You catch a fragment of the conversation between Dr. Ingleby and myself, and immediately jump to the conclusion that the story I allude to has something to do with the death of John Fossdyke."

" Excuse me, sir," replied the sergeant, quietly ; " the little I overheard was the result of the purest accident, but Dr. Ingleby will tell you I have been of opinion almost from the first that Miss Hyde has some previous knowledge of James Foxborough, and that if she could be persuaded to tell that to, say, Dr. Ingleby, it might prove of considerable value in getting at the rights of the Bunbury murder."

"It is true, Phil," observed the doctor, "the sergeant is so far right that Miss Hyde has admitted to some knowledge of Foxborough, although she declares she never saw him, and that the little she knows about him could throw no light whatever on this affair."

"Now, look here, Mr. Soames, you cannot think that I want to annoy or occasion pain to any young lady," interposed the sergeant, "but I know from experience it is just the merest trifle that constantly affords us the clue we seek. I don't say Miss Hyde is in possession of it; she no doubt honestly believes the little she knows is of no consequence, but I do wish she would let me be judge of that. If she could be induced to confide it to Dr. Ingleby, and the doctor then submitted it to me, Miss Hyde would be saved pretty well all unpleasantness; and forgive me, sir, but in the interests of justice I am compelled to gather every scrap of information I can about one of the most mysterious murders it was ever my lot to investigate."

Philip Soames was still indignant at the idea of the lady of his love being mixed up in the affair in any way, but then he reflected she must be slightly so under any circumstances, and then it occurred to him that what the sergeant had first said was very probably true, and that Miss Hyde's story would quite likely include the account of the slight knowledge of Foxborough. He had just been urging his old friend to obtain this confession in his own behalf, and there would be glaring inconsistency in opposing his doing so now just because a detective officer thought a clue to the Bunbury mystery might turn up in the narration; moreover his own love chase depended on the result, and he did not think that Bessie need fear to confide in so trusty a friend as Dr. Ingleby. Love is essentially a selfish passion, say the philosophers, more especially a young man's love, and finally Philip gave his assent once more to his own scheme.

"You rely on me, Mr. Soames. Don't you be afraid of my not considering Miss Hyde's feelings. The chances are there won't be the slightest necessity for ever making public the young lady's information, but it will quite likely just throw a glimmer of light upon what I don't mind telling you, gentlemen, is about as dark a business so far as ever I went into. By the way, doctor, I suppose you never made anything out about that letter?"

"No; I should think there is little doubt it was destroyed. By the way, I saw in the papers some letters had been discovered at the Hopbine."

"Bless you, sir, the papers will say anything in cases of this kind," replied the candid sergeant. "Good-night, gentlemen!"

CHAPTER XXIII.

BESSIE'S CONFESSION.

DR. INGLEBY, the next morning, half repented him of this promise he had made. He was exceedingly fond of Bessie Hyde, and he recollected the girl's distress the last time he had spoken to her about her knowledge of Foxborough. True, this was somewhat different, he was only going to ask her this time to trust in him and let him be judge whether there was reason the happiness of two lives should be wrecked. If she really loved Philip, and he was not the man to say she had made that admission without due and sufficient grounds for so saying, surely she would be anxious to clutch at a chance of clearing away the obstacles to her marriage. "At all events," thought the Doctor, "if I am somewhat overstepping the privileges of an old friend, it is on behalf of two young people whom I sincerely desire to benefit. It may not be quite a pleasant business, I am afraid it won't, it seemed so painful to Bessie before to touch upon, that it would be absurd to suppose it will prove otherwise now; still it's got to be done. I'm not going to have Bessie Hyde and Phil Soames drift apart if I can help it. She's just the wife for him; he's plenty of money, and lots more to come. Oh no! I'm not at all above doing a bit of match-making when I think it desirable, and I'll have the bells ringing at Baumborough about those two, or know the reason why."

No matter this to be put off, and the doctor determined to go over to Dyke, and have the thing out at once. Unlike Philip, he knew he should have no difficulty about a *tête-à-tête* with Miss Hyde. Bessie undoubtedly regarded the doctor as a trusted friend, and he was of that age she might look upon him as not likely to misinterpret her confidences. He called next day upon the two ladies, as was his custom, about tea-time, and after much desultory conversation as was usual, and having quietly informed Mrs. Fossdyke that nothing fresh had transpired concerning her husband's melancholy end, said, as he made his adieux, " Miss Hyde, walk to the gate with me, please. I have something to say to you."

" You wouldn't deceive me, doctor ? " cried the widow. "Surely there can be no more terrible news coming to me ? "

" Not in the least, my dear madam. What I have to say to Miss Hyde concerns herself alone, and is a thing she need feel little misgiving about listening to. Will you come, Miss Bessie ? "

" Yes, of course ; my hat is in the hall. I feel half frightened, doctor," she continued as they passed the hall door. "I don't know what you have to tell me, but I can never forget the night when Phil—Mr. Soames sent for me into the study and told his terrible tale."

" I have nothing terrible to tell you, nor you me, but, Bessie, I want you to comprehend that I consider I stand to you in the light of him who has gone. You know how intimate I have been at Dyke, and it has always appeared to me that poor Fossdyke looked upon you more in the light of a ward than his wife's companion. I was, as you know, one of his most intimate friends, and am now his executor. I want you, Bessie, to regard me in the same light, and give me your confidence."

The girl's face looked a little troubled for a minute or so, and then she replied, gravely, " It is only too good of you to take an interest in me. As for confidences—" and here she indulged in a little nervous laugh,—" what should I have to

17

confide further than it was I upset the cream and not the cat."

" To begin upon," said Dr. Ingleby, " Philip Soames has acquainted me with all that has passed between you."

" Then I think Mr. Soames has been guilty of much indiscretion," retorted the girl, as she reared her head proudly. " He might have relied upon my lips being sealed, and though I have nothing to reproach myself with, still I did not anticipate our affairs becoming common discourse."

"Bessie, Bessie," replied Dr. Ingleby, gently, "please don't meet me in that spirit. It was in no braggadocio vein, believe me, that Phil told me the story of his wooing. It was the wail of a rejected lover—rejected forsooth, as he honestly avers and believes, for some shadowy reason that could he but come by it might be swept away in an instant."

" Mr. Soames did me an honour which for reasons good and sufficient I felt compelled to decline. He has told you that he asked me to be his wife and, further, that for his own sake I was obliged to refuse his request. I think Mr. Soames is not treating me generously. I told him frankly that I could marry no man to whom I had not first told my story, and that I had not courage to do that ; if I had loved him less it would have been easier, but I could not bear the dismay on his face when he learnt who I really was, or to have him stand by his offer from a pure sense of honour. I could not bear," she continued, passionately, "to embroil him with his own family, or that people should whisper and point to Philip Soames's wife as a woman with a shameful story attached to her. No ! Dr. Ingleby, you are very good, but I love Philip too dearly to be a millstone round his neck, or to have him at war with society for my sake. If poor Mr. Fossdyke had lived the decision would have rested with him. He knew all about me, and I told him what had passed between me and Philip, but his advice is lost to me, and I believe I am acting for the best, doing what is right, in adhering to my original decision."

Bessie ceased speaking, but it was evident she was deeply moved, the long dark lashes of her eyes were wet, and the girl's whole frame trembled slightly with emotion. Dr. Ingleby was not a little nonplussed. There could be no doubt that Bessie honestly loved Soames, and that it was entirely for his own sake she refused him. She certainly was a better judge than either he or Philip could pretend to be of the circumstances ; was it fair to wring this girl's story from her only to endorse her own view and acknowledge that the obstacles she deemed unsurmountable really were so ? Then, again, was it not better for Philip that things should remain as they were, and he be free from what might probably turn out an unfortunate marriage, so far as connection went ? Society in country places is even more intolerant than in big cities ; in London, for instance, who you are is not so much consequence now-a-days as what you've got per annum, and can you keep clear of the law your iniquities are not counted against you, provided your cook and your wines are unimpeachable ; but none knew better than Dr. Ingleby that if the ladies of Baumborough once decided the antecedents of a new-comer, made her admission within society's pale inadmissible, it would be a gigantic task to break through the taboo.

"Give me a few minutes to think, Bessie," he said at length. "I want to give the best advice I can, to think what is best for both you and Philip."

And as they strolled slowly on it occurred to the doctor that Philip was in very genuine earnest about winning the girl for his wife, and was not likely to rest passive with things as they were ; that whether he interfered or not the chances were that the young man sooner or later would come at the truth and take his own way then without much reference to the opinion of friends or relations. It would be better, he thought, if he could induce Bessie to yield him her confidence ; he should be judge of the case now while he had yet opportunity to tender advice to both the young people.

" Bessie, you admit the decision of this affair would have rested with poor Fossdyke had he lived. Do you not think it would be best to look upon me as standing in his place? True, in one case, unfortunately, you have a painful story to tell which would have been spared you in the other; but you know I am sincerely attached to Philip. I have known him from a child, and know his character thoroughly—a man very resolute, and difficult to turn from a thing when his mind is once made up, and he is terribly in earnest about marrying you. It will be no light thing that will stop him, and, Bessie, remember by your own confession he has friends in the garrison should he press the place hard."

The girl smiled, as she said softly,

" Too true; I've never denied it, but I'll be staunch to Philip's real welfare, never fear."

" Can you not trust an old friend of his, a man like myself, who knows the world well, and who would be a much clearer and more dispassionate judge than himself, and who would not abet him in doing a foolish thing, to be judge of the case? It may be I shall pronounce your scruples ground-less; it may be I shall say, ' Bessie Hyde, if you have any real love for Philip, run away from the place, and don't bring social ruin on the man for whom you profess affection.' "

The colour came and went in the girl's face, as she listened to the doctor's speech. He had struck the right key; he ignored her and affected to be only anxious about Philip's welfare. That was what she wanted. Would any one decide between them, thinking only of him? If her marriage was pronounced possible she should only be too happy and thankful, but if for Philip's sake it were best she should go, she would depart without a murmur.

" Dr. Ingleby," she said at length, " if you will promise to do that, to think only of Philip and never of me, I can perhaps muster up courage to tell you my story; but, mind, I am never to be cause of reproach to him. Tell me honestly if I am right in my view, and, friends in the garrison notwithstanding, I'll take good care he never has chance to carry the place."

" My dear Bessie, I want to do what I deem best for two young people, of whom I am very fond, but my first consideration here, I think, ought to be Phil."

" Yes," she faltered, " you must not mind me. Remember, please, to be the woman whose sad story was hung round his neck, and socially drowned him, would be infinitely more painful than giving him up altogether. You must not forget, will you ? "

" No," replied the doctor, mechanically, " I will not forget," and as the words passed his lips, he thought to himself, " I have no right either to forget your negation of self or honest love for the man who loves you."

" Doctor," Bessie continued, after a slight pause, " you must know that I am nameless ; that I have no father ; that I am nobody's child. You understand," said the girl, in a low tone, as the blood rose to the roots of her hair, and her voice dropped almost to a whisper.

" You have no father you ever knew, I presume ? " observed Dr. Ingleby, inquiringly.

" I have no father at all, I tell you," rejoined the girl, sharply. " I am a love child. I have been brought up by my aunt, and impressed all my life with the disgrace of my birth. I have only seen my mother now and again. She has always been upon those occasions kind, tender, and anxious to provide me with everything I might want, but my stern aunt used to interfere with her austere ways and language, and remind her sister that when she took charge of me it was upon the express stipulation that she had control of me for good, and that I was not to have my head turned with the frivolities and fripperies of my mother's position. It was long enough before I understood what my mother's position was : she had run away from a serious family at Clapham with a theatrical gentleman, and had naturally taken to the same profession. I was the unfortunate result

of this union, if union it can be called, as I am afraid, Dr.
Ingleby," continued the girl, blushing rosy red, " my mother
never was married."

" There is no very serious obstacle in all this, Bessie ;
unless you have something much worse to tell I shall give
you away yet, my dear."

The girl shot him a grateful glance before continuing her
narrative, and then resumed—

" When my cousins grew up they were no longer to be
repressed, they wanted more life and gaiety, and speedily
overruled their mother, which, of course, included their
father, and got it. Dances, parties, and even an occasional
theatre became the order of the day. My uncle undoubtedly
disapproved of it, but as for my aunt, she thought the new
régime possessed great opportunities of settling her daughters,
and so acquiesced in it. Then came my offending. I unluckily proved more attractive than my cousins, and no
sooner did this become transparent than my home was
made unbearable to me. I was for ever twitted with my
birth, or rather want of it ; and at last confided my troubles
to Mr. Fossdyke, who was an old friend of my mother, and
who often came to see me. He not only offered me this
place of companion to his wife, but counselled my taking it,
saying, " Remember, Bessie, you are not dependent upon
these people ; you have to earn your own living, no doubt,
but while she lives there is always an allowance from your
mother to look to ; this, of course, goes to your aunt at
present, but will be paid down to yourself if you come to
us. I shall allow you fifty pounds a year, which in addition
to your mother's hundred ought to make you a well-to-do
young woman, considering you will live at Dyke for nothing.
And so it all proved."

Still, Bessie, you surely must know there is nothing very
dreadful in all this. Illegitimacy is no such terrible stigma
in these times ; if there are people who would carp at it, there
are plenty of others who would laugh at the idea of its being

any ban to marriage or social advancement of any sort in these days."

"But my mother is an actress," said Bessie, in low tones.

"That may sound very terrible to your fantastical aunt and uncle, but to people who live in the world that is nothing now-a-days. Indeed, from the time of the Stuarts down to that of Her present Gracious Majesty, royalty and nobility have always had a great admiration for the ladies of the theatrical profession. Who is she? I mean what is her stage name?"

"Miss Nydia Willoughby," rejoined Bessie, with eyes rivetted on the ground.

"Miss Nydia Willoughby; let me see, dear me, I know the name. Where did I hear it? I don't think I ever saw her."

"That is her stage name, and I believe she sings at the Syringa Music Hall."

"Good heavens, the Syringa! why that is the place of which this James Foxborough is the proprietor."

"Yes, and my mother is Mrs. James Foxborough," faltered Bessie, in a low tone.

To say that Dr. Ingleby was astounded at this last revelation really did not describe that gentleman's state. He was completely stupefied by the announcement, and for a minute or two remained silent. At last he said, "Foxborough is not your father, though?"

"No, I tell you I never knew my father. I never saw my mother until the year before I came here, except quite as a child, and saw as I told you but little then of her. Mr. Fossdyke, who was her man of business, and an old friend, called upon me about twice a year as a child, and perhaps a little oftener as I grew up; and now, Dr. Ingleby, you know my history. With the stain I bear upon my name, how could I marry Philip? and the last awful tragedy has made matters still worse; I am the step-daughter of the murderer of one of his most intimate friends, though I never even saw the miserable man."

"My dear Bessie," said the doctor, after a slight pause, "I tell you fairly, I am so bewildered by what you have told me that I don't think at present I am quite a clear judge of the circumstances. In all your story it is not quite evident to me there is any impediment to your marrying Philip. You acted like an honest girl when you said you could not consent to do so until he knew your history; that you should shrink from telling it was only natural. Still Philip alone can decide upon this matter. There is nothing in reality against yourself, and if you follow my advice you will keep your own counsel. It is not necessary that, with the exception of Philip, any one in Baumborough should know more about you than they do at present. If you give permission, I shall make him acquainted with your story; but otherwise, of course, my lips are sealed."

"Yes, Dr. Ingleby, I should wish Philip to know all I have told you. It will convince him, at all events, that I am no heartless coquette. Give him, give him my love, and say I wish it could have been otherwise; but he will now see the impossibility of my saying other than I have done."

"Good-bye, Bessie," rejoined Dr. Ingleby, as they reached the gate. "You have a staunch friend in me, whatever may be your future lot; and remember, my dear, I shall feel proud to give you away yet, and claim the privilege should it come to pass."

Bessie Hyde made no reply in words, but her eyes thanked the doctor with mute eloquence as they shook hands.

CHAPTER XXIV.

THE PHOTOGRAPH.

AS Dr. Ingleby walked back to Baumborough and turned Bessie's story over in his mind he could not but reflect that his own situation was now just a little awkward. Prepossessed as he was in the girl's favour, and believing thoroughly that there was nothing which could be alleged against Miss Hyde herself, still it was impossible to shut one's eyes to the fact that she would hardly be deemed a desirable connection by any respectable family. There was not only that matter of her birth, but the very unfortunate accusation under which her stepfather at present lay. Old Mr. Soames and his wife might fairly resent the encouraging of their son in such a marriage, and the doctor felt very loth to give cause of offence to such old friends. He was bound to tell Philip this story, and had a strong idea that the chivalry of the young man's character would only lead him to cling more closely to his sweetheart in her trouble. Well, it could not be helped ; Philip was a man of thirty, and if he could not decide for himself now, would he ever be fit to do so ? He would get a good wife in Bessie, even if her antecedents should be deemed a little against her, and, moreover, as these had been kept a secret for two years, why should they not continue such ? He could trust himself not to speak. Philip would naturally for Bessie's sake keep silence, whilst as for Sergeant Usher the doctor had early taken stock of that officer's open candid disposition, and rightly deemed that he could be close and dumb as an oyster upon anything of importance ; the confidences he made were for the most part of the most innocent and milk and watery description, and might have pretty well been arrived at by diligent perusal of the journals.

That Philip Soames would call that evening Dr. Ingleby felt assured, and that Sergeant Usher would do likewise he thought was more than probable. He was not deceived ; he had not long finished his solitary dinner, and was sitting over his wine and walnuts, when Phil made his appearance.

" Well, doctor, have you any news for me ? " he asked, anxiously, as he took a chair and responded to the mute invitation contained by the pushed-across decanter, and filled his glass.

" Yes," replied Dr. Ingleby, " I have. Whether good or bad is for your own self to determine. I am prepared to tell you the whole of Miss Hyde's history. I may promise at once there is nothing against herself, but many men might hesitate about marrying her. You, Phil, are old enough to judge for yourself. I intend to tell you her story simply, and to counsel you neither one way nor the other," and then without further preamble Dr. Ingleby narrated Bessie's account of herself.

Phil Soames listened attentively, but interposed never a word, though he could not suppress a start when he heard that Bessie was the illegitimate daughter of James Fox-borough's wife. He waited patiently till the doctor had finished, and then said,

" Thanks no end, my dear old friend, for what you have done for me. We have agreed not to discuss this subject, but that is no reason I should not tell you what I shall do. All this makes no difference in my feelings with regard to Miss Hyde. I only honour her more for the delicacy and regard she has displayed towards myself. I shall marry her, for I don't think when I ask her again, with full knowledge of her story, she will say me nay any longer. I don't mean just at once, you know; she couldn't well do that so soon after John Fossdyke's death, but as soon as the conventionalities allow, and, doctor, I don't think it is necessary my future wife's history should go any further."

"Certainly not; and you may trust me in that respect, but remember we are half pledged to let Sergeant Usher know the result. Still, I consider that a question for your decision, and would only remark that I think you may rely upon his making very discreet use of the information."

"I had rather it went no further than ourselves," rejoined Phil, slowly.

"As you will," replied the doctor; "only remember so far, the sergeant has shown much feeling and thoughtfulness in dealing with the ladies at Dyke. If we refuse to take him into our confidence he may discover, and very likely will, the whole thing for himself, and is then of course in no way bound to show any particular discretion in dealing with the information. If we let him into the secret of Miss Hyde's history, of which remember he is already on the trail, I think he will make no public use of it, except in the last extremity."

At this moment the door opened, and the servant inquired if the doctor would see Mr. Usher, and after that official's wont he followed so close upon the heels of his own announcement as to pretty well preclude the possibility of denial.

"Good evening, gentlemen. I have just called in to tell you I can gather no particle of information that is to be called reliable about Foxborough in this town. No one, you see, really knew him by sight. Now, doctor, have you got anything for me?"

"Sit down, sergeant, and help yourself to a glass of port," and as Mr. Usher complied Dr. Ingleby cast an inquiring glance.

"Quite so, sir; I understand," exclaimed that worthy, whose quick eye little escaped that came beneath it. "Now, gentlemen, I'm not such a fool as to be obtrusive, but I see you've got the information I seek, though you can't quite make up your minds to let me share it. You cannot suppose I would make things unpleasant for Miss Hyde. Although what she has told you may be of great use to me, it strikes me as most improbable that her name will ever appear. Of course I can't say for certain till I know what it is, but I can promise this, Mr. Soames, that nothing but the most extreme necessity will permit me to bring Miss Hyde's name into the case." Phil looked Mr. Usher straight in the face for a moment, but the sergeant's keen grey eyes never faltered, and then turning to the doctor he said, curtly, " Tell him everything."

Dr. Ingleby without further delay narrated Bessie's history, to which the sergeant listened without comment.

"I don't think, gentlemen," he said, as the doctor concluded, " that this is likely to be of any use to me, though it unexpectedly may be. It is very unlikely, indeed, that Miss Hyde will ever be called upon with regard to this case further than possibly to testify that the dagger was not Mr. Fossdyke's property. As to what the doctor has just done me the honour to confide to me, my lips, gentlemen, are sealed. But, Mr. Soames, has one singular coincidence in this affair struck you ?"

" No ; what do you mean ? " cried Phil.

"That you and your friend, Mr. Morant, should be each courting a daughter of Mrs. Foxborough."

"It never occurred to me before, but it is extraordinary," exclaimed Soames; " but how on earth did you know it ?"

" Well, if you'll excuse my making so bold, it's no secret that you are sweet on Miss Hyde in Baumborough. Watching Foxborough's house, as of course we've done very close, showed us that Mr. Morant was Miss Foxborough's lover, and of course at the inquest I saw you knew each other perfectly well, and the rest is very simple, that you were old university chums, and a slight knowledge of your previous lives was not difficult to come by."

"And do you always study people after this fashion?" asked Philip, half angry, half amused.

"Only when they have the distinction of being concerned in what I consider a great case," rejoined the sergeant, gravely rising; "and now, gentlemen, with many thanks for your kindness, I have the honour to wish you good-night."

Soames was not long before he followed the sergeant's example, and also betook himself homewards. Phil lived with his father and mother, but in a low wing or rather leg of the house that had been run out expressly for his accommodation. He had a separate entrance, a sort of half ante-room, half business-room, and a library, study, smoking-room, or what you please to call it, on the ground floor. Above were two excellent bedrooms and a bath-room. Having turned up his lamp Phil lit another cigar and began to reflect on the events of the evening. It was curious—deuced curious—that coincidence, as the sergeant described it. To think that he and Herbert Morant were going to marry sisters, at all events half-sisters; and then it occurred to Phil, why on earth should he not have Herbert down at once, and put in motion those schemes for that young gentleman's redemption which had crossed his brain before the miserable tragedy of John Fossdyke's took place? How little did he think when Morant said at the inquest it was odd that the murdered man should be a friend of Phil Soames, while the daughter of the presumed murderer was the girl himself aspired to marry, that they were in love with half-sisters. Phil was a man of decision. Half a dozen more turns in the room, and some slight more consumption of tobacco, and seating himself at his writing-table, he wrote to Herbert Morant, saying he should now be delighted to see him at once. It would be rather pleasant, he thought, as he directed and stamped his letter, to have a chum with whom to talk matters over a bit, and then he wondered whether it would be unwise to tell

Bessie's story to Morant, who, no doubt, was in perfect ignorance concerning it.   No matter, he wanted to do his old
friend a turn, and had not two old friends in love constant
food for discourse.   They would smoke, talk of their sweethearts and poor Herbert's future till the grey of the morning,
more especially as Phil really did see his way into opening a
career for that careless spendthrift, always providing he was
willing to put his shoulder to the wheel in earnest.

When Herbert got that message he read it with mingled
feelings of exultation and despondency.   He was jubilant at
the idea of really making a start in the world, but he was
low at the idea of having to leave Nid and her mother in
their troubles.   Still it was impossible to doubt what it
behoved him to do ; he could be but of negative use to Mrs.
Foxborough, except that his daily visit brightened her now
somewhat sombre life, and was of course of much consequence
to Nid, he could really do nothing for them.   The Bunbury
mystery was for the present in abeyance, and Mrs. Foxborough's theory that her husband was dead had gradually
obtained considerable hold of Herbert's mind.   He had a
sorrowful good-bye to say at Tapton Cottage ; Nid clung to
him, and declared it was cowardly of him to leave her in her
misery, but Mrs. Foxborough had more strength of character.
She rated her daughter pretty sharply for her selfishness,
thanked Herbert for all he had been to them in their affliction, and bade him " God speed " in search of fortune with a
face half smiles, half tears ; reminding him that Baumborough
was within very easy distance of London, and that she should
have no scruples about sending for him if she had need of
him.   Under which assurance, and with a tearful embrace
from Nid, Herbert bade good-bye, and set forth to see what
sort of career that might be that dear old Phil had to suggest
for him—hazy, very, concerning what this career should be,
but firmly convinced that an alarum clock and early rising
were most important factors in all starts of a commercial
description.

Very glad indeed was Phil Soames to welcome his old university chum ; he had always been very fond of Herbert when they were at college together, having for him that strong liking so often conceived by the man of strong character for his weaker brother, and Herbert Morant was essentially one of that class—a continuous doer of foolish things, but no chronicle of anything mean or blackguardly against him. And so Herbert had continued till the present, with nothing against him but want of vertebra in his character.

The greeting between the pair was genuinely cordial, and Herbert having been duly presented to the old people, and dinner being concluded, they adjourned to Phil's peculiar domain for a cigar and gossip.

"I want to have a real good talk with you, old man," said Herbert, as he took possession of an easy-chair ; "have wanted it indeed for some time. I have been a lazy purpose-less beggar all my life, but I've got something to work for now, and I mean to begin just as soon as ever I can see my way. If Foxborough did kill Fossdyke I believe it was done in hot blood, and any way I am going to stand by his daughter. I told her I loved her before her father had this charge laid at his door, and no one can suppose I'm going to be such a pitiful cur as to abandon her in her trouble."

"No, Herbert, I know you too well to think that of you, and you might know that I was not speaking at random when I asked you to come down here. We have an opening for you in our business, and I consider it worth your con-sideration. It will take you a good six months to master the routine, and by that time we shall know if you will suit us, and you will know whether the work will suit you."

While Philip was speaking, Morant had taken up from the table a small photograph book, and was idly fiddling with the clasps, undoing them and snapping them to again.

"It is awfully good of you to give me such a chance," he exclaimed, as the other paused.

"Yes, it is a chance ; might quite possibly lead to a junior partnership in the firm, but mind, Herbert, it must depend a good deal upon yourself. If we can't make you a business man in that time there is no more to be said. We cannot afford to make you a sleeping partner. You must put your neck to the collar, and pull your fair share of the waggon. If you are ever to participate in the profits you must be a *bonâ fide* working partner."

"I'm going to make no protestations, Phil. I can only say try me, and as for sleep, sir, I've brought down an alarum clock that will effectually attend to all that. With Nid to work for I should be a brute to neglect such a chance."

While he spoke he had opened the photograph book, and was carelessly turning over the pages. Suddenly he exclaimed, "Great heavens, Phil! how did you come by this?"

"What is it? That?" he replied gravely, as Herbert showed him the photograph that had arrested his attention,— "that is a likeness of poor Fossdyke."

"Extraordinary!" exclaimed Herbert. "I could have sworn it was meant for James Foxborough, and was a very excellent photo. The two men must have been the very image of each other."

And Morant and Soames stared at each other in blank amazement.

CHAPTER XXV.

"OF course you never saw John Fossdyke," said Phil, after a pause of some minutes' duration.

"Certainly not; nor you, as I understand, Foxborough. The likeness is odd, devilish odd," rejoined Morant.

Phil Soames smoked on musingly for some seconds, and then said:

"It's a curious thing that this extraordinary likeness between the two men has never been touched on as yet by any witness in the case. You were present at the inquest, and know it was never alluded to. You're quite sure you're making no mistake?"

"Quite, if you had not told me that was the photograph of Mr. Fossdyke, I'd have sworn to its being a likeness of Foxborough."

Once again did Phil Soames meditate before he spoke, as if phlegmatic and slow of thought, as the traditional Dutchman. Then he said:

"This is a bit of information that I don't consider I am entitled to communicate to the police without your sanction; but, Herbert, Sergeant Usher, of the Criminal Investigation Department, who has charge of the case, is in the town at the present moment, and I have an idea that he would consider this important."

" Why ? " rejoined Morant, briefly.

" Well, there you beat me," replied Phil. " I don't know ; it's a mere idea of my own, but I'll confess to being con-siderably impressed with Sergeant Usher. He seems to me, to use Mark Twain's expression, a *lightning* detective."

" That may be, but, my dear Phil, situated as I am with the Foxborough family, it is not clear to me that assisting a *lightning* detective at this moment would be for their benefit altogether."

" Certainly not, if you believe Foxborough guilty, but you have already to-night avowed your total disbelief in his criminality. If you stand by that the discovering of the truth is most desirable for his sake. I go for seeing the thing fairly out, and I have a right to speak; little as you may think it, Herbert, we are almost in the same boat."

" The same boat ! Why, what on earth do you mean ? " exclaimed Morant.

" It's rather a singular thing, Herbert ; and the knowledge only came to me some two days ago, but the girl I hope to make my wife is a half-sister of Miss Foxborough."

" Impossible ! James Foxborough has only one child—his daughter Nid."

" That may be, but Mrs. Foxborough had a daughter before she ever married Foxborough—a child who has been brought up by her mother's sister. I don't wish to go further into her history than this. I only mention it now to show that I have almost equal right with you to decide upon what use we shall make of the discovery we have just made. If Foxborough is an innocent man, the more light thrown upon poor Fossdyke's tragical end, the better for him ; and then, again, we have no moral right to suppress an important piece of testimony like this."

" Hum ! I don't know ; I've a sort of idea that standing staunch to one's pals is a primary duty in life, and I don't think I should bother myself much about moral obligations when fulfilling them threatened to turn to their detriment."

" I don't believe, as I said before, that this will be to James
Foxborough's detriment. Like you, I hold that even if he
was the man who caused poor Fossdyke's death it was a case
of manslaughter and not deliberate murder ; but remember
that, except the one fact of the identification of the weapon,
the evidence against Foxborough is all somewhat conjectural.
Look here, we will submit this in the first place to Dr. Ingleby,
and ask his advice about it."

" I don't half like it, Phil," rejoined Morant, gloomily,
"and wish I had never seen your confounded photograph
book."

" But you have, you see ; you have virtually given a bit of
evidence impossible to recall. I cannot tell you why I think
it important, but I do."

" Now," rejoined Herbert, " I'll give in. I know these
two things—that your head is better than mine, and that you
are sure to do what you think best for both the Foxboroughs
and ourselves. That's so ; isn't it ? " added Morant, somewhat nervously.

" Not a doubt, old man. Playing straight may be playing
bold, but it's very often marvellously effective."

As usual the stronger spirit had carried his point, and
before the pair separated that Dr. Ingleby should be informed
of the curious discovery was thoroughly settled.

Morant was somewhat astonished at the importance the
doctor appeared to attach to it, indeed it seemed of more consequence in other people's eyes a good deal than his own, but
Dr. Ingleby was quite clear on the one point that it ought to
be communicated to Sergeant Usher without delay, and the
sergeant was accordingly at once sent for. The message
found Mr. Usher in somewhat gloomy cogitation. The story
of Miss Hyde he had no doubt was a piece in the puzzle, but
by no means a prominent one, and he was just as far as ever
from arriving at one of those centre-pieces upon which those
pictured problems invariably depend.

" We have a bit of news for you, sergeant," said Dr. Ingleby as Mr. Usher entered the room. "Sit down and listen to what we have to tell you."

"Good evening, gentlemen," replied the sergeant, with a comprehensive bow, and without further speech Mr. Usher quietly seated himself. In his vocation the sergeant was perfectly aware of the supreme advantage of the listener, more especially of that very rare specimen, the attentive listener. Was not his business to acquire information, not to dispense it? Loquacity as a rule leaked; silence absorbed. But that Dr. Ingleby's account of the extraordinary likeness of John Fossdyke and his reputed murderer interested the sergeant there could be little doubt with any one acquainted with that officer's peculiarities. His quick grey eyes glistened as the doctor recounted Morant's curious mistake about Fossdyke's photograph. He uttered no word till Dr. Ingleby had finished, and then said quietly, "Would Mr. Morant permit me to ask him a question or two?"

"Certainly," replied Herbert.

"You know Mr. Foxborough well?"

"Fairly so; I have seen him a good many times, but I wouldn't swear to twenty, remember."

"No matter. You cannot be mistaken about his identity?"

"Certainly not! I know him quite well enough to be perfectly sure of recognizing him should I ever meet him again, unless, of course, disguised."

"Thank you, Mr. Morant. Now, Mr. Soames, I am going to ask you to lend me Mr. Fossdyke's *carte-de-visite*; if you have any objection, no doubt I can get it in the town. I don't suppose you have."

"Not at all," replied Phil, "I have brought it in my pocket on purpose; here it is."

The sergeant looked at it attentively, and then said, "I never saw this poor gentleman alive, but I should call this an excellent photograph."

"Undoubtedly," rejoined Phil.

"Excellent," echoed Dr. Ingleby.

" Now, gentlemen," said Sergeant Usher, "you are entitled
to know what I think of all this. Two of you are, at all
events, I presume, somewhat interested in proving James
Foxborough an innocent man. Well, you never did him or
his a better turn than you have done to-night. I have not
ciphered it all out in my own head yet, but I fancy this
means what they call at St. Stephen's, when the Government
works round and takes up the politics of the party it has
turned out, ' a new departure.' "

" You don't seem to think much of the principles of our
legislators,' observed the doctor, laughing.

" Lord, sir," rejoined the sergeant, "I never troubles my
head about politics; all I meant was that, whether they were
Whigs or Tories, Radicals or Irish members, their policy is
pretty much that of the gentry I pass my life in opposition
to, one of expediency. They pass acts of spoliation or levy
taxes just as my clients commit burglaries or pick pockets.
The necessities of the moment must be complied with, and
whether it's supper or place, a man goes for what he wants
badly. But good-night, gentlemen. I shall have something
to tell you before forty-eight hours are over, unless I am very
much mistaken. It's been an intricate puzzle all along, but
it's coming out, although I don't pretend I see it as yet.
Once more, good-night, gentlemen."

" You agree with me this is important evidence, doctor,"
said Phil, as the street door closed upon the sergeant.

" It must be, when we come to think of it. This extraordinary likeness between the two men cannot have been
overlooked. Yet the people at the Hopbine never alluded to
it, nor could the mysterious stranger who sat next Totterdell
have been Foxborough. Neither Totterdell nor any of the
Baumborough people could have overlooked such a startling
likeness as this seems to have been. It must either have
been some other Foxborough—somebody who assumed his
name—or he must have had a confederate."

They continued to talk over the affair in somewhat desultory fashion for some time, but got no further than they should all be extremely anxious to hear what Sergeant Usher might have to tell them when he next condescended to be confidential. The doctor alone knew how very little was comprehended in the sergeant's confidences, and thought it was more than possible that Mr. Usher's next communication would contain nothing, but that he did lay considerable stress on the night's news the doctor felt no manner of doubt.

The sergeant, as he walked homewards, turned this "latest intelligence" over in his mind, and became more impressed with its importance the more he thought about it. "There can be no doubt whatever now about the confederate," he muttered. "In fact, although Foxborough likely enough instigated the murder, it is quite open to question whether he had anything to do with it personally. Armed with that large command of ready money to which Mr. Sturton testified, he could purchase the services of almost any scoundrel he chose, and nothing is more probable than it was something connected with Miss Hyde's history caused his compassing Fossdyke's death. The latter might have been Miss Willoughby's first lover, and Miss Hyde the consequence of that affair. That is probably the case, and what led Foxborough to seek his life is easy of explanation on those grounds. It's curious, and it never seems to have struck any of those gentlemen as yet, that we have not so far fallen upon any witness that knew both men, and yet there were two or three people present at that inquest, Mr. Morant one, who, had they viewed the body, must have been at once struck with the marvellous likeness to the accused. Totterdell, without further questioning, is conclusive evidence that Foxborough was not present at the opening of the Baumborough Theatre. He could not possibly have overlooked such a likeness as this. He is a wandering, very wandering witness, but he tries to tell the truth as far as his conceit and natural tendency to talk will allow him. It strikes me that I had better be off to town to-morrow and see if any of the people at the Syringa recognize this extraordinary likeness."

The sergeant was a man of decision, and the first train next morning saw him on his way to London. He had slept on the thing, and thought it well out, and arrived at the conclusion that further fishing at present in the somewhat stagnant waters of Bunbury and Baumborough would be productive of no results, but that his casting-net next time must be thrown into the wide ocean of the metropolitan waters. The confederate, or rather the real perpetrator of the crime, was the man he wanted. Foxborough at most could be but an accessory in the eye of the law, although probably the instigator of the murder, and that he had fled the country Mr. Usher began to deem probable. That the principal ports had been closely watched was a matter of course, but that his brethren had been beaten before in this respect the sergeant was only too well aware of.

CHAPTER XXVI.

MR. CUDEMORE'S MANŒUVRES.

ERGEANT USHER, arrived in town, lost no time in making his inquiries. Herbert Morant is confirmed in every respect. People perfectly conversant with the appearance of James Foxborough recognize the photograph for him at once, and these are officials at the Syringa for the most part, who all disclaim any knowledge whatever of Mr. Fossdyke, and deny ever having heard his name till his sad fate put it in all men's mouths. Sergeant Usher begins to have a shrewd suspicion of the truth, but is more puzzled than ever as to the identity of the mysterious stranger who graced the opening of the Baumborough Theatre with his presence, and yet the sergeant has little doubt that he was the chief actor in the tragedy. For the present Mr. Usher is at fault; quite undecided, indeed, as in what direction to make a fresh cast for the recovery of the trail. He has called at Scotland Yard to report himself, and learnt that they have no tidings whatever of James Foxborough. Mr. Usher is not much surprised at that; he does not think it probable that any clue to Foxborough's lurking-place will be picked up by his brethren, but has a strong suspicion that he himself can indicate where he is when necessary. In the meantime he wants the accomplice, or the Foxborough of the Hopbine, who evidently was not James Foxborough of the Syringa Music Hall. " It is very odd," mutters the sergeant, " but here I am carrying about in my pocket-book what would probably identify him in a moment if I could only hit off the right person to submit it to. This note addressed to the dead man is in no disguised hand, and there are doubtless plenty of people could identify it if I only knew 'em. Both Foxborough's bankers and the stage manager of the Syringa don't see any attempt at simulating his hand, and from the writing they showed me I also should say there was no effort at imitation. It only wants a little thinking out. Query, was Miss Hyde the cause of the murder ? Why should she be ? She is not Foxborough's own daughter, and John Fossdyke from all accounts has been an exceedingly good friend to her. I know a little more about the thing than any one else, but I admit I am still quite in the dark as to who committed the murder, if murder it was, and why he did it."

" Let me see," muttered the sergeant, as he once more sat meditatively smoking over his own fireside. " Why did Foxborough want all that money he borrowed ? I don't know as yet, but I fancy I can get at that. Next, what has become of Foxborough ? I feel pretty certain I can get at that. Then, how did the dagger of Foxborough, with which Fossdyke was undoubtedly killed, arrive at the Hopbine ? Lastly, who was the Foxborough who went down to stay at the Hopbine, went to the Baumborough Theatre, invited Fossdyke to dine, and undoubtedly caused his death ? I have got his handwriting, which he doesn't know. I've got plenty of witnesses to his identity, which he undoubtedly does know, and I feel pretty sure that he has never left the country. Further, I have made a discovery of which he is not likely to get a hint, and upon which he must principally rely as his safeguard. It's a good game, a very good game," exclaimed Mr. Usher, " but I'll give checkmate for a crown before it is over."

It was a very jubilant evening in Tapton Cottage when Morant's letter from Baumborough reached them.

"My darling Nid," wrote Herbert, "I cannot tell you what, nor could you understand its importance any more than I do, but we have made a discovery about that miserable Bunbury affair, which the celebrated detective in charge of the case deems of the greatest consequence to your father. He told Phil Soames, in my presence, that nobody had served your father better than we had in accidentally bringing to light the trivial circumstance we did. I can't explain it, Nid, because I don't in the least understand its importance for one thing, and I'm bid hold my tongue for another, though I suppose you would say that couldn't possibly apply to you. Any way, dearest, tell your mother it's good news, and that I feel sure your father will be fully exonerated. Dear old Phil has made me a splendid offer, and holds open to me a choice that I shall deserve kicking if I fail to avail myself of. Did you ever hear of a beer king, Mademoiselle? You are, I trust, destined to be a beer queen. Shall you be awfully shocked at treating our friends to beakers of Soames and Morant's extra, or urging them to try just one glass of the Philerbertian stout? The invention of that composite name is my first great stroke in the business. As for the alarum about which you chaff me, there is a hatred between us as yet too deep for expression, but he is master, and I obey his brutal behests implicitly. Time, not his time, may bring about a reconciliation, but his horrible indifference at this season to the glories of sunshine are disgusting. He often appeals to me to be up and about long before it.

"God bless you, Nid, remember you are to be a breweress, so don't adopt the blue ribbon, not the Garter, the other one, nor turn up your pretty nose at oysters and stout. I never did even before I was one of the initiated malt and hops brethren. Love to your mother, and tell her, though I cannot explain it, our best news is good news.—Ever, dearest Nid, your very own, HERBERT."

Yes, a letter like this was certain to spread joy through Tapton Cottage. It was good news to both ladies, and the bright flush of happiness in her daughter's face could not fail to evolve some sympathy from such an essentially sympathetic woman as Mrs. Foxborough. She warmly congratulated her daughter.

"I think I understand Herbert, Nid," she said; "and a man such as he has described Mr. Soames will be the making of him."

"Mr. Cudemore, ma'am," said Eliza Salter, as she entered the room, "wishes to know if he can see you for five minutes?"

"Well, he can't see me," cried Nid; "I hate the sight of him. Oh you, poor mother, I am so sorry for you, but I must run away. Herbert's the only 'disagreeable' I ever take off your hands, and he, of course, has a claim for his pretended gallantry while I was insensible. I have no doubt it was the park-keeper really rescued me, and that he regarded the conflict from a safe distance."

"You don't believe anything of the sort, you silly child," replied her mother, smiling; "but if you don't want to see Mr. Cudemore you had better vanish, because I must see him. He has come, I know, on a matter of business. Off with you."

"Show him up, Eliza."

Nid gathered up her skirts and fled precipitately, while Eliza proceeded to fulfil her mistress's behest.

"Good morning, Mrs. Foxborough," said Cudemore, as he entered. "I am excessively sorry to have to intrude upon you at such an unfortunate moment as this, but business unluckily refuses to be postponed, and your husband's either ill-timed or misjudged absence has occasioned an unpleasant complication which necessitates my appealing to you."

"Pray sit down, I am quite willing to hear what you have to say," rejoined Mrs. Foxborough, who had no very favourable opinion of the money-lender. She knew Mr. Cudemore had, though in urbane manner, most rigidly exacted his pound of flesh on former occasions. She knew that he was their creditor now for a very large sum, about the investment of which she had no conception. She had bowed meekly to her husband's decision to borrow it. It was not wanted to sustain the Syringa, she knew, but about his provincial speculations she was in total ignorance. He had at times made money out of them, undoubtedly; without one of his provincial companies they never could have mustered the money necessary to start the Syringa, and that they had been obliged to borrow money besides, she was only too painfully aware. Mr. Cudemore had been a very exacting bloodsucker in the early days of that concern; paid off at last, but, as Mrs. Foxborough ruefully remembered, once more a terrible creditor.

" It is most unpleasant for me, of course, and more especially under the peculiar circumstances, but please remember, Mrs. Foxborough, I am only the unwilling mouth-piece of others. Your husband's absence has frightened the people who have advanced him this last money on the security of the Syringa, and my instructions are simply to give notice of their intention to withdraw the mortgage at the end of six months. You can't suppose, Mrs. Foxborough, that I wish to be disagreeable, and should you deem this inconvenient, I shall be happy to give you my assistance in raising it else-where."

" That, of course, Mr. Cudemore, will be a thing for future consideration. In the meantime I can only thank you for your good intentions."

But Mr. Cudemore was not to be got rid of like this. He had by no means said his say as yet; in fact, this was mere skirmishing. The battle royal is not always fought at our own discretion, but we at all events can endeavour to exercise some pressure about bringing it about.

" I think you had better take me into your confidence," he urged. " These people may get impatient when the time comes, and if you don't find them their money foreclose, and you would lose possession of the Syringa."

" But how can I take you or anyone else into my confidence when I am in total ignorance myself ? If I have to find the money at the expiration of the time, and can't, well then I suppose the Syringa and I must part. But it is most unlikely my husband made away with such a large sum as £6,000. Some of it, of course, he may have spent, but I am sure there is something to show for it. He invested it in some manner, and I think before the time you mention it is probable I shall discover where he is, or whether he is alive. I don't know, but I am quite sure he never committed the crime laid to his charge, and I hear the police are coming to the same opinion."

" I am very glad to hear it," replied Mr. Cudemore, suavely, "but I need scarcely say I can have no wish to touch upon so painful a subject. Still there are circumstances under which I could find you the money."

" It will be time enough to discuss those circumstances when the necessity for finding the money arises," rejoined the lady, sharply.

Whatever his design Mr. Cudemore felt that he could not prosecute it any further for the present, and took his departure.

" The miserable trickster," said Mrs. Foxborough, as her eyes sparkled. " He means he would find the money if I gave him Nid, as if I wouldn't see the child dead and the Syringa burnt first. I wonder whether the people who lent the money are altogether guided by him, and what induced poor James to borrow so large a sum. What could he want it for ? "

From this date Mr. Cudemore was constantly proffering assistance. He claimed, too, certain authority over the Syringa, and neither Mrs. Foxborough nor her stage-manager were quite clear whether he had such rights or not. He said he had a right to examine the books weekly on the part of the mortgagers, and as Mrs. Foxborough had no copy of the deed, she was not able to gainsay him. Mr. Cudemore said that clause had been specially introduced, as she would see when her husband's copy was discovered. Mr. Cudemore's dogged persistence was remarkable. In vain did Mrs. Fox-borough decline his offers for assistance. She was almost rude to the man, but he still would keep perpetually calling. Then he tried to frighten her about the loss of the Syringa, but Mrs. Foxborough told him plainly she had done without the Syringa before and could do so again. She did not want to lose it, but if her retaining it was to be a matter of favour then she preferred to go. Cudemore was evidently very much in earnest, or he would never have put up with such con-tinuous rebuffs, and aboutwhat his real motive was Mrs. Fox-borough had never had any doubt from the very beginning. He rarely saw Nid upon these occasions, and certainly could not claim to have met with the slightest encouragement from that young lady, but the man was crazed about her, and determined to win her at all hazards. That she had the slightest fancy for him never crossed his brain for a moment. On the contrary, I think a wicked determination to make her pay dearly for her ostentatious indifference should she ever be his wife was much more often in his thoughts.

"Yes, my dainty lady, the time may come when you'll wish you had shown me more civility, ay, and your stuck-up mother too. I shall marry you at last, little as you may think it."

And it did look preposterous, and only that Cudemore was quite off his head upon the subject, he might have seen so himself. Whether she lost the Syringa or not, Mrs. Fox-borough and her daughter would be in no such needy circum-stances that he might look to bend them to his will against their own judgment, and he must have been blind indeed if he failed to see that neither lady favoured his pretensions. As for Nid, her feelings were more than mere indifference towards him; they amounted to actual dislike, and in face of her engagement to Herbert, no pressure would have been likely to make her accept Mr. Cudemore.

"My dearest Herbert," wrote Nid. " So many thanks

for the good news contained in your last letter. It is grand
to hear that the police have no longer any doubt of papa's
innocence."

"Well, upon my word," remarked Morant, as he laid
down the letter for a moment, "that is a most ingenious
twisting of my words. What I meant was 'Seem to have
some doubt of Mr. Foxborough being the delinquent after
all.'"

"We get on pretty well, but mamma frets dreadfully, and
to add to her troubles that wretched Mr. Cudemore is always
worrying her. He claims some control over the Syringa,
though whether he has any real right to interfere we don't
know, but he's always coming here pestering about it, and
poor mamma has quite sorrows enough without their being
aggravated by a monster like that. How very good it is of
Mr. Soames to give you such a nice start. Next time I see
you—ah, when is that to be—I shall expect to find you have
taken a treble x degree. You will grow awfully rich, brewers
always do, you know, and that will be nice, because you will
be able to give me all sorts of pretty things, and I appreciate
pretty things. I don't want to interfere with your work, but
do snatch a day the first time you've a chance, and come
up and see us. It will do mamma good, and you might
make out for us whether Mr. Cudemore is entitled to assume
any control of the Syringa. Good-bye, Herbert dearest
Mamma's love, and believe me, ever your own NID."

Mr. Morant's first impression upon perusing this epistle
was that it behoved him to go straight to town and kick
Cudemore, but upon second thoughts he decided to postpone
that ceremony for the present.

CHAPTER XXVII.

HAT Philip Soames, after what he had stated of his intentions to Dr. Ingleby, would be long before putting them into practice was not very likely, and the very next afternoon saw him striding along the causeway to Dyke—mightily determined Bessie should answer that question in solemn earnest this time, and that there should be no further mystery between them. Miss Hyde, to tell the truth, had passed a sleepless night, a night of starts and shivers, hopes and fears, such as is the luck of few of us to escape experience of; she knew now she had staked her very all upon the case, for she no longer attempted to disguise from herself that she was life bankrupt in love should Philip resign her. She had talked bravely enough about not being a clog round his neck, of never being a social drag upon him, of giving him up for his own good, and she meant every word of it; but still she had never realized his giving her up. That might come to pass, but it was at an undefined distance, not an immediate question. She might still hope at all events this last stain might be removed from her family, that the step-father she had never seen might be absolved from the murder of him who had been so good a friend to her, that Phil's love might triumph over her own resolution. All this was in the future; now she was face to face with it. Thirty-six hours, forty-eight at the outside, and she would know whether all was over between her and Phil Soames. If he had not spoken before to-morrow night the chances were she would never see him again ; if he had not spoken before the night after, she knew if ever she saw him again it would be as no lover of hers.

To say that the announcement of Mr. Soames made Bessie start and colour would barely describe the girl's agitation, but it had to be mastered; and though she had a violent desire to run away, she knew that was ridiculous, that Phil's early visit was an augury of the best, and that it was impossible for the best-intentioned and most ardent lover to propose if the object of his idolatry persistently refused him opportunity. So she held her ground, and showed no sign of shiver in her manner as she greeted him. Mrs. Fossdyke welcomed him warmly, as usual, and Miss Hyde, albeit her hand shook slightly, handed him his tea with very fair composure.

"I am very glad to see you, Philip," said Mrs. Fossdyke. She had aged and become much more subdued in manner since her husband's death. "I hear you have got a friend staying with you."

"Yes, an old college chum, whom I hope you will permit me to introduce to you before very long."

"Ah, it's getting too late for me to make fresh acquaintances. It is not as it was when John was alive. I'm not going to mope or shut myself up, but I do feel all the spring's out of my life, Philip."

"You can't expect to get over such a shock all at once," he replied. "Is it true that you have taken that cottage of old Morrison's close to us ?"

"It is and it isn't," said Mrs. Fossdyke. "I have not as yet, but I am thinking of doing so. It would be quite big enough for me and Bessie, and I don't wish to stay at Dyke even if I could."

"It will suit you admirably, and you will be close to most

19

of your old friends.   But I have come out, Mrs. Fossdyke, to
beg a great favour of you."

Miss Hyde gave a slight start.

" A favour of me, Philip !   You should have come in the
days of my opulence."

" There are plenty of favours to be craved at your hands
yet, as you will find in due time, Mrs. Fossdyke.   What I
have to ask is your permission to win this lady for my wife
if I can," and Philip rose as he spoke and bent his head to
Miss Hyde.   .

" It's madness ! " exclaimed Bessie, faintly.

" Yes, sweet, and with method in it ; but let me only have
Mrs. Fossdyke's permission, and I'll endeavour to explain it."

" She's as good a girl as ever stepped ! " exclaimed the
mistress of Dyke, as soon as she had recovered from her
astonishment, delighted to find that her pet project was on
the eve of accomplishment.   " You have not only my sanction,
but, Bessie, my dear, if you take my advice you will treat
him kindly."

" You know all, Philip ; you are sure you know all ? "
faltered the girl.

" Dr. Ingleby has told me everything, and now I know
your secret I laugh at it, as I have always prophesied I
should ; and now, Bessie, before Mrs. Fossdyke, I ask you
solemnly, will you be my wife ? "

" Stop," cried Mrs. Fossdyke, " I don't like this ; more
mystery ; there's usually misery with mystery, Bessie," she
continued, sadly.   " What is this secret of yours ?   Alas ! it
has brought woe to me already, the bitterest quarrel ever I
had with poor John was about that.   Is every one to know it
but me ?   Am I to be ever hearing of it, but never hear it ?
I think, child, I deserve your confidence better."

Bessie half sprang from her chair, then dropped back, and
with wet lashes cast an appealing glance to her lover.

Philip responded at once—

" Mrs. Fossdyke, spare me Bessie for a short time, and on

her return she shall tell you everything. I trust by that to
have obtained the right to advise her. Come! you came for
a stroll with me not long ago, and I hope you will send away
a happier man to-night than you did on that occasion."

The two ladies seemed swept away by this decisive, dictatorial young man. Mrs. Fossdyke simply pressed his hand,
and wished him success as she bade him good-bye; while
Bessie quietly got up and followed him out of the room, took
her hat and flung a woollen shawl round her as she passed
through the hall, and then they stepped out and he led her
to the now leafless rosary; there he stopped abruptly, no word
had as yet passed between them, and said almost brusquely,
" Bessie, how is it to be ? "

For a few seconds she felt indignant at his abruptness, and
then she reflected that this was the third time this man had
asked her to marry him, that even the knowledge of her
history had made no difference whatever in his steady
devotion; that she loved him dearly, and, lastly, if they once
get over the first shock women more often than not succumb
to these blunt wooers.

" Philip," she said at last, " it shall be as you will."

" Then, dearest, you belong to me," was his rejoinder, and
he clasped her in his arms and kissed her. " Now, Bessie,
I have nothing in the main, remember, to learn about your
history, but I do want to ask you one or two questions.
How much do you know of your mother ? "

" Next to nothing, as I told Dr. Ingleby. I have seen her
only occasionally. Such a fine handsome woman and with
a charming voice and manner. She kissed me and fondled
me, but seemed always under some sort of restraint, and if,
as more than once happened, my aunt interrupted our interview, she immediately became formal and cold in her manner.
I am sure she was bound by some pact to my aunt to be
nothing more than a mere nominal mother to me. When I
implored her to let me come and see her she said it was
impossible, and I never even saw her house, nor do I know

where she lives. I think my mother and I could have loved each other dearly if we had ever been given the chance, but we saw each other so rarely."

" And what about your sister—half-sister, I mean ? "

" Sister ! " exclaimed Bessie, " I didn't know I had one."

" Well, she is only your half-sister, but Nydia Foxborough is, I am told, a very pretty and charming girl."

" I should like that. I should like to have a sister, Philip. Shall I ever know her, I wonder ? " said Bessie, softly.

" Yes, you will know her, and see a great deal of her, little woman, I hope, in days shortly to come. You have heard I have an old college chum staying with me ? "

" You told us so at tea-time."

" Well he, Herbert Morant, is engaged to marry Nydia Foxborough, and I intend that Herbert Morant shall turn brewer and become a partner in the firm of Soames and Son. And it will be Herbert's own fault if it don't all come off, and when a man's really in love I can vouch for his becoming very resolute," concluded Phil, laughing.

" Very desperate," interposed Bessie. " I can't give you back your troth, now, dearest. I'm too selfish, it would break my heart; but I'm afraid, Phil, you are not doing a very prudent thing in marrying me ; but to take care of my unknown sister besides is too good of you, for you are in-directly taking care of her, you know. You must bring this Mr. Morant out and let me know him. I shall be so pleased to talk to him about Nydia."

" Yes," laughed Phil, " and, great heavens, won't he jump at the opportunity. I've a good deal of difficulty in suppress-ing a tendency to talk to him about you, but I doubt whether I should be allowed if I tried, Herbert has so much to say about your sister. She's a sweetly pretty girl, judging from her photograph, but not in the least like you, though I hear she is a miniature edition of her mother."

" Mamma is tall," observed Bessie.

" And Nid, as Herbert calls her, *petite.* She is endowed

with every charm and virtue under the sun. I need scarcely say that the testimony is biassed, and if a man is not biassed in favour of his betrothed he's not in love with her. If she be not all grace and perfection in his eyes, well ! "

" Well, what ? " asked Bessie, roguishly.

" His fetters are not snapped to," rejoined Soames, laughing. "Mine, darling, are well rivetted ; and, faith, when you talk to Herbert Morant I think you'll admit his manacles are satisfactorily soldered on."

" Ah, well, I shall be charmed to listen to him for a long afternoon. I have always so longed for a sister, and you say she is nice."

" No, pardon me, I never said so. Herbert does ; he knows her and I don't. All I say is, if the sun don't lie, she should be a very pretty girl, but I've only seen her photograph."

" When am I to see her ? " asked Bessie.

"Ah! That I can't say. It depends a little upon this miserable murder. I fancy the police have rather changed their views about it of late, but they don't take us into their confidence. Miss Foxborough down here just at present would be an impossibility, you know."

"Yes, and I fervently trust now that Mr. Foxborough will be acquitted of the crime. It would be a wall between Nydia and myself were it otherwise."

" For the present, perhaps, yes, but not of necessity in the future. In the meanwhile we must not speculate on disagreeable subjects."

" But, Philip," said Bessie, in a low tone, as they continued to pace up and down, "am I to tell Mrs. Fossdyke all my story? Would it be best ? "

" Yes ; tell her everything, prefacing it with the intimation that you are pledged to be my wife."

" It shall be as my lord wills," rejoined Bessie; "but I own I think it will pain Mrs. Fossdyke."

Phil Soames gave a low laugh ere he replied—

" To think, dearest, a man's wit for once in a case of this

sort should eclipse a woman's. Mrs. Fossdyke may be a little startled at first, but in telling your story you will of course make her clearly understand you never even saw your stepfather. Well, you will satisfy no little curiosity she feels about your previous life, and the announcement that we are engaged will, I am sure, please her. You know, Bessie, as well as I do, that though she has never been so injudicious as to attempt match-making between us, she has in many little ways never attempted to conceal that she would be pleased if we did happen to take a fancy to one another."

"Philip," cried the girl, as the blood rushed to her temples, "you have no right to talk like that. It seems——"

"Stop," interrupted Soames, "it seems as if you were about to observe that one of the twain was a long while taking that fancy. She can't say it was altogether my fault, for, my darling, if ever a man won a bride by thorough belief in her, devoted love for her, and persistent refusal not to take 'no' for an answer, I think I did. I'll hear no word against Mrs. Fossdyke."

"I wasn't going to say anything against her. What I meant was this——" cried Bessie.

"Which was not in the least the case," replied Phil. "You were going to insinuate that, like Benedick, I was trapped into falling in love with you. Not a bit of it; before I'd known you six weeks I'd vowed to marry you, and on my word, Bessie, there was a time when I thought I was like to be forsworn."

"For your own sake, my love," she replied, softly. "If it had not been for that, Phil, I am afraid I should have surrendered at the first assault, and that the telegraph board on the cricket-field would only have recorded the half of your triumphs."

Soames pressed her arm in reply, and said, "Walk with me to the gate, Bessie, for it is time I got home to entertain your brother-in-law that is to be, after all these family matters are arranged."

" And you are sure I had better tell Mrs. Fossdyke everything ? " asked the girl, as they strolled down the drive.

" Quite ; because, Bessie, she might learn the story in
some shape at any time now. We have thought it best to
let the police know everything, and though they promise not
to make unnecessary parade of the knowledge we have
afforded them it is quite possible that they may have no help
for it."

" Were you right to tell them so much ? "

" Yes, Bessie, I think so. One has no right to keep back
evidence that seems to bear upon a great crime, or for the
matter of that a little one. In our case all I can say is the
officer in charge of the case seems to think we have done
Foxborough good service. I don't in the least understand
how, nor did he condescend to explain, but, my darling,
straightforward policy generally seems to me to be most
profitable in this world in the long run. Now, pet, give me
a kiss, and then scamper home, and remember you've sent a
real happy man on his road home to-night." So saying,
Phil clasped the girl in his arms, and claimed lawful tribute
from her freely yielded lips.

" Good-night ! and away with you," he said, as he released
her. " Don't be afraid, but that, though she may weep a bit
after your story, Mrs. Fossdyke will be very pleased with it
on the whole. Once more, good-night ! "

Bessie sped home with a light heart. Confession to Mrs.
Fossdyke might be awkward, but what did it matter, Philip
loved her. She was Philip's now, spite of everything. He
knew all about her, and clasped her to his breast, and called
her his plighted wife, and laughed at the idea of her poor
biography making any kind of difference in his feelings.
Ah ! yes, as Philip's *fiancée* and authorized by him to tell it,
what recked she if the world knew her whole story ? Personally she knew she was blameless.

CHAPTER XXVIII.

MR. CUDEMORE GETS UNCOMFORTABLE.

THAT men have infatuations about women past comprehension, is an axiom as indisputable in life as that a line is the shortest distance between two points in mathematics. "What does he see in her?" demand his friends, angrily and with justice; she may be vulgar, and even of dubious beauty, but no matter, she has fascinated that man, it may be for days or it may be for ever, but though of mature age he will be blind as a newly-born puppy to her demerits. What does he see in her? Good Lord, he could not answer that question in the least. He would tell you that she was lovely, deny that she was vulgar, and assert upon oath that her English was faultless. Useless to reason with these infatuated ones. Safer far to emulate that astute philosopher, who upon being condoled with about his brother's *mésalliance*, quietly retorted: "What is there to howl about? Charlie would never have been happy with a lady."

Mr. Cudemore was quite off his balance about Nid Fox-borough. He had fair grounds for his infatuation. The girl was very pretty and had been thoroughly educated. There were none of the vulgarisms mentioned above in her, but she had never given him the slightest encouragement, nor had he indeed ever been afforded much opportunity of pushing his suit; but for all that Mr. Cudemore was most

resolute in his determination to marry her. He was
working hard to get the Syringa mainly into his own hands,
and had already, as he knew, assumed a control there, to
which he was by no means entitled. What distressed him
at present was not Nid's indifference to his suit—that he was
prepared for; but her mother's indifference to the loss of the
management of the Syringa.

Mr. Cudemore had already abandoned all hope of carrying
his point as a mere wooer, but he did think pressure about
the Syringa might do wonders for him. To his dismay Mrs.
Foxborough seemed to care little whether she stayed or left.
He had trusted much upon this leverage in the game he
conceived James Foxborough's death had opened out to him.
Another thing which had gone awry with the money-lender
was this. He was, of course, aware that Herbert Morant
was his successful rival. He had held some bills of Morant's,
and Mr. Cudemore's experience of young men told him that
the first bill, like the first woodcock, was but the precursor
of the flight. He had looked forward at no little distance of
time to having the young man most thoroughly under his
thumb, but to his great astonishment Herbert Morant had
promptly taken up his bills as soon as they became due, and
shown no wish to contract fresh obligations; consequent
indeed on his love for Nid and desire to set to work to make a
home for her; but Mr. Cudemore did not know all this, or I
am afraid that maledictions would have fallen from beneath
his well-waxed moustache, thick and thorough.

He could not be said to be having a rosy time of it altogether, this jackal that preyed on the necessities of his
brethren. Your professional affairs may run favourably
enough, but most men have some aim utterly outside that,
and the mark that particularly attracted Mr. Cudemore's
attention at this moment seemed considerably beyond his
attainment. Still he was of that pertinacious temperament
that sometimes achieves the fulfilment of its desires by its
dogged perseverance.

One thing, quietly as he had passed it by, had struck Mr.
Cudemore during his interview with Mrs. Foxborough—to
wit, her statement that the police no longer thought her
husband guilty of the Bunbury murder. It was considerably
to his interest, he thought, that Foxborough should be held
guilty of that crime, and he resolved to call upon Mr.
Sturton, and endeavour to ascertain from him what Scotland
Yard had thought of the information he had brought them.

The great Bond Street maestro was at home, or, to speak
more correctly, at his place of business. As for home, he
resided in a charming house, standing in excessively pretty
grounds out in West Kensington, where were plenty of
servants, saddle and carriage horses, a French cook, a Scotch
gardener and conservatories; his sons were at the univer-
sities, and though far more Conservative in their professions
than their father, with much less real reverence for a lord.
As Coleridge had a contemptuous belief in ghosts such as he
might hold in cabbages, because he had seen so many of
them, so had these young men discovered that hereditary
rank was simply the result of successful spoliation and cor-
ruption in the days gone by, and its descendants by no
means gifted above the sons of men. Mr. Sturton was at
his place of business, and Mr. Cudemore was at once ushered
into the sartorial potentate's private sanctum—a simply
furnished room at the back of the shop, where Mr. Sturton,
seated at his writing-table, was quietly engaged in answering
the heavy batch of letters which each morning brought
him.

"Ah ! Cudemore," he said, in his usual languid manner;
"pray sit down; excuse me for two minutes while I just
finish this, and then I shall be ready to talk to you."

A few minutes, and then Sturton threw down his pen, and
pulling his chair round, said quietly—

"Now, then, what is it ?"

He and Mr. Cudemore were not wont to indulge in cere-
monious calling upon each other.

" What did they say to you at Scotland Yard the other day ? " inquired the money-lender, without further preamble.

" You needn't feel the least uncomfortable about my going there anyway, for your name has never been mentioned, while mine they promised to keep dark unless absolutely compelled to bring it forward, which they did not in the least anticipate. I saw Sergeant Usher, the detective officer in charge of the case, and he said my information might turn out of great value to them, but would probably never lead to their requiring any evidence from me, and that certainly at present they would infinitely prefer my keeping my mouth closed on the subject."

" I am told the police begin to think that Foxborough did not commit the crime. Is that true ? What does Sergeant Usher think about it ? "

" I am sure I don't know," replied Mr. Sturton ; " and from what I saw of Sergeant Usher, I should say he's very unlikely to let any mortal soul know his opinion on the subject till he's got some one on his trial for the murder. I should think he would talk affably and apparently openly with you for a week, and at the end of it you wouldn't have discovered what he thought about anything. I see a good bit of human nature, you know ; you can't help measuring men's minds a little while you are measuring their bodies, that is, if you are an artist. There are customers who never know exactly what they want, and whom you may persuade to do anything. Others who equally don't know what they want, but suspect you if you attempt to assist the wobbling ideas that do duty with them for a mind ; there's the customer you can't please, do what you will, angular in body as in opinion ; there's the man who hates trying on, hates ordering clothes at all, and pays ready money ; there's the man who delights in both the first, but abhors the latter part of the ceremony. Hasn't Carlyle written a book about it ? and, good Lord ! if he had only had me to prompt him ! Ours is one of the great arts, and the day will soon come

when it will be acknowledged as such. You've R.A.'s, and
I don't see why there shouldn't be R.T.'s ; and as the age
gets more advanced, and the general fusion of things begins,
there's no doubt, there's no doubt whatever——" and here
the great democratic tailor stopped abruptly, his tongue
having a little overrun his defined opinions upon the coming
upheaval ; a thing which happens notably to many of our
legislators, and accounts for the consequent abrupt termination of some of the bursts of eloquence with which they are
wont to electrify their constituents.

Mr. Cudemore was of a narrow-minded but practical turn
of mind. He stared with undisguised astonishment while
his friend delivered himself of the above rhapsody, but
would, had his thoughts been put into English, have expressed himself somehow in this wise :

"All men have their faults, I know. It's the weak point in
their organization which, carried to excess, men call madness. Only I know Sturton to be a thorough business,
practical man, I should wonder why his friends didn't shut
him up, that is to say, if he ever lets out in this way to them.
I ! hum, if I could, should charge him another ten per cent.
for it."

"Then this Sergeant Usher didn't really tell you he considered Foxborough had nothing to do with the crime ? "
remarked Mr. Cudemore, at length.

"Certainly not—what put that into your head ?"

"The papers, I believe," rejoined the money-lender, carelessly ; "and then I misunderstood you about your interview
at Scotland Yard."

"I told you clearly," rejoined Sturton, "that Usher, like
a colourless photograph, expressed nothing. Voluble, very,
on occasions ; that is, it struck me, if I didn't talk ; but mute
as a mouse when I'd anything to say. I know nothing about
the opinion of Scotland Yard whatever."

"Ah ! well, I felt a little curious to know what they
thought of your confession," rejoined Mr. Cudemore, rising,

" and also whether the making of it had brought you peace of mind."

" The sooner you understand I mean invariably to take my own way the better," rejoined Sturton, sharply, and with a quickness that the money-lender had never given him credit for. " It is very easy to transfer such business as I have with you to another of the fraternity."

" And suppose I chose to bruit abroad our former relations afterwards," rejoined Cudemore, sullenly.

" I should deliberately and as assuredly ruin you. Fool that you are! Can't you see that small capitalists like you are at the mercy of the bigger men who employ them,' retorted Mr. Sturton, calmly. " All the leading men in my *profession* are reported to lend money to their customers whether they do or not. You can't do me much harm, but, my dear Cudemore, I shall assuredly break you. I pull strings that your limited mind has no conception of."

" I don't want to quarrel," replied the money-lender. " Unless with an object it's always a mistake, but when you run counter to my views I like to know the why of it. We'll change the subject. How about young Morant ? Is he still on your books ? he has taken up all his papers ? "

" No, that's the man who stands in your way with Miss Foxborough, isn't he ? He has squared up and left us, and when they do that of their own accord it usually means that they have taken to the business of life in some fashion. Flying kites and West-end tailors don't quite accord with such utilitarian views."

The conversation was again verging a little too deep for the money-lender, and it may be doubted whether Mr. Sturton really comprehended what he meant by his last observation. A tendency to inflated language is one of the characteristics of all platform oratory of the present day. Mr. Cudemore thought there was no more to be said, and no more to be learned, so he gravely and impressively wished the Bond Street magnate good-bye. Somewhat staggered,

Mr. Cudemore got out of the house, having found this man of so much tougher calibre than he had deemed him, so utterly unmalleable and determinate about having his own way. Still he did recognize Sturton's grim formula that when the brazen pots and the earthen quarrel it is bad for the latter, and felt that to succumb with grace to his principal's dictum was all that was left to him. He had been slow to perceive this, but was quite awake now to the fact that this languid man had a most peremptory will of his own, and was hardly to be turned from it.

Musing over this, to him by no means pleasing discovery, he arrived at his house in Spring Gardens, and proceeded, without going into his office, to ascend the stairs to his own private apartments. As he turned the angle of the staircase, he caught sight of his junior clerk coming, as it appeared to him, out of his, Cudemore's, bedroom.

" What the deuce are you doing up here ? " inquired the money-lender, angrily, as the pair met.

" I came up to see if you were in, sir. There's a gent of the name of Smithson wanting to see you terrible bad."

" Where's his card ? " inquired Mr. Cudemore.

" He hadn't got one," rejoined Tim, for such was the soubriquet by which the junior clerk was known in the establishment; doubtful even whether his master knew his legitimate patronymic.

" Show him up then at once," rejoined Cudemore.

" He's left, sir ; said he would call again in an hour, when he heard you were out."

" How the devil did he hear I was out, you young cheat-the-gallows, when you have just made the discovery ? "

" I told him I thought you were," replied Tim, flippantly, " and he wouldn't wait till I ran up to see——"

" Look here, my young friend, it strikes me you're lying on a pretty extensive scale. You knew I was out to begin with."

" Certainly, sir, but I was not quite sure you had not come in."

" Clients who come to see me generally leave or produce cards," said the money-lender.

" Well, this one wouldn't," rejoined Tim, doggedly.

" And what business, sir, had you to suppose you would find me in my bedroom ? "

" I didn't. I went to look for you in your sitting-room, and not finding you there ran upstairs on the off-chance, the door being open I peeped in, you were not there, and I thought it best to shut it behind me."

" I could have taken my oath, almost, you were coming out of the room when I caught sight of you."

" Well, it may be I'd had my neck and perhaps a foot over the threshold. I'm very sorry if I've done wrong, Mr. Cudemore, but this gentleman was so urgent, and I really didn't know whether you were in or out."

" That'll do," replied the money-lender, curtly, " but remember, if ever I find you above the first floor again, you go, and with no recommendation for further employment from me."

Tim said nothing in return, but disappeared promptly to his legitimate sphere.

" Now what was that cursed young liar prowling about my bedroom for ? " mused Mr. Cudemore, as he entered his sitting-room and lit a cigar.

CHAPTER XXIX.

MORANT MEETS MISS HYDE.

HEN Phil went over to Dyke next day he was most warmly greeted by Mrs. Fossdyke.

"Sincere congratulations," she murmured. "You can't think how happy you have made me; that you two should come together has been the wish of my heart this year past."

"Ah! I suppose Bessie has told you all," said Phil, emphatically.

"All," replied Mrs. Fossdyke, "and I know what a wretch I was to tease her about her past, but it was not altogether my fault, although at my age I've no business to attempt to shift the blame to other people's shoulders."

"Nobody ever doubted who the real culprit was, Mrs. Fossdyke; but where is Bessie?"

"She will be down in a few minutes, but I asked just to have you to myself for a little. I've known you so long, Phil, and you've always been such a favourite of mine that I wanted to make my congratulations in earnest. She will make you a good wife, even though there be a stain in her pedigree."

"I am very glad to hear you say that, Mrs. Fossdyke, for, even assuming her step-father is the guilty monster which he is alleged to be, and which every fresh discovery seems to make more doubtful, it would be too cruel to visit his crimes on the head of this girl who never even saw him."

"I quite agree with you. I love her very dearly, and though, of course, I can't repress a little shiver as yet when I reflect upon her connection with that—that man," faltered Mrs. Fossdyke, "still, Philip, I hope you don't think I could be unjust to Bessie."

"You were so not very long back," thought Philip, but he gave no utterance to the reflection and merely bent his handsome head.

"And now," continued Mrs. Fossdyke, "I want to see the other one, this Mr. Morant who is engaged to Bessie's unknown sister."

"Certainly; I was going to ask permission to bring him out here, as I want him to know Bessie; but if I have leave to introduce him to you also, I shall be only too delighted."

"Yes; I want to know him. Is he nice? is he good-looking?"

"Good-looking? Well, we men never can quite tell what your sex will call so, or I'd say decidedly not; but he is a gentleman, and a real good fellow, Mrs. Fossdyke. He's been an idler so far, but he's got a wife to work for now, and, please God, I'll make a man of him here. I'm bound to say that, so far, he faces his work like a bull-dog."

"With that incentive to work and you as his tutor, Phil, I think he'll do," said Mrs. Fossdyke, laughing softly. "But bring him out to see me, and I'll judge of his appearance for myself."

"Certainly!" And as he spoke Miss Hyde entered the room, and greeted her *fiancé* with a bright smile, to which he responded by warmly embracing her.

"Bessie, I've just obtained Mrs. Fossdyke's permission; nay, I may say more, her command, to bring out your future brother-in-law for your personal inspection."

"You know I am as anxious to hear about my sister and make his acquaintance as Mrs. Fossdyke."

20

"Yes, and I'll ensure your hearing about your sister," returned Philip, laughing; "no intimate friend of Herbert's will miss that at present, I fancy."

"He will find me an interested listener, at all events. When will you bring him?"

"To-morrow, if that will suit you, Mrs. Fossdyke. Lord, what friends you and he will be, Bessie! A woman who will be a sympathetic recipient of a lover's outpourings about the *object* wins his devotion. He will at once pronounce her a very paragon."

"And pray, Philip, who is the confidant of your 'outpourings'?" said Miss Hyde, laughing. "I presume from what you say such a confidant is a necessity?"

"Oh, yes, my dear," rejoined Philip, gaily, "there are times when I feel it a necessity to dilate on your attractions, and then I'll own at first it came hard. Herbert has no idea of fair play. He expects me to listen for hours to prose poems about your sister, but I regret to state he manifests as yet but a cursory interest in hearing about you. Of course I also had to find somebody to rave to; but I hadn't far to seek. I knew an old friend who says, Bessie, if he could only take off twenty years you would have had to decide whether he or I was the best man, and he'll always listen while I chant your praises."

"Ah! that's dear old Dr. Ingleby," said the girl, as she slipped her arm through her lover's. "I hardly dare think yet, Phil, that we are going to be married, but if ever we are he will have had as much to say to it as the clergyman."

"'Ever we are, child?' What nonsense you are talking. You know, dear Mrs. Fossdyke, that out of respect to your poor husband's memory neither of us would wish it at present, but after a due interval I know we shall have your best wishes and permission."

"My very best wishes and hearty congratulations," replied the widow: "now run away, the pair of you. I know you must have a lot to say to each other, unless things have changed a deal from the days when I was young."

"Certainly," replied Phil; "I have got to teach Bessie woman's duties as a wife."

"Oh, Phil, Phil," said Mrs. Fossdyke, laughing. "I know you both better. Only make her love you, and she'll want no teaching on that point; but till you slip the ring on her finger it's woman's prerogative that her word should be law; and, Bessie, my dear, don't be false to your sex and forego the privilege."

"Come along, Bessie, come for a stroll; and as you are strong, be merciful. I bow meekly to Mrs. Fossdyke's decision, but don't command more chariots than a mere maltster can afford you."

"Don't chaff your wife that is to be, Phil," said Bessie, with a low, rippling laugh. "You know very well till she came to Dyke cabs and omnibuses constituted her ideas of chariots. No, dearest, I can promise two things—to love you truly and develop no lavish ideas on the subject of expenditure."

"A wise woman in her generation is Mrs. Fossdyke," replied Phil, "and if you'll only do the first I quite agree with her. I need trouble about nothing else."

A slight pressure of his arm acknowledged the speech, and then Bessie said, "Mind, Mr. Morant brings out Nydia's photograph to-morrow. I am so anxious and curious to see it."

"Of course," replied Philip; "but here we are again at the gate. Still, Bessie, saying good-bye to you now is not what it was."

"I trust not," she rejoined, softly. "You will understand how different it seems to me when I say 'Kiss me, Phil,' and, mind, I must see you to-morrow."

There was no mutiny on Philip Soames's part against his lady-love's first behest, and as he swung into Baumborough at a four-mile-an-hour gait, there was perhaps no happier young fellow in the United Kingdom. Dashing into his own sanctum, he found Herbert Morant staring solemnly at the glowing coals. Lifting his head, that gentleman glanced at him for a moment and then exclaimed—

"No, don't, please; I can't stand it. There's wedding-bells in every line of your face. All very well for you, who see marriage within measurable distance, but for one to whom it seems a mere possibility of the future—Ah!" sighed Herbert in conclusion.

"Don't be a fool, and don't stare into the fire till oppressed with the doldrums," rejoined Soames, sharply. "Your marriage-bells are within very reasonable reach, if you only stick to the collar as you have done since you came here."

"You really think I shall make a brewer?" asked Herbert.

"There's no doubt whatever about it, and marry Nydia, and settle down at Baumborough, and become a vestry man, a town councillor, and half a dozen other things of which you at present comprehend nothing. In the meantime I'm pledged to-morrow to take you out to Dyke to introduce you to Mrs. Fossdyke and Nydia's half-sister."

"You are awfully kind, Phil, but won't it—won't it be just a little awkward?"

"Not at all; that is all smoothed away. Both ladies are dying to see you. Bessie wants to hear all about her unknown sister, and if you give her about a tenth of the confidence you bestow upon me there won't be much left for her to learn."

"Don't talk bosh, Phil; I've never said much to you about her."

"Good Lord!" exclaimed Soames, "am I like this? Are we fonder when we babble of our love——? My dear Herbert, you discourse of little else."

"Come, look here, old fellow," exclaimed Herbert, suddenly rising and lighting a cigar. "I may chip in about Nid when I get the chance, but you are usually haranguing to such an extent about the angelic qualities of Miss Hyde I never get a fair opportunity to tell you about Nid."

"Well, my boy," rejoined Phil, laughing, "you're not going to get it now. That cigar should about settle your appetite for dinner. I'm off to dress."

"Good heavens! it's not dressing time, is it?" said Morant, turning abruptly to the clock on the mantelpiece. "By Jove, you are right," and as he spoke he hurled his fresh-lit cigar into the fireplace. " Off we go, old man, white tie and soap and water time."

That he unduly discoursed about Miss Foxborough was a fact that Mr. Morant could not possibly be convinced of. To use a horribly commonplace simile, he was in the position of a man who snores; unconscious of misdemeanour, he is not to be persuaded that he has ever been guilty of it. But he looked forward immensely to being introduced to Bessie; although unaware that he gave rein to it, he did know that to talk about Nid to any one afforded him considerable pleasure, and, of course, from Phil's account was quite certain that Bessie was prepared to give ear to all he might say about her newly-found sister.

Herbert Morant was duly paraded at Dyke next day, and cordially received by both ladies.

"No, Philip," said Mrs. Fossdyke, in an undertone, as Bessie carried the new-comer off into the window to talk to; "there can be no mistake about it, your friend is not a good-looking man. No woman will ever think so."

"I never thought so myself," rejoined Soames; "but what has that to say to it? He is a real good fellow, and I don't think personal attractions, after all, have so very much weight in love affairs. There are so many of us, both sides, would never get married if we entirely depended on that. I know in old days how I have fought for a dance with the belle of the ball, won it at last, and never pleaded for another. I suppose women are something like us: prone to be smitten in the first place by an attractive exterior; but an angel who can only valse and simper speedily disenchants most men who have anything in them, and a plainer young lady, who can not only dance, but talk a bit, gives her handsome rivals the go by in the long run."

"You've won a wife, Philip, who can do both," replied Mrs. Fossdyke, quietly.

"I know it," he said, smiling; "but I am exceptionally gifted amongst the sons of men."

"I most sincerely trust and believe you are. Nothing can bring my poor, dear husband back to me, and for Bessie's sake and yours, I wish the whole of this investigation could be swamped. I feel no desire for vengeance, and I should like the whole tragedy to be forgotten by the public."

"Spoken like your own true-hearted self," rejoined Soames; and then he thought how marvellously her great grief had transformed Mrs. Fossdyke. The rather petulant, talkative woman he had originally known was transformed into a patient, considerate lady, taking a kindly interest in all those surrounding her.

"I am afraid, dear Mrs. Fossdyke, the authorities, in the interests of justice, will not quite allow that. That the police are quite at fault this minute I firmly believe. You know, and always shall, as much as I can learn. What they may think exactly I can't say, but so far I fancy they really are utterly nonplussed."

"And it would be best they were left so, for many reasons," replied Mrs. Fossdyke, "but this is beyond either your control or mine; but, Philip, should there be anything to know you will let me hear it, will you not?"

"I promise faithfully. Do you think I might venture to interrupt that couple in the window?"

"Certainly," rejoined the widow, smiling. "You've allowed him to do a very fair amount of raving about Miss Foxborough; you are quite entitled to do a bit of raving on your own account now."

Phil Soames moved across to the window, and said—

" Well, Bessie, do you begin to know your sister ? "

" Yes, and have in some sense seen her. No thanks to you though, sir, for it seems you quite forgot my instructions."

" Oh dear yes, about bringing her photograph. I plead guilty, and implore pardon ; but I see Herbert happily brought it."

" Yes," replied Morant, " I thought Miss Hyde——"

" Bessie," interrupted the girl, laughing. " How much oftener am I to tell you that ? I'm not going to be called Miss Hyde by my brother-in-law. We are fast becoming great friends, Phil. I know he's not good enough for Nid, though I've never seen her ; and he owns it."

" Of course I am not ; but then, Miss Bessie, I know nobody ever will be, so it is not worth her while to wait till he comes by, but she'll never find any one to love her more dearly."

" You love her better than Philip loves me," interposed Miss Hyde, not a little amused.

" Oh ! that's a puzzler," rejoined Herbert ; " there are weighing machines—things to calculate how hard you can blow, &c., but science as yet hasn't got as far as weighing your affections. If it had, Bessie, you would see that though Phil would bring the scale down, I should break the machine."

" What a lucky girl my sister is, to be loved like that ! Immeasurable adoration," continued Miss Hyde, demurely ; " we can demand no more."

" Now she's chaffing," exclaimed Morant, rising. " Come, Phil, we had better go."

" I shall keep this photograph, Herbert, as a pledge of your speedy return, though such a high-pressure adorer as yourself I've no doubt has at least a dozen."

" Yes, I can leave you that. I do happen to have another —and now good-bye."

Bessie shook her head at him laughingly, as she replied,

"You'll never see this again. Another! I suppose he s an album full, Philip. Isn't it so?"

"I think he's another or two," rejoined Soames, smiling. "Good-bye, dearest. I'm awful glad you two have made acquaintance."

"Good-bye, Herbert," said Bessie. "Like the dutiful helpmate I've promised to be, I reiterate my lord and master's observation."

"What do you think of her?" observed Philip, curtly, as the young men strode home to Baumborough.

"Bar Nid! she's just the nicest girl I ever met," rejoined Morant."

"Ah! I wanted you two to like each other," rejoined Soames, "and I'm pleased you do. Now, old man, I'll tell you what we'll do. After dinner we'll go over and smoke a cigar with the doctor. He won't say much to you, but he takes as much interest in our love affairs as we do."

"Nonsense! What an old trump! Smoke with him, of course we will, Phil. A delightful termination to a delightful day."

CHAPTER XXX.

SERGEANT USHER was getting quite angry with himself on account of his inability to put his puzzle together. He had so great an insight to the great Bunbury mystery that it made him quite irritable he could not quite explain it. A good deal that the public could not comprehend was quite plain to him; but who was the confederate? where was the writer of that note? It was not Foxborough's writing, nor was it even an attempt to simulate his hand; he had ascertained that from people whose testimony on the point was thoroughly reliable, yet it must be in handwriting perfectly familiar to the dead man or he would never have so promptly attended to its behests. It had become quite clear to Mr. Usher that, much as he desired to keep that note in the background, it was no longer possible; as long as that note reposed in the security of Mr. Usher's pocket-book it was quite evident there could be no opportunity for any one to recognize the writer. The sergeant was an enthusiast in his profession, and had a whimsical fancy for producing an important bit of testimony at the last moment—hence his desire to keep his treasure-trove of the Hopbine a secret. But it was clear to him now the enigma could not be solved otherwise than by the recognition of that handwriting. Nowhere, he thought, was that more likely to be achieved than by some of John Fossdyke's old friends at Baumborough, notably by Dr. Ingleby, and hither Mr. Usher determined to betake himself without loss of time; quite possible even Mr. Totterdell might be the man he wanted.

"And though," mused the sergeant, "he's a blethering old creature to get information out of, still I mustn't throw away a chance simply because a witness is a weariful, wandering old nuisance."

As he whirled down by the afternoon train Mr. Usher pondered a good deal upon where he should commence this fresh inquisition. He knew the Baumborough world by heart by this time. The local gossip had revealed to him a good deal of the ins and outs, the likes and dislikes, of social life at Baumborough, and he finally thought that perhaps he had better begin with Mr. Totterdell.

"Mrs. Fossdyke would be likely to tell her garrulous godfather as much as she knew of her husband's affairs before the quarrel," mused Mr. Usher, "and, hang it, a woman always knows a deal more than her husband gives her credit for. It's quite likely he might tumble to this handwriting at once. I'll begin with him, and try Dr. Ingleby afterwards, if it don't come off."

That Mr. Totterdell would be at home to Sergeant Usher there was very little doubt. The old gentleman was fidgety, and fuming over the non-elucidation of the great Bunbury mystery not a little. What were the police about, he wanted to know? When was he to have an opportunity of coming forward? For he still laboured under the delusion that as soon as his evidence had been taken properly and at length, there would be no difficulty whatever about the apprehension of the murderer.

"Well, sergeant," he exclaimed testily, as that officer entered the room, "what is it now? It is singular you don't seem to be able to move a step in this matter without my assistance, and yet I can't get you to listen to what I have to say."

" That's just it, Mr. Totterdell ; that's exactly what I keep telling 'em in the Yard," replied Mr. Usher. " ' I can't make head or tail of it myself,' says I ; ' there's none of you here can do any better. If there's one man in England who can throw a light upon the truth it's Mr. Totterdell. Just you let me go and have another palaver with him. If this thing's to be worked out, it's he and I have got to do it.' ' Do as you please,' says they; and here I am. With your permission, sir, I'll take a chair to begin with. Nobody knows better than you do that one can't exchange views upon a matter of such paramount importance in a hurry."

" Certainly not, Mr. Usher ; certainly not," replied the old gentleman, with the utmost complacency. " Sit down, by all means ; and now what have you got to tell me ? "

" Well, sir," replied the sergeant, smoothing his hat with his handkerchief, " the boot happens to be on the other leg. I was rather in hopes you had something to tell me. A gentleman like you on the spot, and gifted with your keen perception in these matters, I thought might have picked up something."

" And so I have," chuckled Mr. Totterdell. " It's a queer thing—a very queer thing ; and I got at it by accident. It don't seem much to bear on the case, so we'll talk over what you've been doing first."

"Now what on earth," thought Mr. Usher, " has this blessed old image discovered ? Whether it's any use or not, he of course knows no more than the man in the moon, and the attempt to get it out of him directly I know will be a tedious, if not a hopeless, business. I had better come the confidential dodge, and give him a glimpse of this letter at once, and then, likely enough, he'll boil over."

" Mr. Totterdell, I depend on you not to disclose to a soul what I'm going to confide to you," replied Mr. Usher, in a mysterious whisper ; " but the fact is, I've got hold of a scrap of writing of this James Foxborough, the man you saw at the theatre, and I want to know if you can recognize it as one of the late Mr. Fossdyke's habitual correspondents. You doubtless knew most of their handwriting by sight—so intimate as you naturally were with the family ? "

" Of course," replied Mr. Totterdell mendaciously, for he had no knowledge whatever of Fossdyke's business relations; but he would have committed himself to a very much bigger lie at any time sooner than miss an opportunity of gratifying his insatiable thirst for gossip.

" Well," said the sergeant, producing the note, still so carefully folded that there was little more than the signature to be seen, " do you know that handwriting ? for that is the writing of the man who took John Fossdyke's life."

" God bless me ! " exclaimed Mr. Totterdell, as he put on his spectacles. " You're sure of this, Mr. Usher ? "

" As sure as if I had seen him commit the murder. Do you know the hand ? "

Mr. Totterdell stared at it for some minutes, and then said : " No, I never saw it before."

" Ah well, whenever I can catch hold of anybody who can recognize that writing, I'll clear up the Bunbury murder in less than no time ; and now, Mr. Totterdell, what have you to tell me ? "

" Well, it mayn't be much," said the old gentleman; " but it's odd, odd, you see, sergeant—deuced odd. I'm sure you'll agree with me when you hear it, eh ? "

" I've got to hear it first," retorted Mr. Usher shortly.

" Of course, quite so, and I'm telling you as fast as I can ; you're like that old fool on the inquest who was always interrupting my evidence," said Mr. Totterdell, angrily.

Mr. Usher, exercising wise discretion, made no reply.

" Well, I have made a curious discovery. You must know when the Baumborough Theatre was first mooted there was, of course, a great question how the six thousand or so estimated for its erection were to be raised. Poor Fossdyke proposed an extra rate, and to get at the money gradually in that wise ; but I, who had just come on the

Municipal Council, having ascertained that we had something like that sum out at mortgage, suggested its being called in and used for the purpose instead of levying the fresh rate."

"Ah!" exclaimed Mr. Usher, involuntarily.

"Eh! what? something strikes you?" said Mr. Totterdell, peering over his spectacles into the detective's face.

"Quite right," responded Mr. Usher. "You always are, sir. I was thinking what a thing it was for Baumborough when they got you on the Town Council."

"They might have done worse, Usher," replied Mr. Totterdell, blandly, and utterly blind to the sergeant's flagrant adulation. "Well, it's a rum thing, but though the money was all right enough, though John Fossdyke accounted for it all to a copper, yet there never was such a mortgage effected."

"Ah!" once more exclaimed Mr. Usher, softly, "and what interpretation, Mr. Totterdell, do you put upon that?"

"None, Mr. Usher, none; that is a thing for a judge and jury to determine, like many other facts I can testify to when I get an opportunity."

"Well, Mr. Totterdell, I'll not take up your valuable time any more. You've the keystone of the case, whenever we can really get it complete; but it's growing up, sir, it's growing up. I see my way a little bit further every day."

"Capital," responded the old gentleman; "and just between ourselves—quite between ourselves, you know—where do you suppose the scoundrel Foxborough is? Have you any clue?"

"Well, yes, I have," said Mr. Usher, rising; "but to a gentleman of your astuteness and experience I needn't say mum's the word. You understand, mum's the word," and so saying the sergeant bade Mr. Totterdell good-night.

"Quite right, Mr. Usher, you can trust me to keep things quiet. There's nobody knows how to keep a quiet tongue better than me. Mum's the word! ha, ha! Good-night!"

" Yes, you are right for once, it is," quoth the sergeant.
" You'll tell nobody this time, because you've nothing to
tell; but the puzzle's piecing out beautifully. If anybody can
identify this handwriting I'll tell 'em the whole story pretty
near of the Bunbury mystery. Half-past nine. Yes, not a
bit too late to call upon Dr. Ingleby. I don't suppose he
will know this handwriting, but it's worth trying. At all
events this run to Baumborough has been good business.
I've got an important little bit of evidence out of the Totterdell creature which just clinches the thing."

Thus ruminating Mr. Usher arrived at the doctor's door,
and, after his wont, followed very close on the heels of the
servant who announced him.

He found the doctor tranquilly enjoying a cigar, and
listening to the gay castle-building of Herbert Morant and
Phil Soames. The former especially had one of those con-
stitutionally sanguine temperaments that run up palaces on
the slightest possible foundations. Their palaces, it is true,
come down about their ears like the card houses of child-
hood, but no whit dismayed, they re-erect them with exactly
the same happy carelessness that characterized their nursery
days. Dr. Ingleby enjoyed all this immensely, to the quiet,
sober, matrimonial dreams of Phil Soames, or the resplen-
dent visions of Herbert Morant, he listened with the keenest
interest. He liked both the young men, and it was good to
listen to their healthy love stories, to contrast cool, steady
Phil's strong, steadfast devotion with excitable Herbert's
passionate adoration. They loved, these two, quite as
earnestly as they were capable of; but neither men nor
women experience the passion in quite the same fashion.

" Well, sergeant," exclaimed Dr. Ingleby. " Sit down
first, say what it is to be next, wine or alcohol, and then tell
me what you want. You I know are much too busy a man
to pay calls of ceremony. It's not your health, is it ? "

" No, doctor," rejoined the sergeant, laughingly. " It's
not my health, and I'll call it port if you'll allow me. It's

just a little matter of business. I've got this Bunbury business mapped out to a T but for one trifling bit of evidence, and I thought I'd just consult you and Mr. Soames about that. Here's my respects," said the sergeant, as he topped off the bumper of port the doctor had poured out for him, " and very good tipple it is."

" Well, I'm very glad you are getting at the bottom of the mystery," rejoined Dr. Ingleby, " but it's a question whether these two gentlemen or Mrs. Fossdyke will appreciate it. I fancy they would all rather it died out and was forgotten."

"Now, listen to me, gentlemen. It can't be allowed to die out and be forgotten; it would be an everlasting reproach to ' the Yard' if it was. I don't quite know that you'll any of you like the story when we come to it, and come to it we shall, but if it's relief to your mind to know James Foxborough didn't kill Mr. Fossdyke, either by accident or design, you may take my word, he had nothing to say to it."

The trio started at the speaker in blank amazement.

" No, gentlemen," continued the sergeant, " I don't turn my cat out of the bag until I'm quite certain I can catch her again. What have I come here for ? As the doctor says, if it ain't my constitution gone wrong, what is it ? Well, it is this, both you and Mr. Soames, doctor, must have known something about Mr. Fossdyke's friends and correspondents."

"His friends, yes," rejoined the doctor, " his correspondents, no. He was an extremely reticent man about his business transactions, and intimate as I was with him I knew nothing of them."

" And you, Mr. Soames ? " asked the detective.

"Still less, if that be possible. He was scarce likely to confide in a young man like me what he concealed from an old friend like Dr. Ingleby."

" Unlucky, but I'm afraid then, gentlemen, you can't

help me ; however, as I have come to see Dr. Ingleby for a specific purpose, I'm going to play the cards out."

Mr. Usher dived into his breast-pocket for a moment, and then from the depths of a formidable pocket-book produced the famous letter, folded still so that little but the signature was decipherable. "Do you know that handwriting, sir?" he asked, as he handed it to Dr. Ingleby.

"Not in the least," replied the doctor, after a cool and steady investigation.

"And you, Mr. Soames?" inquired the sergeant, as he pushed the piece of paper across.

Phil stared at it for some minutes, and then replied as he returned it, "No ; to the best of my belief I never saw that handwriting before."

"It's hard, very hard," remarked the sergeant ; "to know who wrote those few lines is to put the prettiest and most interesting case complete before the public I ever took charge of ; and yet, dash me, I'm beat on that point, though there must be hundreds of people who could testify to it. D——d if I don't have it photographed and inserted as an advertisement in all the dailies."

"May I look at it, Mr. Usher?" inquired Morant.

"Oh, Lord, yes. I meant to keep it dark, but anybody's welcome to see it now."

Herbert scanned as much as he was allowed to see of the note for a few minutes, and then as he threw it back across the table to the detective, said quietly, "I am pretty certain I know who wrote that. It was——"

"Hush, sir! for God's sake, hush!" cried Sergeant Usher, springing to his feet. "I'm going to ask you for forty-eight hours to let nobody but myself know the name. If he's in England I shall be able to lay my hand upon him by that, but leakage, gentlemen, is fatal in these inquiries. If you don't know you can't let anything out. Isn't it so? You'll forgive me, Dr. Ingleby, and you, too, Mr. Soames, when I once more say—see me to the door, please, Mr. Morant ; tell me the name, and tell nobody else for two days."

"I think you may do what the sergeant asks you," said Dr. Ingleby; "Phil's curiosity and mine can last out forty-eight hours. Good-night, Mr. Usher; I know you want to be off now. See him to the door, Morant, and breathe your secret on the threshold."

"That's it, sir—that's it; good-night, gentlemen. Come, Mr. Morant."

With which words, Herbert and the detective disappeared.

21

CHAPTER XXXI.

MR. CUDEMORE'S LOVE-MAKING.

DOGGED, persistent, and defiant as Mr. Cudemore is in his resolve to marry Nid Foxborough, still he is not altogether quite satisfied with the way his cards are playing. To begin upon, he had reckoned when Foxborough's disappearance threw the Syringa, so to speak, in the hollow of his hand, that Mrs. Foxborough would be at his feet; that her anxiety to retain the lesseeship of the music hall would render her perfectly subservient to his wishes, and that Nid's hand was to be the price of his assistance he had made up his mind. But Mrs. Foxborough seemed very indifferent as to whether she kept the Syringa or not, whilst as for Nid, she was difficult to catch sight of; still when the pressure really came, when it was actually brought home to her that unless she begged help from him, Cudemore, her anxiety to retain the management of the music hall might be unavailing, he fancied Mrs. Foxborough would be only too glad to come to terms. Another thing, too, that somewhat disturbed Mr. Cudemore's equanimity was the discovery of Timothy on the second floor. What the deuce was the boy doing up there? He might say he was only closing the dressing-room door, but the money-lender was quite convinced in his own mind that he really came out of the room. The boy had never come up to that floor before to seek him, what made him do it this time? His people always knew pretty well whether he was in or out; and it was in the sitting-room on the first floor that they looked for him, if in doubt. He could never recall to mind either of his clerks, senior or junior, seeking him on the floor above. There was no one less likely to stand his affairs being pried into than Mr. Cudemore, and that gentleman speedily made up his mind that Timothy's services might be advantageously dispensed with. He accordingly sent for that acute young gentleman into his private business-room and blandly remarked—

"You are a very intelligent and excellent boy, Timothy, but you might remember I expect my people to keep close to their own business and not trouble themselves about anything further. I engaged you, remember, as second clerk at the liberal salary of fifteen shillings a week, and your duties were confined to the reception of visitors in the outer office, and ascertaining, if I was upstairs, whether I wished to see them or not."

"Well, sir, how was I to know whether you was in or not if I didn't come to see?"

"Just so, Timothy, but you weren't required to look under the bed or into the bath for me, or to overhaul my boots or brush my clothes, Timothy. It was considerate in the extreme taking upon yourself the duties of a valet as well as a clerk, but you see I prefer my people to confine themselves to what I am paying them for, and therefore, my young friend, here are your week's wages, and henceforth I will dispense with your valuable services."

"I suppose I needn't come no more, then, after to-night?" rejoined the boy, doggedly.

"Just so, that's it. I shall have no objection to give you a recommendation, and vouch that you are willing and intelligent; a little too willing, in fact, anxious apparently to do everything. Next time, my boy, whatever it may be, take my advice and stick closely to your own business."

Timothy said never a word, but picked up his money, and with a quiet bow to his employer returned to the outer office, over which he still held sway.

Now, this again somewhat puzzled Mr. Cudemore. He expected the boy to plead vigorously against dismissal, to volunteer further explanation of his conduct, and Timothy had done nothing of the kind, but acquiesced with dogged resignation in his sentence. It was not very likely that anything he could say would have made the slightest difference to Mr. Cudemore, but then that gentleman did expect him to say it, and to one of his suspicious turn of mind this afforded grave food for reflection. Mr. Cudemore engaged in a good many transactions that, though not illegal exactly, were of the kind denominated shady. He was not wont to trust his clerks very much about anything, more especially was he unlikely to place confidence in a boy like Timothy; he certainly could call to mind nothing of the slightest consequence of which the boy had knowledge, and yet he felt uneasy at Timothy's easy acquiescence in his dismissal. Another curious circumstance, too, was that the mysterious gentleman who declined to leave his name had never called again.

Musing somewhat irritably over all these things, Mr. Cudemore seized his hat and determined to call at Tapton Cottage.

He was so peremptory in his demand to see Mrs. Foxborough on a matter of business, that the girl who opened the door succumbed at once and ushered him into the drawing-room before Nid, who was coiled up in a big arm-chair in front of the fire immersed in a novel, had any notice to escape.

"Miss Foxborough," exclaimed Cudemore, "this is indeed an unexpected pleasure," as he advanced to take a hand which was not extended to him.

Nid had sprung to her feet and greeted him with the most formal reverence; and how stately the little lady could

be when she stood upon her dignity, must have been seen
to be believed. Cudemore was a bold reckless *roué*, and
wild about this girl, and both Nid and her mother knew
it, as only women do know these things. A chit not out
of the schoolroom knows intuitively when a man is at her
feet. But to do Nid justice no young lady was ever less
proud of a conquest than she, whilst we already know Mrs.
Foxborough's opinion on the subject.

"Let mamma know at once, Ellen, that Mr. Cudemore
is here," said Nid, imperiously.

"Yes, Miss," rejoined the parlour-maid, and she knew
at once from her young mistress's authoritative tones that
she had done wrong to admit the visitor.

"Pray tell Mrs. Foxborough that it is nothing pressing,
and that my time is hers," exclaimed Cudemore, boldly, as
Ellen turned to leave the room.

Very angry was Nid at the man's manner, but still he
had got into the house and must be treated with some sort
of courtesy. So she motioned him to a chair.

"If you knew, Miss Foxborough, how I have longed for
this opportunity."

"Mamma, I'm sure, won't keep you waiting long," replied
Nid, with wilful misapprehension, albeit a little defiantly.

"It is you I want to speak to more than your mother," he
replied. "Young women are not blind, and there is no need
for me to tell you how passionately I love you."

"You couldn't expect me to listen to such language at this
time under any circumstances," rejoined Nid, nervously.
"You seem to forget, sir, the affliction that overshadows us,
the gloom that hangs over the house."

"I speak, Nydia, because first there is further misfortune
threatening you. Your mother will lose the Syringa unless
she listens to my counsel."

"Meaning," cried Nid, springing to her feet, with her
cheeks aflame and her eyes ablaze, "that my miserable self
is the price you propose for such assistance."

" You're not in the least miserable ; on the contrary, you're devilish pretty," he replied, insolently, " and never looked handsomer than you do this minute."

" I'll not stay here to be insulted," exclaimed Nid. " Were my father alive you would never have dared make that speech to me ; as it is you may chance to rue it bitterly."

" I've not heard of your father's death," replied Cudemore, coarsely, as he placed himself between her and the door. " But if you are threatening me with the vengeance of the red-haired admirer, I tell you I am not much alarmed."

" He's a man, sir," cried Nid, furiously, " which you are not ! He's a gentleman, sir, which you are not ; and were he in the room you would be on your back on the floor this minute ! "

" Bah ! " replied Cudemore, contemptuously. " Listen to me, Nydia. Herbert Morant is a broken man. He has no money ; he never will have ; there are some men who have no faculty for making it : he is one. Marry me, and you shall have carriages, diamonds, and all that woman's soul rejoices in."

" Some women, perhaps," rejoined Nid, with a contempt bitter as his own. " Go into the market, Mr. Cudemore, and buy for your seraglio if you will, but never insult me again with what you are pleased to term your love. You don't even know the meaning of the word."

" I understand it in my own manner," laughed the money-lender, " and a more tempting little morsel was never put before an epicure than you. Don't be ridiculous, child. Do you think your sentimental idealism of that passion will long survive darning socks and cooking mutton-chops for that red-headed calf in a second floor at Pimlico ? I offer you again a good house, a French cook, and your milliner's bills shall be paid and not looked at. What is it you see in him to out-balance all this ? "

Nid drew herself up to the full extent of her small stature, and then said, " He is simply a gentleman, sir, which you neither are nor ever will be. He loves a woman and doesn't propose to buy her. I've never been so insulted in my life. Let me pass."

"Not without a kiss, my beauty," cried the money-lender, his brutal nature stung to madness by her last speech; and as he spoke he caught the girl in his arms and impressed three or four passionate kisses on her cheeks.

"You brute, you beast!" cried Nid, more vehement than lady-like in her language. "Help, mother! where are you?" As she spoke the door opened, and Mrs. Foxborough entered.

"How dare you, Mr. Cudemore!" she cried, all aflame at the sight of Nid struggling in his embrace. "You coward, to dare lay a hand on my child!"

"I apologize," replied the money-lender, as he released the girl; "my passion, I own, overcame conventionalities. I apologize to you; I apologize to Miss Foxborough, though her attractions are enough to turn any man's head. Still, remember in extenuation, I have offered her marriage, and a superb establishment."

"Which have been indignantly rejected," cried Nid, impetuously through her tears. "I would sooner earn my living by sweeping floors than be his wife."

"Listen, little lady. I've tried to win you by fair promises, such as men most dazzle women's eyes with. Now hear the other side of the question. Marry me, or out your mother goes of the Syringa the day the foreclosure of the mortgage can be enforced."

"And out she will go," rejoined Mrs. Foxborough, fiercely, "and reck little about it. In the meantime I'll trouble you to leave this house, and never set foot in it, nor lay hand on its knocker again."

"Good," returned the money-lender, in a low voice that trembled with passion. "You are right, Mrs. Foxborough, to turn from your door the one man who might perchance clear your husband's character. You hold it in great esteem now;

when you are a little more enlightened, perhaps you may change your opinion."

"My poor husband, I have no doubt, I shall never see more," replied Mrs. Foxborough, proudly; "and you can hardly expect his wife and daughter to listen calmly to insults to his memory. You have already, by your brutal insolence, frightened this child to death," continued Mrs. Foxborough, clasping the excited and beautiful girl closer in her embrace. "Leave the house this instant, or I shall call in the assistance of the police; and, mark me, I neither desire nor will continue to manage the Syringa while it involves meeting you in any way."

"I will spare your invoking the assistance of the police," replied Cudemore, brutally; "they have had rather more than their fair share of surveillance of this house lately. You will regret your rude rejection of my offer before many weeks are over, believe me."

Mrs. Foxborough's sole reply was a contemptuous motion to the door, and, with an ironical bow, Mr. Cudemore took his departure.

"I couldn't have believed a man of education could be such an utter brute," sobbed Nid, who, plucky as she had been through the tempest, had now broken down completely. Again she passed her handkerchief across her face, and at last murmured, "Pah! mother darling, I must go and wash it; the stain of his filthy kisses is on my cheek still, and every one an insult, though, thank God, not treachery to Herbert."

"Go and lie down a bit, pet. You are a little upset, and no wonder, at such a trying scene. One word more, darling. I wouldn't say anything about it when I wrote to Herbert if I were you. It would only lead to unpleasantness for him, which I'm sure you don't want, and I'm quite able to take care you shall never be so insulted again. Trust your mother, sweet, and call in Herbert when she fails you."

"As if I didn't always, and as if she ever did fail me,"

cried Nid, impetuously; and having given Mrs. Foxborough a hug, the girl ran off to her own room.

"Confound it," muttered Mr. Cudemore. "I've made a pretty mess of things. I always do lose my head about a woman; that child looked so pretty to-day, and riled me so awfully, I couldn't resist taking the sauciness out of her. Besides, who could guess the little fool would make such a fuss about a kiss? They don't usually, so far as my experience goes."

Mr. Cudemore's experience had been gathered in a somewhat meretricious school, where the prompt, audacious, and especially the wealthy lover, was highly appreciated.

CHAPTER XXXII.

" BREAST-HIGH SCENT."

MEN of Sergeant Usher's profession, like all men engaged in the hard practical business of life, are as speedy in resolve as quick in execution. The detective conned the information he had just acquired on his way to his hotel, where he immediately paid his bill, then threw himself and his bag into the omnibus which, as he knew without looking at the time-table, caught the last train to town. There are many problems solved on the railway in these days; it is bound to be so. Look at the many hours business and professional men pass on it, and that they should think out intricate problems in the easy embrace of a first-class carriage is but natural.

"It's a beautiful case," mused Mr. Usher. "I don't know that I ever had the solving of a prettier puzzle. How beautiful it begins to piece out! I could almost tell the public the whole story now, but I've a few minor links to collect before the chain of evidence is complete. I don't think the public will regard the police as duffers much longer when they've heard my exposition of the Banbury mystery."

"Now, let me see," continued Mr. Usher, "the first person I've got to see is Miss Lightcomb, and the first thing I want is a copy of the *Era* to ascertain where she may be; that

I'll buy at Charing Cross; just a few words at the Yard to tell them what to do, and to-morrow morning I'm off to have a quarter of an hour's talk with Miss L." On arrival at the terminus Mr. Usher, having possessed himself of the principal theatrical journal, took a cab and drove home to his lodgings in Spring Gardens. A few minutes' study of the *Era* showed him Miss Lightcomb was at present enacting leading lady at the Theatre Royal, Plymouth.

"It's a nuisance," muttered the sergeant, "but I am used to it; important witnesses always do get into remote corners when specially wanted; here's this girl plays at Margate, when I can make no particular use of her, and now I want to see her special, of course, she's got to the other end of the kingdom. Well, there's nothing for it but just to give 'em instructions over the way (and here Mr. Usher jerked his head in the direction of Scotland Yard), and be off to Plymouth by the first train in the morning."

Arrived there, the sergeant naturally proceeded to the theatre and inquired for Miss Lightcomb. On explaining who he was he was furnished with her address, and at once departed in quest of the lady. But here he was once more disappointed; the actress had gone to a picnic party, and would only return in time to fulfil her duties at the theatre. Musing sadly over the absurdity of a witness in a great murder case condescending to the frivolity of picnics, and reflecting that after all Miss Lightcomb had very little conception that she could give any evidence whatever concerning the Bunbury mystery, Mr. Usher remembered that it was time to sustain nature, and went off in search of something to eat. Like an Indian on the war trail, the sergeant could do without either food or sleep if exigencies required it, but as an old campaigner he understood the husbanding of his resources, and neglected taking in neither when a lull in affairs permitted. He meant returning to town by the night mail if he could, but he had come down to have ten minutes' talk with Miss Lightcomb, and, of course, was not going back till he had achieved that. But the actress only arrived at the theatre just in time to dress for her *rôle*, which, as it happened, was a heavy one, and sent word upon receiving Mr. Usher's card that it was impossible she could see him till after the performance, so the sergeant was fain to sit and pass critical judgment on Miss Lightcomb's histrionic powers in the " Bride of the Caucasus." But the curtain fell at last, and then Mr. Usher made his way rapidly behind the scenes.

"I cannot say I am glad to see you," said the actress, as the sergeant entered her dressing-room. "You frighten me, and I really know nothing of this Bunbury mystery"

"Now, don't you be alarmed, Miss Lightcomb. Nobody for one moment supposes you do, or that there is any little bit of information you would not willingly put at our disposal if you only fancied it bore the least upon the case."

"I have told you I cannot recollect all who spoke to me that night, there were so many gentlemen complimented me on my acting," rejoined Miss Lightcomb, wearily.

The girl was tired out with her day's pleasure, and her night's acting, and was anxious to get her supper and go to bed, and had no fancy for being cross-examined by Mr. Usher.

"Don't you get fidgety, Miss Lightcomb," replied the sergeant, taking in the state of things at a glance. "I sha'n't detain you three minutes. Do you know the original of this photograph?" and as he spoke he produced the *carte* of John Fossdyke.

"No," rejoined the actress after glancing at it.

"I didn't suppose you would," rejoined Mr. Usher. "Now, do you know Mr. Cudemore?"

"Certainly, of course. Why?"

"Didn't you speak to him behind the scenes on the opening night of the Baumborough Theatre?"

"Yes, now you mention it, I recollect I did," replied

Miss Lightcomb, after a minute or two's reflection. " I remember being so surprised at seeing him there."

"I need not detain you another moment, Miss Lightcomb, that is the one fact I wanted from you. If I don't tell you what it means the daily papers will in three days' time. If you could only have recollected that when I called upon you at Margate."

" I'm sure I'm very sorry, Mr. Usher, but really his name never occurred to me."

"I know it. Of course it is difficult seeing so many new faces, as you must do, to recollect who you may speak to on any particular night, and unluckily I wasn't in a position then to assist your memory."

"But surely I sha'n't be called upon to appear in court ? " asked the actress, somewhat dolorously.

"I am afraid," replied the sergeant, "you will, but you won't be detained five minutes in the box, and you must comfort yourself that disagreeable as it is for a lady it will bring your name prominently before the public, and prove a valuable professional advertisement. If you have only a friend or two on the press it may do you a deal of good in the long run ; and now I'll wish you good-night, with many apologies for giving you so much trouble."

Very polite and considerate was Sergeant Usher, and Miss Lightcomb's horror at the idea of being compelled to appear in the witness-box was considerably mollified at the idea of what a great gratuitous advertisement the being mixed up in such a *cause célèbre* would be for her. More-over, she had so little to do with the whole thing, and was so utterly innocent in the matter that she felt pretty safe from awkward questions. Mr. Cudemore had never been more to her than an ordinary acquaintance.

The ubiquitous Usher was off to town by the morning train, and made, as usual, a first visit to head-quarters, there to learn that, according to his instructions, Mr. Cudemore had never been lost sight of, and could be laid hands upon at any moment; that he had apparently no intention of absconding, but that he was watched day and night, and would be arrested at once should he show a sign of doing so.

"No, let him alone another day or two. It's a lovely case, and upon my soul, when I've got it complete, I must put the bracelets on him myself," replied the sergeant, "but never let him out of sight, mind."

It's risky, Usher," said one of his colleagues. "A cunning fox like this, with command of money, may slip you any moment, watch him close as you like. You know best what reason you have now for leaving him at large, but, mind, once lost sight of, he may take a deal of catching."

"Right you are, Dickinson," replied Mr. Usher, rubbing his hands softly; "but an artist like yourself would do as I do. It's one of the most perfect riddles ever I solved, and I have only two more inquiries to make. One in London, and another in Baumborough. Superfluous, it might be urged, and quite to be gone into after you had jugged your bird, but I do like to get my case quite complete before I pounce."

"I know it, old man," replied Dickinson, laughing, "only don't wait to pounce till there's nothing to pounce upon. Remember a hawk may hover too long."

"Never fear, never fear," rejoined the sergeant, "this one won't slip us, I'll go bail," and with this observation Mr. Usher betook himself to the Wellington Restaurant, Spring Gardens, to dine.

The sergeant greatly affected this place. It was a quiet, modest little dining-room, close to his own lodgings, frequented by sedate, steady-going people who lived in the immediate vicinity. Bank clerks, lawyers' clerks, &c., but nobody who affected swelldom ever appeared across its threshold any more than did the gentish or raffish element of London life. It was too slow for these latter, a *terra incognita* to the former. That a detective officer should be a mere shade, or impersonality, or abstract fact is no doubt true; but still they must be known to some few people, and at the Wellington the famous Sergeant Usher was both known and respected.

"Something to eat, quick, William," he observed to the waiter, as he made his way to a rather favourite corner table.

"Pea soup, sir; a nice slice of cod, and a beef steak would perhaps about meet the case, Mr. Usher," returned William, who was quite a privileged functionary with the *habitués*.

"That's about it," rejoined the sergeant, "with a pint of stout and a little hot grog to follow."

"Very good, sir, I'll give 'em the order at once," and the waiter bustled away. He soon returned, and whisking about the table after the fashion waiters have when business is slack, of putting a knife straight there, shifting a cruet-stand from one side the table to the other here, and then taking a glass into custody on suspicion of not being quite clean, and putting it through a severe course of polishing with the napkin under their arm, combined with a rearrangement of the three or four sticks of property celery always on hand in such places in the winter season.

At last he bustled out and returned with the stout and the soup.

"There's been a boy hanging about here, Mr. Usher, very anxious to see you all yesterday and to-day. Don't know what he is exactly, but he's in one of these offices up the way. He's a plate of cold meat here at lunch time now and again, and is wolfish about the vegetables, but he ain't a bad sort for his time of life. Never forgets his penny, sir, to me, and pennies ain't plentiful with him, neither, I'd bet."

"Then why do you take it from him?" asked the sergeant, drily.

"Now, Mr. Usher, what is the use of talking like that? Did you ever know of a waiter who refused his fees? No, sir; and what's more," continued William, dropping his tones to a mysterious whisper, "if any one of us did, it's my impression he'd quickly become a case for your professional investigation."

" Go and get the fish ! " retorted the sergeant, grimly.

" Certainly, sir, certainly," and William vanished, only to return speedily with a handsome slice of boiled cod.

" But about this boy, sir. I really have to pretend not to see him, he's that wolfish about the greens, and—God bless my soul, sir, here he comes."

As he spoke, Tim entered the room, and at once seeing the sergeant in the almost empty room, for the detective was dining at a rather nondescript hour, walked straight to his table."

" Mr. Usher, sir, isn't it ? " inquired Tim.

" Yes, my lad," replied the sergeant, quietly.

" And I see by the papers you are in charge of the great Bunbury murder."

" Just so."

" Well, there's a deal of money for any one who'll give information concerning it."

" Now, look here, my boy, don't you fall into any mistake of that sort. There's £200 for anybody who can give information that may lead to the apprehension of James Foxborough. Offer withdrawn to-night, because I know where to find him."

" Then if I'd a bit of valuable information to give I should get nothing for it ? " replied Tim, in a disappointed voice.

" No, I don't say that, you would get something, but certainly not £200 nor anything like it. William, you had better go and look after the steak, and you needn't hurry with it for the next five minutes," added the sergeant, significantly.

" Now, my lad, look here, I know all about you. You're Cudemore's clerk, that's what you are."

For a minute Timothy stared in simple awe of the omniscient detective, whose knowledge in this case was by no means singular ; then he replied, " I was, but he's discharged me."

" Ha, what for ? "

" I don't know, exactly, it may be he thought I knew too much. He caught me coming out of his bedroom, where I admit, Mr. Usher, I'd no business. He said he had hired me as a clerk, and not as a valet, and gave me the sack there and then."

" He was about right," rejoined the sergeant ; " you're one of those young gentlemen who are just a shade too sharp to live."

"No ; but, Mr. Usher, if I could tell you where Mr. Cudemore was on the day of the Bunbury murder, what would you give me for that ? "

" Nothing ; what's it got to do with the case ? "

" I don't know, but it might have."

" Precisely, and so might your dismissal ; but it don't strike me as bearing much upon it."

" Then I suppose it's no use saying anything more ? " rejoined Tim, doggedly.

" You know best about that. You know best what put it into your head that Mr. Cudemore's journey to Bunbury had anything to do with the Hopbine murder."

" You know that ? " exclaimed Tim, and his open mouth and utter bewilderment really tickled the detective's vanity more than anything he had encountered for some time.

" Of course I do, and everything else about it. Look here, my lad, I can do perfectly well without you, but if you really have any evidence to give, now's your time, and you must leave it to me to appraise. It may be worth a fiver, but I doubt it. Remember I can find you any time, and make you speak now."

Tim was utterly crushed. He recognized that the great detective carried too many guns for him, and it was quite meekly he replied, " Well, sir, all I know is this, there's a Bunbury railway label on Mr. Cudemore's portmanteau, and that he returned from the country the morning the

22

murder was discovered, and has never been out of town since."

"That'll do, my lad. You'll make a pound or two out of that; leave your address here, and now you can go, I'm tired. Come along with that steak, William, and bring me six of Irish hot, please."

Timothy slowly left the place with a respect for Sergeant Usher that bordered on grovelling.

CHAPTER XXXIII.

SERGEANT USHER over the Bunbury mystery is now a sight for the Gods, as the old books say. One can understand it; when we have achieved the solution of any great mental problem there is always an inclination, speaking figuratively, to stand upon our head or throw our hat into the air; notable especially in the solving of that great annual spring riddle on Epsom Downs, when those who have successfully elucidated the great conundrum are wont to express their satisfaction in fantastic fashion.

"It's a lovely puzzle," chuckled Sergeant Usher, as he smoked his pipe in his own lodgings in Spring Gardens, "and it's all put together now with the exception of the last few bits, and they are obvious."

"First thing is to see if Sturton knows this handwriting," and here Mr. Usher tapped his breast-pocket in which he kept the precious note and the photograph of the late John Fossdyke, "according to my reckoning he will."

"Secondly, to see if that wearisome old creature, Totterdell, recognizes this as the photograph of the man who sat next him at the opening of the Baumborough Theatre, which, of course, he won't."

"Lastly, if I can, to get hold of a photograph of Mr. Cudemore, and then show Totterdell that, and if it don't give him fits well I'm mistaken some. Now, how the deuce am I to get about this last business? Yes, I think my precocious young friend, with his still more precocious views regarding the £200 reward, might really earn a £10 note over this little bit of business. In the meantime," said Mr. Usher, still chuckling with satisfaction at his piecing of the puzzle, "a man of fashion like me really ought to get a new rig out from Sturton. None of your reach-me-down ready-money tailors for a man of my position. Dukes and detectives should be waited on by first-rate artists, and, yes, by first-rate *tickists*; Sturton taking my order for a frock-coat and all to match, and doing my little ninety days' bill for a hundred. O Lord," said Mr. Usher, bursting into a fit of laughter; "just to think of myself as a real Bond Street lounger. It's a rum 'un, it is."

Sergeant Usher had put the obtaining Mr. Cudemore's photograph last in his cogitations because it was by far the least important of the three last bricks in his arch of evidence. Miss Lightcomb, Mr. Totterdell, the people at the Hopbine, and the label on the portmanteau, all sufficed really to identify the money-lender if he was the man, as the sergeant had now no manner of doubt he was; but, as was before said, Mr. Usher was an artist, and liked to hand his cases over to the Solicitors of the Treasury without a flaw in them.

The first thing the sergeant did was to send for Timothy Whipple, that very junior, and now dismissed, clerk.

Gentlemen of Mr. Cudemore's vocation usually find one confidential clerk quite enough for their actual requirements, although a junior or two of the Whipple calibre are useful. Timothy, although he had been sternly disabused of that Golconda-like dream of grasping the £200 reward, still cherished hopes that he might realize something handsome by his information, and responded to Mr. Usher's summons with alacrity. It would have been utterly wanting in accordance with the sergeant's practice to ask any one to call upon him at his own lodgings, so the Wellington Restaurant was the trysting-place he selected. There he found Timothy duly awaiting his arrival over a pint of ale and some bread and cheese.

"Now, my lad," said Mr. Usher, "you really, considering your age, have some little gumption. That portmanteau business is creditable; not much importance to us, but creditable. Now it's just possible you might earn an honest ten-pun note over this business. It might run. to that, although we can easy do without you. But remember this time you're working to orders, and when people don't act strictly to my orders, they'd best lead lives of virtue and circumspection. Now, I shouldn't think, my young friend, that'll be quite your future. If you don't turn gamekeeper you'll become poacher; if you don't join us you'll drift into the ranks of the criminal classes."

"I'm sure, Mr. Usher, I'll do anything you tell me," replied Timothy, meekly.

"Well, look here, my lad. Mr. Cudemore's given you the sack, but still for all that you might be able to get what I want, and that is Mr. Cudemore's photograph. Do you think you can?"

"I can't be sure, sir. He's a book of 'em in his sitting-room, and I'm pretty sure there's one of himself in that; but you know, Mr. Usher, I can't make very sure of getting into that room now."

"There's no making sure of anything much in this world," rejoined the sergeant, sententiously, "but you'll make sure of a tenner if you'll manage that, and to a young gentleman of your sort, who's out of employment, and don't permit his imagination to run riot, that should represent profitable business."

Tim simply thanked the omniscient one, promised to do his best, and withdrew.

"It ain't of much account," muttered the sergeant, "but I do like to send in a case complete."

The next thing that Mr. Usher had to achieve was obviously to interview the fashionable Bond Street tailor, and there, accordingly, the sergeant proceeded next and sent in his card.

Mr. Sturton was at home, and at once sent out word that he should be happy to see the eminent Scotland Yard official.

"Well, Mr. Usher, what can I do for you?" inquired the Bond Street maestro urbanely.

The humour of the situation tickled the sergeant, and it was with a grim smile that he retorted, "Well, you know a gentleman in my profession wants a good many costumes at times. Now, suppose I ask you to pitch me out as a real swell about town?"

The great sartorial artist was some two or three minutes before he made reply, during which he eyed his visitor gravely, at last he refused. "No offence, I trust, Mr. Usher, but it's best to be candid in these cases. I'd do my very best for you, but you couldn't look it, not if we did our utmost to oblige you. Now, please, don't get angry, because I shall be only too willing to do all I can to assist. Listen to me! as the slightly eccentric member for West Broadacres, member of the Carlton, and with violent Conservative tendencies, I can turn you out to the nines, or if you like it better as the advanced Radical member for Flareupperton, rejected of the Reform, because he goes a little too far for that played-out institution, I also can do you justice. As a man of fashion, Mr. Usher, you won't come off."

The sergeant gave vent to a grim chuckle at his little joke, and said, "Well, Mr. Sturton, it's not quite true then that men are what their tailors make them."

"Good heavens, Mr. Usher!" cried the enthusiastic Sturton, who really did believe in his profession, "it isn't every clay suits the sculptor, and goodness knows it isn't every clay that suits the tailor. No disparagement, my friend, but it's not in the power of broad-cloth, tweed, serge, or angola to turn out a lord."

"And you wouldn't if you could," retorted the sergeant, perfectly aware of Mr. Sturton's weakness, "not you; nobody knows better the days that are coming, and that coronets will be amongst the relics of history, eh?"

"Well," replied Mr. Sturton, who, despite his professed Radical opinions, entertained a servile adoration for the aristocracy, "they are not quite to be overlooked as yet by my profession."

"Quite so. Now, Mr. Sturton, we'll come to business," rejoined the sergeant, curtly. I suppose you're a judge of handwriting?"

"I don't understand you," replied Sturton, in blank amazement.

"Well, I mean this: in the course of your business you must have had ' a wrong 'un ' given you occasionally."

Again did the eminent tailor stare blankly at his questioner.

"What I mean is this," said the sergeant, confidentially, "you've taken a cheque or two in your time when the drawer's imagination had proved too much for him; when, in fact, he had forgotten his own name."

"Ah, yes," said Mr. Sturton, "that, of course, has happened, but you know, Mr. Usher, as a rule they are rather lucrative things than otherwise; the family always pay to avoid an exposure, and never object to a pretty stiff percentage under the circumstances."

"Just so," rejoined the sergeant, quietly, "but to return to my original observation, you're a judge of handwriting. What do you think of this?" and here Mr Usher produced the famous note that was so nearly burnt at the Hopbine.

It was folded after the mysterious manner in which the sergeant invariably had shown it, so that you could see little more than the signature, but one glance at it sufficed for Mr. Sturton.

"Yes," he said, "I know that hand, but I have no intention of telling you whose it is."

Mr. Usher broke into a low laugh as he replied, "I don't want you to tell me whose handwriting it is, because I know, but you will be wanted to give a court of law your opinion before three weeks are over your head, and I can only tell you with what I am in a position to prove, it would be madness on your part not to speak out."

The collapse of Mr. Sturton was quite equal to that of Timothy Whipple. He knew well that there could be no fencing about his relations with Mr. Cudemore in a witness-box. The more candid he was, the less harm would it do him, but he saw to his dismay that the detective meant to have him in the witness-box, and so replied quietly, "Yes, it's Cudemore's. I know nothing about the note, and you have given me no chance of knowing; but even if you did I fancy it is a thing with which I had nothing to do."

"Not you, Mr. Sturton," replied the sergeant, as he picked up his hat. "I know that well enough; but you'll have to testify to that handwriting. Good day, sir, and it's real trouble to me to think you could not make a genuine Bond Street 'toff' of me."

Very uncomfortable was Mr. Sturton after the detective left him. He was far too shrewd a man not to thoroughly comprehend the whole situation. He saw that he should be called upon to identify Cudemore's writing in court, and quite understood how very unpleasant a sharp cross-examining barrister might make it for him. That he lent money to his clients was no particular mystery in a select set, carefully as he endeavoured to make it so, but he certainly did not want that fact advertised in the journals. Mr. Sturton d——d the Bunbury mystery with no little energy, fascinated as he was by it, as soon as Sergeant Usher had departed. It had never occurred to the great Bond Street maestro before that he might be actively and disagreeably inculpated in the elucidation of the crime.

"That little bit of business is settled," mused Mr. Usher, as he wended his way leisurely back to the Wellington

Restaurant in Spring Gardens, where he had appointed Timothy Whipple to meet him.

As he expected, Tim was waiting for him.

" Well," said Mr. Usher, " have you got what I wanted ? "

" Yes," said Tim, " I have, and a good deal of trouble it's caused me. I had to watch the governor out, and then wait for my chance to steal upstairs ; but I've got it, Mr. Usher, and here it is."

" Good, my lad," said the sergeant, as he took a capacious pocket-book from his breast. " Now," continued Mr. Usher, as he dropped the photograph into one of the pockets and extracted a bank-note from another, " there's ten pounds for you, and, remember, my young friend, it's not many of us can ever knock that out of their first murder case."

" It ought to run to more, Mr. Usher, indeed it ought. You know you've incited me to steal that photograph. There's penalties, you know, for prompting any one to commit a felony."

The sergeant's face really was a study at this retort. He looked Tim Whipple over for a moment, and then said solemnly—

" My young friend, your sole chance of escaping the gallows is joining ' the Yard.' If you don't devote your talents to hanging your fellow-creatures, they will some day undoubtedly hang you. I told you to, if possible, procure a photograph of Mr. Cudemore. I never authorized your stealing it ; and if I did what I ought, should take you into custody now on that charge. I should know then where to lay my hands on you. I should save this ten pounds, and, in fact, damme, I believe that's the best way out it."

But here Tim Whipple's audacity utterly gave way. He burst forth into no end of apologies for his presumption, declared he was perfectly satisfied with his remuneration, that his address was always at Mr. Usher's disposal, and that if the sergeant would at some future time recommend him as a candidate for the police force or the criminal investigation department—his ambition would be satisfied. He quite grovelled before the great detective, and even offered to restore the ten-pound note.

"Well, my lad," said Mr. Usher, at last, "I think you've the making of an officer of my department in course of time. The sooner you get over bumptiousness and thinking things out for yourself at present the better. We don't stand that sort of nonsense amongst our subordinates. We do the thinking, and merely expect them to do what they're told, and any one who can do that satisfactorily in our line is certain to come to the top of the ladder if he's any gumption in him at all."

"Oh, Mr. Usher, if I thought that," exclaimed Tim.

"Beware of bumptiousness," rejoined the sergeant, solemnly, "and it's possible you may escape the gallows yet. Now, my lad, hook it—I've done with you."

CHAPTER XXXIV.

LAST LINKS.

ONCE more did Mr. Usher take train for Baum-borough—the riddle was solved, the whole story of the Bunbury mystery was clear as noonday to him, with one exception. What had been Cudemore's motive? Why had he killed John Fossdyke? and about that, rack his brains as he might, the sergeant was compelled to confess himself beaten. He had no doubt whatever about Cude-more's guilt; he had no doubt whatever about proving it in a court of justice; still, just as a great artist insists upon either having back, or detaining, a picture for a few final touches, so did Mr. Usher want to complete two or three trifling links before arresting Cudemore.

The first person the sergeant desired to see in Baum-borough was Mr. Totterdell, and no sooner had he deposited his modest luggage in the hotel he affected than he started off to that gentleman's residence. Mr. Totterdell had gradually taught himself to believe the Bunbury mystery could only be elucidated by himself; that the police "were born fools, sir," he expressed to every one unguarded enough to listen to him; and if that idiot of a coroner, and still bigger imbecile, Mr. Trail, had only listened to his evidence that the murderer would have been arrested was a fixed fact in the Totterdell brain, and fixed facts in the Totterdell brain were apt to become just a little hard upon other people, especially those of an irresolute turn of mind, who had not nerve to risk the loss of a lapel sooner than submit to button-holing.

Still Mr. Totterdell was conscious of having been some-what snubbed by Mr. Usher at their last interview, and with all his contemptuous opinion of the police in the abstract, had a dim idea that the sergeant in particular was a little awkward to put down; while, on the other hand, his curiosity was insatiable, and therefore when Mr. Usher's card was put into his hand he gave prompt directions for his admittance. The sergeant, after his wont, trod close on the heels of his name, and the fussy Town Councillor received him with no little effusion.

" Ha, Mr. Usher," he exclaimed, rubbing his hands, " so you're come back to me again, eh ? No getting at the bottom of this complication without my assistance, eh ? Well, sir, what is it now ? if I'd been listened to earlier the whole affair would have been cleared up long before this."

" I'm beginning to be of that way of thinking myself, sir," replied the detective. " I'll take a chair with your per-mission, and then, perhaps, you'd answer me a question or two."

" Sit down, sit down, by all means," replied Mr. Totterdell, with pompous patronage. " I'll help you all I can, my good fellow; anything, you know, to forward the ends of justice."

" Quite so," replied the sergeant. " I know I can rely upon you. Now, Mr. Totterdell, you couldn't possibly be mistaken about the identity of the man who sat next you at the opening of the Baumborough Theatre, I presume ? "

" What, James Foxborough ? Certainly not; I'd swear to him anywhere."

" Just so ; you never saw him before, and, like everybody else apparently have never seen him since."

" No, I never saw him except on that occasion," rejoined he; " but I tell you what, Mr. Usher——"

" Half a minute, sir," rejoined the detective, as he took the stout pocket-book from his breast; " half a minute, if you please," and producing a photographic *carte*, he handed it to Mr. Totterdell, and said abruptly, " Is that him ? "

The old gentleman glared at it for a minute, and then exclaimed, " Good God, no ! Why, that's poor Fossdyke, any one could recognize him ! "

" Dear me, dear me," said Mr. Usher, " how stupid I am, I've given you the wrong *carte*! Excuse me, sir, but this is the one I want you to look at," and as he spoke the sergeant exchanged the photograph for that of Mr. Cudemore.

" That's him, that's him, Mr. Usher," cried Mr. Totterdell ; " that's the scoundrel who sat next me in the stalls ; that's James Foxborough. It's an awful thing, sergeant, so to speak, to think you've hobbed and nobbed with a murderer."

" Well, I don't know about the hobbing and nobbing," rejoined the detective, " but, you see, I've had intimate relations with so many in my time that it don't strike me that way. They're, as a rule, inoffensive creatures, and one rather wonders how they came to do it."

" Well, Mr. Usher, this was a nice, civil-spoken gentleman—the last person in the world you'd have suspected of any, any sad, any——"

" Sad games," rejoined the sergeant, curtly. " Bless you, sir, they usually are. The worst of 'em generally goes to church pretty regular, and you wouldn't think would wring the neck of a sparrow, much less, as one I made professional acquaintance with, polish off a whole family."

" Dear me," rejoined Mr. Totterdell, with both eyes and mouth wide open, " you don't say so ! Now, Mr. Usher, I really should like to hear the particulars of that case."

" Well, sir, one of these days, if you'll give me a dish of tea, I'll be proud to tell you the story, but just now I really am pressed for time. We can't afford to let this fellow slip through our fingers, eh, Mr. Totterdell?" said the sergeant, as he gently withdrew the photograph from the old gentleman's fingers.

"Certainly not ; and you know where to lay your hand on him, sergeant ?"

"Undoubtedly, and you shall be face to face with him before many days are over. Yes, sir, I'm going to hang your friend of the theatre, and you may take Silas Usher's word for it. I don't make many mistakes, and this is about as lovely a case as ever I worked out."

"All right, sergeant, if you'll just ring the bell they'll bring you some tea, and then if you'll just tell me the story as far as you've got it worked out, why I'll give you my advice about it," rejoined Mr. Totterdell, his face all aglow, and his inquisitive old eyes positively glistening with excitement.

"That's just it," replied Mr. Usher, rising. "You're the very man I want to talk the whole thing over with ; but time, Mr. Totterdell, don't admit of my doing it just now. There are telegrams to send off, sir, orders to despatch, other people to see, so I'll bid you good-day, sir, for the present. Once more thanking you for your valuable assistance," continued the sergeant, as he brushed his hat with his coat-sleeve, "allow me to wish you good-day."

"They can't get a step without me in the business," murmured Mr. Totterdell, with a complacent smile as Mr. Usher's footsteps died away in the distance. "When it comes to a question of law,—ha, ha,—I fancy they've nobody quite so good on the Bench. Usher sees it at once. Good man, Usher. This case will probably make him, and who's worked out this business for him?—why, *me*." And then Mr. Totterdell threw himself back in his chair, and indulged in ecstatic slumber.

"Darned old fool," muttered the candid detective as he walked leisurely away from Mr. Totterdell's residence.

"Still I've got the one fact out of him I wanted. Cudemore was the man at the Baumborough Theatre. Well, I
fancy Cudemore is one of those this world must suffer by the
loss of. The next thing is just to show old Marlinson and
one or two of the Hopbine people the photograph, and then
the case is just as complete as ever I turned one out. But
the motive. Why did Cudemore kill Fossdyke? why did he
think of it? I'm dead beat about that; if he meant going in
for money and bleeding him, it was the last thing he'd have
done. Wringing the neck of the goose that lays the golden
eggs is not done in practical life, whatever may take place in
fable; especially philosophers like Cudemore, who make their
living out of the weaknesses of their fellow-creatures, don't fall
into such mistakes. Cudemore has owned too many geese
of this kind in his time to do anything so foolish as that.
Well, we shall perhaps have it out of him at the trial and,
moreover, a man goes to the gallows for conclusively proved
murder, even if the why of it is never made clear. Some of
the most remarkable on record have never been cyphered out
in that respect."

The next day saw Mr. Usher lounging leisurely into the
Hopbine at Bunbury, to the extreme horror of old Joe
Marlinson, who, by his surly greeting, quite gave the
sergeant to understand that he had no desire for his
patronage.

"I'm glad to see, my old friend," said Mr. Usher, easily,
"that you've not forgotten me. As for me, you know, I
never forget anybody."

"If you could make an exception in my case," rejoined the
landlord of the Hopbine, "I'd take it as a favour; I don't
want any more murders or inquests committed in this house."

"No, my man, and you don't want to appear in a witness-
box, no doubt," observed the sergeant, jocularly.

"It's a scandalous thing at my time of life, if I'm dragged
into court to be worried about an affair I know nothing
about. Do you suppose I keep a throat-cutting hotel? Do

you suppose murder and robbery is licensed on these premises? I ain't going to have it, nor inquests either—no, nor detectives loafing about my place."

"Now, look here, Mr. Marlinson," rejoined the sergeant; "it's not a bit of use your getting shirty over the matter. The murder was committed in your house, and if you didn't actually do it, I'm not quite so clear you didn't have a hand in it. Just you pay attention to what I've got to say to you, or you'll find yourself in the dock instead of the witness-box."

Mr. Marlinson's face was simply a comic study for the moment, then he went deliberately to a cupboard, from which he produced a couple of glasses, and taking a greenish bottle from the liqueur-rack of the bar-parlour, solemnly filled them.

Mr. Usher was quite equal to the occasion; although an abstemious man, he tossed off the Chartreuse or Kümmell proposed to him, and then said, "Now, Mr. Marlinson, you'd know this Foxborough again if you saw him; could swear to him anywhere, I suppose?"

"I should think I could, and I should rather think I would," replied Mr. Marlinson, excitedly, to which no doubt considerable absorption of liquors contributed. "D——n him, what's he mean by coming to a respectable hotel to commit his murders, when there's any amount of hedge ale-houses about the country that seem special for him? I don't want no more inquests here, Mr. Usher. I don't want to have anything more to do with the business; but I don't mind swearing to a scoundrel who's brought disgrace upon the Hopbine. Hanging he deserves, and hanging I trust he'll get, dash me."

"Quite so," replied the sergeant, quietly; "now look here," and somewhat to Mr. Marlinson's dismay the detective produced that fat leather pocket-book, which might almost have been called "his familiar." It was the black poodle of Faust.

"You see this photograph," continued Mr. Usher, as he

produced from its depths Mr. Cudemore's *carte*. "Who is it?"

"That's him—that's the——villain who has caused all this trouble. I could swear to him anywhere."

"We sha'n't trouble you to do that; if you'll swear to him in a court of justice it's about as much as we shall ask you to do. But now, I just want Eliza Salter and Thomas Jenkinson, the waiter—a mere matter of form, Mr. Marlinson, but when people outrage respectable hotels, houses with a county and crusted port reputation, they must be punished, Mr. Marlinson, eh?"

"They must be thinned, sir, that's what it is. Have another glass, Mr. Usher, it's mild as mother's milk, this Chartreuse, and comforting under affliction," and as he spoke Joe Marlinson poured out a couple more glasses of the insinuating compound. "We can't have such vipers about, sir, they must be scotched. I don't quite know what that means, but I believe it's a term applicable to vipers."

"Well, just send for the waiter and chambermaid, my friend, you may rely upon it that this particular viper won't come across your path any more."

"I hope not, Mr. Usher; it's upset me altogether. For all I know, I've been harbouring and entertaining murderers for years. Here's a gentleman comes here with all a gentleman's manners, and shows a taste in wines and cookery that stamps him as a member of the upper circles, and then he just in the middle of the night sticks a fellow-creature as if he were a pork-butcher. I give it all up, sir. I never believed the aristocracy were up to such rigs as this, and now they tell me there was a French duke took to it only a score or so of years back."

"Don't you trouble, Mr. Marlinson, and take my advice and be a little careful of your fine Chartreuse. Good tipple, but demoralizing. Now run in for Salter and Jenkinson, for I've no time to spare, and must catch the next train to Baumborough."

Thus advised, the landlord of the Hopbine speedily summoned those servitors, and Mr. Usher exhibited the *carte* of Cudemore for their delectation. Neither had the slightest doubt about it. Yes, that was No. 11; Mr. Foxborough, as they knew him to be afterwards. The photograph was an excellent one, and they could swear to him anywhere. Was there any chance or immediate prospect of apprehension ?

" You needn't fret yourselves about that. I, Sergeant Usher, tell you that I know exactly where to find James Foxborough when I want him, and that there's never a man in England less likely to change his abode. That you will be all able to recognize Foxborough when you see him in the dock is all I want. And now just tell Bill Gibbons I'll run down in the 'bus."

That stolid, open-mouthed admiration characteristic of country folks was visible upon the faces of the whole Hopbine establishment, from the landlord to the boots, as the great detective took his departure.

Arrived at Baumborough, Mr. Usher made his way straight to Dr. Ingleby's, and was at once admitted. He found the doctor alone.

" Sit down, Usher, and have a glass of port," remarked the *medico*. " Am I to have the story of the Bunbury mystery to-night ? "

" Well, sir," said the sergeant, as he filled his glass, " to tell you the truth, that's just what I came to do; but I should like both Mr. Soames and Mr. Morant to be present when I relate it."

" Ha ! a little unlucky. I'm not going to make any mystery to a man so completely behind the scenes as yourself, but Herbert Morant took Miss Hyde up to London to-day to introduce her to her half-sister. The girl was mad about it; and young Morant, well, I suppose, he was pretty keen too to get a look at his sweetheart."

" Yes, sir, yes," said the sergeant, with a low chuckle, " that's human nature, about one of the few cards you can depend upon being played straight in the world. But I'll tell you·what it is, I'll put off telling the story of Mr. Fossdyke's death till they come back if you'll allow me. The story is all plain as noonday, but I want to tell it before Mr. Soames, Mr. Morant, and Miss Hyde. I'm beat about the motive, and I've a strong idea that either Mr. Morant or Miss Hyde might give me the clue to it. As for who killed John Fossdyke, he'll be in custody to-morrow, and to prove the case is as simple as possible; but why he did it I'm beat about still. Good-night, doctor; nobody keeps such port as you, but fine Chartreuse at the Hopbine in the afternoon is not the best foundation for it," and with this profoundly philosophical remark the sergeant vanished.

CHAPTER XXXV.

THAT Miss Hyde should be anxious to make the acquaintance of the mother she hardly knew, and of the half-sister she had never seen, was only natural; but her feelings had been so aroused by the enthusiastic manner in which Morant spoke of them that her desire to do so had become feverish. Herbert spoke of Mrs. Foxborough as one of the noblest, greatest-hearted women it had ever been his lot to know; and it is not every day that sons-in-law elect show such passionate admiration for the mothers of their sweethearts. That he should rave about Nid was only natural; if a man of Herbert's age don't express himself in somewhat extravagant fashion regarding the girl he is about to marry, he must be either of a very phlegmatic temperament, or very mildly in love, and of those failings nobody could possibly accuse Mr. Morant.

Phil Soames too could not resist feeling some curiosity to see people to whom he was likely to be allied so nearly as Mrs. Foxborough and her daughter, and it took very little persuasion on Bessie's part to induce him to agree to run up with her and Herbert to London, and be presented at Tapton Cottage.

"You must come, Phil, dear. You know what Herbert

is. When he once gets beside Nid, I shall never see him
again, and be left to take care of myself; and though
Herbert in his reckless way declares that mamma will be
delighted to see me, I don't feel quite sure about how she
will brook my intrusion on her home. She has always
been charming and tender upon the rare occasions on which
she has come to see me, but she has never hinted that
I should come and see her "—a speech that shows Mr.
Morant and Miss Hyde had speedily arrived at terms of
easy confidence.

"What reasons there might have been, Bessie, for Mrs.
Foxborough handing you over to the care of your aunt I
can't guess; but I think no mother is likely not to be proud
to own you as a daughter now."

"Oh, Phil, Phil," cried Bessie, laughing, "to think of
your giving utterance to such shameful flattery!"

"I don't know that there's much flattery about it,
darling," replied the young man as he wound his arm
round her waist. "If after a hard struggle one gains the
prize one's set one's heart on, I think one's justified in
being just a wee bit proud of the prize."

"How you do spoil me, and how was I ever so mad as
not to tell you my story at once?" replied Bessie, as she
dropped her head on his breast with the inevitable result.
"But you'll come to town with Herbert and me to-morrow,
that's understood?"

"You don't suppose I'd give a chance, child, for any
other fellow to run away with my property?" and then
came some further assertion of his being the rightful owner
of "the property," scarcely interesting to readers or lookers-
on.

And so the very morning that Usher, the ubiquitous,
was upsetting Mr. Marlinson's equilibrium at the Hopbine,
Phil Soames, Morant, and Miss Hyde took the train for
London. They were not, however, destined to depart
altogether unchallenged. Mr. Totterdell, in his thirst for

information concerning the doings of everybody and everything, was on the platform buying newspapers. He was
a great frequenter of the station. He liked to know who
came to, and who departed from, Baumborough; and
the why and the where of their journey was a special
object of interest to the old gentleman. The sight of
Phil Soames and his friend Herbert Morant, with Miss
Hyde, all evidently awaiting the London train, was like the
trumpet to the war-horse.

" Going to London, Mr. Soames ? " exclaimed Mr. Totterdell, as he sidled up to them. " Can hardly be pleasure,
I suppose, while this terrible mystery, in which we are all
so interested, remains unsettled ? "

" Yes, I'm going to London," rejoined Philip, drily.

" Got a bit of shopping to do, eh, Miss Hyde ? "

" A lady always has that, Mr. Totterdell; but I'm not
going to London for that purpose."

" On business of importance, eh ? "

" Just so," rejoined Herbert Morant, cutting into the
conversation. " We are all going up to see the pantomimes."

" Pantomimes, my dear young friend," said Mr. Totterdell;
" why, bless you, they don't commence for another six weeks."

" No," rejoined Morant, serenely, " but there's nothing like
being in time to get a good seat. Never, Mr. Totterdell
neglect that golden advice on the playbills, ' Come early.'"

Here Phil Soames and Bessie could control their laughter
no longer; but just then the London train fortunately glided
into the station, and they jumped hastily into a first-class
carriage, leaving Mr. Totterdell jabbering impotently in his
wrath.

Arrived in town, they drove straight to Tapton Cottage, and,
as pre-arranged, Morant jumped out and knocked, leaving his
companions in the cab. Bessie was fearfully nervous. She
feared how the scarcely-known mother might take this un-
authorized intrusion; and, poor girl, she so yearned for some
near relations she could love. The bitter experience of her

puritanical aunt and waspish cousins had left sad memories in her mind; and though Phil Soames had in great measure succeeded in obliterating them, still Bessie craved for the love of that handsome mother she had so seldom seen.

"Do you think she's very angry at my coming, Phil?" she whispered, as she stole her hand into her lover's.

"Nonsense, child!" he replied, as he pressed it. "Don't be foolish. Morant must be given a few minutes to explain matters."

Suddenly the door opened, and a tall, handsome woman, with a wealth of chestnut hair crowning her head, rushed down the steps, and exclaimed as she impetuously wrenched open the cab-door—

"Bessie, my darling, where are you? Come in at once, dearest, and you too, Mr. Soames, for of course you are Mr. Soames. To think, child, that your mother would not be glad to see you in your own home. Oh, my darling, I've a long story to whisper into your ears when I get you inside."

When they entered the drawing-room, Nid was standing, her face all aglow with excitement, waiting to welcome her new sister. For a second or two she regarded her shyly; then the girl's impulsive nature asserted itself, and without more ado, she made a rush at Bessie, threw her arms round her neck, and kissed her passionately.

"There, that will do, Nid," said Mrs. Foxborough, in a low voice, as she gently separated the two girls. "Take her into the library, Herbert, and let her there make acquaintance with her brother-in-law that is to be. You will forgive me, Mr. Soames, but I have a full confession to make to my daughter, and I am sure," she continued, addressing herself to him as her voice sank almost to a whisper, "you do not wish to make the story of a woman's weakness harder for her to tell than necessary."

"I assure you, Mrs Foxborough——" interposed Phil.

"No," she continued, still speaking to him, and recognizing instinctively that he was the master spirit of the party, "I know you don't, and lowering her head as few people had ever chanced to see the proud Nydia Willoughby do before ; " but Bessie must learn the truth from my lips at last. You and she, I dare say, know the outline of it already. Spare me its being further bruited abroad."

She presented so sad a sight in this her hour of humiliation, and the low tremulous tones vibrated so painfully on the heartstrings of her hearers, that the two girls burst into tears, while Mrs. Foxborough stood silent and abased. Phil Soames, however, rose promptly to the occasion.

" Kiss and comfort her, Bessie ; go to her, child," and he placed the weeping girl in her mother's arms, and raising Mrs. Foxborough's hand to his lips, kissed it. " Take Nydia to the library ; I will follow you and try to make my sister-in-law's acquaintance."

For a second Nid hesitated to give way to Morant's light grasp upon her arm, then she mutely clasped Phil's hand, and yielding to her lover's gentle compulsion, drew him after her as they left the room.

" Oh, Bessie, darling," exclaimed Mrs. Foxborough, as she wound her arm about her daughter. " It is a terrible story for a mother to have to tell, how she ever came to desert a child like yourself, but there are really extenuating circumstances—that is, if anything can excuse a woman so doing. Listen, child, to a very commonplace story. Your grandfather was a Presbyterian minister at Plymouth, and we—that is, myself and your aunt—were brought up after the fashion of girls in a very serious family. There were only us two, and Augusta cheerfully conformed with the views of our parents. It may have been the romantic name which my mother, with ' The Last Days of Pompeii ' still seething in her mind, insisted upon bestowing on me ; but from the very first I rebelled against the solemnity of our home. While your grandmother lived it was somewhat mitigated, but after her death your grandfather and my sister, who was some five years my senior seemed to think even laughter a crime. Novel reading, theatre-going, and all the innocent amusements that a girl most delights in were in my case sternly repressed. Can you wonder that I fell into a state of chronic and sullen revolt against the gloomy existence I was condemned to lead ? As long as my sister remained at home, despite my having no scruples about indulging in any of the forbidden pleasures whenever I could get a chance, my opportunities were few. A woman is not easily blinded by another woman, and Augusta was not easy to deceive ; but when she one day married the son of a prominent member of our congregation and went away to her new home in London, it became comparatively easy. The bribing the two maids that comprised our modest household were hardly necessary, their sympathies were entirely with me ; they agreed that Miss Nydia ought to see a little more life and have a little more amusement. Novels I obtained now as many as I liked, and I may say lived in the fairy-land of fiction, while now and again I enjoyed the stolen delight of a visit to the theatre in company with Ruth, our parlour-maid."

"Poor mother," murmured Bessie. "No one, as you know, could understand your dreary life better than I."

Mrs. Foxborough, who was seated in a low chair, fondled the head of the girl who was crouched at her feet.

"Then, Bessie sweet, came my agony. I met there upon one occasion a very good-looking young man, who was excessively civil about getting us a cab. It was a wet night, and cabs were somewhat scarce. I soon found that he was the *jeune premier* of the company, but not being wanted in the last piece had strolled round in front. I was only seventeen, Bessie, and we met and met again. To a romantic fool as I was then an actor was a species of demi-god. I fell violently in what I thought was love, and when the company left Plymouth was easily persuaded to elope with him. A little more than a year afterwards I found myself a mother, and deserted, with the additional agony of discovering that my betrayer was already a married man. What was I to do? Thanks to my *soi-disant* husband, I had already got a footing on the stage, but how to carry you about with me and take care of you I knew not. My salary, I need scarcely say, was scanty, while in the matter of new parts country managers are simply merciless, and one has to play almost any *rôle* at forty-eight hours' notice. What with study and rehearsal I could simply take no adequate care of you. Go back to my father's house I couldn't—I really had not the courage to undergo the humiliation that awaited me there even if he would receive me, which was not exactly certain. At last I bethought me of your aunt. I took you there, and bore meekly the reproaches that were showered upon me, and then, Bessie, I assented to the cruel terms proposed to me— That I was to give you solely over to her; that it was her duty, if possible, to snatch a brand from the burning, and her duty she would do; but that she must make it a positive condition that I saw you but rarely, and never attempted to remove you from under her care even for a day. What cruel justice Augusta dealt out to me at that time I forgive her for your sake, but I can never forget it. She did her duty by you honestly according to her own narrow lights, and I, God help me, did not."

Here Mrs. Foxborough ceased, and in a second Bessie's arms were wound round her neck, and the girl was seated in her lap.

"Oh, mother," she whispered, "what a hard life you must have had!"

"No, I don't know that it was harder than is the lot of most of us, except the having to part with you. Soon afterwards I got a lucrative opening in the music-hall line, and there I have continued ever since. It was at that time I met poor James, and we were married, but I told him about you before I became his wife. He didn't

get on well on the stage, and was too proud to live upon
me, so we agreed to separate for a little. Fond as he
was of me, and though he would have lavished money on
me if I would have let him after he began to make it, he
was always strangely reticent about his business. He did
well whatever it was, and bought and rebuilt the Syringa
entirely for me. He called his business, Bessie, the managing
of country theatrical companies. I always affected to believe it, but I very much doubt whether that was what
it was really. But he's been a good and dear husband
to me, child, and had nothing to say to this murder I'd
stake my life, though I've a presentiment I shall never
see him again. And now about yourself, child—do you
love this bonnie wooer of yours ? "

"With all my soul, mother. You can't think how kind,
courteous, and considerate he is, and he must care a good
deal about me, or he'd never take such a penniless child as
me to keep."

"Oh, darling !" replied Mrs. Foxborough, as she toyed
a little nervously though fondly with the girl's hair, " there
are plenty of men about who would gladly take you with
just the gown on your back. May you be happy, child!
and now we'll go and call back the others. I have hardly
seen this tall sweetheart of yours."

CHAPTER XXXVI.

MR. CUDEMORE GETS UNEASY.

MR. CUDEMORE was getting somewhat uneasy in his mind. He did not at all like Mr. Sturton having put himself in communication with the police relative to the large sum of money that James Foxborough had borrowed. He would have liked it still less, had he known of Mr. Usher's visit to Bond Street, but of that he was in ignorance. He had called once or twice to see Mr. Sturton lately, only to be told he was not in. This in itself disturbed the suspicious money-lender. He had never found any difficulty about seeing the fashionable artist before, why should he now? The truth was, Mr. Sturton kept purposely out of the way. Although Mr. Usher, after his wont, had kept his own counsel pretty close, yet he had made no secret that Mr. Sturton would be called upon to testify to that handwriting, and, further, it was clear to the latter that the sergeant attached great importance to that note. Mr. Sturton had always followed the Bunbury murder with morbid interest, and he had arrived vaguely at the conclusion that Cudemore was somehow implicated in the crime. He could be cool enough on all matters of business, but he had no nerves for horrors, and the Bunbury mystery, which had absorbed him from the first, now kept him in a state of nervous irritability.

Mr. Cudemore was very dissatisfied with the progress of his love-suit. His chance had not looked a particularly rosy one before he lost his head that afternoon in Tapton Cottage, and now he knew that nothing but coercion remained to bring it to a successful termination. Not that Mr. Cudemore would have cared about that, had it only promised a favour-able result, but it did not. He interfered more and more in the affairs of the Syringa; he insisted upon it that he must see the manageress on matters of business. Mrs. Foxborough steadily refused to take the slightest notice of him. In spite of her prohibition he had again called at the cottage; the door remained closed in his face. He had written to apologize for his conduct, but no reply was vouchsafed him. He had written once more, pointing out that if the six thousand pounds borrowed by James Foxborough was not forthcoming at the expiration of the notice given the mortgagees would foreclose, and the Syringa Music Hall go altogether out of Mrs. Foxborough's hands, and Mrs. Foxborough again was perfectly indifferent, and abstained from answering his letter. Then the money-lender had pushed persecution as far as he knew how, and was fain to admit with no result.

He was infatuated with his mad passion for the girl, and it to a certain extent lulled to rest that shrewd instinct of coming danger now newly awakened. In the days before he had avowed his admiration he had begged a photograph from Nid, and she, who was turning over a lot of freshly-executed sun likenesses of herself, gave him one without hesitation. Musing one afternoon in his rooms over his mad desire to make Nid his wife, he suddenly bethought him, as he could not see the girl herself, he would look at her picture. He fetched his photograph book from a side-table and turned over the leaves till he came to her likeness, and then he was struck with something else— the opposite *carte* had been removed. He knew perfectly well whose it was. It was his own. He had placed it there as men will at times in order to see themselves coupled with the object of their idolatry. Who had taken it? and why? The division from which it had been abstracted was slightly torn, as if it had been removed with some haste, and once more a feeling of uneasiness came over the man. He had no intimate friends likely to commit such petty larceny, in fact, friends were a luxury Mr. Cudemore professed himself unable to afford. He was a great admirer of the fair sex, but his *liaisons* were transient and of that meretricious order that involves no great amount of sentiment on either side.

He lit a big cigar and sat there for an hour brooding over various little suspicious circumstances, all tending to confirm his views that Scotland Yard had come to suspect him of being concerned in the Bunbury mystery. What was young Whipple doing in his dressing-room? why did Mr. Sturton persistently avoid him? and, lastly, with what object had some one abstracted this photograph? He wondered if he was under surveillance; whether he was watched as he knew the police could watch a man upon occasion. Then he thought it would be as well to realize some securities, so as to have a good bit of ready money always at hand, in case it might seem good policy to abscond. Bah! he was losing his nerve. Let them suspect, he was in no danger; it was little likely they would ever penetrate the mysterious disappearance of James Foxborough, and until they did that he was safe. No, while there was a chance of securing Nid Foxborough for his wife he would stay, happen what might, and then he actually began to muse over impossible schemes for her abduction. His fierce lustful passion for the girl—love it cannot be called— was of that kind that led to savage outrages of such sort in the seventeenth and eighteenth centuries, but is fortunately not quite so feasible in the days we live in. Did he but know it, Mr. Cudemore was as well policed as the Prime Minister or the Lord-Lieutenant of Ireland.

Still the more he reflected the less he liked the aspect of affairs. He looked at the clock; yes, with a good hansom there was just time to catch his broker and give him instructions to sell Guatemala bonds sufficient to realize a thousand. He would do it. "I shall want money for either tour," he muttered grimly, "whether it be a wedding one or the other."

On the track of his hansom stole another tenanted by a wizened little old man dressed something like an old-fashioned bank clerk, but one of the deadliest beagles in all the detective pack. He was not a man of anything like Mr. Usher's calibre, he was not good at finding his game; but once shown his quarry, and he hung upon the track like a sleuth hound. Old Nibs, as he was affection-ately termed by his brethren of the yard, was a very valuable officer in his own line; a very difficult man to slip when he had once sighted his prey.

Mr. Cudemore arrived in time, and a little surprised his broker. Guatemalas were now going up and promised to be an uncommon good thing ere the month was out. Did not Mr. Cudemore think it would be advisable to hold on a week or two, or, if he must have money, realize some other property? No, Mr. Cudemore didn't think so. His orders were peremptory to sell Guatemalas to realize a thousand the next day, and that done he drove off and recreated himself at the Gaiety Restaurant, and went into the theatre after-wards; but let him go where he would, that little wizened old bank clerk followed him like his shadow till he finally reached his home in Spring Gardens, and there another member of the force was ready to take up the watch.

Mr. Cudemore slept the sleep of the just. Whatever his connection with the Bunbury mystery might be, it affected him no more than it might make it advisable for him to leave town, and this, in consequence of his wild infatuation about Nid Foxborough, he did not wish to do. The money-lender thought that he could easily baffle the police whenever he should deem it necessary, and though he had pictured himself watched, had little idea that such watch had actually commenced. He thought he might to some extent have fallen under their suspicion, but he deemed they had barely got hold of the clue as yet, much less unravelled it. Uneasy he was, he felt there was danger in the air; but he'd no idea he was already completely in the toils, that the indefatigable Usher had his, Mr. Cudemore's, photograph multiplied, and that there was not a leading police-station in England without both that and a complete description of him, more especially all the principal seaports, so that even should he evade the vigilance of " the Yard " he was not likely to get very far.

The next morning Mr. Cudemore, having had his breakfast, betook himself to the Syringa Music Hall, where he, as was his habit, harassed the stage-manager with business inquiries and demanded to see Mrs. Foxborough.

" She's here, I know," said the money-lender, " for I saw her brougham waiting in the street."

" I've Mrs. Foxborough's express commands to say she will never see you, that she doubts whether you really have any right to interfere with us at all until your time comes. I don't quite know what she means by that, but I give you her message as I have given it you before."

But Mr. Cudemore was determined to see Mrs. Foxborough this time, and he lingered in the entrance until she came out, and then, taking off his hat, boldly requested to speak to her on business.

The manageress of the Syringa drew herself up proudly and passed on towards her carriage without a word or hardly even a glance at him, and Mr. Cudemore fell back discomfited as the stage-manager put her into the brougham. He was verily not doing much with this game of persecution, and Mr. Cudemore walked moodily away. " She must have a good bit more than I thought," he muttered, " or she'd never take the prospect of the loss of the Syringa so lightly; and yet I thought Foxborough had pretty well all he had sunk in it; but of course I know now he had other resources."

Now it so happened that the very morning upon which Mr. Cudemore made the last attempt to intimidate Mrs. Foxborough was the day upon which the party from Baumborough, under Morant's guidance, arrived at Tapton Cottage. If Mrs. Foxborough kept a brave presence before the money-lender, she was in reality considerably dismayed at the loss of the Syringa. Her husband might have other property, but she knew nothing about it, and it was the Syringa that kept Tapton Cottage going. Of course she could fall back upon her profession and command a very fair engagement, but it would mean a very different income from that which she derived from the music hall. She wondered whether Cudemore had the rights he claimed over the place at present; but the mortgage she knew was a fact, and where to get six thousand pounds she didn't know. She had come down to the Syringa early in order to avoid observation, and hurried back to the cottage in consequence of a letter from Morant received that morning.

When she and Bessie had fetched the other three back from the library, as it was the custom to call James Foxborough's own den, Mrs. Foxborough sat down to make acquaintance with Phil Soames, while Morant was left to entertain the two girls. Mrs. Foxborough was a quick-witted woman, and she had heard of Phil's business qualifications from Herbert. She was much struck with his quiet, shrewd remarks, for she had turned the conversation on his (Soames') own business and position, and what he thought of Herbert's chance of prospering in the opening his firm had so kindly afforded him, and her heart felt light about the prospects of her daughters as she listened to Phil's clear exposition of the future. Suddenly it flashed across her that she sorely needed some one to advise her. Why should she not confide her trouble about the Syringa to this clear-headed son-in-law that was to be?

24

She paused for a moment and then said, "Mr. Soames, I want your advice," and without further preliminary, she poured into Phil's ears the stories of her difficulties with Mr. Cudemore.

"Don't be alarmed, Mrs. Foxborough," replied Soames, quietly, as she concluded. "I've no doubt, in the first place, when this bullying money-lender is confronted with a sharp solicitor we shall find his power over the Syringa to be mythical. Secondly, I have no doubt that when the mortgage has to be paid off I can obtain the money for you if the property is anything like what you represent it to be. Lastly, with your permission, I'll call in my partner in embryo. I've a notion in days gone by he also patronized this Cudemore; he might give us a hint, and mind, Mrs. Foxborough, I'm training him to business. Come here, Herbert, we want you for a minute."

"Yes, and he's rather popular on this side of the room just now," replied Nid. "Mamma monopolizing two young men is sheer tyranny."

"We only want him for two minutes, Nid," replied Soames, laughing. "A matter of business."

"Oh! dear; we don't require him in that capacity in the least; you had better go, sir."

"What is it?" said Herbert, as he crossed the room.

"You told me one night at Baumborough, if I don't mistake, that you once had some dealings with a money-lender of the name of Cudemore?"

"Yes, the thief, he's slippery as an eel. What about him?"

"May I tell him, Mrs. Foxborough?" asked Phil.

The manageress nodded assent, and then Soames told the story of Mr. Cudemore's audacious claim to look into the books, see the receipts, and otherwise interfere with the management of the Syringa.

"The confounded scoundrel," exclaimed Morant, "I've half a mind to break every bone in his body, only I've an idea it is unnecessary. Listen, Phil, the forty-eight hours stipulated is up. We came prepared to stay the night in town. Let Bessie stay here as originally proposed, but let you and I, instead of going to an hotel, take the train back to Baumborough. Be guided by me this time, Phil."

"Herbert's quick enough, Mrs. Foxborough, when he takes the trouble to think. He knows what he's talking about now and I don't, but I have no hesitation about putting myself into his hands."

"Good! Mrs. Foxborough," said Morant, "I may be mistaken, but I've an impression Cudemore will trouble you no more."

"And I feel sure," said Philip, as he bade his hostess adieu, "that mortgage can be arranged. Remember, you've a right to claim my assistance now."

Then the two young men made their farewells to the girls. Bessie kissed her *fiancé*, and shook hands with her future brother-in-law; if they thought it necessary they should go, no doubt it was so; but Nid was not to be dismissed so easily. The little coquette affected to pout, and said that if Herbert and her new brother were satisfied with such a flying visit as that she was afraid the sight of her was not good in the king's eyes, and here she looked at Phil; but at this juncture her lover caught her in his arms, and, lifting her off her feet, snatched half-a-dozen kisses, then putting her down breathless and indignant, rushed out of the room, followed by Phil.

"Ah!" said Nid, when she was able to speak, "that's what it is to be little; nobody, not even strong tall Phil, could subject you to such an outrage."

"Oh, yes," rejoined Bessie, laughing, "I fancy he could if he tried, and I don't think, my dear, I should feel any worse about it than you do."

"Miss Hyde, I'm ashamed of you," rejoined Nid, demurely; "come and have some tea."

CHAPTER XXXVII.

NO LONGER "AT FAULT."

AS soon as Phil Soames and Morant arrived in Baumborough, they hurried off to the home of the former, and had just time to tumble into their evening clothes previous to joining the dinner-table, at which their unexpected advent occasioned no little surprise on the part of Phil's parents. However, as this worthy pair were completely ignorant of what had taken the young men to town, some vague excuse about having changed their minds amply sufficed to allay their curiosity. The meal over, Phil and Morant adjourned to the former's sanctum, as they often did for an after-dinner cigar.

No sooner had they gained it upon this occasion than Morant said, "Of course, Phil, we didn't come here to smoke to-night. We'll just light our cigarettes, and then we must go across to Dr. Ingleby's, and see if he has any news of Mr. Usher. He should have."

"All right," rejoined Soames; "you're in command, you know."

So off to Dr. Ingleby's, only some quarter of a mile away, the two started. The doctor was as much astonished to see them as had been old Mr. and Mrs. Soames.

"Why, I thought you were not coming down till to-morrow," he exclaimed, the customary greetings over.

"Quite right," replied Morant; "but something we heard in London made us think it desirable to see Mr. Usher as soon as possible. He promised me to be here to-night."

"And he has been. He came, he said, to tell us the complete story of the Bunbury mystery ; but when he found you two were not here, he asked permission to postpone his story, as he seemed to think it probable you might clear up one or two points about which he is still doubtful, if you only heard the story. He hasn't been gone a quarter of an hour."

"How deuced unlucky!" exclaimed Morant.

"Nonsense, Herbert," cried Phil Soames. "He can't have left the town. Where does he put up, doctor?"

"At the Woolpack ; and we shall probably find him there, if I send for him."

"Nonsense, doctor ; I'll go myself," exclaimed Morant. "You two just wait quietly here, and I'll be back with Mr. Usher in a quarter of an hour at furthest," and with these words Herbert vanished.

Little was said between the doctor and Phil Soames during the interval of Morant's absence ; they were both too anxious to listen to the coming revelation to speak much.

The quarter of an hour had hardly elapsed when Herbert entered triumphantly, closely followed by Sergeant Usher.

"Good evening, Mr. Soames; and once more good evening, Dr. Ingleby. I'm very glad, gentlemen, you came back, and that Mr. Morant came and fetched me, for I should like to tell you the whole story of the Bunbury murder before I leave Baumborough, as you have been, so to speak, all a bit mixed up in it, and are certainly all interested in the riddle. I must leave for town by the 11.30, but I've got a good hour and a half to spare, which will much more than suffice to tell my story."

"You can easily imagine, sergeant, we are all extremely anxious to hear it," replied Dr. Ingleby ; "indeed, these two gentlemen came back from London for nothing else."

"So Mr. Morant tells me, sir," rejoined the sergeant, as he quietly seated himself and commenced his narrative :—

"James Foxborough (and as far as I know that is his real name) started in life as articled clerk to an attorney in London. Like many of that class, he had a great fondness for the theatre. Somehow or other, at one of the minor suburban theatres, he scraped acquaintance with Miss Nydia Willoughby, then a struggling young actress, and concerning whose earlier history I know no more than I learnt from Mr. Soames in this room a few weeks back. Nor is it in the least necessary I should. The two fell in love, and after a little married. James Foxborough broke his articles, and managed, through his wife's influence, to obtain a small engagement on the stage. But unluckily he was not possessed of what the literary people call histrionic powers. His wife kept steadily fighting her way upwards, but he just as steadily dropped into a mere super. He was entrusted with letters to carry on, and about two lines to say ; and his salary, gentlemen, was about as short as his part. Well, to do Foxborough justice, he was clear grit; he'd no idea of living on his wife's earnings, and as soon as he had satisfactorily ascertained that he couldn't earn bread and cheese on the stage, he announced his intention of seeking it elsewhere, and they parted, quite amicably. Mind now, you may ask how can I know all this? I only reply, I know the main facts of the case so far, and have filled in the remainder by inference, as any one of you might, and probably would do.

"Now," continued the sergeant, "the idea that had occurred to James Foxborough, by way of earning his living, was to fall back upon his old profession. His experience as an actor had made him pretty sick of the stage as a profession ; the gilt was all off the gingerbread as far as he was concerned ; but remember, he had broken his articles ; and though I don't suppose—though I honestly confess I don't know—that there is any very severe penalty for that,

still it was quite sufficient to make him change his name,
and leave London. To begin upon, he was not an attorney,
and how he managed to get his name on the rolls I can't
say—I lose sight of him here for two years or more; when I
next pick him up he's practising in Baumborough, under the
name of John Fossdyke."

"What!" cried Dr. Ingleby, "you mean to tell us that
John Fossdyke and James Foxborough are the same man?"

"Not a doubt about it," rejoined Mr. Usher.

"Impossible!" exclaimed Morant. "Very much alike, if
you will; but the same man—ridiculous."

"I told you it was a beautiful case," rejoined the sergeant;
"and the reason we could never find the slightest trace of
James Foxborough is that he is buried in John Fossdyke's
grave."

"But, good God! Mr. Usher, if your story is true," said
Dr. Ingleby, "poor Mrs. Fossdyke was never married."

"Undoubtedly not. Her husband's name wasn't Fossdyke, for one thing, and he was already married, for another.
Now Foxborough," continued the sergeant, "when he first
came to Baumborough was a very poor man. He constantly
ran up to town, and received, I fancy, a good bit of assistance still from his wife. And now, Dr. Ingleby, I should
feel much obliged if you would continue the story."

"Certainly," replied the doctor, "and the bit you want
nobody can piece in better than myself. Fossdyke, or I
suppose I should say Foxborough, gradually began to
acquire a fair practice here; he was a pushing man, who
would have his finger in every pie that was baking. He was
a plausible man, with great command of words, a popular
man, and to some extent a clever man, and the farmers
around especially took to him. You see he had some
sporting proclivities, liked a day's hunting, a day's shooting,
or a day's steeple-chasing, when he could find time for it,
and in those days he was clever enough to know that it paid
in the long run to make time for it. His practice rapidly

increased, and he became a man of mark in the town ; then he made his great hit in life—I'm speaking of him as Foss-dyke—he married Mary Kimberley. This at once gave a status it would have taken him some years yet to acquire, and thanks to the interest his marriage gave him, he shortly afterwards acquired the post of Town Clerk. I have got nothing further to add than this, that though his income was an exceedingly handsome one, and though he apparently lived well within it, yet there were invariably tales about the difficulty the tradesmen had in getting money from him.

"Yes, doctor," interposed Mr. Usher, "that's where it was ; that'll be about the time he went into a good many provincial theatrical specs which terminated all the wrong way, and it was on these speculations he contrived to make away with the best part of Mrs. Fossdyke's money. Then at last came his first theatrical hit—he built and started the Syringa Music Hall, and to do that, doctor, he appropriated between five and six thousand pounds of the Corporation funds."

"Impossible, Mr. Usher, if such a thing had not come out in his life-time it must have done at his death."

"And that is just what has happened," replied the sergeant, "that wearisome Totterdell creature has discovered it, though he is not exactly aware of the real meaning of his discovery. When the Corporation, as I'm told at Mr. Totterdell's instance, voted for the calling in of that mortgage on the houses and buildings belonging to the railway company near the station in order to pay for their new theatre, the discovery of Foxborough's fraudulent appropriation of their moneys was imminent. It was then that he went to one Cudemore, to whom he had often applied before, indeed, had recourse to him about the building of the Syringa, the misappropriated money not proving sufficient, and raised from him, with the assistance of Mr. Sturton, the great Bond Street tailor, the requisite sum to cover his deficiencies, and but for Mr. Totterdell, who is always nosing round like a truffle dog about his neighbours' affairs, I don't suppose any one would have ever known anything about that quiet borrowing of the Corporation's money. He somehow found out that no such mortgage was ever effected, although five per cent. interest was regularly credited to the Corporation on account of it."

"Most extraordinary," said Dr. Ingleby. "I can't conceive this never having come to my ears."

As for Phil Soames and Morant, they sat silent and absorbed in the extraordinary history that Mr. Usher was slowly unfolding for their edification.

"Not at all, sir," replied the sergeant. "Mr. Totterdell so very imperfectly understands his discovery that he is actually unable to talk about it. You must bear in mind, gentlemen, that though I can prove all my leading points, I am filling in my story here and there from what I suppose to have been the case. We next come to the opening of the Baumborough Theatre, and here for the first time the author of the Bunbury mystery appears upon the scene. What brought Mr. Cudemore there I honestly say I don't know, but——"

"Good gracious! you mean to say, then, that the money-lender was the murderer of poor Fossdyke?—I should say Foxborough," exclaimed Dr. Ingleby.

"Just so," replied the sergeant, perfectly unmoved. "These two gentlemen have heard his name before, I fancy, at all events Mr. Morant has. As I was saying, what brought him down to that ceremony I can't fathom, but I do know this, that for the first time he became aware that John Fossdyke and James Foxborough were one, were the same individual. That a man of Cudemore's stamp should attempt to make capital out of such knowledge is a mere matter of course; that he wrote the note which took Mr. Fossdyke over to Bunbury I can prove. Mr. Morant, there, can swear to the handwriting for one, and I have another unimpeachable witness to testify to it besides. Now, gentlemen, just consider what that note meant to the dead man. He, of course, recognized the handwriting, and the signature, James Foxborough, told him his secret was discovered. He goes over to Bunbury to see what terms he can make with the man who has surprised his secret. He knows Cudemore well, and no doubt is prepared for exorbitant demands on the part of the money-lender. What Cudemore did ask we shall perhaps never know. It may be he demanded a very large slice back of that six thousand which he, in conjunction with Mr. Sturton, had lent. That, as we know, Foxborough could not comply with. He had already used the whole of the money to conceal his breach of trust in connection with the funds of the Municipal Council. But whatever Cudemore wanted, we may feel pretty certain it was not Foxborough's life. That he did slay him I believe, but it was undoubtedly an unpremeditated murder. When men of this stamp get a hold over their fellows, and intend to make them what my brethren in Paris call " sing," or, as we term it, black-mail them, of course the victim's life is the last thing aimed at. They want perpetual hush-money from him, and his death naturally puts an end to all that. Now, gentlemen, if any of you can give me any clue to what Cudemore's motive can have been—that is to say, what it was he wanted to wring from Foxborough—I shall be obliged to you."

"All we know amounts to this," said Soames. "Ever since the murder Cudemore has shown a great desire to get the Syringa Music Hall into his own hands. He has given notice of foreclosing the mortgage, evidently relying upon Mrs. Foxborough's inability to find the six thousand pounds with which to meet it."

The sergeant thought for a few minutes, and then said to Mr. Soames, " I can't think that could have been the cause of the murder. Has Cudemore any quarrel with Mrs. Foxborough that you know of ? "

"Certainly Mrs. Foxborough thinks he has treated her very badly about the Syringa," replied Morant, "and declines to have anything to do with him, saying when the time comes if she cannot find the money he must take the music hall."

Neither Soames nor Morant were in the least aware of the money-lender's mad passion for Nid.

"No," said Mr. Usher, "that is a consequence of the murder, but certainly not the cause of it. Even in his first moments of exasperation at finding he couldn't have his slice back of the six thousand he had lent, Cudemore would never have been such a fool as that. With the hold he had over Foxborough he could have become a partner in the Syringa on his own terms. Well, gentlemen, it's no use trying to guess a riddle now, which the trial will probably solve. We have brought the thing down now to this: Cudemore, at the opening of the Baumborough Theatre, convinced himself that James Foxborough and John Fossdyke were one man. Whether he suspected it before I don't know, nor does it matter. Taking advantage of his discovery, he summons Fossdyke to dine with him at Bunbury, and what concession he demanded to hold his tongue we don't know, but in the sitting-room the two men quarrelled, and either by accident or design Cudemore stabbed his companion to the heart. He then carried him into the adjoining room, divested him of his dress coat, and placed him as he was found."

"But don't you think," said Soames, "that a man like poor Fossdyke might be stung to such madness by finding his secret at the mercy of a man like Cudemore as to lay violent hands on himself?"

"Quite possible, sir; but first Dr. Ingleby will tell you that from the peculiar direction of the wound it could hardly have been self-inflicted. Secondly, if he is an innocent man why did not Mr. Cudemore come forward and tell his story? and, lastly, there's that third point,

which was pretty well proved at the inquest, if the door
was not locked from the outside, where was the key?"

"It might have been thrown out of the window," said
Herbert.

"Now, really, Mr. Morant," rejoined the sergeant, with
a deprecatory smile, "that's a cutting observation to a
crack officer of 'the Yard.' You can't suppose but what I
had every inch of ground under that window searched that
very afternoon as far round as it was possible for a man
to throw a key. No, it was an off-chance, but I didn't
overlook it; and now, gentlemen, I must say good-night,
as I have to catch the mail train."

"One word more, Mr. Usher," said Soames. "I suppose
Mrs. Foxborough need fear no further molestation from Mr.
Cudemore?"

"Neither she nor any one else for a very considerable time
to come. Mr. Cudemore will be in custody about breakfast time to-morrow morning. Once more, good-night,
gentlemen."

"Usher's case is beautifully clear," said the doctor, as
the detective left the room, "but there'll be no conviction
of murder, I fancy."

"No," said Soames, "he'll get off with manslaughter,
I'm inclined to think."

CHAPTER XXXVIII.

MR. CUDEMORE'S ARREST.

ON his way home from the Syringa Music Hall after his final rebuff from Mrs. Foxborough, Mr. Cudemore first awoke to the fact that he was dogged. A rather less expert tracker than Old Nibs had for a little taken that worthy's place, and the money-lender's eyes had fallen mechanically upon a shabby genteel young man as he left the Hall. Coming down Portland Street he rather suddenly struck into one of the side streets leading into Portland-place, then suddenly recollecting the want of some small article of haberdashery such as he was accustomed to purchase at a shop in Oxford Street, turned about abruptly to retrace his steps. At the corner he ran almost into the arms of the shabby genteel young man he had noticed outside the Syringa. In an instant all the money-lender's suspicions were aroused, he pursued the even tenor of his way into Oxford Street, but like a woman now he had eyes in the back of his head. He walked home quite leisurely, and knew perfectly well that shabby young man followed him like his shadow. To take a cab Mr. Cudemore knew would be useless. If he was, as he had no doubt now, under the surveillance of the police, they knew perfectly where he lived, and any attempt to evade his unwelcome attendant was ridiculous. Besides, go home he must, if it was only to get that thousand pounds which he had just procured for this very emergency. Peeping from behind his curtains, Mr. Cudemore caught occasional glances of the shabby young man lounging pensively up and down the street. He was a young officer, new to his business, and undoubtedly rather too pronounced in his manner of conducting it.

"If they were only all such duffers as that," muttered the money-lender, "the idea of not being able to slip the police at any moment would be preposterous."

And then he prepared to go out and dine and enjoy himself. He dined and drank a bottle of champagne at the Criterion, and then once more adjourned to a theatre. He did not see the shabby young man any more, but felt quite sure that he was accompanied by an attendant Sprite, and troubled his head little about it. To-morrow he would make a bolt of it. He would complete all his preparations that night, and disappear from London next day at such time as might seem to him most favourable. He had no doubt about compassing this little matter of evasion of the police, but still he regarded it as a delicate operation, and not to be carried out at any fixed period. After the play, Mr. Cudemore felt that his spirits required sustaining to the extent of a pint of champagne and a dozen of oysters, and accordingly so sustained them. Then he drove quietly home to make preparations for his flight. These consisted for the most part in the burning of several letters and papers. Then he packed a small hand-bag with great care, and laid out his overcoat and railway rug. Finally he took from his writing-table a well-stuffed note case, and placed it on the dressing-table, and then Mr. Cudemore undressed and went to bed.

As to what direction his flight was to take Mr. Cudemore was not so clear, but he had a leaning towards Scotland. As for baffling the police at the rate of abandoning his hand-bag, railway-rug, &c., that he thought would not be difficult. He thought that once he had taken his ticket and his seat with such slender baggage they would feel quite sure of his absconding, and fancy they knew all about it. His idea, then, was to get into a second-class carriage at the last moment, and leave the train at the very first station. For this purpose he intended to take two tickets—one first right through for Edinburgh, say if he took that line; the other second for the first station out of London, and it need scarcely be said he had no intention of travelling by express. The idea was ingenious, and it is much to be regretted that Mr. Cudemore was never destined to put his scheme to the test, but his passion for Nid Foxborough was destined to prove fatal to him as the candle to the moth. Mr. Cudemore might have left the country at one time without let, hindrance, or suspicion, but that time was now gone by. The toils were around him, and that mighty Nimrod of criminal humanity, Mr. Usher, had marked him for his own.

Having ascertained from one of his myrmidons on his return to town that Mr. Cudemore was in his own house, the sergeant, with that consideration for his victim which always characterized his proceedings, resolved to allow him one more night in his own comfortable rooms, and having warned another officer to come over to his (Mr. Usher's) quarters punctually at eight, the sergeant returned to Spring Gardens, and tranquilly slept within fifty yards of his intended prisoner.

The appointed time found Mr. Usher all dressed and ready for business. No sooner did he see from his window the approach of the constable than the sergeant descended rapidly to the street and joined his colleague. The habits of Mr. Cudemore's establishment were accurately known. The charwoman who cleaned out the offices arrived at eight, the office-boy (or third clerk, as he loved to designate himself) at nine, and the other two clerks at ten; consequently when Mr. Usher presented himself he found the charwoman sweeping the steps, banging the mats against the neighbouring railings, and the door wide open.

"Lawk-a-mussy, it's the perlice!" chimed that lady as Mr. Usher, followed by the constable in uniform, pushed past her. The sergeant knew all about the house quite as much as if he had lived in it all his life, and ascended at once to the second floor; there he paused, and turning round, said to his follower:

"Wait here, Brooks, and don't come in till I call you;" and then Mr. Usher quietly opened the bedroom door and found himself face to face with Mr. Cudemore, half-dressed, and grasping a hairbrush in either hand.

"Who the devil are you? What the deuce do you mean by coming up here in this sort of way?" exclaimed the money-lender angrily, but even as he spoke his lips tightened and he knew that the avenger was upon him.

"Now, Mr. Cudemore, it's no use making a fuss about it. I'm Sergeant Usher, and I've come to arrest you for the murder of John Fossdyke, at Bunbury, last September."

"Arrest me for the murder of John Fossdyke!" repeated Mr. Cudemore, and putting down the brushes he fell back some three or four paces and stole his hand towards the lid of a small davenport in a corner of the room.

"Yes," said the sergeant, as he sprang forward, quick, agile as a wild cat, and pinned Mr. Cudemore by the wrist. "None of that nonsense! What's the use of your fumbling for a revolver. Bless your innocence, you'll find another man on the landing, and another at the door, and will never get fifty yards without being arrested. Do you think shooting me is the way to prove yourself not guilty? Don't be a fool; just finish dressing yourself before I slip on the bracelets, and we'll have a cab and go across to 'the Yard' quietly till it's time to go down to West-minster."

"All right, Mr. Usher," said the money-lender. "Excuse

a slight error of judgment owing to the excitement of the moment."

Cudemore then proceeded leisurely to complete his toilet, and at last emerged from the dressing-room with that particularly well-stuffed note-case in his hand.

" Shall I be allowed to keep this ? " he asked. " There's a good lot of money in it."

" Chuck full of bank-notes, I can see," replied Mr. Usher. " Of course, it will be yours till you are committed, and you will be that before midday. Then, you know, we take care of it for you, or hand it over to any one you please to name."

" Yes, there's a good deal more than *two hundred pounds* here," said Cudemore, slowly. " I've nothing to say to this Bunbury affair, of course, but the mere accusation is an awful stigma for a professional man like myself. I've often heard men of your craft have made more money by missing a thief than finding him."

" Stow that, Mr. Cudemore. I understand what you mean of course, but Silas Usher's never worked on the cross yet, and he isn't going to begin. Now, sir, as soon as you're ready I'll send Brooks for a cab. All right," continued the sergeant, as the money-lender signified a sullen assent; then putting his head outside the door, Mr. Usher briefly observed, "growler, Brooks, quick as you can."

They had not many minutes to wait before Brooks announced the cab was at the door, and then Mr. Usher advancing said, " I don't want to be uncivil, but I must slip these on."

" One moment, please," exclaimed Cudemore; " reach me an envelope out of the davenport behind you. They will never take this from me ? " he asked anxiously, as he removed a photograph from the book.

" No," said the sergeant, eyeing him curiously. " I fancy you'll be allowed to retain that."

25

Cudemore put the photograph carefully into the envelope, and then placing it with the note-case in his breast-pocket, simply held out his hands and said, "I am ready."

In an instant the steel handcuffs snapped round his wrists, and he quietly preceded Mr. Usher to the door at which Brooks stood waiting. Mr. Usher followed him down the stairs, and having seen the money-lender and the constable into a cab, delegated to the latter worthy the task of conveying the prisoner to Scotland Yard, some two or three hundred yards' distance only, and turned back into the house to make a cursory overhaul of Mr. Cudemore's apartments.

It was not that Mr. Usher expected to get much out of the investigation, but it was a piece of mechanical work that he never neglected. None knew better than the sergeant the curious monomania that compels murderers to preserve some damning evidence of their crime. It is always so trivial that in their eyes it cannot matter, and yet that little link is just the thing that knots the noose round their throats. Few now recollect the great Stansfield Hall murder, and yet the want of a wedding certificate brought Rush to the gallows. He was hung on the evidence of his mistress, whose evidence, had she been his wife, was inadmissible.

Mr. Usher flitted and peered about the sitting-room and dining-room like a magpie, but without any result; though it is fair to say the money-lender's locks were respected and only his open repositories subjected to search, and then the sergeant once more ascended to the second floor. His investigations here met with little more result till he came to the dressing-table and threw open the drawers; the first contained simply some half-dozen razors and a packet of shaving-paper, but in the second, amidst a lot of knick-knacks, such as old studs, disabled pins, and broken sleeve-links, Mr. Usher observed something which set him a pondering.

"It would be odd if it were," said he, "but nevertheless it's odd its being here by itself. Still, it's so astonishing the mistakes they all make that the man who can bring off a great murder is a genius almost. Anyway I'll take you," and what Mr. Usher put into his pocket was an ordinary chamber key.

CHAPTER XXXIX.

" THE TRIAL."

THE Bunbury mystery had pretty well died out of men's minds, and when alluded to people shook their heads and opined the police would never take Foxborough now; so when the first edition of the *Globe* came out with the " Bunbury Mystery—Arrest of the Murderer," in the largest type, there was quite a sensation in London. Newspaper boys trotted along, bellowing at the top of their voices what sounded like " Bum'stery arrest of the murdrer," and got double prices for their wares. At the clubs tongues were wagging; and when it was known Mr. Cudemore, the money-lender, was in custody on the charge, wagging faintly expressed the pace at which they oscillated.

There were members, for instance, at the Theatiné who could speak with undoubted authority regarding Mr. Cudemore, and not in that loose and desultory fashion in which they had manufactured biography for James Foxborough. Although the money-lender had been prone to invest his money in theatrical circles, Mr. Sturton sent him many a client from the *jeunesse dorée*, and there were members of the Theatiné who pondered gravely how this would affect certain acceptances, the renewal of which would be so infinitely simpler than the taking of them up. And the members of the Theatine being, as a rule, like the Heathen Chinee, of a disposition "childlike and bland," always preferred the simpler course.

The arrest of the murderer sufficed to fan the waning interest of the public once more into a flame over the Bunbury mystery. That the accused should be one whose trade was usury added an additional whet to the public appetite, always prejudiced against these philanthropists, regarding them invariably as endowed with hearts of granite and no bowels of compassion—a view of the London moneylender which the Northumberland Street tragedy of some twenty years ago tended much to strengthen. Arraigned of any such crime, and public opinion is apt to condemn the luckless usurer without waiting for the production of evidence. The later editions contained an account of the prisoner's appearance at Westminster, which, of course, ended in his being remanded.

In these days, as we all know, a man accused of a capital crime is generally tried three times. First, before the coroner; secondly, before the police magistrates; and thirdly, before a judge and jury. Our system of justice is doubtless perfect, but no one can say it is either speedy or inexpensive. It will be only necessary, therefore, to say that after some few days, during which the public were once more roused to fervent interest about the great Bunbury murder, Mr. Cudemore was committed to Newgate, there to await his trial.

A great artist was Sergeant Usher. If ever there was a man, to speak metaphorically, who delighted in keeping a few trumps up his sleeve, it was him. Very little of the real story oozed out at Westminster. He confined himself entirely to proving that Cudemore was the stranger at the Baumborough Theatre, that Cudemore was No. 11 at the Hopbine, and that Cudemore was the writer of the note, and the man John Fossdyke dined with. Quite sufficient this to justify a committal, and concerning the identity of John

Fossdyke with James Foxborough the sergeant adduced no evidence whatever. To his intense disgust, even Mr. Totterdell was not brought to London to give his evidence, Mr. Usher preferring to rely upon Miss Lightcomb's testimony as to Mr. Cudemore having been present at the opening of the Baumborough Theatre, while he only called upon Morant to testify to the prisoner's handwriting. In the smoking-room of the Theatiné it was agreed that if more evidence on this point was desirable they could furnish it, and then some astute rhetorician started the problem as to whether when a usurer came to his death by premature strangulation, acceptances become void or payable to the Crown, and this knotty point led to much wordy argument and consumption of drinks.

But the very fact of so little having come out in the public court only further awoke the curiosity of the public. Where was Foxborough ? What had become of him ? He, of course, was in the background ; the man couldn't be a myth. Foxborough, lessee of the Syringa, was a fact, an undoubted fact. There were plenty of people who knew the Syringa, and knew that James Foxborough was the lessee, but when it came to any knowledge of the man's personality, these people were lamentably abroad, and constrained to admit they had never seen him. Still, the Bunbury murder was once more the topic of the day, and Radstone assizes were looked forward to with absorbing interest by no inconsiderable section of the community.

A *cause célèbre* in these days of diffusion of universal knowledge, like libel and scandal, is apt to attract considerable attention. It attracts two large sections of the public, those who have nothing to do, and to whom a public scandal or case of this nature is a boon inasmuch as it gives them something to think about and talk about, and that busy division to whom it is something like a great realistic novel, unravelling itself day by day. Further, it must be noted that Mr. Cudemore was a man of resources, and in a position

to engage equally eminent counsel to those retained for
the Crown.

Mr. Baron Bumblesham, elected to try the case, was
doubtless as incorruptible and impartial as English judges
invariably are, but we cannot help our proclivities. Baron
Bumblesham's were aristocratic. He metaphorically sat up
like a poodle on his hind legs to a Duchess, he stood literally
on his head to Royalty. He delighted in presiding over a
sensational trial. It enabled him to gratify his aristocratic
friends with "orders," and, like a judicious theatrical
manager, he usually kept "his show" running as long as it
would draw. In short, there were all the elements of a
sensational trial about the Bunbury mystery, and, as said
before, a sensational trial is a thing loved of the people.

Fashionable London, like fashionable Rome, takes a great
interest in seeing a fellow-creature hounded to his death,
although the matrons of the earlier empire city enjoyed the
more extended privilege of seeing them die by the dozen,
while the ladies of London must be content to see one man
wrestle for his life at a time. Civilization, in spite of all
our bragging, does not advance very much, and the inherent
cruelty of human nature is ever seeking to gratify its taste..

Radstone was within such easy distance of London that
many of that mysterious "upper ten thousand," the fragment
of the great city not condemned to labour for their living,
determined to attend the trial. Mr. Baron Bumblesham
found himself inundated with applications from the mag-
nates of the land for seats on the bench, and Mr. Baron
Bumblesham smiled, smirked, and promised to do his best
for His Grace and My Lord, and threw the cards of Jones
and Smith contemptuously into the waste-paper basket. It
was widely rumoured that this would be one of the most
sensational trials of the age; and that the police should
suddenly arrest a man for the murder whose name had never
as yet been mentioned in connection with it, and in defiance
of the strong presumptive evidence there was against the

missing Foxborough, seemed to warrant such belief. When Sir Horace Silverton rose to open the case for the prosecution you might have heard a pin drop in the court, so anxious were the densely packed audience to hear the mysterious story unfolded by one of the most gifted and fluent speakers of the Bar. Quietly and smoothly did Sir Horace run through all the preliminary story of the murder with which the public was well acquainted, and those who knew him best felt that he was simply clearing the ground for the effect he felt confident of producing.

"When Silverton begins in that way he has a devil of a case in the background," remarked a leading counsel on the circuit. "I'm going into the other court, just send round for me when he wakes up. He's not going to talk like that all the time, I know. He'll be worth listening to before he sits down."

The preliminary ground cleared, Sir Horace, as fine a judge of dramatic effect as ever appealed to a jury, paused for a moment, passed his handkerchief across his brow, and then continued his address in a totally different tone. The quiet, clear, well-modulated voice was now exchanged for the impassioned, fervid accents with which men enunciate great creeds to the world. "Gentlemen," he said, "one James Foxborough, lessee of a music hall called the Syringa, has so far borne the odium of this crime. I am about to acquit that luckless person, I trust, of any concern in it. At all events I shall produce, in the first place, evidence before you to prove that James Foxborough, of the Syringa, and John Fossdyke, solicitor of Baumborough, were one and the same person. Evidence, gentlemen, past all dispute." Here the sensation in court was such that Sir Horace had to pause for a minute or two. "It is curious, it will be hard for many of his friends in Baumborough to confess that their trusted co-mate of so many years has been a living lie all this time; more especially, gentlemen, will it be hard," and here Sir Horace dropped his voice to that intense whisper with which all real masters of oratory are conversant, "to those two ladies who have each in their different sphere regarded themselves as his wife. I purpose to trespass upon the private history of James Foxborough, *alias* John Fossdyke, no more than is absolutely necessary. This inquiry, as I have already pointed out, must be necessarily painful to many people, and it is no wish of the prosecution to make it more so than is unavoidable. The identity of Foxborough with Fossdyke I am compelled to prove, but I desire to go no further into his dual history. We next, gentlemen, come to the accused. Evidence will be brought before you to show that this was undoubtedly the person who stopped at the Hopbine, and with whom the deceased went over to Bunbury to dine. His note of invitation, signed James Foxborough,"—and here Sir Horace paused as the prisoner, hitherto immovable, could not refrain from a slight start—"happens by a curious accident to have been preserved, and I need scarcely say we shall have no difficulty in identifying the handwriting to your entire satisfaction. What it was that the defendant sought to extort from the deceased we don't pretend to know, but there can be little doubt that at the opening of the Baumborough Theatre he surprised James Foxborough's secret, became aware of his dual existence, and that he took advantage of this knowledge to attempt the levying of black-mail in some form or other. You will, of course, have observed, gentlemen, that in addition to the charge of murder we have included the minor plea of manslaughter against the prisoner, and I am happy to inform you,"—and here Sir Horace became confidential to the jury, and apparently confined his address entirely to them with a total disregard of the judge and general public—"that the theory of the prosecution and the evidence we shall adduce in support of it is more in accordance with the secondary charge. My learned friends on the other side will doubtless be able to put forward many most legitimate reasons in favour of that view of the case, and it is very possible may argue that the deceased committed suicide; but that James Foxborough did not die with his own hand I feel sure of demonstrating to your entire satisfaction," and here Sir Horace sat down amidst a subdued buzz of applause, and left the examining of the witnesses for the present to Mr. Trail, his junior.

To recapitulate all the evidence we have had about the Bunbury murder would be simply wearisome both to myself and my readers, but for the proper understanding of the story we must just briefly glance at the salient points in the case.

The first witness called was Miss Lightcomb, the actress, who looked very pretty and flustered, making a most attractive and interesting witness with which to commence a sensational trial. Her testimony was brief, and simply associated with the fact that she was acquainted with Mr. Cudemore, and had met him behind the scenes at the opening of the Baumborough Theatre. The counsel for the defence declined to cross-examine her, and it was of course transparent at once to Sir Horace Silverton and Mr. Trail that their opponents meant to put forward the theory that John Fossdyke met his death at his own hands. This was only what they expected, and it rather amused them to think of the terrible trump card they held in the background.

The next witness was our old friend, Mr. Totterdell; the supreme moment of his life had at length arrived, and it is no hyperbole to say that he swelled, so to speak, in the box like a turkey-cock with his plumes *en evidence.* Mr. Totterdell was the man who could speak to the identity of the prisoner at the bar. Mr. Totterdell was the man who had formed his theory concerning the great Bunbury murder, and Mr. Totterdell was about to explain to a listening impatient world how Cudemore, the paid agent of the old villain Foxborough, had compassed the death of John Fossdyke. But, sad to say, the coroner, in his arbitrary curtness, was as nothing to Mr. Trail, the examining barrister for the Crown. Some half-dozen questions amply sufficed to establish the identity of the prisoner at the bar with the stranger who sat next to Mr. Totterdell at the opening of the Baumborough Theatre; and, then, not only did Mr. Trail intimate that he had nothing further to ask, but the counsel for the defence equally seemed no more desirous of Mr. Totterdell's views or knowledge on the subject. When Mr. Totterdell, clutching frantically at his fast diminishing opportunity, commenced, *apropos* to nothing, to say, "And it's my opinion, my lord," he was sternly informed that his opinion was not required, and when he faltered forth that he "wished to explain," he was sharply told that if he did not hold his tongue and immediately leave the witness-box he would be committed for contempt of court. Mr. Winkle, after giving his evidence in the famous case of Bardell *versus* Pickwick, was not more hopelessly crushed than was Mr. Totterdell as he retired from the arena in which he had contemplated immortalizing himself. He was like a man stunned, and could hardly realize his opportunity had been and was lost.

The next witnesses were the people of the Hopbine. Old Joe Marlinson, in a mingled state of trepidation, exasperation, and rather too much liquor, was a comic witness whom Mr. Trail handled tenderly. He was simply, of course, called upon to identify the prisoner with the gentleman who had taken No. 11 bedroom last September, and with whom Mr. Fossdyke had dined. A little erratic and irrelevant in his testimony no doubt, as was William Gibbons, the boots, who followed him, but both quite clear as to Mr. Oudemore's personality. But when Eliza Salter, the chambermaid, entered the box, and Sir Horace Silverton himself took her in hand, a stir ran through the court, and without knowing why, people began to feel that one of the great sensations of what was rumoured would be a great

sensational trial was about to commence. Her recognition
of the prisoner as No. 11, afterwards known as James
Foxborough, of course created little interest; but when
Sir Horace skilfully drew from her the discovery of the note
in the empty fire-grate the court was positively breathless
with excitement.

"Yes, she remembered the little old gentleman, whom
she now knew to be Sergeant Usher, the famous detective,
ordering the fire in that room. She recollected his suddenly
stopping her as she was about to throw the waste papers
she had taken out of the empty fireplace on the fire she had
just lit. Remembered perfectly his keeping one of them;
was scolded by her master for having allowed him to do
so; did not know in the least what the paper was Mr. Usher
preserved; it seemed to be a small note of some kind, but
she could say nothing more positive than that."

Close observers noticed that for the first time the prisoner
looked uneasy at the turn things were taking, and that
Mr. Royston, the counsel for the defence, manifested marked
attention.

Further examined, Eliza Salter said she could swear to
the key of Mr. Fossdyke's room being in the door when he
occupied it. The door was locked, and had to be broke
open on the afternoon his death was discovered, which was
not till five or six hours after the prisoner had left the
Hopbine. Did not know what became of the key which was
missing, and she had never seen it since till three days ago."

Great sensation in court.

"It was shown her then by Sergeant Usher. She believed
the key shown her to be the identical key of the bedroom
in which John Fossdyke was discovered dead. Had seen
it tried, and it undoubtedly fitted the lock as if made for
it. It was, of course, difficult to swear to a key of that
description, but she was of opinion that was the missing
key."

For the first time Mr. Royston indulged in sharp cross-

examination, but upon the two points to which he directed
his endeavours, he failed utterly. Eliza Salter professed
to know nothing whatever about the scrap of a note, which
she had raked out of the empty grate, and which Sergeant
Usher had impounded, but that he had so seized upon a
piece of paper and kept it, she was very firm and decided
about. That the key of John Fossdyke's room was in the
door the night he dined at the Hopbine, she was equally
clear about; that it was missing next day and she had never
seen it since, till Mr. Usher produced what she believed to
be it, she was equally positive about, and when she left
the box there was a growing impression that things were
not going altogether well for the prisoner.

And now came a point in the trial which not a little
discomposed Sergeant Usher. That eminent detective
always prided himself upon handing a case over so complete
that the attorneys had nothing to do but put it on paper for
counsel's information. It had never struck Mr. Usher,
keen, shrewd judge as he was of evidence, that there could
be the slightest difficulty in proving John Fossdyke and
James Foxborough to be the same man, but that was now
just what came to pass. The whole thing became a question
of photographs, and wonderful as these sun likenesses are
at times, still it is within the knowledge of every one that
now and again, and by no means unfrequently, comes the
carte that we fail to recognize. There were plenty of people
who knew John Fossdyke, there was no lack of folks who
could speak to the identity of James Foxborough, but to
lay hold of any one who had known the two men, or rather
the one man under the two aspects, unless it was the
prisoner in the dock, was curiously enough unattainable.

Mr. Usher was troubled considerably at this point. Mr.
Morant testified, as did some other witnesses, to their
belief that the photograph of John Fossdyke represented
James Foxborough, and there were numerous people, including the photographer himself, to swear that it was that

of the Town Clerk of Baumborough. Mr. Royston saw his opportunity, and on cross-examination so shook this evidence as to leave it open to question whether Foxborough, lessee of the Syringa, was not an entity after all, despite the theory of the prosecution; but the great eminent lawyer who had rescued many a graceless neck from the gallows was no way blind to the fact that though he might establish a mythical Foxborough in the background, there was no getting away from Cudemore, his client, having been the entertainer of the dead man at the Hopbine. That John Fossdyke committed suicide was of course the defence he intended to set up. So far the prosecution could advance no theory of black-mailing on the part of his client. The key alone threatened to be an awkward incident, and knowing his friend Sir Horace as well as he did, and having the experience he had of Sergeant Usher, Mr. Royston felt sure that key and that note were the two awkward features in the case as far as his client was concerned.

The next evidence produced for the prosecution was that apparently innocent invitation to dinner which had lured the dead man to his doom; curious, like most of the minor links in a great crime, on account of its prosaic simplicity, and horribly suggestive of how little separates our every-day, humdrum life from that lurid melodrama we read of in the newspapers.

Both Morant and Mr. Sturton swore clearly to this being the handwriting of the prisoner at the bar. The former clearly and staunchly, the second in that nervous, hysterical manner which, though apt to be terribly disconcerted by cross-examination, carries irresistible conviction to the hearts of a jury. Such a witness may be bullied and frightened by the fierce battery of questioning to which he finds himself subjected, but his hearers still feel he is telling them the truth to the very utmost of his ability.

And then stepped into the witness-box Sergeant Usher, and everybody knew that the great sensational scene of the

tragedy was on at last. A quiet, trained, practical witness
this, who was neither to be flurried nor disconcerted, who
understood exactly how much reply to give to the questions
addressed to him, and volunteered no uninvited matter. The
Court was so still you might have heard a pin drop, as the
saying goes, while the famous detective clearly and audibly
trickled forth his discovery of that famous note in the empty
grate of the room occupied by the dead man. Judge, jury,
and the public listened in that entranced way they yield to
the great effect of a skilled dramatist, when he has what is
technically termed "caught his audience," and when Sir
Horace went on to draw forth the story of Cudemore's arrest,
and the finding of the key, the excitement of the hearers
found vent in such a murmur of applause that the judge
threatened to clear the court if it was not instantly suppressed. And then came that tinge of bitterness for Mr.
Usher which the Roman poet tells us lurked at the bottom
of all fountains of perennial bliss, that *surjit amari aliquid*,
as Sir Horace endeavoured to draw from him his theory
of John Fossdyke and James Foxborough being one and the
same person. Nobody knew better than the accomplished
counsel the risk of endeavouring to prove too much; nobody
could be more morally convinced that this story was true
than he was, and also of the great difficulty of demonstrating
it legally; but the fact had been introduced into the case,
and was not now to be passed over. Now, like everybody
else in the case on this point, Sergeant Usher was a worth-
less witness. He had never seen John Fossdyke till he saw
him lying dead in the Hopbine at Bunbury, while he had
never seen James Foxborough at all. He tried to insinuate
some of the evidence he had collected on this point, but
it was not likely that an old hand like Mr. Royston would
allow that, and after Mr. Usher had left the box that eminent
counsel felt quite assured the identity of the two men would
never be established legally in that trial. That it was so
in reality he had no more doubt than his opponents, but

it was most decidedly against his client's interest to admit it.

Ellen Maitland followed, and again gave evidence as to the dagger having been the property of her master Mr. Fox-borough; had missed it, but could scarcely say how long before the inquest at Bunbury. Knew Mr. Cudemore as a friend of her master's. He might certainly have had the opportunity of taking the dagger in question, but could not say for one moment that he did so.

And then came the medical testimony. An admirable witness was Dr. Ingleby, clear and terse, but strongly of opinion that the wound which caused John Fossdyke's death was not self-inflicted. His colleague wobbled, and eventu-ally may be said to have gone all to pieces in the hands of Mr. Trail.

Sir Horace Silverton addressed the court with all that practised fluency that had done so much to make his reputa-tion. Glossing over the double identity business as a thing which, though admitting of no moral doubt, he confessed to the prosecution having failed legally to establish, he pointed out how little the guilt of the prisoner depended on that. Did Cudemore write that note? Was Cudemore the man at the Hopbine who entertained John Fossdyke? And was the key found in the drawer of Cudemore's dressing-table, the key of the room in which John Fossdyke died? Surely on these three points the jury could have no doubt. The theory of the defence was the dead man committed suicide, but the story of the key negatived that. He would simply submit this case to them: Did not the prisoner induce the late John Fossdyke to dine with him under a false pretence for some hidden purposes of his own? Did not Fossdyke meet with his death on that occasion, and did not the prisoner Cudemore never come forward about the affair till brought before them by the police. They had listened to the evidence of Sergeant Usher, and if after that they did not feel it their duty to return a verdict of " Wilful Murder " against the prisoner, he should feel more surprised and pleased than he ever felt in his whole professional career.

And then, after a two hours' speech, Sir Horace resumed his seat.

The summing-up of the Judge was both lucid and exhaustive, but it was too close a repetition of Sir Horace Silverton's argument to admit of introduction into these pages, and when the jury withdrew it was felt that the sole chance for the prisoner was that they might possibly arrive at the conclusion the dead man died by his own hand, and yet in the face of that evidence concerning the key it seemed a decision hard to come to.

Ten, twenty, forty minutes passed ; it was close upon the hour when the jury once more trooped into their box, and the Foreman in low tones delivered a verdict of " Wilful Murder " against the prisoner.

Brief and solemn was the Judge's address, but it concluded with his assumption of the black cap, and that short, terribly plain announcement concluding with " God Almighty have mercy upon your soul," which nobody that has once heard it can ever forget.

CHAPTER XL.

IT has occurred to many of us to carry our lives in our hands at times. In the savage surges of the Mid-Atlantic. In the fierce tempestuous storms that rage round either of the famous Capes—those southern extremities of Africa and America, where winds and waves seem never at rest. In the treacherous shoals of the James and Mary, where the Hooghly and the Ganges join hands, and combine in the sinking of ships. In the petty skirmishes of Alma, of Inkerman, Balaclava, and the storming of Lucknow which preceded that terrible twenty-five days' campaign in Egypt, culminating in that awful twenty-five minutes' action at Tel-el-Kebir. If it is given to statues to smile, and after the late wearisome trial who shall say that "artistic grace" is denied them, "the Iron Duke's" effigy at Hyde Park Corner must have been a study that day when the Egyptian heroes strode past him and he recalled the memories of Talavera, Ciudad Rodrigo, Badajos, and Waterloo.

But to be told you are to die a dog's death in the grim grey of the morning, that you are to suffer that excessively brutal extinction peculiar only to the fierce Anglo-Saxon race, who, under the pseudonym of justice, put their fellow-creatures to death in the most degrading fashion it is possible for human beings to compass; well, that is ugly to think upon. Cudemore was no coward, but it is easy to imagine a shudder running through a strong man's veins at the prospect of terminating his existence in such miserable fashion. The crucifixion of the Romans might be more cruel, but it was infinitely less debasing. With all our brag about civilization, who can say that the Greeks, with a bowl of hemlock, were not infinitely before us in this respect?

Still Ralph Cudemore is condemned to die, and though the public have great doubts about that sentence being carried out in its integrity, and even the prisoner himself has received a hint that from what transpired on the trial the making of a clean breast of it would probably tend very much to his advantage, yet he has so far not spoken. Mr. Royston, indeed, has exerted himself on all sides to obtain commutation of the sentence, and risky though it may be, he believes if Cudemore could only be induced to speak there will be no chance of the extreme penalty being resorted to. Sir Horace Silverton and the counsel for the Crown are of the like way of thinking; in short, the motive for the deliberate murder is palpably wanting, whilst it is so easy to show cause why it should never have come to pass.

And the sole man with a faint dim perception of the truth is Mr. Sturton. Very vague indeed even is his theory concerning it, but it has mistily crossed his brain that the money-lender's love for Foxborough's (now pretty conclusively proved to be Fossdyke's) daughter might have had a good deal to say to it, while in the seclusion of his cell Ralph Cudemore occasionally smiled triumphantly as he thought of that afternoon at Tapton Cottage when he had caught Nid Foxborough in his arms and snatched half a score of kisses from her lips in the frenzy of his lustful love. He would muse over this till it maddened him and seemed utterly regardless of the position in which he stood; the nearer approach of that grim grey morning which was to give his throat to the rope, and his last gasp to this world, troubled him no iota; that he could not possibly take Nid with him no doubt did. He could not have expressed it, but he felt like the savage hero of Swinburne's *Les Noyades.*

> "For never a man, being mean like me,
>   Shall die like me till the whole world dies.
> I shall drown with her laughing for love, and she
>   Mix with me, touching me lips and eyes."

Like the rude peasant who met this doom on the Loire bound hand and foot to the dainty aristocrat idol of his distant idolatry, when savage Carrier daily published the banns for what he termed "Republican marriages," Cudemore could have died with a laugh on his lips, providing Nid Foxborough was locked in his arms. It was well for Nid that he was laid by the heels in prison, for when a man contracts such fierce love for a woman he is capable of almost any crime to gratify his passion. He sullenly rejected all consolation from the chaplain, saying with a bitter sneer that if a man didn't know how to die without priestly teaching, he was either fool or coward. But one morning he suddenly expressed a wish to see the Governor and Sergeant Usher, "the man who," as he said, "had tracked him to the grave." If the expression was not exactly correct the authorities quite understood what he meant; the great detective had brought a good many men in his time to that leap into eternity which few face in the grey of the morning without a shiver.

The Governor of the gaol arrived, bringing Mr. Usher with him, and commenced explaining that he, Cudemore, must build no hopes of a remission of his sentence on whatever he might be about to confess.

"Hopes," rejoined the prisoner, ironically; "no, if I had any hope left I shouldn't come whining to you for my life, and it's not for that. I've sent for you to tell you how the whole thing came about. The sergeant there is the first man that's bested me since I was twenty. He's the only man in England, I believe, that could ever have solved my riddle. He's not done it quite, but he's got so near that I am going to tell him the true story. I thought you might like to write it down, you know, and so asked you to hear it too. How he "—and here by a gesture Cudemore indicated the sergeant—" got the clue to Fossdyke and Foxborough being the same man of course I don't know. I believed it a thing known only to myself; and, as he rightly conjectured, it only came to my knowledge by the sheerest of accidents at the opening of the Baumborough Theatre. Now don't ask questions, Mr. Usher, because I'm going to tell you all you want to know. What took me to Baumborough? A combination of business and bad luck, for which I am about to pay the penalty. Pooh! a bad night at baccarât has put men quite as much out of their world as a bad night's luck is about to put me. I came down to Bunbury to look after James Foxborough. He had borrowed, as you know, six thousand pounds of me and my friends, and I was mighty curious to know what the speculation was that he meant to put it into.

"Yes, Mr. Usher, you're quite right," said the money-lender, in reply to the detective's inquiring look, "I undoubtedly meant to force my finger into the pie if I could and thought it worth my while. And a new theatre was an affair I was sure to look at, and without a thought of James Foxborough I ran over for the evening to see it. With what results you know. It killed him, and is about to kill me.

"Now I didn't even know Foxborough's whereabouts. It was a mere accident—life's a succession of them—which led me to look for him down in these parts. But when I discovered the secret I knew exactly I thought the price it would cost him to silence my tongue, and but for his terrible irritation and dismay at my discovery, I still think things might have gone right. He lost his temper, a stupid thing to do, and both our lives, as it turned out. Am I penitent?" Cudemore continued, turning sharply to the Governor, "not a bit; if I'd to play the cards over again I don't think I'd change my lead."

"You haven't mentioned the stakes," observed Mr. Usher, sententiously.

"No, you'll perhaps hardly understand quite how high they were," rejoined Cudemore, slowly. "I wanted to marry his daughter."

"Good lord!" exclaimed the sergeant; "what, that pretty girl mixed up in the game? Well, I'm cornered this time. If her sweet face was in it I'm surprised at nothing you've got to say."

"Was in it?" retorted the prisoner, fiercely. "Is in it? you may ask at this moment. If I didn't know I'd irretrievably lost her, I'd fight for my life this minute. You, of course, don't understand such things," continued Cudemore, with a contemptuous wave of his hand to the Governor; "but you do, sergeant. In the course of your experience you've met men who could sell their soul for a woman's love, or the possession of the woman they do love. To have called Nid Foxborough my wife I think there's mighty little in this world I'd have flinched at. Murder! I'd have walked over six men's graves providing they led her and me to the altar. Foxborough and I had quarrelled about this very subject before. I could have taken care of the girl as a lady, and was good enough mate for her, I thought, but he wouldn't give her to me. Can you be surprised that when I found I held all the trumps I put the screw on? My note! I forgive Sturton, poor weak fool; once you'd got the clue, which you did through that young brute Morant, there were clouds of witnesses to identify my handwriting. Of course, I told Foxborough I knew the secret of his life. Foxborough knew perfectly well that when I asked him to dinner it was simply to arrange at what price my tongue could be stilled. I named it, and again we had angry words on the subject.

But we stood on a different footing this time. It was for me to dictate, for him to submit, and he had the wit to see it could not be my interest to expose him. Of course it was not. I could make nothing out of showing him up to the public, but a dead hold over a man is always worth having, eh, Mr. Usher? let him be the poorest pauper that ever crawled. You can use a poverty-stricken wretch, if you've got him in irons in this fashion, at times to advantage. Well, as I said, we quarrelled and parted over it. He wouldn't give me Nid, and I would take nothing less. He went off to his room furious but frightened. Though he knew it could not be in my interest to expose him, he lacked the sense to stand by that knowledge. He wouldn't give in, but he was so obviously upset by the discovery of his secret that I thought I could carry my point, and that my best chance was before he could pull himself together. I went to his chamber after we had parted in the sitting-room and recommenced the argument. We had drunk a good bit of wine and he got furious, and at last, saying he would kick a scoundrel like me out of the house, advanced in most threatening manner towards me. No, Mr. Usher, I'm not particular, and I'm no coward, but I do know when I've the worst of the weights, and I'm not keen about being kicked; for the matter of that never knew but one low class attorney that was; but when Foxborough or Fossdyke 'went for me' I had to meet a bigger man than myself. That cursed dagger lay on the table. He had put it in his bag, no doubt, as a paper knife; I snatched it up instinctively to defend myself, and when that brief two minutes' struggle was over John Fossdyke lay dead at my feet. Whether he ran on the dagger—I think and hope he did—or whether I struck at him with it I can't say, but it don't matter much now to either of us. He's dead, and I soon shall be. That, Mr. Usher, is the true solution of the riddle you have spent such time and patience over, and solved near enough to hang a man."

"Most folks," remarked Mr. Usher, gravely, as Cudemore paused, "think a man with the grave gaping ready for him can't lie. I know better, but I ain't, take it all round, a bad judge of truth when I hear it, and it's truth, sir, he's telling us now;" and as he spoke the sergeant glanced sharply towards the Governor, who was rapidly committing the prisoner's confession to paper previous to reading it over to him.

"Shake hands," cried the prisoner, warmly; "you've tracked me to the gallows, but you recognize that I'm a man, Usher. You see that I'm no more afraid to die for mad love of a woman than scores of others have been before me. Once more I say, Foxborough met his death at my hands as I tell you, and by accident, though I would have killed him, or half a dozen more, if I had thought it would get me Nid for a wife. To lock the door, return to town according to my original intention, and rely upon my assumed name to avoid detection, was so obviously what appeared to be my game, that I should accept it can surprise no one. If it hadn't been for the fluke of your finding that scrap of paper, Mr. Usher, I should be at large this moment, and you would be still hunting for James Foxborough. If either of you know the game of poker you will understand what it is to have four aces in your hand, and be beat by a flush sequence. That's my case, the aces would be good enough to back for fifty years, but there is just that one off-chance, they may be rolled over. There, I've said my say, and open my mouth no more; ask the Governor there next month whether I died with my heart in my mouth, or as a man who dared to play dice with the devil for a woman and lost should."

"You'd die game enough," whispered the detective, as he gripped Cudemore's hand, "but it isn't likely to come to that. I'd to run you down, mind, as a matter of business; but I'm just as sorry, now it's over, as any of the swells down Melton way are at the death of a stout fox." And with that comforting assurance Mr. Usher followed the Governor out of the cell.

    *   *   *   *   *   *

The play is over, the curtain and the lights are down, and the audience are seeking cabs and carriages, omnibuses and overcoats, and it is perhaps well for him that the author cannot respond to " a call." We have all heard of Artemus Ward's artist that painted *the* famous picture of his show; how the New York public couldn't rest till they saw him, and how, when they did, *they hove chairs at him:* and that fate awaits author, artist, and dramatist at times, though they may give the best that is in them. If hard it is righteous; we gamble for public approbation, and it is childish to whimper because one casts " the dog's throw" occasionally.

What more am I to tell you? that Cudemore's confession, under Mr. Royston's skilful manipulation, resulted in the extreme penalty being commuted to some seven years' penal servitude, you have already settled for yourselves; that Morant, under steady Phil Soames's guidance, became a prosperous brewer in Baumborough, you can also easily imagine; while that the steeple chimes of the old church rung out blithely for a double wedding some few months after Cudemore's trial is superfluous to mention. That Baumborough should be much divided over which was the prettiest of those two brides is a question Baumborough will probably wrangle over till sweet Bessie Hyde and coquettish little Nid are laid—and long may it be hence—in their graves. You may think these people don't exist, ladies and gentlemen. I can only say for the last six months they have been terribly alive to me, very much more so than they will probably ever be to you. How Mr. Totterdell became an " Ancient Mariner," whose crooked forefinger was dreaded as that of him who slew the albatross, can be also easily conjectured. He was the terror of Baumborough for some few years, although his particular views of the famous trial were never exactly ascertained.

Two women there were to whom this was an infinitely sad and sorrowful story, and these were the two wives of the dead duplicate man. To keep the truth from either of them was impossible, but from the day she learnt it, to her death, the name of her husband never passed Mrs. Fossdyke's lips. She knew, poor thing, that she had never been his wife, and that to a woman means much. With proud Mrs. Foxborough it was different; there was no doubt about her wedding-ring nor marriage certificate. She managed the Syringa for many a year after Nid had left Tapton Cottage, and successfully, too. Like most histrionic stars, she had no wish to retire. She visited her daughters at Baumborough now and again, and was made much of by each, but she and--well--Mrs. Fossdyke never were allowed to meet.

THE END.

UNWIN BROTHERS, THE GRESHAM PRESS, CHILWORTH AND LONDON.
6-13-0-83-20 × 39-64-v14.

By CHARLES LEVER.

By HARRISON AINSWORTH.

By E. P. ROE.

By WHYTE MELVILLE.

London: WARD, LOCK & CO., Salisbury Square, E.C.

London : WARD, LOCK & CO., Salisbury Square, E.C.

THE SELECT LIBRARY OF FICTION.

By VARIOUS AUTHORS.

London: WARD, LOCK & CO., Salisbury Square, E.C.

London: WARD, LOCK & CO., Salisbury Square, E.C.

THE SELECT LIBRARY OF FICTION.

London: WARD, LOCK & CO., Salisbury Square, E.C.

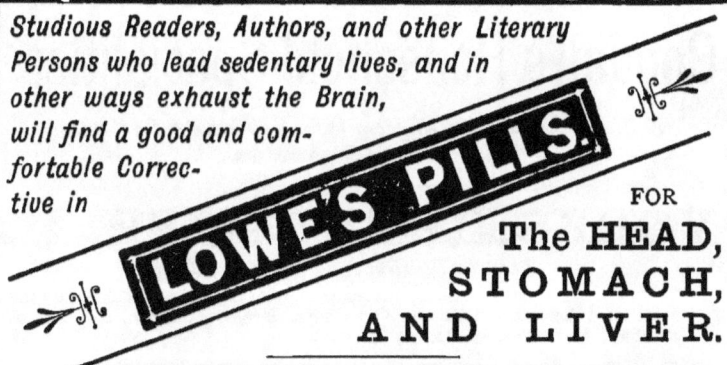

www.ingramcontent.com/pod-product-compliance
Lightning Source LLC
Chambersburg PA
CBHW021334110726
47900CB00005B/1463